Praise for *A Density of Souls*

"A chillingly perverse tale . . . Rice can be given
credit for his energy, brashness, and ability to capture the real misery
of the teenage years."
—*USA Today*

"Bold, ambitious."
—*The New York Times*

"In his debut, Rice charms with his lovingly embraced evocations of
genteel Crescent City and its gay French Quarter."
—*Kirkus Reviews*

"He has a good sense of pacing . . . the plot rackets along."
—*The Village Voice*

"Rich and loving depiction of an exotic and intoxicating city . . .
The characters are compelling . . . vivid and intense."
—*The Boston Herald*

"An intriguing, complex story, a hard-nosed, lyrical, teenage take on
Peyton Place."
—*Publishers Weekly*

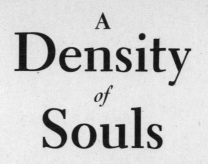

A
# Density
*of*
# Souls

# A
# Density
## *of*
# Souls

**CHRISTOPHER RICE**

TALK MIRAMAX BOOKS
HYPERION
NEW YORK

Library of Congress Cataloging-in-Publication Data

Rice, Christopher.
    A density of souls : a novel / Christopher Rice.—1st ed.
      p. cm.
    ISBN 0-7868-6646-2
     1. New Orleans (La.)—Fiction. 2. High school students—Fiction.
    3. Young adults—Fiction. 4. Friendship—Fiction. 5. Murder—Fiction.
    I. Title.

PS3568.I2717 D46 2000
813'.6—dc21                                     00-035072

PAPERBACK ISBN 0-7868-8646-3

FIRST PAPERBACK EDITION

10  9  8  7  6  5  4  3  2  1

FOR MOM AND DAD
*Rocks rot. Only the chant remains.*
*But overhead, the moon is always beaming.*

FOR BRANDY EDWARDS PIGEON
*Fate can deny us sisters, only to deliver them later in life.*

FOR SPENCER RYAN DOODY
*Salvation can come with the first man*
*who inspires us to lift our hands to the keyboard.*

# Author's Note

While locations are referred to in terms of existing New Orleans streets, the houses—like the characters who inhabit them—exist solely in the author's imagination.

*Part One*

# The
# Falling
# Impossible

*"Plants of celestial seed! if dropped below,*
*Say, in what mortal soil thou deignst to grow?*
*Fair opening to some court's propitious shine,*
*Or deep with diamonds in the flaming mine?"*

—Alexander Pope, Epistle IV
"An Essay on Man"

# 1

Cannon School occupied an entire block of New Orleans, its sprawl of manicured lawns and neocolonial brick buildings dividing the neighborhood in half. The back end of Cannon's football field had drained the blocks behind it of property value, turning the neighborhood into a welter of shotgun houses with crumbling front porches. The façade of the school's main buildings faced the wealthier Creole cottages of uptown. The school announced its name on a bronze plaque above its entrance doors, both of which bore the Cannon seal frosted onto glass panes set in polished mahogany frames. The entrance doors led into the administrative hallway where the business of the finest private school in New Orleans was conducted in gentle whispers punctuated by gracious laughs.

The commerce of the front wing of Cannon School was softened and padded by wall-to-wall carpeting in all the offices, interrupted by the occasional clicking of high heels over the hallways' hardwood floors. Beneath crown moldings, Cannon's finest alumni stared out from eight-by-ten picture frames.

There was no hallway connecting the locker room and the administrative offices. To get from one to the other, a teacher would have to leave the building completely and re-enter the campus through the side parking lot. This was a bone of contention for most of Cannon's faculty, because the faculty lounge was located at the far end of the administrative hallway. Thus, there was no easy access between Cannon's classrooms and the over-decorated faculty lounge with its worn, soft sofas and massive mahogany coffee table.

At the far end of the campus, a wrought-iron breezeway connected the three-story Athletic Complex to the smaller, squat Theatre Building; it was almost as if the athletic department were taunting its less popular cousin. The handful of theatre enthusiasts at Cannon were often forced to exit quickly through the breezeway onto the side street, for fear of meeting up with the varsity football players who always seemed to have leftover steam to vent after afternoon practice. Play rehearsals in the Theatre Building were sometimes interrupted by footballs hitting the side of the building; the actors knew the field was too far away from the pigskins to be simply misdirected passes.

The Senior Courtyard sat in the exact center of campus, separating the Administrative Building from the English Building and its ground floor locker room, and featured rusted wrought-iron furniture. Fringed with yellowing banana trees, the Senior Courtyard was so exclusively reserved for the graduating class that any underclassmen found sitting in it without an invitation would promptly be shoved into the nearest empty locker. But the only way for students to reach the classroom hallways from the locker room was through the Senior Courtyard and up a concrete set of steps which led to the second floor of the English Building. During this time, nervous underclassmen would scurry up the steps, trying to avoid the glare of seniors awaiting an opportunity to assert themselves as the top echelon of Cannon's aristocracy.

Half of Cannon's lessons were taught by its queer architecture. Its passages and connections were illogical, subjecting its students to intermittent bursts of pain and confusion. Over four years, Cannon's students were forced to find the proper mix of aggression and grace to guide them through passages that led from one ritual to another, in a seemingly endless succession of hierarchies, before finally depositing them back into the city that had given them birth—the same city that had given birth to Cannon itself.


As Meredith Ducote learned on the first day of her freshman year and the last day of her life as a child, students were forced to enter Cannon every morning through the side gate, rounding the outside of the main campus buildings before coming to a single entrance of glass doors. The locker room took up the entire ground floor of the English Building. Even with its expanse of benches and blue-painted lockers, it could barely contain Cannon's three hundred students.

The glass doors were gliding shut as Meredith turned the corner of the English Building. The doors were tinted and a green poster taped to them read WELCOME FRESHMAN! Its edge was torn where it had been caught between the opening and closing doors.

Meredith's sweaty palm slid off the door handle. She gently kicked one of the doors inward with her foot. It didn't budge. She wiped her hand across her skirt and pulled the door open, revealing what seemed like three hundred faces that all seemed to stare back at her, if only for a second, before they collapsed into laughter and conversations.

Earlier that morning, Meredith had argued with her mother about the halter top she had bought from Contempo Casuals a week before freshman orientation. The argument had culminated in a tug-of-war with the halter top during which Trish Ducote kept intoning, "Meredith, you are *fourteen!*" It was her mother's voice, high-pitched through clenched teeth, that came to Meredith through the locker room racket. The admonishment became an accusation.

Her breasts suddenly seemed huge. She could suddenly feel them pressing against the halter top and her exposed arms went hot and clammy with sweat.

She found herself paralyzed, paces past her locker and surrounded by laughing, bellowing classmates. At fourteen, Meredith had experienced few moments from which there seemed to be no escape, but this was one of them. She glanced behind her and saw a group of girls (all wearing shirts with sleeves) gathered around the door to what she was pretty sure was her locker. They looked back at her like conspiring thieves.

Someone brushed Meredith's shoulder with his book bag. Meredith almost let out a startled yelp before she saw Brandon.

He was sitting on a bench against the far wall. Meredith didn't recognize the guy next to him; his face was concealed under the bill of a baseball cap that read CANNON KNIGHTS and he was hunched over with his forearms on his knees, obviously whispering the punch line of a joke. Brandon erupted into laughter and rocked back on the bench.

When he saw Meredith, his laughter stopped. Meredith felt a smile tighten her face, but it died as Brandon's eyes rolled up and down her body, his face suddenly expressionless. He nudged the guy sitting next to him.

Greg Darby looked up at Meredith from beneath his cap.

For a brief moment, as Greg took her in, Meredith understood what the four weeks of pre-season football training had done to Greg and Brandon. It had made them men. Or at least look like what Meredith thought men should be.

When Greg smiled, Meredith felt her heels sink to the floor. She realized she had been walking on tiptoe since she had entered Cannon.

Stephen was waiting by Meredith's locker, trying to guard it from the posse of girls. They had giggled at his approach and whispered after his arrival, but he held his back on them. Knowing this was the only way he could wait for Meredith alone. He told himself that Meredith would hardly want to ask a bunch of strangers to move out of her way so he'd keep a clear passage open for her.

She had looked right at him. And then away.

Meredith took a seat between Greg and Brandon, and Greg curled one arm around her shoulders. She playfully batted it away. Stephen stared at them; he was perfectly within their line of vision. None of them looked his way. When the three of them finally rose from the bench, with Greg extending a hand to help Meredith to her feet, Stephen made no move to follow them out the doors into the Senior Courtyard.

Something dark uncurled inside of him.

During his first morning at Cannon, Stephen's only companion was the collective din of whispers, snickers and openly disdainful glares he received as he passed. All of which made him acutely aware of the flop of blond bangs that partially concealed his eyes, the strain of his backpack straps as they pulled at his gaunt frame, and worst of all, the reflexive cock of his wrist as he extracted a book from his backpack during class. It all culminated in the nightmare of PE, the aftermath of which propelled him to the back freight door of Cannon's Theatre Building and the smell of cigarette smoke wafting through the open door of a brightly lit office down the musty, darkened corridor of the backstage.

Stephen had deliberately gone to PE early. He had been frightened by the idea of having to take off his clothes, so he had planned to change quickly and make it to the gym floor before everyone else. Then the football players had exploded into the locker room, slugging metal doors and bellowing war cries intended to clear a path before them. Their heads had all been shaved during freshman varsity initiation. Stephen thought of Nazis. At Cannon, athletes were exempt from physical education classes, but the first week of the semester was dedicated to endurance testing, mandatory for everyone.

They had assembled on the gym floor, where it seemed all eyes inspected Stephen. He relaxed slightly when he saw that neither Brandon nor Greg were in his class. The football players had mangled their PE uniform shirts to protest a week of third-period gym classes. Daniel Weber had torn holes for his nipples on either side of the Cannon logo across the shirt's breast. Coach Stubin ordered him to put duct tape over them. Stephen looked from Daniel's nipples to the polished gym floor, where he saw his own reflection between his tennis shoes. He lifted his head to stare off into some distant corner of the gym, and found himself taking in the series of banners that hung from the banister of the jogging track circling the gym's ceiling, proclaiming the various District Title wins of the Cannon Knights.

But now, in the theatre, there was smoke and light, tattered costumes and old set pieces, the ragged edges of stage flats. Carolyn Traulain threw open the office door and a blinding rectangle of light fell across Stephen. She looked startled when Stephen didn't raise a hand to block the glare from his eyes.

"Are you here for the meeting?" Carolyn asked.

Stephen stuttered a yes, hating the sibilant *s* on the end. She nodded and disappeared into a thicket of curtains and darkness. The overhead lights flickered to life, illuminating the theatrical debris that surrounded him. There were so many flats he could have tripped over.

Carolyn Traulain had a white scar that scooped beneath the collar of her black T-shirt before resurfacing on the opposite side of her neck. She occasionally glanced at Stephen as she set up a small battalion of metal folding chairs, kicking each chair's legs out. "You came from Polk?" she asked.

"Yeah," Stephen said as he moved to a faded green sofa against the wall. It had obviously been a set piece in every production since the school's founding in 1905.

"We get a lot of kids from Polk," Carolyn said. She was the first person all day to speak to Stephen like an ordinary person, and he immediately loved her for it. She met his eyes with each question and he saw no laughter in them.

But the mention of Bishop Polk Elementary School, so much closer to home and now abruptly transformed into a memory, tugged at something in him. He brought his book bag onto his lap and began to tear at one of the seams with a fingernail he had not yet chewed off. He tried not to think of the old morning bike rides to school. As the battalion of students turned onto Jackson Avenue, they would pass beneath the bell tower, its portico towering high enough to catch the first rays of a rising sun that had not yet mounted the tree line.

Over, Stephen thought. That's over now.

Carolyn's voice startled him. "The first day can be rough."

A flicker of genuine emotion softened her eyes. Stephen could only manage a forced smile in response. Carolyn nodded, as if a suspicion of hers had been confirmed.

They both jumped at the sound of the freight door thrown open.

A shadow was advancing through the darkness. Stephen could make out the bulky outline of a letter jacket and his breath caught in his throat. For an instant, he thought it was Greg.

It wasn't. The shadow was shorter, thicker. It moved with an ease of strength over the discarded dresses and sequined shirts. A powerful arm pushed a curtain out of its way.

A short, dark-skinned boy turned and regarded Stephen with drowsy brown eyes. On the shoulder of his letter jacket a miniature cartoon Knight raised a sword.

"Wassup?" he asked.

Stephen tried a nod that resulted in a stiff jerk of his neck.

"Glad to see you could join us, Jeff," Carolyn announced, emerging from her office with a folding chair under one arm.

Jeff looked from the chairs to Carolyn.

"Sorry, Miss T. See, Coach called this meeting 'cause we're playing Buras on—"

Carolyn threw up one arm to steady herself, releasing the chair. It smacked onto a pile of paint-speckled plastic tarps.

"Right. No surprise," Carolyn said, plucking up the chair and kicking the legs out.

Jeff turned to face her. "Look, I'm sorry—" he began, both arms thrown open.

"You're always sorry and you never show up at meetings!"

Carolyn turned and disappeared into the prop closet. Jeff's eyes moved to the empty folding chairs all around him and then to Stephen and back again.

"And if you ask me about the musical again, I'm going to strangle you." Carolyn's voice blew in from the prop closet, followed by a metallic crash.

"You're killing me with the waiting, Miss T!" Jeff called out.

"And you'll wait even longer, if you keep calling me Miss T. Goodbye Jeff. Get your cudgel and go to the field!"

"What's a cudgel?" Jeff asked with a smile.

"Bye, Jeff!"

He pivoted and found himself facing Stephen, whose presence he had apparently forgotten. Stephen looked away from the boy whose profile was broader and thicker than his own entire frame.

"Freshman?" Jeff asked.

"Yeah," Stephen answered, dropping his voice so suddenly and ridiculously that Jeff smiled, which made the discomfort worse.

"Junior," Jeff said. "Gets better, dude."

As Stephen tried another nod, Jeff stared at him for a second before turning and leaving. When Stephen finally heard the freight door slam shut behind Jeff, the aftershock of sudden desire congealed. He finally understood the whispers that had followed him around all day. He knew what was being said. And he knew it was true.

Because Meredith had spent the morning with Brandon Charbonnet and Greg Darby, she could easily introduce herself into the posse of girls who spent lunch period on the hill next to the cafeteria with their sleeves and hems rolled back to the tanning powers of the sun. Kate Duchamp had immediately rolled over onto her stomach, pushed her Oakley sunglasses up off her face, and said a word hardly anyone said as a freshman on the first day of high school. "Hi."

"Hey," Meredith replied with forced indifference as she took her seat.

"You went to Polk, right?"

"Yeah."

"That's why you're friends with those guys?"

"One of them is so hot . . ."

"Greg," a voice finished.

"No . . . Brandon is so fine! Have you ever seen his brother?" asked another female voice Meredith couldn't identify. All the girls around her were lying flat on their backs beneath the glare of the sun.

"Who's the other one?" Kate asked.

Meredith felt as if the patch of earth beneath her butt had shifted and sunk several inches beneath her. The other one!

"Omigod . . ." Now Meredith recognized the voice. It was Cara Stubin, the football coach's daughter and the only other freshman girl to make varsity cheerleading along with Meredith. "He's like . . ."

"Stephen. He's kind of cute . . ." another voice from the grass offered.

"I heard his mom is like so fucked up," Cara continued. Meredith's first instinct was to rise up and stomp one foot into Cara's stomach.

"My mom said she came to this parents' meeting in this dress with, like, her tits hanging all over the place . . ."

Other girls laughed. Meredith realized Kate had not taken her gaze off her.

"I'm sorry. But I think I'd be a little screwed up, too, if my husband blew his brains out!" another girl said defensively.

"Do you know him?" Kate asked Meredith.

She remembered a cemetery pummeled by rain. She remembered a tangle of mud-flecked legs. The memory led Meredith to commit an act that would carve itself into her memory with the building precision of regret.

"He's a fag," she said flatly.

Some flame guttered inside of her, quietly and without protest. She felt hotter, but she assumed it was the sun on her bare arms.

Kate laughed, signaling that Meredith's pronouncement was more of an accusation than a joke.

Ten minutes before the lunch bell rang, Kate Duchamp invited Meredith to go to the bathroom with her. Meredith followed silently as Kate led her through the desolate English Hallway, past classrooms where teachers savored lunchtime silence at their desks. Once inside the bathroom, Kate said, "Watch the door," gesturing toward it with one thumb before moving slowly down the four stalls, checking for feet. She opened the door to the first one. Meredith braced herself across the door.

"So how long have you been friends with them?" Kate asked, as she gathered her platinum blonde hair behind her head, holding it tight in one fist.

"Since we were kids. We all live near each other."

"Brandon's fine. You're not, like . . . You guys don't . . ."

"No!" Meredith responded so quickly that Kate laughed before she sank to her knees on the stall floor. Meredith listened to the sound of Kate vomiting into the toilet bowl. She rose, butt first, out of the open stall door, wiping the corner of her mouth with a triangle of shredded toilet paper.

"That crap they serve isn't even meat. It's like meat juice with, like, extra fat poured on top."

Meredith managed a laugh. Kate hadn't even had to gag herself to force her lunch out of her stomach.

"What about the other one?" Kate asked, stepping clear of the stall door.

"Greg?" Meredith asked, with a note of ambivalence in her voice that suggested even she—his childhood friend—was not sure of his name.

"Yeah," Kate said, her eyes darting back and forth between Meredith and the open stall door. Meredith guessed that if she hesitated Kate would lose interest in the conversation and ask right out why she hadn't tried to throw up her lunch.

"Well . . ." Meredith said.

Kate smiled.


By Friday, Meredith Ducote and Greg Darby were declared "together" by their classmates.

Stephen overheard the news in his fourth-period history class. "Greg Darby and Meredith Ducote are going out." The whisper from the next desk over was still resonant. The teacher, Mr. Humboldt, was asking a question. Stephen knew the answer. He looked down to his open textbook at a Mesopotamian ziggurat and felt something between nausea and acute pain. Without thinking, he raised his hand.

The classroom bristled. Mr. Humboldt couldn't conceal his surprise. Stephen had not once raised his hand the entire week.

"Yes, Stephen?"

Stephen answered. The fall of ancient cultures would become more familiar than the students sitting around him.

# 2

Stephen's mother was named after the mispronunciation of a violent moon, the yellow of rot or cancer, that rose over the Irish Channel rooftops on a sticky June evening in 1943.

The moon drew the porch-bound residents into the middle of Constance Street, where they pondered its holy significance. This was, after all, a poor neighborhood, and its shotgun houses (nicknamed so because if someone fired a shotgun through the front door, the slug would sail cleanly out the back) that spiderwebbed from the wrong side of Magazine Street across from the Garden District to the wharves along the river's crescent had always been the bend in the river where the least popular New Orleans residents would settle.

In 1943, these were the Irish, whose ancestors had come to America on vessels nicknamed "coffin ships," thanks to the hordes who died of famine and disease during the long journey across the Atlantic. Along the eastern seaboard, the hollow-eyed immigrants were turned away by prosperous Americans again and again, labeled as bringers of death and plague.

It was more than fitting that New Orleans—a city built precariously on a bank of mud—would welcome the Irish. They found their best jobs in the lavish front parlors and kitchens of Garden District mansions across Magazine Street. The Irish Channel was routinely swept with malaria, and sometimes the dead were abandoned in the street. The swamp of New Orleans made a better home for mosquitoes than humans.

Beatrice Mitchell had removed the flat cake from the oven and set it on the stove before parking Mother Millie in her rocker on the front porch. At a viciously unyielding seventy-two, Beatrice's mother-in-law had angrily expressed her desire for "something sweet on the teeth."

Although Mother Millie habitually mangled common expressions, she rarely suffered reproach from her daughter-in-law.

Their house on Constance Street was a house of requests that provoked silences, which allowed plenty of space for the pungent memories of sons, husbands, and daughters lost to yellow fever. The framed photographs of John Mitchell—smiling and in uniform—inspired nightmares of his fighter plane's plummet into the Pacific and served as frail evidence of the only link between Mother Millie and Beatrice. A shared death.

Several days after the telegram came, Beatrice realized she was pregnant.

On that June evening in 1943, when Beatrice returned to the kitchen she froze in the doorway, one hand going to the child in her womb and the other to the door frame. What she saw on the stove shocked her. Two fat gray rats were mired in the steaming cake batter. Their bellies slid across the hot surface and their long pink tails whipped at the side of the cake tray. One of them let out a hiss.

Without a thought, Beatrice moved to the oven and sent the cake tray somersaulting out the open window above the sink in a flash of silver tin and the last vain whip of a pink tail. She heard the clatter of the tin on the concrete alley below, and as the rats squealed, she realized that the tray must have flipped, pinning them beneath the batter.

Good, she thought. Let them die a slow and painful death for entering my kitchen.

As she heard the first clamor of voices from the street, she noticed that her hands were trembling. She contemplated whether Satan was an actual, real thing or if he had chosen to sprinkle himself about the world in rats along the rivers and in fevers that melted the body. A better fighting tactic, she thought.

She returned to the front porch to tell Mother Millie there would be no cake that night when she saw the street clogged with dark forms, their arms raised toward the sky. Mother Millie's rocker was empty. Beatrice spotted her sitting on the curb with Margaret O'Connell, the widow from next door whose husband had stumbled off the First Street wharf. The Mississippi's swift and unpredictable currents carried him into the prongs of a paddle wheeler that lifted him up in full view of a cluster of tourists on the boat's deck.

In the glow of the moon, Beatrice could see Margaret tapping three fingers into the center of her palm as she delivered a biblical pronouncement. Beatrice walked to the edge of the porch. At first she saw the distant spire of St. Mary's Cathedral rising over the sloping rooftops several blocks away: the landmark of her neighborhood. But it was suddenly a black crucifix set before an enormous yellow moon.

"Moooon . . . . . . . . auh . . . . . . . . cuuuuuuu-oahmmmme!"

The crowd in the street craned their heads around at the shriek. Beatrice knew the voice. It was coming from the porch directly across Constance Street, the porch where eight-year-old Willie Rizzo spent most of his days.

Willie Rizzo had gone swimming in the river with some Negro children when a dock pile slammed against the side of his head, fracturing his jaw and almost knocking one eye from its socket. The other children, terrified at being blamed over the death of a white boy who had dared to swim with them, dragged him to shore. Willie managed to live, but with a voice forever mangled by his slippery lower jaw. He walked with a wooden cane his father made for him. Margaret O'Connell had disclosed to Beatrice and Mother Millie that Mr. Rizzo had cut the cane from the very dock pile that almost killed his son, as a constant reminder of the boy's crippling stupidity.

Now Willie stood on the edge of his porch, balancing on his cane, one wild wandering eye filled with the yellow light of the moon. The residents along the block had never heard him wail with this kind of authority before. Months afterward, Beatrice would recognize the same tenor in the voices of the priests who delivered mass at St. Alphonsus.

All eyes had moved from the moon to Willie. He used his cane to propel himself off the front porch, loping across the street toward Beatrice, stumbling past the shocked glances of Margaret O'Connell and Mother Miller.

"Da . . . mhooon . . . uh . . . come!"

Even before Mr. Rizzo barreled across the street toward them, Beatrice decided Willie might have the gift of a strange, holy tongue, the language of the half-dead who spoke from both sides of the divide. Even as Willie's hands were ripped from her pregnant body as his father carried him down the steps with one powerful arm around his son's waist, Beatrice made sense and reason of the language. She made her daughter's name.

Monica.

•  •  •

"Some people thought I was a witch," Monica Conlin said in a melo-dramatic whisper as she brought her wineglass to her lips.

In celebration of the end of his first week in high school and in recognition that he had no Friday night plans, Monica had taken her son out to dinner. Houston's Restaurant was abuzz with the sounds of clinking glass and alcohol-induced conversation. Soft ambient light-ing blended with the halos thrown by the lamps on every table.

The rumble of a streetcar passing down St. Charles Avenue filled the silence between Monica and Stephen.

Monica could not tell if Stephen's air of vacancy resulted from boredom or from the initial stages of a perpetual sullenness she had always feared Stephen would inherit from his father. So, at the end of dinner, she continued the story of her childhood, moving from the tale of her name to her exploits in Catholic school.

"The nun used to go from desk to desk and make us stand up and read aloud out of the textbook. So you want to know what I did?"

Stephen looked down at where his plate had been.

"I calculated just how much text she was making each girl read. So when she called on me, I stood up and read it aloud from memory. And do you want to know what she made me do?"

"Stand in the wastebasket for the rest of class," Stephen said. "You've told the story a hundred times. And you stood in the waste-basket every time."

Monica stared so sharply at the sarcastic curl of her son's mouth that he blushed and looked away from her. She followed his eyes to where a waiter was staring openly at the ethereally beautiful woman in her early fifties with the shock of blonde hair spilling down her back and then at that rail-thin androgynous boy sitting—unwillingly, it seemed—across the table from her.

"You haven't said an entire thing all night." She reached for the check and removed her credit card from her wallet. "Someone had to talk."

She signed the receipt. They sat amid frost.

The silent anger that had overtaken her son was too similar to the impenetrable silence that had captured her own husband in the years before his death. Until Stephen's first week at Cannon, Monica had been convinced that Jeremy had not bequeathed his darkness. And that seemed just. Jeremy had forfeited part-ownership of Stephen when he took his own life, leaving his widow to battle any lingering traces of the man who abandoned them both.

She had been taunting Stephen, boring him deliberately, trying to lure him out of his shell.

"It's late," Stephen murmured.

He lifted his eyes to hers. She was startled by something she saw there.

Pain. In one week, Stephen had developed a type of penetrating gaze that comes out of a fine silt of resignation that settles upon the soul. It was a gaze so rare in young men of his age that its absence usually made them what they were.

He held her gaze.

"I love you, Stephen." She was surprised by how easily the words came out of her mouth. "There will be times when you don't think that means a lot. Or when you take it for granted. Or when it's not as important to you as approval from . . . other people. But trust me, you need it. And you're going to need it later, so . . ."

Monica nervously looked to her hands folded across her lap and then lifted her gaze to see Stephen raise one clenched fist to his right eye, before the tears could trickle down his cheek.

"It's important for you to know that I love you," she finished.

He nodded, suddenly, as if to shake her words from his ears. He lowered his fist. Tears sprang from his eyes despite the fact that he had shut them. He continued to nod his head dumbly. Monica rose, moved to his side of the booth, slid an arm around his shoulders, and walked him out of the restaurant, meeting the curious glances with the hostile glare she had perfected as a child.

They drove home in silence. Monica repeated one thought in her head, almost whispering it aloud: Goddamn you, Jeremy.

On the third floor of the Conlin residence, Jeremy Conlin's study remained just as it was the day he had shot himself.

A child of the Garden District, he had courted Monica with poetry. She often came up the stairs to visit his study late at night when Stephen was asleep one floor below. The streetlight through the single window threw spiderweb shadows of oak branches across walls plastered with quotations—drawn from both his own writing and that of his idols, Theodore Roethke and Thomas Mann. He had published one book of poems, *The Upstairs Stories*, which had met with miserable reviews but had secured him tenure in the Creative Writing department at Tulane University. Monica kept a copy of the book on

Jeremy's desk. It was the only thing she ever touched in the room.

As Stephen slept, she flipped through its pages. She knew the poems by heart. Anger kept her from ferreting out Jeremy's wisdom, from decoding it from the lines of his poems. Yet she never became so angry that she could clear out his study, pack the notebooks into boxes, and paint the walls. After several hours sitting silently there, Monica would relax. She knew she was communing with Jeremy's ghost. He did not haunt their house as an apparition. Rather, Jeremy Conlin was a constant, silent presence on the third floor, his substance the papers and shelves and a desk with a typewriter. If he had a wisdom to impart, it would have to filter from the study to where she and Stephen made their lives downstairs.

# 3

"**W**ho read last night?"

Yale-educated David Carter knew enough not to let a single fresh-man English class compromise the reputation he had built with his students over four years. By November, however, a week before Thanksgiving, David realized that an after-lunch section of English I had forced him to do something he swore he'd never do: hate a student.

He cocked his hip, bringing the paperback copy of *Lord of the Flies* to his waist in one clean motion, as Stephen Conlin quite obviously peered to decipher David's notes in the margins. Stephen's face was wrinkled in thought. Nineteen faces stared back at David, wearing expressions of feigned fascination as they chewed the ends of their pens.

David's Yale classmates had laughed at him when he announced he was going to spend several years teaching at the high school level. Bewildered, his parents declared their son's goal a waste of their tuition money. For three years, he had proved them all wrong. His junior and senior classes allowed him to cement a reputation as a handsome young maverick who knew what Cannon's limits were. He could say "shit" rather freely, but "fuck" would stir only useless, nervous laughter. By now he could slide Dickens and Chaucer into the minds of students without major objection. David was the teacher the male students confided in and the female students thought was hot.

But all of that was slowly being devoured by the crooked grin of Brandon Charbonnet, seated in the back row next to his twin in the testosterone brotherhood, Greg Darby.

"The boys find the wreckage of the plane," David offered, trying to control his voice. Brandon and Greg exchanged a look that resulted in stifled laughter from them both.

"Meredith, you care to jump in here?"

Meredith Ducote tilted her head at him with mingled desperation and annoyance as if to say, Don't you have anything better to do than bother me?

David pondered answering her aloud: Yes, like grant work, a Ph.D., a book I've had in me for the last seven years—but no, I love chiseling at the gold-plated lock you have on your mind, Meredith. That's why I do it.

"Which plane?" Kate Duchamp piped up with the hollow assertiveness common to the most popular girl in class.

David rolled his eyes.

"There are two plane wrecks," she declared righteously.

Stephen barked out a laugh.

David tensed. The book in his hand straightened slightly against his waist as his fist clenched its spine. Stay out of this, Stephen. They'll eat you alive.

Kate was glaring at Stephen's back, three rows ahead of her. David caught Brandon staring at the nape of Stephen's neck, but with an amusement as threatening as it was cocky. With a simple laugh, Stephen had strayed into Brandon's turf—namely, the back of the class, where the budding football player conspired alongside Greg Darby, with Meredith Ducote and Kate Duchamp sitting in front of them like puppets they could manipulate.

"They find a fighter plane," Stephen said.

Meredith found herself listening unwillingly. Stephen kept his head bowed as he spoke. But Meredith was suddenly distracted as the girl sitting behind Stephen slipped his book bag out from under his desk, dragging one of the straps with the corner of her shoe. She kicked the book bag back to Kate Duchamp, who slid it back to Brandon with her clog.

"The boys find the wreckage of a fighter plane that's crashed on the island and . . . The Pilot. He's still in there and there's this parachute attached to him. And he's got his mask on, so . . ."

Greg was writing in big block letters. As he gently tore the page from the notebook, Meredith stared straight ahead. David Carter was seated behind his desk now, holding his forehead in one palm.

"So they think he's this monster. But really, see . . . what's happening is that—" Stephen was mumbling now. Meredith knew he was embarrassed by the amount of time Mr. Carter had given him to talk. "It's a dead man. It's not a monster . . ."

The book bag traveled across the classroom floor. Meredith did not look down as she heard the straps sliding past her desk over the dusty linoleum.

"They're the monster. The boys. Because they're out there with nobody and . . . They make up this monster to cover up the fact that they've turned into . . ."

Stephen shifted in his seat as the girl behind him wedged his book bag under his desk with the heel of her shoe.

" . . . beasts, basically."

"Thanks, Stevie!" Brandon said in a high-pitched squeak from the back row. Meredith caught Stephen staring down at his desk. "Fuck you," he mumbled so audibly it frightened her. She saw Mr. Carter's head slip off his hand in surprise.

The bell exploded through the classroom. Stephen went for his book bag and slid it over both shoulders, then bolted for the door, making his typical fast escape. David Carter stared after him, his eyes widening. Meredith saw Kate Duchamp double over in her desk with the clownish guffaws of someone laughing for everyone around her. Greg rose out of his desk first, rushing past the spot where Meredith sat frozen, staring at Stephen's back as he disappeared. She waited for the sound of laughter to erupt from the hallway as Stephen walked down the middle with the word **FAG** dangling on a piece of looseleaf paper taped to his backpack.

There was a rat in the prop closet. Carolyn could hear it from her desk. It was trapped and whining and she prayed it would either die or free itself and vanish into the auditorium.

The noise from the closet collapsed into breaths. She rose from her desk without thinking, abandoning her cigarette, and found Stephen Conlin curled into a fetal position on a bed of lamé draperies she had used in the living room set for *Lost in Yonkers* the spring before.

A piece of paper was crunched into a ball inside Stephen's clenched fist. Carolyn squatted and forced Stephen's fingers open, unfolding the piece of paper. Run through by wrinkles in the paper was the word **FAG.**

The freight door slammed so hard that Carolyn dropped the note. Jeff Haugh was bounding across the floor toward her. He leapt over a pile of newly painted flats. When he saw her, he faltered in uncharacteristic awkwardness. His eyes—usually drowsy with a sexual frankness Carolyn did not like to see in teenage boys—widened slightly.

Caught, Carolyn thought, as she crouched over Stephen. She saw fear in Jeff's eyes. She saw her suspicions of the boy suddenly written across his face. He had come to hear Stephen's sobs and perhaps taunt him further. She felt a flicker of disappointment. She had thought Jeff might actually be better than his crude jock brethren.

Jeff's gaze shifted—from the note in Carolyn's hand to the rectangular view of Stephen's butt through the prop closet door. She stood up and held the note in one hand so the word was visible to Jeff. She waited for Jeff to muster some response as he surveyed the result of what she now believed to be his crime.

He said nothing.

"Get out," Carolyn hissed.

"*What?*" Jeff's anger was incredulous and immediate.

"I said, get out of here. Go to the football field and stay there! Don't ever come anywhere near my office again! Do you understand me?"

His upper lip trembled in what looked to Carolyn like a sneer.

She held her ground.

Jeff gave one last look to what he could see of Stephen through the doorway before turning and leaving the theatre building, his gait more strained. When the freight door slammed behind him, Carolyn brought both hands to the top of the note, to rip it down the center. Then she was struck by the odd thought that for some reason Stephen might want to keep it. And if he didn't, she just might.


After escorting Stephen to the nurse's office on the ground floor of the Athletic Center—he had said nothing to her, but as his tears subsided he had let himself be led—Carolyn made her way beneath the framed photographs of Headmaster's Award winners hanging along the walls of the Administrative Hallway to find David Carter at the coffee maker in the faculty lounge.

His eyes jumped as Carolyn slapped the note down next to his coffee mug. A few teachers looked up from their conversations about impending Thanksgiving plans and their stacks of yet-to-be-graded papers, then looked away just as quickly.

"Did you see this?" she asked.

"Yes, but . . ."

"You saw this note? You saw . . ."

"No I didn't . . ." He backed away from her.

"Well, what are you saying then, Dave? Did you or didn't you see the goddamn note?" She felt the effect of her suddenly raised voice rippling through the faculty lounge.

"I'd appreciate it if you stopped yelling at me," David said gravely.

From his tone, Carolyn could tell he thought she was violating the rule of all high school teachers by being too emotional, getting too involved. He would tell her to calm down, get a little distance, and realize that they were only children.

"Have you spoken with Phillip?" she asked. Phillip Hartman was the headmaster.

"I didn't see who did it, Carolyn," David whispered.

Carolyn's shoulders sagged. She had just been told a lie she didn't have the energy to expose.

"Carolyn." David took an exaggerated, deep breath. "Have you ever heard the argument that if you confront the issue at the moment you might end up embarrassing the victim more than the perpetrator? There's a point where . . . well, kids want to take care of it on their own. It's humiliating to have a teacher intervene . . ."

Carolyn snorted, then looked from the note to David. "We have auditions for the musical a week after Thanksgiving break," she began, her voice quaking with each word. David furrowed his brow in confusion, but Carolyn continued. "Stephen wants to audition. I want him to. If he doesn't make it until then, or if he"—Her teeth clenched, her eyes flared—". . . if he's too *embarrassed* to get up on stage, then expect this note in your mailbox!"


In the nurse's office, a sophomore girl had just been hooked up to an aspirator by Mrs. Schwartz, a member of the Cannon Mothers' Club whose only qualification for tending to the young was the ability to speak gently. As the plastic tube pumped oxygen into her asthmatic lungs, the girl stared blankly at Stephen, who was sprawled flat on his back on a gurney. Stephen studied the ceiling.

Nurse Schwartz approached and laid a hand softly on his shoulder.

"Do you think you're ready to go back to class, Stephen?" she asked.

"No," he whispered.

"Well . . ." Nurse Schwartz seemed baffled. Her hand lifted off his shoulder, then touched him lightly again before she withdrew it completely. Her eyes wandered down the length of Stephen as if there was some solution in the way his legs attached to his hips.

"It's never a good idea to cry like you do," Nurse Schwartz said quietly, so the girl would not hear. "Kids can be mean, but if they see you cry that usually makes them meaner."

"When will it stop?" Stephen asked.

"I'm sorry?"

"When are they going to leave me alone? They don't have to like me. But I just want to know when they're going to leave me alone," Stephen said.

He raised his eyes to meet Nurse Schwartz's pained gaze. There was no answer to his question.


After the final bell rang, Stephen spared himself the torturous walk down the English Hallway, which he knew would be crowded with juniors and seniors heading to practice on the field. The Administrative Hallway afforded a quiet and easy escape. The pine office doors and framed pictures of prominent alumni would not snicker or giggle at him.

Stephen shuffled toward a framed eight-by-ten portrait of the Headmaster's Award winner, vicious white smile shining from half a hallway away. Hesitantly he passed the closed door to the headmaster's office. A small bronze placard was affixed to the bottom of the frame. Its calligraphic script announced the name of the previous year's recipient:

### JORDAN CHARBONNET

Stephen stared blankly at the name. At first it didn't register.

His eyes traveled up to the young man's face. Jordan Charbonnet's black hair was as sculpted as the proportioned, muscular figure that was clearly contained beneath his blazer and tie. Jordan's brown eyes and slightly full, auburn lips gleamed against immaculate olive skin.

Dread left Stephen. As he gazed up at Jordan Charbonnet, he felt a sudden quiet pass over his soul. Jordan Charbonnet was a vision, a god, and Stephen Conlin was hungry for the divine.

Jordan Charbonnet.

Finally, it registered. Brandon's brother.

Stephen had only glimpsed Jordan several times, years before. His only knowledge of him had been the tales of his sexual conquests that Brandon had related to all of them—stories that repulsed Meredith, fascinated Greg, and flushed Stephen with an excitement he could not yet understand.

On that November day, Jordan Charbonnet stood before Stephen Conlin smiling with a pride that Stephen felt had been stolen from him. The purity of desire filled him for the first time with sustenance rather than envy. Jordan Charbonnet's beauty spoke to Stephen louder than the whispers of the three friends who had abandoned and branded him. And Stephen knew that a feeling so strong and so immediate could not be destroyed by the cruelty of others. His desire offered him promise. It would, he hoped, armor his soul, protecting the most vital parts of who he might someday be allowed to be.

I must dream about you, Stephen thought, I must take you from this picture and place you firmly in my soul.

Five minutes had passed. Stephen thought it had been an hour. He gauged the distance between himself and the picture, and the front doors. He took one step forward, and then lifted the picture off its nails. Without a single witness, Stephen walked out of Cannon with Jordan Charbonnet under one arm.

# 4

Meredith's fifteenth birthday came one month after Thanksgiving and her father gave her a car, a brand-new Toyota 4-Runner fully equipped with CD changer and leather seats, to which Trish Ducote commented, "He could at least have waited until Christmas!" As Meredith would realize later, her father had an ulterior motive for making a gift of the car. When Ronald Ducote divorced Trish, he unprotestingly departed their Garden District mansion, the Dubossant residence, which had originally belonged to Marie Dubossant, Trish's grandmother, and surrendered any claim to Trish Ducote's sizeable inheritance and mutual funds. The car was meant to prove that Ronald now had money of his own and Trish could finally just give in and go back to her maiden name. Why Trish kept her married name baffled most people, but Ronald had told Meredith he thought it was a deliberate gesture meant to intimidate his girlfriends. Ducote was a "yat" name, indigenous to the less wealthy residents of New Orleans who were more Italian than French and lived in the suburbs hugging the shore of Lake Pontchartrain. A "yat" had a Brooklyn-esque accent, a mother with big hair, and a tendency to use the expression "Where y'at?" when inquiring about someone's well-being. Hence the term yat, and hence the reason Meredith's parents had divorced. Meredith knew her father had been a yat, much in the same way that Stephen's mother, Monica, had been a poor Irish girl from the wrong side of Magazine Street. While Trish Ducote had spent her youth at debuts and Mardi Gras balls, Ronald had attended crab boils and gone on fishing trips to Manshack.

Christmas break was several weeks away the day Meredith skipped cheerleading practice and drove to an area along the Mississippi River known as "the Fly," a stretch of grassy, hillocky riverbank that was home to middle school soccer games and several jungle gyms. Meredith came here to contemplate most things she wouldn't dare think in the halls of Cannon School.

An unseasonably cold winter stained the air. The sky was a flat gray and the oaks of uptown New Orleans stood out in a ferocious shade of green against the stone-colored clouds. After the final bell, Kate had snuck her a Marlboro Light she had stolen from her father's hidden pack. Kate was taken aback when Meredith put the cigarette in her coat pocket and said she wanted to smoke it alone.

By the time she was fifteen, Meredith did not feel awe for many things. The Mississippi River was one exception. Staring at the river from where she sat on the 4-Runner's hood, her cigarette smoldering between her fingers, Meredith thought of a poster Mr. Carter had on his classroom wall—a drawing of a man in a black trench coat poised on the edge of a cliff, staring out at a stormy sea. She thought the man was supposed to be a poet but she wasn't sure. Now she felt slightly like the man in the picture: the thought occupied her mind and eased the lingering burning sensation in her lower jaw. Only the wind wasn't strong and the Mississippi was quiet and sluggish.

Meredith and Greg had not said a word about the note in the month since Greg had written it and Brandon had taped it to Stephen's book bag. The night before, she and Greg had been studying, which usually consisted of looking sidelong at their books for a while, and then falling back onto Meredith's bed, where Greg would lift up her shirt and start gnawing her nipples through her bra, then manage to yank the cups down over the bottom of her breasts before finally undoing the hooks and taking it off. He had taken his shirt off, which made it better than usual.

But then Greg had started in. *Baby, baby, baby*—over and over again, in low breathy moans. She had finally retaliated with an impatient, "*What?*"

"Huh?" Greg gasped, his mouth still pressed against her breasts.

"Baby . . . What?" Meredith asked.

He hopped off the side of the bed and retrieved his T-shirt, which was dangling on the back of Meredith's desk chair. He stabbed an arm through one sleeve. "You don't have to be a bitch about it. If you don't want to, then just say so . . ."

"I didn't say that," she answered, her head hitting the pillow again.

"No. You were just being a bitch!"

"You know what, Greg . . ." Meredith began and then stopped, bringing both hands to her forehead. Greg shot her a look of baffled frustration. Five more seconds and she knew he would be angry.

"Whatever," she whispered.

"So you think I'm some moron?" Greg asked.

He had read her mind. For an instant, Meredith thought that she might be wrong about him. Greg knew things the way she did, but he just couldn't articulate them. Maybe she and Greg often shared the same thoughts, but neither of them could know for sure because they were always too afraid to express them.

"Yeah, whatever!" Greg was getting breathless with fury. "You know, like, since we started high school you've become, like, this totally different person. It's like you think if you're as bitchy as Kate then you're going to . . ."

"I am *not* a different person!" Meredith cut in, jumping off the bed. "Jesus. Just go before my mom comes in."

"Meredith, if you think being a bitch is going to make you homecoming queen in four years, then just forget it because—"

"What the hell is that supposed to mean? Homecoming queen?" Her anger was rising uncontrollably. She had been reaching for her bra, but now her arm had drifted to her side and she no longer cared that her breasts were still exposed. Greg had cut deeper than he realized. She liked to think that there was still a part of herself that was sanctioned off, a small portion that still connected her to the girl she had been before entering Cannon. She was outraged that Greg would be the one to try to convince her that her connection to the past did not exist.

"So you're exactly the same?" she asked, harsh as she could make it. "You haven't changed at all? Yeah, right! Why don't you ask Stephen's opinion?"

Meredith looked away from him. Silence followed. When she finally looked back, Greg had gone rigid. His face was fixed, like her own mother's, indignant and speechless, to let her know that she had violated something—gone too far and cut to the bone.

Suddenly, his arm arced through the air in a clean sweep, his hand forming a fist in the instant before it struck her right beneath the jaw. When it hit, she felt her mouth rear up, pressing her right eye against its socket. Then she was staring into her bedspread.

"Shit," Greg whispered.

Meredith lay with her face pressed against the comforter. Maybe she had gone too far. Stephen's name could propel both of them back into anger.

"I didn't . . ." Greg stammered, "I didn't . . ."

"Go," Meredith said.

After he slammed the door behind him, she righted herself. She lifted her bra off the comforter and strapped it on. She didn't bother to put her shirt back on as she crept to her bedside mirror and stared at the first signs of a bruise beneath her bottom lip.

Greg had a dozen good defenses he could use against the mention of Stephen. Brandon had made sure of that. Stephen was a fag; he broke the rules; he betrayed the world they now lived in, and had never even apologized for doing it. Why did Greg have to hit her to prove that? Hadn't the note they taped on Stephen's book bag made it all obvious?

*I know things.*

The thought struck her instantly. She cocked her head as if fascinated by the developing bruise. *I know things.* Greg's fist had shown her that her words were more powerful than she realized.

Now, the *Cotton Blossom* was rounding the bend in the river, just off the bank of the Fly, its brightly lit decks and harsh calliope music a sudden disruption. She felt the winter chill in the air and shivered before the smoldering butt of the Marlboro Light stung and she released it from between two fingers with an angry hiss.

The *Cotton Blossom* cruised down the river in front of her, a trail of wavering light on its wake. She tried to focus on it. She was being forced back toward memories she didn't want to face.

It had been a Sunday during the summer before their sixth-grade year at Polk.

Meredith's mother had left her with Aunt Lois, who wanted to teach Meredith how to make macaroni picture frames. Meredith had called Brandon's mother. No, the boys weren't there. She'd called Miss Angela, Greg's mother, and got no answer. So she went to Greg's house, where she plucked out the hidden key from beneath the geranium pot on the back porch. (Stephen's hidden key was buried in one of the flower beds outside the back door; Brandon, as far as she knew, didn't have one.) As she walked down the side driveway of the Darby residence, she noticed the family mini-van was missing, which meant that Mister Andrew and Miss Angela had probably taken Greg's younger brother, Alex, to the aquarium. Had Greg, Brandon, and Stephen gone with them? And if they had, why had they gone without her?

Once inside the house, she was overcome by the giddy sensation of trespassing in empty rooms. Her only company was the stuffed Mr. Toad perched precariously on the piano bench in the living room. (Alex was infatuated with *The Wind in the Willows.*)

Then she heard the boys upstairs.

She craned her neck and stared at the plaster molding around the crown of the chandelier. She continued to listen—but voyeuristic excitement collapsed into an icy bath. What she was hearing was not laughter. It sounded like a series of giggles, but it was too urgent, and there were too many in a row. She couldn't recognize any voices. If only one of them would talk.

She heard what sounded like a dog's yelp.

"For the love of God . . ."

It was Greg's voice. But something was wrong with it. He didn't sound like himself.

Then she heard Brandon's laughs, high pitched yet striving to be the loudest. Angry tears stung her eyes. What was there for them to laugh about without her? What would the three of them be doing that they had to shut her out?

Meredith locked the back door to the Darby residence behind her and slid the key back under the geranium pot. She started to run down Philip Street. The faster she ran, the harder it was to cry.

The muddy river sprawled before her and Meredith thought once again, *I know things.*

"Hey!"

Greg was standing ten feet away from where she sat on the hood of the 4-Runner. His father's Bronco was parked comfortably far away. He had wanted to take her by surprise. Despite the chill, Greg was wearing his practice shirt with the sleeves shorn off, revealing his bulking shoulders and broadening forearms. His hair was sweaty. If Greg was going to endure this conversation at all, he'd do it only after he had spent two and a half hours on the football field proving he was invincible.

"Look, I get it if you, like, don't want to talk to me right now . . ." Greg said.

"How did you know I was here?" Meredith asked.

"Kate."

Meredith's breath hissed between her teeth.

"What I did was stupid . . ." Greg trailed off, his hands fumbling, trying to clasp one another. He studied the patch of pavement between his cleats. Meredith had never seen him so deflated, so in need of something from her.

"It wasn't stupid," she answered, her gaze moving back to the river. "It was something . . . else."

She heard Greg let out a snort. When she finally worked up the nerve to look at him again, she saw that he was crying.


Hours later, Meredith was unable to fall asleep. Eventually, she kicked the covers to the floor. She got out of bed and crawled silently downstairs to her mother's liquor cabinet, which was routinely un-locked. She was about to pour herself a glass of Stoli when she de-cided to take the bottle and the glass upstairs with her.

Meredith knew why she couldn't sleep. She couldn't forget the moment when Greg began to cry. She downed half a glass, wincing as the vodka burned a path through her throat. Her skin felt warmer, her feet lighter. At her desk, she opened her Biology notebook to a section of blank pages. If the memory of Greg's weeping was plaguing her so much, maybe there was a way to rid it from her system.

She wrote. The words flowed almost effortlessly. She grew frustrated with how much her hand could not keep up with her thoughts, the spe-cific details—Greg with his muscular shoulders hunched, head bowed, face contorted with anger at his own tears. She found herself describing the river behind him. Meredith paused; she felt dizzy. The spiral notebook originally intended for Biology would become her journal. By day, it would rest under her bed next to the bottles of Stoli she would begin to swipe from the liquor cabinet.

By three A.M., Meredith had filled three pages. By the fourth page, she found herself writing Greg Darby a letter she would never give him.

*I don't want the responsibility of you. Because some day some-thing's going to tear open that hole I pierced last night—like two fingers gouging through a tiny slit in paper and wiggling until they tear the entire paper in half. And when that happens, Greg, you're going to fall through. And the chances are you'll try to take someone with you. And if that someone isn't me, if you try to take other people into the fucked-up madness that you're trying to coat with muscles, then I'll rush to save them before I even think about you.*

To Carolyn Traulain's quiet pleasure, Stephen made it to auditions for the first musical of the Cannon Drama Club season. She cast him in the role of the tenor in *The Mikado*. The theatre budget being absurdly small, she staged the elaborate musical as a concert version with three microphones across the front of the stage and cast members dressed in coat and tie and evening gown. The four performances were poorly attended, but Saturday night's closing performance garnered the best crowd—twenty parents and friends in an auditorium that seated three hundred. In the front row, Monica realized she had had no idea her son could even sing.

In the back row, Meredith watched the performance, after lying to Kate and Greg that she was having her period and didn't feel like sneaking into Fat Harry's with Kate's sister's expired ID.

In the wake of David Carter's altercation with Carolyn, he and his wife broke tradition and did not attend any of the performances.

After the performance, Monica tried not to cry as she handed her son a bouquet of white roses. Stephen opened the card, which read "I'm very proud of you and I'd like to take you to Rome this summer so you can see some Michelangelos."

Meredith did not go backstage. She snuck out during the curtain call.

Their freshman year, Greg Darby and Brandon Charbonnet were members of an accomplished football team that nearly won the state championship before losing to the Thibodaux Boilers. Coach Stubin often compared Brandon—his best defensive tackle—to Brandon's older brother, Jordan, who was, he declared, "the best wide receiver

I've ever seen." Meredith cheered them on with a dedication that was as emphatic as it was hollow. Jeff Haugh was elected cocaptain for next season's team; he had given up the theatrical ambitions that his parents, friends, and coach had all found so puzzling, and he had played without distraction. Still, he did not want the position and in the ballot he had not voted for himself.

In January, the school receptionist finally noticed the absence of Jordan Charbonnet's picture outside the headmaster's office. The headmaster eventually dismissed it as a student prank, and he told his secretary to put any of the Charbonnets right through if they called to inquire about the missing picture. They never did.

By March, Meredith Ducote was downing a bottle of Stolichnaya a week. It helped her vomit after lunch. Trish Ducote had fired two housekeepers over the missing bottles. Meredith's secret notebook was half-full.

Greg decided not to go out for basketball. Brandon did, causing Greg to quickly reverse his decision. To Meredith's delight and the boys' shared fury, Brandon and Greg warmed the bench all year, neither of them having the skill necessary to move the ball with grace and panache.

Brandon ended up passing David Carter's freshman English class with a D-minus. He was the first and last student David Carter ever let pass with such a grade. The thought of having to teach Brandon for another year quelled any delight David would have taken in failing him. Stephen made honor roll with straight As, except for a B in Algebra, a course he hated. Meredith finished her freshman year with four Cs and a B, out of deference to Greg and Brandon. Kate's mediocre grades reflected the fact that she had routinely copied Meredith's work in the three classes they had together, and that Meredith had decided to answer many multiple choice questions incorrectly because she felt it would not be right for Kate to get As. Greg had lied to Brandon about his own "even Cs" and Meredith found out that he had actually earned two As and three B-minuses. She never asked him about it, but after several glasses of vodka late at night she dedicated a journal entry to detailing the scenario of telling Brandon that Greg had deceived him.

In early May, Stephen heard from Carolyn Traulain. Her cancer had recurred. He asked her what that meant. She would not tell him so he would not cry.

They sat alone in her office for several empty, quiet moments before Carolyn said anything more. She told him she wanted to enhance the profile of the Cannon Drama Club: They could raise money through bake sales, schedule regular meetings, and name a chairperson—him. When Stephen jumped up to embrace her, Carolyn believed that for an instant she could feel the lump the ultrasound had discovered in one of her lymph nodes.

As he left her on that day—the last day of his freshman year— Stephen walked numbly past Jeff Haugh in the English Hallway. Jeff nodded to him and mumbled a "hey" as he passed. Stephen didn't notice.

By the middle of June, the time of the year when two years earlier four children would have been riding their bikes to Lafayette Cemetery and chanting rhymes in the rain, Stephen and Monica left for Rome, Brandon was relieved of his position as a runner in his father's law firm for calling one of the senior partners "an asshole," and Greg and Meredith decided to have sex.


Greg parked his father's Bronco several yards from the lone street lamp illuminating the muddy bank of the lagoon in City Park, and turned to grab Meredith. He cocked his head toward the rear of the car. "More space in the backseat," he said. She knew he was proud to have been considerate enough not to lose his virginity in his own room, which was right next to the Power Rangers–studded bedroom of his seven-year-old brother, Alex. Greg loved Alex hugely and dumbly, Meredith knew, and he probably treated him with more tenderness than he was exhibiting with her now, as he parted her clothes and her legs, pressing himself against her prone body, before shoving himself all the way in.

Fire lit the base of Meredith's spine. She bit her lip. Greg mistook it for arousal.

She waited for the pain to subside, the way she had been told it would. It didn't. He held her breasts as if they were handlebars and rode her as if her vagina was his own fist. Meredith tried to tell herself not to feel disappointed after he finished, dressed hastily, and kicked open the back door, letting in the sticky night air, which played over her body as she lay pressed to the leather. The drone of cicadas wafted into the car. After this night, Meredith would always associate the buzz of insects with the feeling of sudden, flushed exposure. Greg had not even bothered to remove all of her clothes.

"Did it hurt?" he asked her, standing several feet away from the open door and smoking a cigarette from a pack he and Brandon had shoplifted earlier that evening.

"No," Meredith lied.

He nodded, without looking at her. "We gotta go to Brandon's," he said, dropping the cigarette in a flutter of sparks.

Brandon's parents had flown up to New Jersey to visit his older brother Jordan, who had just completed his freshman year at Princeton, and was threatening not to come home for the summer, mentioned taking some time off—which spurred Elise and Roger Charbonnet to book themselves on the first available flight.

When Greg and Meredith arrived, Brandon had already set out three bottles of Tanqueray he'd retrieved from his parents' liquor cabinet. Brandishing a Gatorade bottle, Brandon let his gaze drift from Meredith to Greg, who was standing behind her. Meredith felt a hot blush cross her cheeks before her neck stiffened and her hands curled into fists.

A smile broke across Brandon's face. He knew.

He laughed and leaned against the kitchen counter, surveying the two of them as if sex might have lengthened their limbs. He picked up a Gatorade and gin off the counter and extended it toward Meredith. "Congrats, Mer!" he said, laughing.

She took it. Greg stepped from behind her and Brandon shot one arm around his shoulders and wrestled him into a headlock. Greg let out a grunt muffled against Brandon's chest. Meredith looked from the green-tinted drink to Brandon, whose face leered like a child's, his tongue poking from between his teeth. He drove the knuckles of one fist into Greg's scalp.

"Dude! Stop!" Greg spat. Brandon was threatening to bring Greg to the linoleum floor.

Meredith watched in rigid silence as Brandon spun Greg around by his neck. Brandon's laughter was growing more high pitched as the other boy struggled. Their tussle had turned into a mad dance of flailing arms and stumbling feet. It was the first time she had seen anger, envy, and joy so confused.

She brought the plastic cup to her mouth. The first slug tasted foul, but she drained the entire cup and felt the veins in her neck constrict her burning throat. Brandon finally hurled his friend to the kitchen floor. Greg landed on his back, both hands going up to block any possible blows. Greg's smile was weak and defeated.

"You dog, man. You're a *fucking* dog, Darby!" Brandon shouted.

He pivoted and faced Meredith, looking her up and down the way he and Greg had done on the first day of the school year.

"Am I any different?" she asked, with gin-induced bravery. She managed a sarcastic smile.

Greg lifted himself off the floor with one hand clenching the edge of the counter.

"Naw, you look pretty much the same. Course, if you were naked maybe I'd be able to—"

"Brandon, man! Shut up!" Greg groaned between guffaws.

Meredith and Brandon locked eyes, but Greg didn't notice. She often directed the same glare at Greg, but he had met it with only bafflement. Brandon, on the other hand, gazed back at her evenly.

Greg moved into the adjacent living room and flopped down on the sofa beneath a photograph of Jordan, a Gothic building with naked vines behind him. Jordan looked like his brother, but a larger more perfect version executed by a master sculptor who had known better than to give Jordan the sharp angularity of Brandon's rigid features.

"You're happy for him?" Meredith whispered to Brandon.

Greg switched on the television and flipped through the channels. He had lost his virginity and wrestled his best friend—plenty of accomplishment for one night.

"What's up with you, Meredith?" Brandon asked softly.

"You're relieved, aren't you?" Meredith said.

His dark, narrow eyes slanted with suspicion.

He's afraid of me, she thought. He snorted and followed Greg's path to the living room. He sat next to Greg, who was intently watching the big-screen image of a car flying through a bridge guardrail in a shower of sparks. Meredith poured herself another drink.

"Brandon?" she called.

"What?" he barked back.

"You're not supposed to mix alcohol and Gatorade. Gatorade's got electrolytes in it and it puts the alcohol right in your bloodstream . . ."

"That's the idea . . ."

He lowered his voice, finishing to Greg, ". . . you stupid bitch."

Greg exploded into laughter and cocked his head toward the kitchen with a mischievous grin.

Later that night, she wrote in her journal what she had wanted to tell Greg when he smiled at her so wildly. Drunk, she had to tense her entire shoulder to keep the pen against the page.

> *I know more of your whispers than you think I do. And sometimes I think both of you would do to me what you did to Stephen. But instead, you both kept me. That's really why you wanted to do it, isn't it, Greg? Not because you like my body. But maybe because the only way to keep me from being a link to the past, a link to what you want to forget, is to fuck me. Am I different now? I think so. One time, a time that seems so long ago but really isn't, I was one child among four. Now I'm owned by two.*

# 6

During his first days in Rome, Stephen seemed intoxicated. Monica watched with pleasure as the city's Baroque beauty caught him by surprise, transforming his jet lag into gleeful delirium. Monica had booked the penthouse suite of the Hotel Hassler. Situated five stories above the Spanish Steps, their suite's plate glass windows offered a spectacular view of the Roman skyline more believable on a postcard. The terrace was larger than the entire suite and the bellhop informed them in broken English that heads of state sometimes held banquets on it.

After his mother had drifted off to sleep, Stephen would rise from his bed and pad silently to the sliding deck door.

From the edge of the terrace, Stephen breathed in the city from a safe distance. Five stories below, the melodic pump of European dance music drew Stephen's attention to the throng of Roman teenagers gathered on the Spanish Steps, jiggling to their handheld stereos. Their allegiances shifted easily, boys and girls drifting from group to group. Their laughter echoed up the Hassler's façade. Boys groped girls visibly, even from the height of five stories.

Herded with the other tourists through the Vatican Museum, Stephen and Monica wound their way down the corridors leading them through a labyrinthine series of frescoed rooms. Stephen became frustrated. And then all of a sudden, as they trudged through a single doorway that seemed to promise another empty library and unimpressive frescoes, they landed beneath the ceiling of one of the greatest works of art ever painted. Monica watched the reactions of surprise all around her as, one by one, the members of their group found themselves stepping into the Sistine Chapel.

Stephen moved deep into the crowd. He found a clear spot on the floor and lay down on his back to stare up at Michelangelo's ceiling with a wonder he had last felt watching summer sunsets with his three best friends.

A security guard had to ask him three times to get up off the floor before he complied, his eyes still on Adam's pointed finger.

At night, Stephen and Monica descended the Spanish Steps. To steady herself, Monica would reach one arm out awkwardly and Stephen, his mother's well-trained child, would take it and support her without being asked. While exploring the winding streets, Stephen would suddenly feel his mother's hand in his, and he would leave it there. He was the escort—the male Conlin who had not died.

As Stephen tossed a penny over his shoulder into the Fontana di Trevi, he caught the open gaze of a beautiful Italian boy sitting amid the guitar-playing students next to the fountain. The boy looked at Stephen with what Stephen realized was fascination tinged by lust.

Jeff Haugh saw Carolyn Traulain's obituary in *The Times-Picayune*. He was working that summer as a stock boy in his father's office supply company and was leafing through a discarded copy of that day's paper left in the stockroom. He sat sweating and smelly on top of a stack of shipping crates staring dumbly at the brief paragraph sketching his old drama teacher's entire life, noting her few survivors. He knew he couldn't attend her funeral. She had died thinking the worst of him and it was now too late to correct the misunderstanding that occurred outside her office.

He got a pair of scissors out of the supervisor's office and clipped the obituary from the paper.

Jeff looked up Stephen's address in the Cannon directory before driving to the darkened, shuttered Conlin residence on the corner of Third and Chestnut Streets in the Garden District. He slid the clipping into the mailbox attached to the wrought-iron front gate and noted how much bigger Stephen's house was than his own. A peculiar sensation burned in his stomach as he held the spokes of the front gate with both hands.

The night before they were to board a flight for New York, Stephen asked Monica how she had met his father.

The question surprised her. "At a streetcar stop. I told you," she said flatly.

They were eating dinner at the Hassler's rooftop restaurant. Monica had allowed Stephen several glasses of red wine, which had slightly stained his teeth and tongue and left him peculiarly curious.

"I know that. But I mean . . . what happened after that? You just met and then what?"

With her food untouched on her plate, and the skyline of Rome sparkling behind her son, Monica felt weighted with the responsibility of being Stephen's sole source of information about his father. Her words would shape Stephen's memory of him. A daunting prospect, when she felt he might do better without any memory of his father at all.

"He rode the streetcar to school. I rode it to work. We met one day at the streetcar stop. Well, we didn't really meet. He saw me and I saw him looking at me. So when we boarded, he walked by my seat and dropped a piece of paper into my lap. It was a poem. A very sweet one . . ."

Actually, the poem had baffled and offended Monica. On that afternoon in 1964, Jeremy had been staring at her as Monica attempted to dig a cigarette out of her tattered leather satchel. At nineteen, Monica interpreted "Angel of Smoke" as an insult about good girls and nicotine.

"What did it say?" Stephen asked.

"It was about how beautiful I was," Monica responded flippantly, taking her first bite of food.

Stephen furrowed his brow.

"It was a love poem, Stephen," she said.

"What kind of love poem?"

Monica went silent. She recalled the words as they had been written in Jeremy's severe cursive:

> her eyes cut knives
> through the smoke she breathes,
> a dragon mistaken for a witch.
> What beauty waits to come
> From an angel hidden in her smoke.

When Stephen looked into his lap, embarrassed, Monica realized she had been silently mumbling the words of the poem. He changed the subject.

• • •

That night, after Stephen had drifted into sleep, the memories he had stirred in his mother came to life. Monica lay awake in her double bed next to Stephen's, listening to her son's slow and easy breaths punctuating the sounds of Rome winding down into the deeper part of night.

Jeremy Conlin was the first person not to laugh when Monica told him she had been named after a moon.

Monica was working the candy counter at Smith's Drug Store on a hot, sticky afternoon in June of 1964, doling out scoops of ice cream that was practically milk. Other girls were sauntering in, sporting longer hair and bared midriffs, sashaying over the dirt-caked linoleum floors with a freedom Monica envied. Jeremy made his entrance at around three o'clock in the afternoon—the moment when the day seemed interminably stuck and Monica was forced to polish the counter furiously to rid herself of the panicked feeling that the day would never end. As Jeremy perched on one of the stools, it seemed that the counter was the only thing in the entire store that had been touched by human hand. It glistened with care, courtesy of Monica Mitchell, her blonde hair spilling over her face and threatening to conceal her ferociously blue eyes.

Jeremy slid a second poem into the path of Monica's rag. She slapped the cloth down with exaggerated annoyance, unfolded the piece of paper, and began to read. Jeremy pressed his stomach against the edge of the counter, looking dizzy with a joy that seemed guiltless and earned.

Monica read the new poem without concentrating on a single word. She had to keep her eyes off of Jeremy's gaze. He was obviously torturing her. She could tell he was one of the well-heeled Garden District boys. Darkly handsome, olive skin, undeniably attractive broad frame. He obviously thought he was better than she, simply because from birth he was rich enough to fend off fever and rats.

"You look like someone who has watched people die," Jeremy finally said in a low voice. She glanced up from the poem.

"People who've watched people die"—his tone was almost clinical—"they aren't as easily distracted by loud noises. Things don't bother them as easily."

"My mother died last year." Monica could almost not hear the sound of her own words.

"I'm sorry . . ."

"She was . . . She was a drunk," Monica said evenly. "She didn't want to go to the hospital, so I watched her, if that's what you mean!"

"I didn't mean to—"

"She used to throw up in the bed and I had to clean it up, if that's what you mean!"

Monica's voice had tripled in volume. A customer threw a startled glance in their direction.

"I didn't want to—" Jeremy stammered.

"Then just what the hell are you doing here, then?" she hissed.

Jeremy eased back down onto the stool, looking defeated, something Monica needed to see. Her hand rose to her neck. She found she would repeat this gesture often, each time Jeremy pierced something inside of her.

"What's your name?" he asked quietly.

Monica decided to test him. "My mother named me after a moon," she said flatly.

She was prepared for any response: The cock of the head that hinted at some lunacy in her lineage, or the look of amused surprise that told her she lived outside of a big joke she didn't get, possibly because she had never been privileged to hear the punch line in full.

"What kind of a moon?" he asked.

# 7

hree weeks after they attended Carolyn Traulain's funeral, Monica bought Stephen a car. He did not yet have his driver's license but he did have an overwhelming need to drive. Stephen wept so openly at Carolyn's service that when he looked up through blurred eyes he realized to his horror that some mourners were paying more attention to him than Carolyn's wig-crowned body in the open casket.

The Jeep Grand Cherokee was delivered with a giant red ribbon on its hood to the corner of Chestnut and Third Street, where it sat for three hours as Monica waited for Stephen to emerge from the house and stumble upon it.

Stephen first saw the Jeep as David Carter dropped by his house to pick him up for a coffee date. Stephen slid silently into the passenger seat of his teacher's station wagon, his eyes on the Jeep. To break the silence, David asked whose car it was. Stephen answered that his next-door neighbor must have bought a new Jeep for his wife. When he looked up, he saw Andrew Darby's Bronco coming down Third. As David pulled away from the corner, he watched as the Bronco slowed slightly next to the Jeep. Before David rounded the corner, he saw Greg and Meredith staring openly at the Jeep with its garish red bow.

Stephen realized the Jeep was his.

David bought Stephen an iced coffee. Stephen could tell he was trying to atone for what had happened the day they had discussed *Lord of the Flies* almost a year earlier. The teacher talked about his experience in college theatre, and gradually Stephen realized that the coffee date had a purpose: David was letting him know that he had been picked to replace Carolyn as the head of theatre. Stephen hardly listened, watching the teacher's nervousness spell itself out in darting glances and hands that repeatedly embraced his coffee mug.

"Carolyn was quite a person and I'm sure she was quite a director," David said.

"She was really great," Stephen offered blandly.

"She wasn't someone you wanted to mess with, was she? I mean, she was really . . . Don't tell any of the faculty I said this . . . but she didn't put up with bullshit, did she?"

There was a long pause. Stephen watched a harried woman rap her fingers on the counter, waiting impatiently for her cappuccino. He halfheartedly wondered if Mr. Carter was going to apologize for doing nothing the afternoon some student slapped a brand on his book bag for all the school to see.

Instead, he said, "Well, I'm looking forward to the coming year. I think it should be really great. And wherever Carolyn is, I think she's looking forward to it, too."

He smiled. Stephen glared at him. "And where is Carolyn, exactly?" Stephen asked.

"I have some belief in a life after this one," David Carter managed.

Stephen nodded slightly. "I don't believe in God."

There was another empty pause. David broke it by rising from his chair. Stephen followed. On the ride back to Stephen's house, they hardly spoke. They rounded the corner and discovered Monica with one hand poised on the hood of the new Jeep.

"I can't drive," Stephen mumbled, as he climbed out of David's car.

After his new drama teacher pulled off down the street, Stephen hesitantly fingered the enamel. Monica stood firm on the sidewalk with her hands on her hips. "I'm going to teach you. In this." She gestured to the Jeep.

Stephen looked back at her, startled.

"You deserve a car. How's that, Stephen? Can you allow yourself to be excited now?" she barked. "Oh shit . . ." she whispered, as Stephen bowed his head with the first sign of tears. Monica curved one arm around her son's waist and set her chin into the nape of his neck. She held him.

"All right, all right," she whispered. "I didn't raise you Catholic. You don't have to atone for everything."

Stephen's laughter punched through his tears. "It's a beautiful car, Mother," he said with forced determination as he slipped out of her grip. He studied the Jeep again, walking in a slow circle around the sparkling vehicle until his mother smiled with triumph. Stephen knew she thought she had brought on his tears.

Kate Duchamp decided to have a party. Her mother and father were in the Mediterranean on a cruise, and Kate had free rein of the four-bedroom Victorian, complete with swimming pool and wet bar. Meredith Ducote would help Kate set up. In Kate's words, Meredith "knew stuff about drinking."

It was an August evening. The air was thick and heavy. By eight o'clock, the street outside Kate's house was clogged with sport utility vehicles and luxury sedans borrowed from parents. Jeff Haugh arrived driving his Honda Civic. Cameron Stern—the closest Jeff had to a pal on the team—had pressured Jeff into going. As Cameron explained it, they were both obligated to go because they were football players. But Jeff knew that Cameron not only needed a ride but was participating in a pool of senior football players who had placed bets on who could sleep with the youngest Cannon girl. Jeff had bowed out of entering the pool, but he had been pressured into attending the party nonetheless.

More people showed up than Kate expected. Jeff found a corner in the kitchen, sipped his beer, and watched with mild amusement as Kate had the requisite panic attack before downing three shots of Southern Comfort that Cameron poured for her, before the two of them disappeared upstairs into Kate's parents' bedroom.

Jeff wandered the house, pretending to ignore the admiring glances of underclassmen, some of them beaming at being in the presence of next year's first-string quarterback. Most of the guests were outside around the pool and he found a spot in the relatively empty living room, where he struggled to concentrate on the ten o'clock news. Then he heard Brandon Charbonnet's voice tear through the backyard.

"That fuckin' faggot gets a brand-new Jeep and I've gotta drive my dad's shitty Cadillac!"

"Got a big pink bow on it, too!" Greg Darby chimed in.

"That's what you get if you fuck your own mother!" Brandon yelled.

"How can he fuck his mother if he's a fag?" Greg asked.

"Maybe she straps on a dildo and gives it to him doggie-style!"

Jeff rose from the living room sofa amid the chorus of squeals and the obligatory shouts of "That's disgusting, dude!"

If Cameron Stern could get Kate Duchamp into the bedroom after only three shots, he could find his own ride home. Jeff left.


Brandon's pantomime of Monica Conlin sodomizing her own son provoked drunken laughter and high-pitched cries that lifted Meredith out of her drunken haze, as she lay in a dark corner of Kate's lawn flat on her back. She sat up on her elbows. The pool area was a halo of light a few yards away. The Brandon and Greg act was finished. A fellow cheerleader was standing on a pool chair, making an earnest speech about how next week they would be sophomores, and then a year after that juniors, and then seniors, and then they would never be together again, and they had to enjoy the moment before . . . The girl exploded into tears and was embraced by her friends.

Meredith noticed that Brandon and Greg had suddenly vanished.


On his way home, Jeff Haugh was cut off at the intersection of Jackson and St. Charles by Brandon's father's "shitty Cadillac." Jeff slammed on his brakes and cursed before he saw the Cadillac veer right onto Jackson. As it rounded the corner in front of him, Jeff recognized the two teenagers behind the wheel. He also guessed where the Cadillac was headed.

Jeff gripped the steering wheel for a full minute. The car behind him was honking at him in staccato beats. Jeff felt his mouth open, as if he were going to say something to himself, but then he pursed his lips shut as he eased his foot off the brake and coasted through the intersection, safely on his way home.


Earlier that night, Monica had let Stephen drive her around in the Jeep unlicensed. He had never driven above twenty-five miles per hour, and he had taken them both on a meandering journey through the streets of the Garden District. He expressed his enthusiasm for the car with excited questions about the gauges on the glowing red dashboard and whether or not it was true that running the AC would drain the gas tank faster. Monica had answered all of them with a slight hint of a smile in her voice. Her son seemed at once boyishly curious and mannishly competent, which led her to believe the gift had served its purpose.

Now Stephen was upstairs and Monica was listening to Mahler's Second Symphony, "The Resurrection," which was escalating to its grand crescendo. At first, the sound of shattering glass was nearly lost in a peal of strings. But then Monica heard it again.

She sat paralyzed in her favorite reading chair, a Sidney Sheldon hardcover spread across her lap.

The symphony had almost concluded by the time she remembered that the Jeep did not come with a car alarm.

She heard Stephen's footsteps on the stairs.

Monica rose from her chair, the book falling to the floor. She heard the front door slam behind Stephen.

Through the frosted glass panes of the front door she saw her son's spidery shadow before the black silhouette of the Jeep. She opened the door with a hand so sweaty it greased the knob.

Something was wrong, but at first she could not tell what. Gradually, she realized that the Jeep was slouched on its carriage, as if the tires and axle had suddenly failed to distribute the weight of the car evenly. She went down the front steps to see what had happened.

The driver's-side rear tire had been gouged repeatedly. It sat like a cluster of molten rubber around the hubcap. A clean white line ran down the passenger side, arching in an erratic sweep before angling up to meet the side-view window. The front passenger window had been smashed in; the pieces of glass glittered like diamonds across the plush leather of the seat. Over Stephen's shoulder, she could see the word spray painted across the windshield, but in reverse. It took her a minute to make out the proclamation: COCKSUKR.

When Monica appeared on the sidewalk next to her son, he jumped, and then his knees buckled. She held him as he moaned. There was nothing she could say.

She clasped Stephen to her for five minutes, her own heart trembling with each sob. When he finally managed to breathe again, he said, "You can't do anything, Mom. You can't do anything . . ."

She guided him into the house. "You can't do anything, Mom," he kept saying. "It'll make it worse. Just don't do anything, Mom, okay?"

She lied to her son and agreed before giving him a shot of Chambord Royale and tucking him into bed.

Three hours later, as Stephen slept, the tow-truck driver arrived.

Monica handed him three twenty-dollar bills. The driver peered under the Jeep. Both driver's-side tires had been eviscerated by a knife—"A big one!" he added clinically. The white lines had resulted from a car key held in one fist and gouged through the paint. As the driver struggled to his feet, Monica informed him that she had special instructions.

At two-thirty in the morning, he deposited the Jeep in front of the Charbonnet residence on Philip Street. Monica knew that Elise Charbonnet would discover it in the harsh morning light when she woke up.

# 8

The next morning, her head pounding with the pulse of the previous night's Southern Comfort, Meredith retrieved her secret notebook from under her bed, wrote "I'm sorry about your car," and then tore the page and threw it in the wastebasket.

Monica got out of bed at eight A.M. after having slept three hours. She went to her son's bedroom door, cracked it, and saw him curled beneath the comforter. She would keep to herself the memory that had plagued her all night.

She went to Jeremy's study. On the wall above the doorway, printed starkly in his own handwriting, hung his favorite quote from *Death in Venice* by Thomas Mann: "For passion, like crime, does not sit well with the sure order and even course of everyday life; it welcomes every loosening of the social fabric, every confusion and affliction visited upon the world, for passion sees in such disorder a vague hope of finding advantage for itself."

In the disorder created by his parents' deaths, Jeremy and Monica had found distinct advantage.

In July of 1964, Jeremy Conlin decided to break the vow he and Monica had made together—that they were never to see each other's houses. Jeremy's parents were leaving town for their annual trip to the Gulf Coast. He asked Monica if she would like to come over.

Until now, their courtship had centered mainly around the St. Charles Avenue streetcar line. Each evening at six, they would ride the streetcar down St. Charles to Canal Street, before reboarding for their return trip. The red sunlight filtered through oak branches, glinting off Monica's blonde hair as she leaned against the window. Jeremy would attempt to compose poems in his leather-bound notebook. Sometimes Monica and Jeremy would get off the streetcar at Audubon Park. They would wander deep into the park, past children playing hide-and-seek around fallen oaks, crossing the bike path where other couples flew past them leaving a laughter in their wake that Monica found to be more contented than her own. One night, half a month into their courtship, darkness took them by surprise and the park became a jungle of shadows. She clutched Jeremy's hand and talked away her fear.

"I think you write because it's easier than talking," Monica announced.

"You're wrong," Jeremy corrected her, in the manner of someone convinced the world does not think and suffer as much as he does. "It's better than talking. There's a space between the words you don't allow yourself to slip into. Maybe it's because everything I write is about you. You don't hear the music of the words because you're just waiting for me to call you a dumb Irish girl or laugh because your drunk mother named you after a retarded boy crying at the moon."

Monica dropped Jeremy's hand like a hot plate. He kept walking a few steps before he stopped, bent his head toward a patch of night sky visible through the oak branches, and sucked in a deep, agonized breath.

"If you think I'm stupid why do you show me your damn poems?" Monica bit back.

"Because you're not stupid. You're too afraid," Jeremy told her.

Monica had not been afraid to clean up her mother's vomit. She had not been afraid to scare the rats out of her mother's bedroom. Jeremy Conlin was accusing her of being afraid of paper.

"I try to write about the truth," he said, his gaze nearly lost in the dusk. "If you don't like the truth, or if you blame me for it, well then, maybe you *are* a little bit stupid!"

The silence between them was punctuated by the drone of cicadas and the bleat of a horn as a ship pushed up the Mississippi.

"I want to make love to you!" he finally declared to the darkness.

She convulsed with laughter that bent her at the waist, then put her hands to her lips.

"You're laughing?"

"Yes," Monica gasped.

"Why?"

"Because you sound like a little boy!" she said, patting back the locks of hair.

"People want other people," Jeremy said in a measured, authoritative tone. "And the only way for them to get—"

He halted. She saw the shadow of him shake back and forth, as if to shed itself of the thought.

"I write about you all the time. Even when you're sleeping, I write about you. And take something from you with everything I write. I won't do that anymore unless I'm sure I can give you something in return."


Every July, Samuel and Amelia Conlin drove out of New Orleans, stopping in Biloxi, Mississippi, for dinner and then staying at the Grand Hotel in Point Clear, Alabama. When Jeremy announced he would not be going with them, they were neither surprised nor upset. A listless unease had overtaken their son since his graduation from Jesuit High School. However, they both knew it could be worse. Jeremy's room did not reek of marijuana and he preferred classical music—Mahler, in fact—over the Beatles. They had no idea he planned on copulating with a girl from the wrong side of Magazine Street in every room of the house.

When Monica first entered the Conlin residence, she was struck most by the way the light from the chandelier sparkled across what seemed at first to be a sea of glass—a profusion of glass etageres housing sets of crystal and mirrors that forced her to realize that with the exception of two front windows and a bathroom mirror there was not a shard of glass in her own shotgun house on Constance Street. She exclaimed over the front parlor drapes, to which Jeremy responded, "All that cloth to make a window seem more purposeful!"

When Monica laughed, Jeremy stayed still in the doorway. His gaze on her softened. She met his eyes, seeing that he seemed more comfortable in his own home with her now in it.


One stifling August night, when she was sixteen, Monica awoke to find the half-crippled Willie Rizzo standing over her bed. She screamed, flailed one arm at him, and sent him stumbling backward across her bedroom on his bad leg until he fell with a pathetic gasp. Monica's anger turned to pity. Just the sight of her naked body was a gift Willie desired. Feeling like the possessor of some strange secret, she let him stare at her for three minutes before she slid into her nightgown and guided him through the house and out the front door.

It was the closest Monica had ever come to sex, and she assumed that lying pinned and burning beneath Jeremy Conlin wouldn't be much different. All pain with a tinge of awe. But the burning of Jeremy inside her turned into a warm bath that washed through her legs. His black hair brushed against her chin, sending tingles down her sternum, making Monica aware of every single inch of skin she possessed. And beyond that skin was the hard and dedicated press of Jeremy Conlin—who, for all his passion, brooding, and poetry, had finally organized his muscles toward a single goal.

That night, as Monica slept with her head on Jeremy's bare chest, Samuel Conlin's Buick lost a back tire. The tire went spinning out from the car with such velocity that the driver behind him thought it was an animal darting across the foggy highway. The Buick plunged through the guardrail and a green wash of water slammed into the windshield. Samuel and Amelia Conlin were carried to the bottom of Lake Pontchartrain.

The answer was simple. Monica had to marry Jeremy immediately. Jeremy's vision of haunting Parisian cafes with Monica beside him was subsumed by a mansion, an inheritance that could last for decades, and a family obligation that would break his spine if he had to tend to it alone.

By marrying Monica, he gained a companion and a refuge from the surviving Conlins. Likewise, taking up house with a girl from the wrong side of Magazine Street would be an ideal rebellion against his parents' legacy of old money. Jeremy asked Monica to marry him less than an hour after he heard of his parents' deaths. He went to one knee with a force and determination that bordered on desperation. Jeremy's desire for her was so obvious, intense, and new that Monica could not think of saying no.

Stephen didn't knock before entering the study. Monica let out a small cry. He recoiled slightly into the doorway as if he had been slapped.

"You're awake," she said stupidly.

Stephen nodded. "Sorry," he said.

"What are you sorry for?" Monica asked.

But they both knew. It was an unwritten rule that Stephen never ventured into his father's study, especially when his mother was in it.

"Let's go to lunch," Monica said, standing abruptly and glancing at the office around her as if it were a foreign landscape.

"All right," her son said and then disappeared from the doorway.

Monica felt strangely guilty as she heard the rush of water through the pipes and into Stephen's shower a floor below. She knew she could not tell Stephen that she had his car dumped in front of Elise Charbonnet's house—not simply because she knew Brandon Charbonnet had probably been one of its violators, but because something had happened between her and Elise years before, before either of them had children whose wounds could drive them to a night without sleep.

# 9

Jeff Haugh had taken up his post on an ice-cold stone bench just outside the door to the locker room. He had brought no book with him to feign studying (which Julie Moledeux and Kelly Stockton were doing quite nicely at the adjacent table, as they chewed over the latest Cannon gossip). To keep his mind from freezing up with nervousness and anticipation, Jeff ran through all the things he should have been doing instead of waiting. He had a calculus test tomorrow morning. The first playoff game of the season was Friday, but he refused to join Cameron and the other guys who had coagulated on the far side of the courtyard to debate strategy against the Thibodaux Boilers, a team Cannon had not defeated in over a decade. These obligations were white noise as he waited for the door to the locker room to open.

"Aren't you cold, Jeff?" Julie finally asked. Her AP Biology textbook was spread open on her lap to justify the past fifteen minutes she'd spent getting Kelly's opinion on whether or not patent leather was too 1950s. He knew that Julie's eyes said another thing entirely—"I've been trying to blow you in the front seat of your car for two years, and I'd like to know why you haven't even given me a ride."

"I'm all right," Jeff said, with an obligatory smile.

Julie smiled back. She was a smiler by nature.

"Psyched for Friday?" Kelly asked.

Jeff almost asked what Friday meant before he remembered the playoff game, which could keep Cannon out of the finals. He nodded, and then sucked in a deep breath. A shiver shook his entire body. Julie frowned at him. The first warning sparks of what he called his "stomach problem" ignited at his sternum.

"Jesus, Jeff . . ." Julie said.

"If you get sick, the team's screwed. Just go inside," Kelly said.

"I think I will," he answered weakly. He rose from the bench and crossed the Senior Courtyard, giving Cameron a high-five as he passed. He mounted the steps, pausing to look back as the English Hallway door glided shut behind him. Stephen Conlin had just walked out of the locker room. Damn.

Three days later, after a grueling practice, Jeff sat in his idling Honda outside of the annex's single gate. The faculty parking lot had emptied out an hour earlier. Jeff's stomach had threatened to act up twice during the scrimmage. But worst of all, Brandon Charbonnet had opened his mouth in the locker room once again, and the only thing he had talked about was Stephen Conlin.

Something was happening to Jeff. It started with small tongues of acidic warning he could feel just above his navel, a replay of the sensation he'd felt when he watched Stephen Conlin walk down the middle of the English Hallway with **FAG** taped to his book bag. Now, almost a full year later, acid seemed to coat his entire stomach, as if a bottle of vodka had suddenly been uncorked inside of him.

He used to be ravenous after practice. He'd devour four Quarter Pounders in a row, consuming them in a heated rush. Now he was afraid to eat at all. Eating provoked a revolt throughout his body.

Minutes earlier, in the locker room, Brandon had all but declared he was the one responsible for defiling Stephen Conlin's Jeep three months before. His swaggering acknowledgment got lost in the locker room chaos Brandon often dominated—and those who did listen reacted less than Jeff expected. It wasn't that Brandon's teammates had suddenly decided to have sympathy for the wispy kid who performed in plays. It was more that Brandon's and Greg's harangue had gotten boring. If Brandon and Greg wanted to keep everyone laughing, Jeff thought, they would have to pick a more imposing target—someone the team thought was worthy of their contempt.

That afternoon, as Brandon had concluded his monologue with "Too bad his mommy has to pick him up from school!" a brief silence fell. Then Jeff slammed his locker door and the room lurched back into its usual melee, voices rising and towels tapping.

Jeff had pressed his ear to the freight door. On the way to his car, he had heard voices singing and tried to determine if one of them was

Stephen. He couldn't. He had driven his Honda into the parking lot, headlights strobing on the back wall of the Theatre Building.

The sky was washed in winter darkness. He slouched forward, his bent arms bracing his stomach against the steering wheel. Waiting. He heard the horn honk before he realized he had pressed it with his chest.

When he looked up, he saw Stephen Conlin staring back at him, caught in the glare of the Honda's headlights. Stephen was squinting. He was facing the headlights without wavering, as if prepared for a fight.

"Do you need a ride?" Jeff asked.

All the windows were rolled up. Jeff muttered a curse before popping open the door and craning his head out of the car. "Do you need a ride?" he asked again.

Stephen said nothing.

"I heard about your car," Jeff offered.

Meredith stared ahead through the windshield as Greg drove and talked about the game. The passenger seat of Mr. Darby's Bronco felt like a padded leather prison cell. The wipers squealed at the thin splatter of rain. According to Greg, there was no good reason he shouldn't be starting quarterback. Jeff Haugh wasn't better, he was just a senior. Boredom led Meredith to interrupt him.

"You shouldn't have done that to Stephen's Jeep," Meredith said.

In the brief silence before he punched her, Meredith could feel the air around her shift and make way, as if the interior of the Bronco were expecting Greg's fist to cut a swath through it. His knuckles dove into the soft part of her cheek, against her molars, bringing blood to the surface. Her forehead struck the window before the rest of her face followed, and she felt the strange warm sensation of her own blood matted to her skin by cold glass.

She opened her eyes.

Stephen stared back at her.

As their eyes met, she thought she was hallucinating. But then Greg pressed his heel on the gas and Stephen's face, framed in a car window, slid instantly out of sight.

"Fuck you, Meredith!" Greg bellowed.

"Take me home," she mumbled.

"I mean, shit . . . Meredith, God . . ." Greg was nearly hysterical.

"Greg, take me home or I'm jumping out of the fucking car right here!" she hissed, parting her lips enough so that Greg could see the blood smeared across her teeth.

Jeff heard Stephen make a sound that caught in his throat. He turned and glanced at Stephen in the passenger seat as the Bronco that had been waiting at the stoplight next to him surged forward through the intersection.

Jeff looked away. St. Charles Avenue stretched ahead of them in a dark tunnel of oak branches that obscured most of the street lights. He felt a pang of guilt for having looked away from Stephen so quickly. Stephen was behaving like someone who had just confessed a guilty secret and was hesitant to speak again.

"What play are y'all doing?" Jeff asked.

Stephen looked at him as if startled out of a trance. "*Carousel*," he muttered.

"Don't know it," Jeff said flatly.

There was another silence filled only by the rush of tires over pavement.

"You used to do plays," Stephen said quietly.

Jeff knew this wasn't a question. "Yeah, I saw you that day . . ." he stammered.

"Right," Stephen finished for him.

There was another silence. "How did you know about my Jeep?" Stephen asked.

"A lot of people talked about it," Jeff said.

He heard the sound of Stephen slumping back in his seat. Stephen held his face to the window as he started to cry.

"Hey . . ." Jeff recognized the tone of his own voice. It was the tone his father had used when Jeff told him he hadn't been cast in his first musical. It was the "hey" of other things—*there'll be other plays . . . you've still got football . . .*

"Take a left on Third," Stephen said, his voice choked and his face still pressed to the window.

"You ever been to the Fly?" Jeff asked.

For a moment Stephen looked like he was collecting himself. When he finally turned his face to Jeff, his eyes were so blue and luminescent with tears that Jeff almost gasped. He realized his face had gone lax at the sight of Stephen's eyes alone and found himself fumbling for his next words.

"I totally hate it when my parents see me cry," Jeff managed. "I can pick up some beers and we can go to the Fly for a little while. Watch the river. Just till you chill."

Stephen nodded, slowly, trying to conceal his amazement. "All right," he answered.

Cameron had made Jeff's fake ID because he possessed the secret knowledge required to pry the lamination apart and alter the final digit of Jeff's birth year. The woman behind the checkout counter at the EZ Serve gave it a bland look before accepting the wad of crumpled bills Jeff handed her. He slid the case of Bud Light under one arm and left the store, forgetting to get his change.

As he approached the Honda, Jeff saw that Stephen's head was slumped back against the headrest as if with weary fatigue, although his eyes seemed sparklingly alive as he watched Jeff's approaching steps. Jeff averted his gaze as he rounded the nose of the Honda, guessing that Stephen's eyes were following him with each step.

He slid into the driver's seat and, rather than passing the case off to Stephen, turned and dropped it on the backseat. When he righted himself, he saw that Stephen's eyes were locked on him. Jeff caught their pointed glare, which seemed suspicious, and managed a smile as he started the Honda's engine.

Swept desolate by the icy winds off the river, the Fly had become a shadow play of jungle gyms and grassy sloping lawns running along the bend in the dark river. Jeff parked his Honda with its nose to the curb, his headlights shining out over the several steps of rocks that lead down to the lapping bank of the river.

They sat on the Honda's hood, both of them safely fixing their gaze on the river. Stephen had obviously never had a beer before. He drank it from the can as if he were sipping from a wineglass. Jeff suppressed a chuckle, which he knew Stephen would take as an insult, and which Jeff suddenly realized was more truly tender affection. Jeff had pulled on a pair of sweats from the backseat, but they were both shivering, and the beer cans tucked between their thighs rattled slightly against the Honda's hood.

"I used to be friends with them," Stephen said.

"Who?" Jeff asked.

"Meredith Ducote . . . Brandon Charbonnet . . . Greg Darby."

Jeff could only nod. The massive black hulk of a cargo ship eased by them, its engines churning a dull roar beneath the whip and snap of the wind. Its wheelhouse towered above them, a suspended island of light.

"My dad has this room . . ." Stephen said, "well, it was like his office before he . . ."

He paused. Jeff knew the story of poor suicidal Jeremy Conlin. Every Cannon student did.

"Sometimes from his room you can see over the tops of the trees," Stephen continued, "and all of a sudden, I'll, like, see this building that starts moving, before I realize it's the top of a ship passing down the river."

The beer was warming Stephen. Jeff could tell. "Brandon's afraid of you," he said in almost a whisper.

Stephen shot him a sudden, violently incredulous look. His features curled into a sarcastic, offended sneer.

"Just trust me . . ." Jeff said. "You never hate someone that much unless you're afraid of him."

Stephen shook his head, studying the beer can between his thighs. He lifted it in both hands as if warming himself with a mug of cider. "I just have to wait, right?" he snapped.

"What?" Jeff asked.

Stephen slid off the car's hood. He moved away from Jeff toward the bank, balancing on the curb before the several steps leading down into the river. He held his back to Jeff.

"Now I might just be some little fag who does plays. And who hates PE. But my day will come. I just have to *wait*!" He said the last word through clenched teeth, and Jeff heard the sound of the beer can crumple in one of Stephen's fists before he hurled it into the air.

It took a moment for Jeff to realize that Stephen was walking away down the curb. Something in Jeff murmured, Wherever he's going, don't let him go there. His legs tensed up, forcing the beer can to upend and clatter to the asphalt. Jeff was about to reach for it when he saw that Stephen had stopped several yards from the Honda, his head cocked toward the night sky. And then Jeff saw it, too.

Jeff's first thought was: Impossible.

The halo of the streetlight just beyond Stephen was frenzied with flecks of white. They looked like moths. Jeff felt icy pinpricks across the back of his neck. He reached up instinctively and brought his hand away: moisture on his palm. Stephen was set in place. The air was filled with it, tumbling flecks of white that dappled the pavement around them.

"Snow," Stephen said, his voice resonant with revelation. He reached out and lifted his head, squinting. Laughter broke from within him.

For a brief instant, Jeff believed that Stephen had caused it. But no, he was the angel embracing it—a tall, wiry silhouette, head thrown back, arms thrown out to embrace the falling impossible.

Jeff wrapped his arms slowly around Stephen's waist from behind. His hands did not clasp around Stephen's stomach until Stephen tilted his head back slightly, opening his eyes only to be blinded by the snow. Jeff felt Stephen go rigid for a second, before his body slowly rocked back against Jeff's, allowing Jeff's entire weight to support him. Stephen's arms wilted to his sides. Jeff's lips met the nape of Stephen's neck with a hot rush of breath. He held his mouth there as Stephen's head gently rolled backward, fitting perfectly onto Jeff's shoulder.

Jeff's bottom lip became delicately caught between both of Stephen's. Half a minute passed before Stephen opened his mouth. For a while they shared breath. Both felt for the first time what it was like to be lost in another person and momentarily free of one's self.

Seven-year-old Alex Darby awoke to the sound of a monster tapping against his second-floor bedroom window. He sat up in bed with a sharp cry before he saw falling pieces of sky blotting out the glare of the neighbor's yard light. When he began to scream, Angela Darby sat up in bed with a jerk that awakened her husband, Andrew, from his Scotch-induced slumber. "What the hell?" Andrew grunted.

"It's Alex!" Angela managed, sliding out of bed and grabbing her robe on the way to the bedroom door.

"What the hell is he screaming for?" Andrew asked before smothering his face in the pillow to blot out his son's wails.

In the next room, Greg and Brandon leapt from Greg's bed at the sound of Alex's shrieks. The porn movie they had stolen from under Andrew's bed kept playing silently until Greg slammed one fist against the VCR's control panel and the frozen image of a woman's penetrated vagina was the room's only illumination. Both boys froze as they heard Alex's door slam shut and Angela's panicked voice before they could make out what Alex was screaming, "Mommy! Snow! Look, Mommy! Snow!"

Several blocks away, Meredith first saw the snow in what she thought was a swarm of roaches crawling across the liquor cabinet. All the lights in the living room were out and she was the only one home; she had drained her last bottle and crept downstairs for another before discovering that Trish Ducote had not replaced the Stoli. Meredith spun around. Both living room windows were dotted with snowflakes, their shadows swarming eerily across the walls and floor of the darkened living room. "Someone's kidding," Meredith whispered to herself.

At her kitchen table, Elise Charbonnet had composed the fifth draft of a letter to Monica Conlin, admonishing her for dumping her son's Jeep in front of her house and thus implicating Brandon in the vandalism. Roger Charbonnet had told her if she was that upset about it she should consult their lawyer. But to Roger's dismay Elise had refused, opting instead to draft a letter that after three months of composition was only three lines long. Elise glanced up into the adjacent living room to see her eldest son Jordan's picture had somehow been horribly stained. Jordan's smile was now splotched, his handsome face carved into a colorless pattern of shadow. And then the stains on his face shifted and slid down the frame as Elise turned to see the small drift of snow tumbling down the window opposite, from where it had become caught in the upper corner of the ledge. The letter forgotten, Elise rose numbly from the table and moved to the back door. For several minutes she stared out at the snow fall that had turned the Bishop Polk bell tower rising over their backyard into a looming, hazy shadow. She realized she was smiling. She had never seen real snow before in her entire life.

On the bank of the Mississippi River, the headlights of Jeff's Honda winked out and the only other light amid the blanketing snow was the iridescent green glow of the dashboard.

# 10

"**W**here the hell have you been?"

The front door slammed shut in response, cutting off the harsh echo of her words.

A dark shadow at the foot of the stairs didn't answer her.

Monica had waited for Stephen outside of the Theatre Building for over an hour. Panic had set in and she did not know a single parent or friend that she could call. She had finally strode into the Theatre Building and found David Carter sweeping the stage. He seemed too unnerved to offer up a coherent answer as to where Stephen might have gone. Then, as she drove home, the snow had begun to fall and Monica thought that the world had cracked down the center.

"I was with someone," Stephen said.

His voice seemed lower. Could it have been dropping for months now and she hadn't noticed? "Who?" she yelled back.

"What does it matter?" Stephen asked, but without any sarcasm she could detect.

"It matters because I thought something had happened to you. I waited outside the theatre for an hour. Mr. Carter didn't know where you were. Jesus, Stephen, I thought something was wrong. I thought maybe you'd done . . ."

Monica's thoughts careened into the wall of her real fear. On a June afternoon in 1983, Monica had driven frantically around the city after Jeremy neglected to meet her for lunch. She had tried his office in the English Department at Tulane. The departmental secretary didn't know where he was. She'd returned home to find a police cruiser parked in front of their house. A neighbor had reported a gunshot.

Monica didn't realize Stephen had ascended the staircase toward her until he took her in his arms, and she thought for a moment that the shadowy figure in the darkened foyer was not her son but an impostor.

"I'm not going to end up like Dad," he whispered.

She heaved in his embrace. He held her easily.

"Dammit, Stephen," Monica said, defeated, as Stephen walked her to her bedroom.

For the first time ever, Stephen tucked his mother into bed.

Monica watched as Stephen turned out the lights, shutting off the television where the weather man was announcing that the unpredicted snow fall had tapered but ice warnings were still in effect for all the Big Easy.

"Stephen?"

He halted in the doorway.

"I want to tell you something."

"Yes?" he asked.

His voice was too steady. Monica thought that he might be drunk.

"I want to tell you what Brandon's family did to me once," she said.

In June of 1976, Monica Conlin became the first and last woman ever to be the subject of a "Special Memorandum" by the Garden District Ladies' Society. Its chairwoman, Nanine Charbonnet, wrote her missive in finishing-school cursive, filling up half a page of perfumed stationery to issue her response to Monica Conlin's application for membership into the GDLS.

"Many of you are already aware of the unusual circumstances under which Jeremy Conlin came to take his wife, Monica. Many of you are also aware of the effect their marriage had on the Conlin family's involvement in the neighborhood we seek to preserve and protect," Nanine wrote.

"I do not wish to deny Monica Conlin membership simply because her entrance into the Conlin family seriously endangered the historical preservation of the Conlin-Dobucheaux house, where she now happily resides."

The memorandum was read aloud to a convocation of the society's thirty members on a Sunday evening. Among those present were

Nanine's new daughter-in-law, Elise, and Angela Gautreaux—recently married to Charles Gautreaux—who had already decided on the name of her first child: Greg. (Angela's children would be sired by her second husband, Andrew Darby—and her second child, Alex, would be a happy accident).

"I wish to deny Monica Conlin membership on the basis of one undeniable fact," the memo continued—read aloud by Melissa Dubossant, whose daughter, Trish, would soon marry a handsome, crude man with the harsh last name of Ducote.

"She has failed to raise a garden," Melissa read aloud. "Our neighborhood is one of verdancy within a city devoured alternately by concrete and the effects of forced integration. I am hereby requesting that we deny Monica Conlin membership on the basis that she has failed to raise a garden in keeping with the traditional landscape of our neighborhood."

Thirty hands wearing expensive but discreet platinum wedding bands and diamond engagement rings rose.

Several weeks later, Nanine Charbonnet was released from Southern Baptist hospital after an intense bout of what the doctors thought was pneumonia. Her son, Roger, and his pretty new wife, Elise, picked her up from the hospital and dropped her at her house, where she told them to leave her bed so she could resume her routine. Nanine owned two Pekingese, Hershel and Stanwick, and she walked them every afternoon at four.

Nanine's route brought her to the corner of Third and Chestnut around four-fifteen. On the day she was released from the hospital, Monica was waiting on her front porch with a gin and tonic.

When Nanine rounded the corner that day and saw the Conlin-Dobucheaux house, she clutched her pearls in shock, inadvertently releasing Hershel's and Stanwick's leashes.

Bougainvillea burst up the front two columns of the house. Morning glory vines curled up the house's side porches. The front lawn had been cut through by flagstone paths that wound between meticulously placed beds of crocus and azalea. Elephant ears poked through the corners of the high wrought-iron gate. Two medium-height banana trees stood like sentries on either side of the house.

From where she sat, on a wrought-iron patio chair purchased just three days earlier, Monica raised her glass to Nanine and wished for a heart attack to strike the woman right there on the corner.

Nanine retrieved her two dogs and hurried home to phone Elise. As new daughter-in-law, Elise had warmed to her duties as Nanine's lady-in-waiting quite well.

Several days later, when she was sure Jeremy was ensconced in his third-floor studio, Monica called Nanine and invited her over for tea.

*"Tea!"* Nanine exclaimed over the phone at Elise, a half-hour after she accepted Monica's invitation. "Does that woman really know how to serve high tea? Should we be expecting scones or doughnuts?"

Before their visit, neither Nanine nor Elise bothered to consult Monica's immediate neighbors about the new Conlin garden. If they had, they would have discovered that Monica had become one of the first women in their neighborhood to hire a landscaper. For a hefty fee, he had redesigned and replanted the entire front yard in just one month.

Still, Monica's application to the GDLS and the subsequent denial had driven a wedge between Monica and Jeremy that would never be bridged, not even by the child they would have five years later. Jeremy felt betrayed. His angel from the wrong side of Magazine Street had sold out, and the magic he had dreamed of creating with her was dwindling in the process. Occasionally, depending upon the amount of Merlot he drank, he would stumble downstairs. Monica would start awake with the thud of Jeremy hitting the mattress beside her. The night before Nanine and Elise called on Monica, she had opened her eyes to find Jeremy's mouth against her ear. His breath was hot from wine.

"Poor little Irish girl," he whispered.

Monica froze.

"Go upstairs," she hissed back.

"What are you serving tomorrow? Let me guess . . ."

"Jeremy. You're drunk. Go upstairs. I don't want you in the bed."

". . . tea, scones, and bite-sized portions of your own soul."

She shot up in bed so fast her shoulder cracked Jeremy's chin. He stumbled backward into the night table. Monica said nothing as Jeremy struggled to his feet with the help of the bathroom doorknob.

"I guess I'm not invited then," he mumbled, slamming the bedroom door shut behind him.

Monica did not sleep for the rest of the night. Nanine and Elise arrived at the Conlin residence on a July afternoon to find a pitcher of iced tea and three glasses set up on the wrought-iron table on the front lawn. The front door was open. The roar of Mahler's Second Symphony could be heard from the third-floor studio. Nanine squinted at the sound of the music; Elise's jaw fell slightly in awe. When Monica emerged from behind an azalea bush, Nanine cried out and grabbed Elise's arm. Monica smiled and swung open the front gate.

The three women took their seats. Elise fiddled with the lap of her dress to such an extent that Monica asked them both if they would like to go inside. Perhaps it was too hot? Nanine responded with a firm no. As she reached over to fill Nanine's glass, Nanine glimpsed the fleshy cleft of Monica's right breast through the armpit of her sundress. Monica caught her gaping, letting her eyes stay on Nanine's until the old woman realized she had been caught.

"And how is Jeremy?" Nanine asked as soon as their eyes met.

"Very well," Monica said, resting back into her chair.

"He's teaching now, I understand?" Nanine asked.

"What does he teach?" Elise said.

"Jeremy claims to teach his students about the lies that humans perpetuate to mask their own fear of mortality," Monica said easily.

Silence fell before Nanine managed a giggle. Elise gazed at Monica with almost reverent awe.

"His mother would be proud," Nanine said. Her tone suggested that not only would Amelia Conlin not have been proud of Jeremy but she probably would've tried to throw Monica over the front gate.

"The garden is . . ." Nanine began.

". . . beautiful," Elise finished.

"Thank you," Monica said, lighting a Benson & Hedges from a pack she kept in the breast pocket of her sundress, before exhaling through her nostrils. "The true secret to working with plants is understanding what ferocious beasts they truly are. Simply because they don't eat meat, we assume all plants are docile creatures."

She had lifted the insight from Jeremy almost word for word, except that Jeremy had articulated the thought to her years before as an explanation for why they should not have any front yard at all beyond a lawn.

Elise nodded her head emphatically.

There was a lengthy pause before Elise tilted her head toward the front door. Nanine noticed it and both of her hands tightened around her glass in response.

"Would you like to go inside?" Monica asked her.

"Would you mind? Just to look around?" Elise posed this question more to Nanine than Monica.

"Not at all. Have a look," Monica said. "Don't mind the Mahler."

"The what?"

"Nothing. Go on," Monica said sweetly, lifting a hand as if to nudge Elise through the front door.

But Elise had already shambled through, her hands clasped to her chest like a child entering a haunted house. Nanine sipped her iced tea. Monica smiled blandly at her as she swallowed, took a breath, and set her glass down.

"We all know your husband's crazy, Monica. You don't have to lie for us," Nanine said.

The younger woman twirled her cigarette in one hand, elbow propped on the arm of the chair as if at any point she might hurl the cigarette directly into Nanine's eyes.

"We are not responsible for our husbands," Nanine whispered.

"But our gardens are another matter entirely," Monica said.

Nanine offered a crooked half-smile. Touché, her smile said. Points earned. "Would you like me to tell you why you were really denied membership? Will you still be able to serve iced tea and try to dazzle us after I tell you the real reason?

"You're a guest here," Nanine continued, her voice almost a whisper again. "This city is dying all around us. My father helped to build this city. He laid this sidewalk, in fact. But now I am of the belief that all of it will someday be devoured by the river. You know the river, don't you? You grew up next to it?"

Monica didn't answer.

"My point," Nanine continued, "is that guests tend not to appreciate what we have here. These blocks, this neighborhood. They must be preserved. And that is a job best done by those who gained an appreciation for this neighborhood from the day of their birth."

Monica sucked another drag off her cigarette. Upstairs, Mahler's Second Symphony was resetting itself on the record player. "However," Nanine said, lifting her glass to her mouth and taking a sip, "I must admit, that no matter how extremely, you have demonstrated a . . . how should I put it? A sense of appreciation." She gestured to the garden around them.

"As for Jeremy, don't try to fool us. We all know that if he had his way this house would be a crumbling wreck. But he has you. And I guess whether we asked for it or not, we have you, too." Nanine set the glass back down on the table with just enough force to convey that she would not be lifting it to her mouth again.

Neither of them spoke. The Mahler played on. Elise was lost somewhere inside the house. In the trees overhead, the birds and cicadas were beginning their tribute to the slanting sun.

Forgive me, Monica thought. Forgive me, Jeremy, for letting this woman do this to me. Forgive me for wanting our children to have a neighborhood and a history. If you ever do forgive me, try to understand that I did this for my mother, who died in the company of rats, with many ghosts to lead her toward death and only one daughter to remember her.

"I accept," Monica finally said.

"Our next meeting is on Sunday," Nanine announced before rising from the chair and moving out the front gate, leaving her daughter-in-law behind. Monica sat and watched as Nanine disappeared around the corner of Chestnut Street.

Her new yard had been a small triumph. Yet a heavy defeat kept her sitting in the middle of it, glued to her chair for long minutes she didn't bother to count.

Shattering glass startled her from her stupor. Elise appeared in the doorway, holding half of a picture frame.

"I'm sorry," Elise mumbled, "I just bumped into it."

Monica rose from her chair slowly and took the shards from Elise's hand. Elise's palm was slightly scored by the frame's jagged edge and her whole body seemed flushed and sweaty with embarrassment.

"Where's the picture?" Monica asked without offense.

"It's on the floor in there. I'll sweep it up. I'm really sorry, I didn't mean to . . ."

She was trembling. Monica set the glass down and gripped Elise by both shoulders. "It's all right," Monica whispered, looking into the other woman's dark, doe eyes.

Elise nodded.

"I'll see you on Sunday evening," Monica said as she released Elise's shoulder, and promptly turned away from her.

"She . . ." Elise faltered, surprised, her jaw dropping. Monica turned and nodded.

"I'll see you then," Elise managed, then turned and descended the front steps.

Monica did not watch her go.

That night, she found Jeremy at his desk, bent over a notebook, his pen clutched in one hand and a half-empty bottle of Merlot on the desk next to him. He did not glance up at her as she lingered in the doorway for a moment. The frame Elise Charbonnet had broken contained a snapshot of Monica and Jeremy minutes after they had been married in a chapel just outside of Reno. Monica held the tattered picture in her hand. Jeremy finally noticed the picture. "Have you been accepted?"

Monica nodded.

Jeremy looked back to his notebook.

Monica shuffled into her bedroom, making it to the bed where she curled into a fetal position without bothering to untuck the covers. She cried for an hour. Jeremy was right.

She had lost her husband. The thought crippled her before another displaced it. I need a child, Monica thought.


Behind Stephen, the windowpane was fogged with ice but the snow on the ledge had melted. Monica could not look at her son for a while. He finally broke the silence.

"Why did you tell me this?"

She leaned her head to one side of the pillow to meet her son's eyes. "Never give in to them," she whispered. "No matter what they do or how important you feel it is to get their acceptance. Never kill part of yourself for them. Because other people will notice that part is missing before you do."

Stephen pressed the knuckles of his right hand into his left palm, as if testing their heft.

"I never went to one meeting," Monica said.

They both burst out laughing. Stephen crouched by the bed and rested his head on his mother's stomach. They continued to laugh. Monica's abdomen rose and fell, lifting Stephen's head in short gasps as his hand reached out to clasp hers.


Jeff Haugh awoke from a half-dream of Stephen's naked skin bathed in the green glow of the Honda's dashboard lights, and he tasted blood in his mouth. His hand grabbed for the pillow, slipping in a puddle of blood next to his jaw. He tried to cough, but the contraction only brought another spasm of blood up from his throat. When he sat up, he felt as if he were going to split down the middle.

When Jeff finally stood in his parents' bedroom door, his mother screamed when she saw him. Jeff tried to speak as his father pushed him into the bathroom. His mother stared dumbly at the trail of blood Jeff left across the carpet as she called 911. Jeff could not form words through the blood caking the insides of his mouth. If he had been able to speak, to tell them why he was vomiting blood across their bedroom late at night, they would have been baffled by his explanation—Stephen Conlin had ripped his stomach open.

# 11

The rain had frozen in the gutters overnight, and Meredith awoke to the glare of morning sun reflecting off ice. She sat up, slowly bringing her knees to her stomach. Her notebook lay open on her desk, but the sunlight blotted out her handwriting. An empty bottle of Stoli sat on her desk. She heard her mother's footsteps in the hallway and leapt from her bed, grabbing the bottle. She barely had time to slide it under her bed.

Meredith vomited into her closet. She had no choice; her mother was in the hall and would have blocked her way to the bathroom. When she finished, she lifted her head and found herself staring at her cheerleading uniform. With a sudden dread that cloaked her nausea, Meredith remembered today's date. December 8.

Several blocks away, Stephen opened his eyes to the sight of the oak branches outside his bedroom window frosted in ice crystals. He slipped out of bed and moved to the window.

Maybe Jeff Haugh wouldn't speak to him in school that day. But it wouldn't matter.

Stephen stared out over his ice-shrouded neighborhood and realized that what had happened the previous night was inviolable; it could not be taken from him the way his childhood had been. Jeff Haugh's arms and lips had held him, and no words or actions could undo that.

Jeff Haugh. Stephen rolled the name back and forth in his head. He found himself unable to think of him as just Jeff. His full name seemed more appropriate. With Jeff Haugh in his history, Stephen would always be part of something beyond his window.

He remembered the date: December 8. Jeff Haugh would in fact not be speaking to him that day—he had obligations in their little world that would draw him elsewhere, Stephen reasoned. That evening the Cannon Knights would face off against the Thibodaux Boilers in the game that could decide the state playoff teams. As first-string quarterback, Jeff bore the weight of Cannon's honor. Stephen's added weight would be too much to bear.

But when Stephen saw the ice, he imagined a football field covered in it. He smiled.

"Your future football prospects will be complicated . . . to say the least," said the heavy-voiced doctor as Jeff gazed emptily at him and his parents hovering over his bedside. The doctor addressed his parents next, as if the news had deafened their son. "He has a preponderance of stomach ulceration atypical in someone his age. Stress and strenuous exertion will aggravate it."

With these words, Jeff knew the doctor had virtually killed his football scholarship to the University of Michigan, insuring that he would go to Louisiana State University as his mother and father had. Jeff said nothing as the doctor delivered a death notice to his life plan.

"Did you do anything high stress last night?"

Jeff looked at him evenly.

"I had a few beers with a friend but that's about it."

Nodding, the doctor turned his attention back to Jeff's parents as he broached the topic of laser surgery.

As Meredith entered the locker room, Kate Duchamp grabbed her by the shoulder so hard that her book bag slid down her left arm. They were both dressed in their cheerleading uniforms, ready for the pep rally at three o'clock that afternoon. The locker room was packed with students talking and arguing louder than usual.

"Okay, like, where have you been?" Kate began as she led Meredith by one arm. "You want the good news or the bad news first?"

"The game's canceled," Meredith answered immediately.

Kate let out an audible gasp of disgust. "Okay, no! We're still waiting. Supposedly, like, they didn't get any snow in Thibodaux but they have to check to make sure the field doesn't have any ice because they had a freeze or something. Okay. Whatever! That was the bad news. You want the good news now?"

Meredith spotted Brandon and Greg amid a small cluster of letter jackets. Greg seemed to be the focus of attention, which was odd because he was surrounded by mostly junior and senior players. Kate took Meredith by both shoulders and pulled her in close.

"Jeff Haugh was rushed to the hospital last night. I don't know the details except that it's, like, some stomach thing."

She paused for effect. Meredith burped slightly, the acidic flavor of vomit blossoming in her throat.

"Do you know what that means, Mer?" Kate asked, louder. "Greg's going to play! He's going in as QB in the most important game of the year. Aren't you psyched?"

Meredith felt the threat of vomit now in her sternum. She knew if she didn't get Kate out of her face, Kate would feel it, too. She tried a smile and bowed her head

"Get your shit together! This is only, like, the most important day of the whole year!" Kate hissed before disappearing into the crowd.

"Did you hear?" Greg called out. Meredith turned to see that he was staring at her from his throng of letter-jacket cronies. She moved toward him, trying to force the nausea down into the base of her stomach. She clasped his face in both of her hands and kissed him on the lips. He went rigid. A few players snickered into clenched fists.

"Congratulations, baby," she whispered, before releasing Greg's face with too much force. Other players whistled under their breath. As she strolled off toward her locker, Meredith heard Brandon mumble, "She's fucked up, dude."

Greg didn't respond. During the brief kiss, Meredith had pressed his upper lip against her front tooth, the one he had chipped the night before when he slammed her head against the car window.

"It can't be fucking canceled, man!" a player said, breaking the uneasy silence.

Meredith was at her locker, unpacking her books with all the focus she could manage. Then she heard it. A soft singing coming from a few banks of lockers away. She went rigid.

"That fucking sucks, dude! Snow? I mean give me a fucking break . . ." Brandon stopped. Meredith turned her head back toward the group. She realized Brandon was hearing it, too. He cocked his head at the sound of the low-pitched male voice singing softly. Greg heard it, looked at Brandon, and followed his gaze to where Stephen Conlin was emptying books from his locker. Meredith watched, gripping the door to her locker, as Brandon and Greg charged toward Stephen.

Stephen didn't see them approaching. Greg hung back several paces. Brandon leaned against the closed locker door next to Stephen's open one.

When Stephen glanced up, Meredith speculated that it must have been the first time he had met Brandon's gaze in years.

"You gonna sing us a little song, Stevie?" Brandon growled.

Meredith was probably the only one in the locker room to recognize Stephen's song—his major solo from *The Mikado*, a production she had been the only Cannon student to attend. When Stephen had sung it before the audience of twenty on his closing night performance, Meredith had fought tears and briefly pondered what a life might be like without Kate and Greg and Brandon.

But Stephen looked paralyzed, one hand splayed against his locker's open door. Greg loomed behind Brandon, staring at the back of Brandon's head. The other football players had lost interest. "Just fuckin' leave the fag alone. Jesus," one of them mumbled as they filed out the side doors.

Meredith watched as Stephen managed to hold Brandon's gaze.

"You celebrating, Stevie?" Greg asked from behind Brandon.

Meredith was now gripping her locker door because it was the only thing keeping her standing. Please say something, Stephen. Say something.

"Did you use a knife?" Stephen asked, his tone even and quiet.

"What the fuck are you talking about?" Brandon hissed.

"On my car. Did you use a knife to flatten the tires?"

Brandon punched Stephen's locker door closed. It missed Stephen's face by several inches but sent his book bag falling from its hook, tumbling to the floor and emptying his books. Stephen did not move to retrieve them.

"Fear cannot touch me," he whispered.

Meredith stifled a gasp.

Brandon and Greg seemed paralyzed suddenly as Stephen bent down in front of them and slowly began repacking the mess of textbooks at his feet. When he finally stood, sliding his bag over his shoulder, Greg had turned his back, but Brandon still glared at him.

Meredith watched as Stephen moved past them, with Brandon's glare following his every step toward the side doors. Stephen disappeared. Meredith was halfway to the doors by the time Brandon had made his first bounding leap toward them. Her head was spinning as she threw herself in front of them, arms shooting out in front of her.

"Enough!" she screamed.

Brandon halted in mid-leap, one fist pawing the air.

"You've got a game tonight, remember?" Meredith said. "Save it, Brandon!"

Coach Henry Stubin slid a notice into the daily bulletin box during third period. The headmaster's secretary immediately plucked it from the box and hastily made copies for all the homeroom teachers. When David Carter read it during fourth period, a cheer ripped through his homeroom that he could hear matched throughout Cannon School.

"Remy Montz, coach of the Thibodaux Boilers, has reported that the football field of Thibodaux Senior High School has been cleared of ice and other weather-related obstructions. The game will take place tonight as scheduled," David read.

As his homeroom students embraced and slapped each other on the back, David sunk down behind his desk and realized that all hope of learning for the rest of the day had been killed by one memo.

During lunch, he sought out Stephen Conlin, looking for him in the locker room, the English Hallway, and some of the empty classrooms. He wove his way through the students thronging the stretch of grass between the locker room and the cafeteria. A group of football players had sneaked a stereo onto campus and the cafeteria manager was attempting to unplug it, elbowing through a crowd dancing to the tinny sound of the Spin Doctors.

Then David saw a blond figure sitting on the distant stands, across the football field. Stephen was eating his lunch in the bottom row of the desolate bleachers. He had fanned out the contents of his brown paper bag on the silver bench. As David crossed the field toward him, gusts of wind flapped the hand-painted banner hung between the goal posts. BASH THE THIBODAUX BOILERS! it proclaimed in bloodred letters.

As David approached, the noises of the lunchtime crowds were distant echoes. Stephen seemed so placid that David looked for a bottle of alcohol at Stephen's feet. There was none. He sat down beside Stephen.

"Selena Truffant was just in my office, Stephen," David began. The silver bench was cold. David shivered.

"What about?" Stephen asked, studying the cheerleaders as they practiced their dance on the lawn.

"It seems the girl who was supposed to play the knight in tonight's game has detention. They need someone for the pep rally. I thought of you," David said, pinching his hands between his knees to keep them warm.

Stephen laughed, low and brief, before taking another bite from his sandwich. The Cannon mascot was a squat blue-skinned knight, with an oversized foam rubber head emblazoned with a cartoon grimace, its angry slanted eyes embedded in a silver helmet. The mascot typically brandished a foam rubber sword as he gyrated around the cheerleaders.

"Why me?" Stephen asked.

"You're an actor. It's performing, isn't it?" David asked.

Stephen smirked, still not looking at David, who shifted against the frigid metal of the bench.

"It's a costume. No one will know who you are," David tried. He felt instantly ashamed. He jerked his chin away from Stephen and fixed his gaze on the empty bleachers behind them. When Stephen laughed again, David stood quickly, hoping to escape. "It's just for the pep rally. Not the game," he said through chattering teeth.

"I'll do it," Stephen said casually, pulling a bottle of orange juice from his lunch bag.

"Good." David said, feeling somehow satisfied.

In the ensuing silence, a corner of the banner tore free and fell slightly before the wind picked it up and battered it against the top of the goal post.

"Big game tonight. Are you going?" David asked.

Stephen looked at David for the first time. "I don't go to football games, Mr. Carter," he said.

At two-thirty that afternoon, Angela Darby and the seven other members of the Football Mothers' Club arrived at Cannon and began dressing for their satire pep rally skit "Da Thibodaux Mommas' Club." Angela had the lead role, toting a crab trap and railing against rich Cannon boys and their fancy cars in a mangled Cajun accent.

As Elise Charbonnet decorated Angela's costume with fish netting and rubber cockroaches, other mothers congratulated Angela on Greg becoming starting quarterback.

At three P.M., when the final bell rang, the Mothers' Club assembled in the locker room as the students of Cannon School funneled into the Senior Courtyard.

In the English Hallway, Meredith stood poised with the other cheerleaders in front of the door to the Courtyard. They would make their entrance, leaping and squealing down the steps onto a raised concrete platform. Idly, she watched as the Cannon Knight hobbled out of Selena Truffant's office and took up a post behind the file of cheerleaders. Meredith rolled her eyes and looked back to the crowd assembling in the courtyard. Marine Hillman, the girl inside the costume, had made the mistake of telling several cheerleaders she didn't wash her hair every day, so nobody talked to her. Better she's in costume so we don't have to look at her, Meredith reasoned.

"That's so sad about Jeff," Julie Moledeux said.

The Knight's head jerked. Meredith heard a startled gasp waft through the foam rubber helmet. Then its arms bounced limply to its sides.

Meredith listened with one ear as out on the patio, Bryan Hammond, football cocaptain, invited Greg Darby to say a few words, "since Jeff can't be with us today." Brandon let out a war whoop, and with five other sophomore players he buoyed Greg across the courtyard before depositing him in front of Bryan. The courtyard was filled with shouts of "Darby! Darby!" Jeff Haugh had never gotten that kind of reaction. It always seemed to Meredith that the few cheers he did receive during pep rallies embarrassed him.

The crowd hushed. The cheerleaders aligned themselves behind the English Hallway doors. The costumed Football Mothers' Club clustered behind the locker room doors. Someone was complaining about how their entrance was blocked by students.

"Big game tonight," Bryan boomed. "Hope you guys can all make it up to Thibodaux."

He elbowed Greg.

"What can I say? We're gonna kick ass!"

The crowd roared and in spite of herself Meredith jumped. The stereo blared Tina Turner's "Simply the Best" and she let herself be swept with two other cheerleaders as they burst through the English Hallway doors and descended the stairs, pom-poms held aloft, a few doing split leaps as they rushed forward. The Cannon Knight stumbled down the steps behind them, the foam rubber sword lowered to his side.

In the front row, nausea bubbling inside her, Meredith saw the arms around her curl into formation, beginning the dance.


Stephen was suffocating inside the costume, Julie Moledeaux's words resonating inside his head. Suddenly he felt the dull impact of Kate Duchamp's fist on his shoulder. "Dance!" she ordered.

He lifted his head and stared out at the gyrating crowd of Cannon students. No one knew who was inside. He felt a sudden, unprecedented freedom. He shot one hand over his foam rubber crotch and the crowd hollered and applauded. In front of Cannon, the buses idled, their droning engines waiting to transport parents and students two hours up the river to Thibodaux. The Pep Band loaded into a Cannon school bus. Stephen danced. Jeff was not here and so he danced for himself, masked, a naked man among the blind.


Thibodaux sat upriver from New Orleans. The cavalcade of school buses made their way up Highway 90, the subdivisions of the river's west bank giving way to swamp punctuated by pools of black water. Eventually they pulled alongside the blaze of Dobie H. LeBlanc Field of Thibodaux Senior High. Beyond the field's far fence, the plume fires of oil refineries on the horizon flickered over the expanse of swamp beyond.

Thibodaux was a small town. The high school's long-standing rivalry with Cannon had prompted a half-day of work that Friday. Students, parents, and college students from nearby Nicholls State had decorated the swampy banks of Highway 90 with painted banners that prophesied doom to all spoiled, Mercedes-driving Cannonites. Looking out the window of the cheerleaders' bus, Meredith saw a banner that exclaimed CURSE CANNON! Beneath its slogan, she glimpsed a crude rendering of a Mercedes-Benz spraying blue Cannon football gear as it smashed into a brick wall.

Behind the school buses trailed the custom cruisers transporting parents and Cannon fans who paid a nominal fee to join the convoy. In their plush seats, Elise Charbonnet and Roger Charbonnet shared a gin and tonic from Roger's thermos, the alcohol fueling their growing indignation as they passed beneath homemade signs that announced the dire fate of the Cannon Knights.

Angela Darby's eyes looked from the clock on the mini-van's dashboard to the profile of her husband behind the wheel, his Scotch-sluggish eyes trying to focus on the thin swath of pavement furiously ribboning away beneath them. She could hear Alex in the backseat, desperately excited, his breathless chirping quieted for the moment as he struggled against his seat belt. The boy was wearing one of Greg's old jerseys, which hung down to his knees like a nightgown.

"Slow down," Angela whispered to her husband.

"We're late," Andrew said.

"And we don't want to get pulled over, either!" she hissed.

"Are we going to be late?" Alex Darby asked. "We can't! I'll miss Greg!"

She turned to face her seven-year-old son, his eyes shining as if it were Christmas Eve. "Of course not. In fact, I called ahead and made sure your big brother would hold the game just until you got there! So don't worry!"

Alex smiled slightly, a smile Angela could barely discern in the darkened backseat. She could feel Andrew bristle. Thickly corded with muscle, her husband had the body of Mr. Clean and a temper she countered with sarcasm that she felt sometimes ran painfully thin. Except for Alex, who had in seven years grown from a "happy accident" to a disarmingly innocent and radiant young presence in their lives, Greg's glory was the only thing the two of them shared. How could Andrew fuck that up, too?

"Next time, I drive," Angela whispered.

Greg Darby had thrown two first downs, and the Knights had to run the ball in to score. In the stands, drunken Cannon fathers pantomimed the sequined Thibodaux Dance Battalion's elaborate and high-stepping routine. Meredith shifted her weight from one tight shoe to another as the cheerleading squad performed a clipped routine that looked like they were directing airplanes on a tarmac with their pom-poms held aloft. Her eyes passed over the Thibodaux side of the stands, which looked to her like a mass of angry, crab-fattened parents, blowing plastic trumpets—dressed in a patchwork of gaudy Wal-Mart sweaters featuring airbrushed cats and Christmas garlands. The Cannon side of the stadium was a sea of L.L.Bean winter jackets, thermoses filled with the contents of home wet bars tucked between legs. To Meredith it seemed as if Cannon couldn't hold a candle to the pure rage of Thibodaux, and she was suddenly cheered by the thought that the Knights might lose.

The routine done, Meredith turned and watched from the sidelines as Brandon got tackled and lost the team five yards. She knew fellow cheerleaders mistook her intent concentration as loving concern for her boyfriend, Greg. They would have been shocked to know she did not want to miss it if Greg got injured.

Players were peeling off Brandon. Bored, she glanced behind her to the front row where Elise Charbonnet clasped her hands in her lap, obeying her belief that if she kept her eyes on her son at all times he would not be hurt. "It worked for Jordan," Meredith's mother told her. "She thinks it'll work for Brandon, too."

"I can run it in! It's twenty yards!" Brandon growled, as the players huddled, their adrenaline rushing through their veins despite the time-out Coach Stubin had called after Brandon's sack.

"Yeah. Twenty yards your ass has gotta run, Charbonnet!" Cameron Stern shot back. "You just lost us five!"

That hurt, and Brandon's eyes shot to Greg's, wide and desperate through the face guard of his helmet. The rest of the huddle was breathing in rattling grunts. Cameron Stern noticed. "No fucking way!" he shouted right at Greg. "You hear me, Darby?"

Brandon saw Greg's helmet flinch slightly in Cameron's direction.

"Fuck off, Cameron!" Brandon barked. "You know I can fuckin' run it and Haugh's not here to throw you a bunch of pussy passes you're not even open for . . ."

Cameron leapt back, breaking the huddle. The players on either side of them stumbled to right themselves. Brandon shot a glance at the sidelines. Coach Stubin was eying the huddle suspiciously.

*"Twenty yards?"* Cameron bellowed. The other players started backing up. Greg was still crouched, paralyzed with indecision. Brandon straightened, mirroring Cameron's posture and ready to fight. If Greg wasn't up to a fight, he sure as hell was. "I can run it!" Brandon growled.

"Bullshit. *Jordan* Charbonnet maybe. But we're not throwing this play just because you and Darby here are blow buddies!"

Brandon slammed into Cameron Stern, their helmets cracking together loud enough for Brandon to think he'd gone deaf. He jabbed one hand into the face guard of Cameron's helmet and as Cameron's arms flailed like propellers, he yanked his head three feet from the cleat-trodden grass where they had fallen before slamming it back to the earth. Brandon could hear his mother screaming at him from the stands just as Cameron got one hand around Brandon's face guard and twisted his helmet against his neck, sending him stumbling sideways where he crashed into Greg's stomach.

He saw Coach Stubin running across the field toward him. Thibodaux Boilers watched as the other Knights backed away from Brandon's and Cameron's kicking legs.

Coach Stubin grabbed Brandon by the back of the neck, yanking him off Cameron, the boy's legs still pumping empty air before Coach Stubin threw him to the side. Brandon collapsed into the mud. The other players glared, their shoulders hunched, as peals of laughter tore through the Thibodaux stands.

"What the fuck is wrong with you, Charbonnet?" Coach Stubin roared.

Brandon opened his mouth. No response came. He spat at the mud clinging to his face guard, angrily wiped at it with one hand. One of the players knelt down next to Cameron Stern.

"Coach?"

Stubin whirled around.

"He's not moving, Coach!"

Stubin studied Cameron as he lay prone against the grass, his helmet listing to one side.

"Get your ass to the bench, Charbonnet!"

Brandon struggled to right himself. He held his helmet up, averting his eyes from the angry glares all around him—except for Greg Darby, who had bowed his helmet. Two medics dashed across the field. As Brandon neared the sidelines, the Cannon stands fell into silence. He saw his mother sink back to her seat in the bleachers. The look on her face was something between anger and shame.

Humiliation welled inside of him and he felt an urge to rush to the stands, to tell his mother what Cameron had called him. But she had already looked away from him, shooting nervous glances at the disapproving glares of surrounding parents.

When he realized embarrassed tears were moistening his eyes, Brandon ripped off his helmet and slammed it into the bench. Nearby cheerleaders jumped.

"Brandon!" he heard Elise shriek.

But he was charging down the sidelines, bound for the locker room.

No one could talk to him like that. No one.

And as he had learned early on, rage was the best weapon against pain.

Silent shock fell in his wake. Cheerleaders turned away, embarrassed. But Meredith approached the bench, staring down at where the two pieces of Brandon's helmet lay on the grass. He had slammed it against the bench hard enough to crack it in two.


"Shit!" Angela hissed before she could stop herself.

The stadium was a halo of light thrown against the night sky. The stands grew visible up ahead, along with the shadows of a hundred bodies sitting in them. Andrew slowed the mini-van as he pulled down along the side road that ran behind the stands. The parking lot was choked with cars.

"Just pull over, Andrew!"

"Oh, God!" Alex wailed from the backseat, "They started! Mom, they staaaarted!"

"Andrew, pull over!" Angela shrieked.

She heard her husband whisper a "Goddamn it" under his breath as he nudged the steering wheel to the left and the mini-van's tires thudded into the mud on the shoulder of the road. The van rolled to a halt.

"Next time, Andrew! Consider me your watch!" Angela shouted.

"We're not getting into this now . . ."

She reached for her seat belt buckle. "Okay. We'll wait until after your ninth scotch and water. How about that?"

"Angela, I swear to God, if you don't . . ."

Andrew stopped, anger drained from his face. Angela's next thought came in the form of a question—What was that woosh? And then she thought what a funny, made-up word *woosh* was. What did she mean, *woosh?* She was more frightened by the sudden fear on her husband's face than the sound she had heard. Woosh. Air. The sound of air. The sound of a door opening.

"Baby?" Andrew whispered. He had not called her that in ten years.

They both heard the screech of brakes. Angela glanced over to see the fractured word —ANITATION perfectly framed in the driver's side window. She heaved against her seat belt without unbuckling it, looked over her shoulder, and saw the arc of her son returning to the earth through the two-foot crack in the mini-van's back door. The brakes of the Thibodaux sanitation truck hissed as Alex Darby's neck gave way under the weight of his upturned body.

It started as light.

A swath of red danced across the field, followed by a swath of blue.

Meredith and the other cheerleaders had just led the crowd in a triumphant roar as Cameron Stern got to his feet with the help of two medics, before walking across the field on his own. She had watched grimly as he removed his helmet. The hair on the back of his head was matted with blood and his jaw was bruised.

Light erupted from beneath the stands. The younger Cannon fans climbed up onto the highest rail, craning their heads over.

Meredith Ducote had no idea what had happened, but what she saw amazed her, as three hundred fans rose numbly to their feet and turned their backs on the field. She stared dumbly at the sea of backs—the blue and red flashes of police lights throwing them into silhouette.

Then Meredith heard it. A human, female wail, a torrent of vocal pain she had never heard given breath before. Meredith felt the wail pass through her body. She trembled. For a brief instant, it was as if the sound had ripped back the veil across Meredith's own grief.

An ambulance's siren devoured the woman's screams.

The pieces of the tableau were falling into place and a voice inside of her spoke, assuming the tone of her mother's voice, all gravity. *Something just broke*, it said. *Something that can't be fixed.*

# 12

The sun had set by the time Elise Charbonnet left Alex Darby's funeral at Bishop Polk Cathedral and drove to the EZ Serve on Prytania to buy a pack of Parliament Lights, her first in fifteen years. In a black cocktail dress, which even with the matching scarf was more appropriate for dinner with Roger's clients than for funerals of seven-year-old boys, Elise stared into space. The cashier slid the pack in front of her. "Three-fifty," he said.

Elise did not react. Over the cashier's left shoulder she reran, like a video loop, the image of Andrew Darby dragging his wife out the cathedral's side door as four hundred mourners watched in horror after Angela had jumped from her pew and slugged her husband in the shoulder. "*They* did it! *They* did it!"

"Three-fifty, ma'am," the cashier repeated.

When Elise looked back at the woman, her eyes were filled with tears. The cashier's annoyed glare softened a little, and she bowed her head. Elise fished the money from her pocket book and nudged the Parliaments into her purse with her free hand.

"You just come from a funeral?" the cashier asked hesitantly.

Elise nodded.

At home, Elise double-checked her house even though she knew Roger had hurried from Alex's funeral to a meeting with a potential client. Brandon, she assumed, had left with Greg. At first, she was glad that there would be no one around to see her smoke the first of her cigarettes. And then a hollowness settled over her and she shuffled into the kitchen. She pondered calling Jordan.

Elise cracked the kitchen window, revealing the spire of the Bishop Polk bell tower over her backyard. Twilight threw the portico's windows into deep silhouette. She lit the Parliament and took her first drag.

• • •

Monica and Stephen had walked the four blocks from Bishop Polk Cathedral to their house. Stephen had not cried during the funeral, and Monica did not cry until they were a block away from the church. Stephen curved his arm around her shoulders, walking her the rest of the way. They were almost to their corner when Monica said, "There's nothing worse than losing a child."

She looked up at Stephen and he took her face in his hands. He seemed strangely detached.

"I promise to live longer than you do," he whispered to her, and kissed her gently on the cheek.

Once inside the house, Monica went to her bedroom, Stephen to his. It would be the last time she saw her son that day.

Later that evening, Monica sought comfort in Jeremy's study. Her husband had kept meticulous records of the progression of each of his poems. First drafts had their own notebooks. January through August, 1976 contained one of her favorites, "To a Child Not Yet Born," but Monica could not locate the first draft. Monica believed Jeremy had written it for Stephen but she had never told her son about it. She found herself reading through Jeremy's poetry for the first time in a long while. When she heard Stephen's door open and shut, she assumed he was going to the kitchen for something to drink.

Roger Charbonnet returned home around eight P.M. By then, Elise had sprayed the kitchen down with Lysol until she was confident there was no lingering cigarette odor. Roger set his briefcase down on the counter and moved toward the living room, where Elise was watching the rebroadcast of the Channel 4 evening news. The funeral for Alex Darby was the lead story. Elise watched the footage of confused children—Alex's classmates gripping their parents' hands—and teenage mourners leaving Bishop Polk in angry silence. Roger sat next to her on the couch.

"Classes at both Cannon School and Bishop Polk Elementary, where Alex Darby was in the second grade, were suspended so that students could attend the funeral. There's no word yet on whether or not the playoff game between the Cannon Knights and Thibodaux Boilers, interrupted by tragedy, will be rescheduled . . ."

"Jesus Christ," Monica muttered. She watched the same report at ten P.M. that night as she sat propped up in bed, a Chambord and Absolut on the bedside table.

"Mourners told reporters outside Bishop Polk Cathedral that the boy's mother was so distraught she had to be removed from the service by her husband," the reporter continued.

Monica sipped her drink, praying it would help sleep to come. She heard what sounded like a bell—a strange metallic note with an echo that was drowned out by the anchor's amplified voice. She ignored it. She often found herself mistaking background noises on television for sounds in her own house.


Roger was in bed by the time Elise took a pen to a pad of floral-bordered stationery. In an hour, she managed to compose two lines.

Dear Jordan,
Things are bad here.

She sat in her nightgown at the kitchen table, staring at her pad. A Parliament Light smoldered in a coaster. The back door was open to a night that had gone quiet following the strange noise Elise had heard moments earlier. She assumed the noise belonged to a ship's horn on the nearby river.

She dragged on her cigarette and lifted the pen again. "Sometimes nightmares come true," she wrote.

She studied the words. She was disgusted with herself for being so melodramatic. After all, she had not lost a child. But the sight of Angela Darby being dragged from the church, screaming and clawing at her husband's arm, had somehow struck something inside of her with more force than the sight of Alex Darby's miniature coffin draped in the Episcopal flag had. Angela Darby's screams had convinced Elise that they could all lose a child at any moment. But wasn't this a fact of life? How foolish I am, Elise thought, to realize it only now. She ripped the piece of paper from the pad, crumpled it, and tossed it into the kitchen wastebasket. She massaged her forehead with her hands and inhaled.

Elise jumped when the phone rang.

"Elise?"

"Trish?"

"Did you hear?" Trish Ducote asked her.

"No," Elise responded, with quiet dread.

"Angela Darby's in Bayou Terrace. Andrew just admitted her. My cousin Missy works over there and she's on call tonight. Missy told me they put her in confinement. Seems she went nuts!"

"Jesus," Elise whispered, leaning against the side of the cabinet with the phone pressed to her ear.

"Meredith isn't over there, is she?" Trish asked.

"I don't think Brandon's around," Elise responded weakly. She took another drag off the Parliament.

Elise dropped the phone. A loud crack sounded. The reverberation had made it seem so close that she instinctively hunched her shoulders and bent down over the counter. She heard Roger's footsteps barreling down the stairs. She groped for where she'd dropped the receiver on the counter. "God! Did you hear that?" Trish practically shrieked through the phone.

Roger appeared in the kitchen doorway in his T-shirt and boxers. He noted the cigarette in Elise's hands.

"The Projects?" Elise asked Trish.

"Too close," Roger answered.

Elise had only one thought. *No. It isn't possible*. The anguish of the day had been complete already.

Roger drifted to the open back door.

"I'll let you go . . ." Trish said weakly.

Elise mumbled something inaudible and hung up the phone. At her husband's side, she followed his gaze toward the night sky where she assumed he was trying to trace the origin of the sound.

"Put it out, Elise," Roger commanded, and she complied.


Monica stood on her front porch and searched the shadows of oak branches. The air was bitterly cold and the glass in her hand seemed melded to her palm. She lifted it to her mouth and gulped. For a brief moment she pondered whether or not she had imagined the gunshot; maybe the day's grief had sparked old fibers of pain, some hallucination of Jeremy's suicide.

She realized she was wrong when she heard the low wail of sirens in the distance.

*Part Two*

# The Bell Tower

"I was that silly thing that once was wrought,
to practice this thin love;
I climb'd from sex to soul, from soul to thought;
    but thinking there to move,
Headlong I rolled from thought to soul, and then
From soul I lighted at the sex again."

—William Cartwright, "No Platonic Love"

# 1

Two weeks before he was to graduate from Princeton University, Jordan Charbonnet had a nightmare about his younger brother, Brandon. Jordan awoke to a darkened dorm room, thick with shadows of half-packed cardboard boxes.

In the nightmare, Jordan was younger, running after his brother and three of his friends as they rode bicycles down Philip Street in the Garden District. The surreal landscape featured a shockingly blue sky unobstructed by oak branches, houses seemed to melt and wrought iron gates tilted and sank in twisted patches of filigree iron. Brandon had left something behind at the house, and it was desperately important that Jordan catch him. In the nightmare, Jordan kept calling out his brother's name, but Brandon continued to pedal. At Brandon's side rode Greg Darby. Greg—like Brandon—appeared as Jordan best remembered him, as a well-developed boy of fourteen. The other two friends were unrecognizable as they swerved out of Jordan's path as he neared the rear wheel of his brother's bicycle. At the moment when Jordan could have reached out and touched the spinning rubber tire, Greg Darby turned his head to Brandon, revealing a fractured face, its cracks filled with blood. Greg pursed his lips like a blowfish and spat a thin geyser of blood into Brandon's face. Jordan halted, breathless, and watched as the two boys pedaled off down the street, Brandon wiping the blood from his face with one hand and shouting, "Aw, gross, dude!" through peals of laughter.

Jordan Charbonnet was graduating with an A.B. in English. It had taken him five years to get it.

After his freshman year, Jordan decided to take a year off. His parents had been horrified and blamed a girl, Katie, a graduating senior who encouraged Jordan to spend a year with her living in New York City. Katie put Jordan up in her new apartment for a year. The following summer, when Jordan told her he would be returning to school after the summer was done, Katie changed the locks on "their" apartment. Jordan returned to begin his delayed sophomore year and never bothered to tell Katie that despite her elegant beauty, her voracious sexual appetite, and the glimpse she offered of a glitzy world of New York money and society, she had not been the reason Jordan had left Princeton behind for a year.

That first year away from New Orleans had been dizzying, at times sickening. He had found himself tossed into a throng of young minds suddenly liberated to embrace the heady pain of their own lives. He sat awestruck and alienated on dorm room floors, listening to fellow freshmen confess their traumas, usually defining their entire lives in terms of mistakes made by other people (namely, their parents). Jordan felt like he didn't belong and he was forced to ask himself, Why do these people like pain so much? And how did all this pain pass me by?

At those moments, when he could gaze unblinking at his past, Jordan could acknowledge what had eased his way. He had spent the previous four years as a poster boy for the Cannon School ideal. He had learned from the batting eyelashes of prom dates and the lascivious glances from the Garden District Ladies' Society that his physical beauty was a weapon capable of spurring admirers to lapses in decorum. His physical appearance reduced people to their hunger, desire, and dependence—three qualities Jordan had to admit he did not seem to possess. His world was fascinating, but it rarely threatened him. His six foot two frame of solid muscle, stretched across broad shoulders, crowned with a handsome face, an immaculate olive complexion—all of it had somehow exempted him from the pain that seemed to make most of his classmates what they were. But it wasn't something that stirred either pride or guilt in him. His beauty was not an accomplishment; it was a fact.

Katie had snatched him up like a trophy and whisked him off to a year in Manhattan that was studded with wild sex, shopping trips to Versace, and loud parties hosted by Katie's boss at her advertising firm. Being Katie's kept boy gave a certain sense of purpose to the physical beauty he felt had alienated him from his classmates. As conversation between them grew thin, Katie's only response was to recommend notoriously noisy restaurants in SoHo for dinner each night with increasingly large groups of coworkers, most of whom were married couples.

Jordan would have had to spend a great deal more time placating his parents about his departure from college if tragedy had not shaken his hometown when seven-year-old Alex Darby was struck and killed by a garbage truck and, in response, Greg Darby, Brandon's best friend, killed himself. The phone calls from his mother stopped as Jordan's parents were subsumed by the grief that had overtaken his younger brother.

After more than half a year of silence following his move to New York, he finally worked up the nerve to call his mother. He had what he thought would be good news for her, but decidedly bad news for Katie, which is why he thought his parents should be the first to know. Elise Charbonnet sounded tired, almost winded, and unaffected.

"How's New York?" she asked him, with a note of sarcasm that he had never heard in her voice.

"I'm going back," he said. "To school. This fall."

There was a long pause. "That's wonderful," Elise said, without enthusiasm.

"I thought you'd be glad to hear," Jordan said.

"I am," Elise said, sounding bored. "Does Katie know?"

Elise said *Katie* as if she had taken a bite of undercooked steak. "No," Jordan responded.

There was another silence.

"What's wrong?"

"Your brother's not doing too well."

Elise offered nothing more. The last Jordan had heard, Brandon had been skipping school. But that had been months ago. "Have you thought about therapy for him?" Jordan offered. Elise laughed wryly, which unnerved Jordan. "I'm serious . . ."

"I've got it covered, Jordan. Thanks," Elise said tightly, and Jordan was too angry and embarrassed to offer anything more. He returned to Princeton that fall.

Phone calls from Roger became routine. His father's enthusiasm over his return to school was unconcealed, and Jordan didn't want to jeopardize the approval he had regained by broaching the subject of Brandon. When Jordan asked about Elise, Roger's responses were stilted and vague. "She blames herself . . ." Roger once offered.

"What do you mean?" Jordan had asked.

"That winter . . . it really affected her . . ."

Still, Jordan found himself unable to broach the topic. Roger's off-handed term—"that winter"—seemed to be a theatrical production that had taken place without his knowledge but involved all of his family as players.

For the next three years, he spent his summers doing internships and his holidays with friends in the Northeast. Neither Roger nor Elise complained about a single missed Christmas.


"Your problem is that you're perfect, Jordan."

Melanie McKee threw back beers like a frat boy, yet tugged her dark hair out of her face with one fragile hand during each drink. She didn't lie about masturbating and, like most of Jordan's girlfriends at Princeton, she had money. Not Garden District, look-to-the-history-books money, but well-heeled constantly maintained, Newport cottage money. Unlike Katie, she spoke without searching his face for a response when she was finished. Unlike Katie, she showed no interest in keeping him in one place. Jordan considered Melanie to be the first real woman he had ever met. She had no trace of the Southern belle behavior he was so used to—that veil of manners built upon the belief that if a girl made her desire for a man obvious then she would bring about her own ruin.

They met at the beginning of Jordan's final semester. She was a graduate teaching assistant for one of his last required lecture courses. Jordan spotted her sitting toward the front of the lecture hall on the first day of class. He took a seat several rows back and was surprised to look up several moments later to find her staring back at him with a smile of confident admiration.

Melanie asked him out. Jordan said yes. After class that day, he went home and called Princeton girlfriend number-four, Claudia, a geology major with whom he had had several dinner dates, some good sex, and complete lack of interesting conversation. After Jordan offered a casual explanation as to how his work load would make dating difficult Claudia had ended their call with a breathy, "I guess it's for the best," and slammed the phone down in his ear.

On their third date, Melanie McKee indicted Jordan's personality with the same fervor she had used to pursue him. "Perfection isn't normal, Jordan," Melanie said. "See, you're naive enough to think that you've attained everything. That there's nothing out there you couldn't get just because you're a walking wet dream. So you think life is boring. Well, that's not your problem."

"What's my problem?" Jordan asked with a cocky smile, his beer bottle halfway to his mouth. He was prepared to write off her evaluation of him as evidence of her hunger and need, as usual.

"You're a freak!" Melanie announced drunkenly, her fist slamming into the bar.

Jordan laughed loud enough to draw the attention of the bartender.

"I'm not kidding, Jordan. Someone as beautiful as you, it's not normal. You're an outsider everywhere you go. But let me tell you something . . ."

She leaned in close enough to kiss him. "You better use it, buddy! Because freaks, they have a better view of the world than anybody else. They see things coming that others don't. So watch out, 'cause if you keep walking around like you're this god you're going to miss seeing the devil until it sinks its teeth into that nice ass of yours!"

Jordan had spent most of his life thinking that all desire was secret and sordid, that people who admired him secretly resented him for drawing out the ferocity of their desire. But now Melanie McKee seemed to give his beauty a sense of place in the world, and a sense of purpose. He was a freak. He kissed her right there at the bar.

Roger and Elise Charbonnet flew in the day before Jordan's graduation. To Jordan's and Melanie's frustration, they had requested that Melanie come along to dinner. Jordan had mentioned her in passing to Roger.

Melanie protested that a dinner with Jordan's parents would be pointless and stress-inducing. After graduation, Melanie was moving to France and Jordan was returning home to get a job before applying to law school. His father was a Tulane Law alumnus with the network to obtain Jordan a job after he passed the bar. They had their fling and it had been enjoyable, but neither of them had any delusions about marriage. Melanie insisted, despite his declaration to the contrary, that Jordan's parents would automatically assume otherwise.

They drove to the restaurant in silence, Melanie nervously re-applying her lipstick in the visor mirror. Jordan was suddenly made queasy by the fact that he would be seeing his parents in person for the first time since they had visited during his freshman year. The casual way he had eluded his parents for five years seemed too enormous to mull over. But the hard reality of it ambushed him as he drove to the restaurant.

As they approached the table, Jordan watched Elise's face as she took in Melanie McKee. Roger rose from the table first, pushing out the back of his chair and extending his hand. Jordan expected Elise to rise with him and give Melanie that gentle and firm handshake Southern women apply only to other women, a handshake that holds someone in place for a moment while they are surveyed. But Elise did not get up from the table at all. Once he took his seat, Jordan leaned over and kissed her on the cheek. Elise smiled numbly in response. She looked older, as did his father. They both appeared to be pinched, dehydrated versions of the parents he remembered.

She's still mad at me for going to New York, he thought, angrily settling into his chair.

Roger handed Melanie the wine list. She took it reluctantly. "You're the one going to France after all," Roger quipped nervously. Melanie obliged with a chuckle as if she had been poked in the ribs.

Jordan had expected Elise to study Melanie piercingly, as she had every girl Jordan ever brought into the house. But Elise sat listlessly at the table. Gone was the nervous, fidgeting woman at Cannon football games. She hardly looked at Jordan.

"So where are we?" Roger finally asked with a laugh. "I hate not being able to drive. I feel like my fate is in the hands of some cab driver."

Melanie smiled weakly.

"You could have rented a car," Jordan mumbled.

"Or you could have been a gracious host and picked us up at the airport." Roger said, without malice, propping open his menu.

Melanie adjusted and readjusted the napkin across her lap. "Where did you fly into?" she asked, eyes downcast.

"Newark. We had a limo bring us down—Route One, is it?" Roger directed his eyes at Jordan.

Jordan nodded. The waiter arrived. They ordered and a stilted silence fell over the table. "How's Brandon?" Jordan asked.

Slowly Elise's eyes moved across the patch of wall she was staring at and landed on Jordan.

"Not well," she responded with an even tone that forced him to look away from her. He turned to Melanie, who was staring at him distantly. He had mentioned his younger brother only a couple of times. Melanie was surprised he was bringing him up now.

"Now there's a story . . ." Jordan began. "Did I tell you about all that stuff that went down at my old high school?"

Melanie shook her head. Roger picked up his fork and began running the prongs along the edge of the tablecloth.

"Okay, my brother, Brandon . . . well, his best friend's little brother was hit by a car on the way to this football game. Killed instantly. It was nasty."

"That would be an understatement," Roger mumbled. Elise's gaze remained locked on Jordan.

"So anyway, the kid's mother—"

"The *kid's* name was Alex. His mother's name is Angela Darby," Elise interrupted.

Melanie's eyes widened slightly at the ice in Elise's voice. Jordan shot his mother a glance.

"Right," he continued. "So anyway. At the funeral, Angela Darby, like, freaks out. See the football game was in your standard hick, bayou town—Thibodaux. And that day at the pep rally they'd done this skit satirizing the Thibodaux Mothers' Club. Angela Darby had been the star. So because Alex happened to get run down by a local garbage truck, Angela convinced herself that her son had actually been murdered. That it was, like, some conspiracy—"

"That's what we heard. She was very upset," Roger said, without looking up.

"Understandably," Melanie said.

"Right, so it gets better," Jordan continued. He felt like an excited child recounting one of his favorite ghost stories. "That night, after his brother's funeral, Greg, Brandon's friend, climbs to the top of the Bishop Polk bell tower—the very same church where he went to grammar school and where his brother's funeral was. And he . . . he killed himself. You heard the gunshot, didn't you, Mom?"

It took Jordan a second to understand the look on his mother's face—contempt. He thought she was about to speak. When she kept silent, he felt flushed and light-headed.

"Are you going to finish, or should I?" Elise said quietly, but with a low note of fury. Roger bowed his head into his chest. Melanie whispered something that Jordan thought might be, "Jesus Christ."

"So following the suicide of his closest friend in the world, Brandon—*Jordan's younger brother*—undergoes what you might call a mental collapse," Elise stated. "He doesn't show up at the house until after one in the morning every night. Cannon finally calls us and tells us he's exceeded the maximum absence days for an entire year over the course of four weeks. When Roger confronts him about it, Brandon hurls a chair across the living room at him. It misses Roger, but it bangs me in the shoulder."

Elise paused, took a sip of wine, and proceeded with the ease of a seasoned storyteller. "So Roger and I lie to ourselves. It's just grief. It's just a phase. It could be worse. Brandon could be in Bayou Terrace right along with Angela Darby. But about a week later, the police find Brandon smoking pot inside a car he'd stolen only three hours earlier—"

"*Elise!*" Roger hissed.

"I'm telling a story, Roger. Do you mind?" Elise swallowed, looked at Jordan. "Of course, Brandon didn't just decide to steal a car at random. No, see, the reason he needed a car is because he'd totaled our Mercedes a week earlier. Drove it right into a fence three blocks from our house.

"So what do we do?" Elise asked rhetorically. "We do what any parents do when they see their son turning into someone entirely different before their eyes. We sent Brandon away. To some place where his little phase could come to an end."

"You what?" Jordan asked, stunned.

"It's a place called Camp Davis. Across the lake . . ." Roger tried to intercede. "Jordan, it's not as bad as it sounds . . ."

"A military camp?" Jordan looked from Roger to his mother. "You never told me . . ."

"I think you were in New York at the time," Elise said before taking a slug of wine.

Anger and humiliation kept Jordan from reacting.

"Meanwhile," Elise continued, "miles away, Jordan finds the sad story of his less-than-perfect younger brother to be perfect dinner conversation. Sordid, entertaining, and tragic. Isn't that right, Jordan?"

"That's uncalled for, Elise," Roger said.

Elise let out a torrent of laughter that chilled them all. Melanie winced. "Oh, Roger, it was all pretty uncalled for, don't you think?" Elise said to the ceiling.

Jordan waited several stunned seconds before rising slowly from his chair. He excused himself and made a beeline for the bathroom.

He threw cold water over his face. Camp Davis. The name alone made his stomach tighten.

When he returned to the table, Elise's eyes had wandered back into space. Melanie had stepped up to the task and engaged Roger in conversation about Princeton, about France, about the food. They were the only two who spoke for the rest of the meal.

Outside, they gathered to say their good-byes.

"We'll see you at the ceremony tomorrow," Roger said, shaking his son's hand weakly. Jordan moved to his mother and embraced her as if she were glass.

"It's all right. Don't let it touch you," Elise whispered into his ear.

Jordan was too confused to look at her as she slipped out of his embrace.


Melanie slid out from under the sheet and pulled a cigarette from the pack on the nightstand. They had driven back to campus with Melanie respectful of Jordan's silence. Back in Melanie's apartment they immediately fell into her bed. As Jordan's graduation day had grown closer, their sex had become more desperate and immediate.

"What did she say to you outside the restaurant?" Melanie asked, standing over him to light the cigarette.

"Don't let it touch you."

"A mother's irony, I guess," Melanie mumbled before exhaling a long stream of smoke.

"What do you mean?" Jordan asked, sitting up.

Melanie shook her head. Her face remained fixed. He knew the look.

"You know, I thought you were all for me getting rid of that Southern hospitality bullshit," he said. "That smile-and-have-a-drink-and-everything's-all-right . . ."

Melanie cocked her head, eyes flaring with angry surprise. "Jordan, what are you . . ."

"I can't pretend to ignore what happened to my own family!"

"Oh, really? Then how come you never told me about it?" she asked evenly.

Jordan fell back against the pillow.

"It was just embarrassing, Jordan. I mean, to bring all that stuff up. They don't even know me . . ."

Jordan sat up. "Why do women always think they shoulder more of the burden than men do?"

Melanie's eyes widened. A sarcastic smile stretched her face. "You're kidding, right?"

"No. I'm serious. How come my mother gets to own the story of Brandon now?"

"Because it isn't a *story*, Jordan! You turned it into one tonight!"

Jordan shook his head. He knew he was pouting, but he was helpless to prevent it.

Melanie approached the bed tentatively. "Look, I think you should reconsider," she began haltingly.

"Reconsider?"

"There's so much distance between you and them, I mean . . ."

"Melanie, what are you talking about?"

"Jordan, I don't think you should go back to New Orleans."

Jordan went rigid. "France, then?"

"Fuck it," Melanie hissed, withdrawing to the bathroom.

"I was still born there. I don't care what happened. It's still where I came from." His voice was rising with each word.

"Then why haven't you gone home once in five years?" Melanie asked, returning.

Jordan felt flushed again. His mouth opened, but nothing came out.

"Brandon . . . He's your own brother and you didn't even know they'd sent him away to a military camp."

"They didn't tell me."

"Did you *ask*?"

Jordan shook his head, slowly sinking back into the bed again. A silence fell before he felt Melanie slide into the bed next to him. She slid one arm around his chest. He felt as if he were about to cry, but the feeling was too unfamiliar to know for sure.

"No, I didn't ask," he finally managed.

Melanie rested her head against his shoulder. "It's all right . . ." she whispered.

Jordan waited before he told her about the nightmare he had several weeks ago. About four kids on bikes, his own brother in the lead.

Melanie listened, trying to keep her cool. He waited and watched her, but she couldn't summon a response.

"I want to go home," he whispered.


Jordan awoke to the sticky feel of the plane's window against his cheek. He had slept for almost the entire flight and now the engines of the 737 droned as the plane began its steep descent toward Moisant Field Airport. Below, the Mississippi River looked like a water-filled path left by a giant snake that had crawled its way to the Gulf of Mexico. The refineries lining its banks looked like miniature gas vents—white tufts of smoke sprouting from the carpet of green swamp. Somewhere down there was a city he used to call home. For a moment, he panicked. There didn't seem to be anywhere to land down there. Just black water and patches of floating green. Who would put a city in the middle of all that? How did such a city stay afloat?

# 2

Trish Ducote awoke at four in the morning with the phone pressed to her ear, listening to a young woman who was not her daughter and who had obviously been crying for some time. Trish fumbled for the lamp, switched it on, and almost reached for the husband she had divorced ten years ago.

"Mrs. Ducote? I'm sorry. I know it's so late . . ." the voice was saying.

"Meredith?" Trish asked with sudden alertness. She sat up in bed. For no reason, she grabbed a pen from the nightstand.

"No, Mrs. Ducote. This is Meredith's roommate, Trin. Do you remember me?"

Trish Ducote had no memory of Trin. "Yes, of course . . . Is something wrong, Lynne?" she asked.

"Well," Trin began, "Meredith's in the hospital."

Thirty minutes later, Trish Ducote was driving eighty-five miles an hour down a freeway bound for Oxford, Mississippi, where Meredith had been a student at Ole Miss for almost two years. She had not bothered to call Meredith's father.

She arrived at Oxford General just after noon, where she was met by a doctor who looked young enough to date her daughter. Trish listened to the details before interrupting young Dr. Lupin. "Is she going to be all right?"

"Yes . . . It was touch and go for a while, but we're out of the woods now," Dr. Lupin told her.

"Can I see her?"

"Yes. We just moved her out of ICU. I can have a nurse . . ."

"No. I don't . . ." Trish brought a hand to her forehead to muffle her headache. "I have something to do first."

Trish recalled the way to Meredith's dorm; she herself had attended Ole Miss and her sophomore dorm had been next to Meredith's. She sneaked through the front door, grabbing it before it glided shut behind a student who opened it with a slide of his ID card through the electronic reader. Students sitting in the hallways stopped their conversations as the older woman marched past them. Trin Hong, Meredith's roommate, was in their room talking on the phone, which she almost dropped when Trish Ducote barreled through the door.

"I need to use that phone."

"Are you—" Trin managed.

"I'm Meredith's mother. I need to use that phone if you don't mind."

"Sure . . ." Trin agreed. "I have to go," she said into the receiver, then clicked it off and handed it obediently to Trish.

"Thanks, Lynne," Trish said before the girl hustled out of the room.

Trish Ducote's first call was to the local Ship 'N' Pack. She needed a number of cardboard boxes and she needed them fast. She then called Federal Express. She had a large pickup for around six that evening—could they accommodate her? Yes, they could. Trish's third and final call was long distance. The message she left was brief. "Ronald, it's Trish. I just thought you should know that your daughter almost drank herself to death last night."


Meredith awoke to the sight of her mother at the foot of her hospital bed flipping through a copy of *Cosmopolitan*. When Trish looked up she closed the magazine and set it on her lap, as if Meredith had something to say.

Meredith said nothing. Her throat was inflamed from the respirator tube in her throat. As Trish glared at her daughter, the IVs in Meredith's right arm came to life in fiery pinpricks.

"I called your father. I left a message," Trish said, as if offering her something.

Meredith just kept her eyes open.

"I packed up your room. Everything's been FedEx'ed back to New Orleans. You're coming home," Trish said, before taking a seat beside her.

"And if I don't want to?" Meredith rasped.

"Well . . ." Trish began, her voice quavering with anger, "considering that you apparently wanted to drink until you changed color and your heart stopped beating, I think what you want is going on the back burner."

Meredith rolled her head away from her mother to the window and the view of the parking lot across the street.

"They've given you a little Dilaudid, so don't try to explain yourself because everything you say right now is going to be a little . . . kooky," Trish said as she plucked up the *Cosmo*.

"Was I dead?" Meredith asked.

"For a little while, yes," Trish replied.

Meredith saw the *Cosmo* start to tremble in her mother's hands. "How come I didn't see anything then?" Meredith asked. "Don't people see things when they die?"

Trish did not answer. She just peered at her, as if her daughter might exist amid the swirl of her medication.

Meredith began whispering. Trish could barely make it out.

"Fear cannot touch me, it can only taunt me. It cannot take me, just tell me where to go . . ." When she finished the rhyme, she said, "Poor Greg" and felt herself fall off into sleep.

# 3

Sanctuary had the façade of a typical French Quarter town-house, but its shutters were thrown back to reveal a dizzying flicker of strobe lights. Its second-floor wrought-iron balcony was hung with rainbow flags and packed with men in tank tops and T-shirts. Gas lamps lined the bar's outer walls. The bar's name was emblazoned in rainbow-striped letters on a sign that dangled over the queue of men outside the front entrance.

On most Saturday nights, unsuspecting male tourists would wander too far down Bourbon Street, past the crowded stretch of jazz clubs and strip bars where the music was either karaoke or belching rock. As the bass pulse of synthesized dance music wafted out of Sanctuary, the young men would turn quickly around, realizing what lay ahead, grabbing the hands of their girlfriends who would laughingly pull their boyfriends toward the bar on the excuse that it had good dance music and looked like fun. But if they strayed too close they were subject to the hoots and catcalls of gay men on the balcony who knew how to spot a foreigner with the precision of an exile.

As Devon Walker dragged him across Bourbon Street, Stephen felt as queasy as he had the first time Devon steered him to the bar two years earlier on another muggy June evening. He had met Devon three weeks before he graduated from Cannon. Devon—with his perpetually bright eyes and ferocious fidelity to the sexual orientation Stephen had spent four years regarding as an affliction—had introduced himself at Rue de la Course, a coffeehouse on Magazine Street frequented by college students. Devon offered Stephen his first cigarette. Now, Stephen smoked two packs a day. A political science major and aspiring politician, Devon was wearing blue jeans and an oxford shirt that stretched taut across the football player's barrel chest, the feature that Stephen had first admired in him.

On their first date, Devon spoke animatedly about mobilization efforts to repeal the Defense of Marriage Act. Devon went on for five minutes before Stephen stopped him and asked him what the Defense of Marriage Act was. Titillated by Stephen's ignorance, Devon was more than happy to explain in elaborate, gesticulating detail.

Stephen had held his glass of iced tea in front of his mouth with both hands as he sipped. He had barely managed to get a word in since the date began. As Devon talked, his eyes widened and his arm swept over their empty dinner plates as if he were clearing a space for the future of the gay community.

Stephen heard little. The notion of a "gay community" had never even occurred to him. Stephen's desire was defined by the two hours he had once spent in the backseat of a Honda with his head buried between Jeff Haugh's legs. He assumed his date with Devon would end the same way. When Devon asked if he had ever been to Sanctuary, Stephen said no at the same time he decided he was falling in love with the bright-eyed young man.

After three weeks of seeing each other, at just the moment when Stephen felt he had written enough love poetry to hand Devon a stack of messy loose-leaf pages, Devon showed up at his house one afternoon and announced that Stephen was a "cold, emotionally withdrawn person suffering from only-child syndrome," and their relationship was over. He offered evidence. "A week ago we went to see a movie. Before the movie you purchased a pack of Dots. You consumed the entire pack without offering me any. In the middle of the movie, I rose and went to purchase my own pack. When I sat down, the first thing you asked me was, 'Can I have some Dots?'"

Devon paused, allowing his indictment to settle over Stephen. In response, Stephen picked up the copy of Reports from the Holocaust by Larry Kramer off the nightstand and hurled it at Devon's head. Devon had given Stephen the book a week ago, "to educate" him. After reading the first page, Stephen had decided to stash it under the bed along with Devon's other gifts, a copy of The Out Encyclopedia of Gay History and Dancer from the Dance by Andrew Holleran. All 284 hardbound pages of Reports from the Holocaust sailed over Devon's shoulder. Devon lifted one hand to his ear and stared back at Stephen, shocked. "Please get the fuck out of my house!" Stephen requested.

They did not speak for three weeks. By the middle of the fourth week, Stephen received a memo printed on the stationery of the Tulane University administrative office where Devon was working part-time.

RE: Your Emotional Issues

Stephen—You exhibited a violence I find unacceptable when you threw a book at my face. While I do not mean to mitigate any of the pain you might be suffering as a result of my decision to end our relationship, you seem to be of the belief that your pain is larger than everyone else's and therefore the feelings of others do nothing more than get in your way. Call me if you wish to discuss this over coffee.

Stephen did not call Devon. Instead, he delivered a case of Dots to the door of Devon's dorm room. Charlie—Stephen's replacement—ended up opening the box as Devon read the attached card: "Knock yourself out—Stephen."

"Hey, candy. Awesome!" Charlie remarked as Devon wadded the card and hurled it into a wastebasket. He called Stephen. "We have to talk!" he announced.

"Talk about what?"

"Did you get my memo?"

"Yes. It was my first memo ever. Thank you," Stephen answered back.

"There's something I need to tell you," Devon said.

An hour later they met at Rue de la Course. Stephen smoked half a pack of his own cigarettes during their conversation. "I have certain needs, beyond candy, which you can't meet," Devon said, his voice tinged with the same melodrama he used when he discussed his one casual friend who had contracted HIV.

"What kind of needs?"

"Do you remember . . ." Devon stopped to glance around and make sure no one was eavesdropping.

"I need a partner . . . sexually . . ." Devon continued, ". . . who is . . . a little bit more dominant than you."

Stephen went rigid. His Camel Light froze halfway to his mouth.

On their first date, fumbling naked on Stephen's bed, Devon had asked Stephen to call him a bitch. Stephen had adamantly refused for reasons he could not explain. He remembered Devon's words of accusation, "Your pain is bigger than everyone else's." Now he whispered, "I understand."

On the way back to their cars, Devon had hugged him forcefully, an embrace that Stephen returned. And in keeping with his missionary zeal, Devon embarked on a relentless quest to set Stephen up with someone else. So far the mission had yielded a Colombian stripper who had babbled drunkenly about "true love" before growing angry when Stephen denied his repeated requests for anal intercourse. Devon had also set his ex up with a rugged Mississippi native who was also a divorced father of three and a cocaine dealer. A day after the date, "Hottie McHottie," as Devon nicknamed him, fled the city when he discovered that his apartment and truck had been bugged by the DEA.

Now Devon was serving up a new candidate. He had called Stephen that afternoon. "This guy is hot! Like, your kind of hot, too. Total, like, frat boy look. Backward baseball cap. But he has an earring—"

"What does that mean?" Stephen asked.

"I talked to him for, like, twenty minutes last night. He's a bartender but he's very sensitive. I told him all about you. He wants to meet you."

"The earring, Devon? What does the earring have to do with anything?" Stephen repeated.

"Okay. Word isn't in on the guy yet, but personally I think he's queer as a three-dollar bill!"

"Devon!"

"Stephen, please. He wanted to know all about you."

"I'm not prostrating myself to some straight-boy bartender."

Devon was unfazed. "I told him you were cute. Blond hair, blue eyes. That always seems to work. You could have a seven-inch nose and two front teeth but as long as you've got the blond hair . . ."

He agreed to go.

Devon was pulling him through Sanctuary's downstairs. He felt hands glide over his ass as he bumped into the sticky press of several dancers. The music and lights blinded him, causing him to feel like an alien even in the gay world.

"Pool Bar!" Devon bellowed over the music, guiding Stephen across the dance floor and to the back staircase, where they waited behind three coked-up drag queens arguing on the back stairs, shouting, "Hurry up, bitch! My pussy hurts!" and "Tired old bitch can't even make it up a set of stairs!" On the second floor, Devon steered Stephen along the atrium balcony where plainly dressed men in their fifties surveyed the gyrating male bodies on the dance floor below.

The Pool Bar occupied a tiny corner of Sanctuary's second floor, where patrons hunched over a single tattered table. Devon sauntered ahead of Stephen, passing through the Pool Bar's single door. Stephen lingered in the doorway as Devon walked right up to the bar, obscuring his view of the potential Mr. Right. Stephen heard Devon shout, "This is my friend I was telling you about!"

He turned to reveal Jeff Haugh.

# 4

The music stopped. Stephen gripped the door frame, paralyzed by a single thought—Jeff Haugh has an earring. Jeff looked blankly back at him in the moment before the DJ's voice shrilled through the bar. "Ladies and *ladies!* Sanctuary would like to ask you to proceed calmly to your nearest exit . . ."

A bored groan went up from the crowd. Devon grabbed Stephen by the arm and yanked him out of the doorway. In a second they were lost among the sweaty, shirtless men stumbling toward the exit. Stephen glimpsed Jeff slamming the bar's French door behind him. A drag queen shrieked, "Fuck 'em all, honey! If a bomb takes this place out, me and my hair are going with it!" and the bar hooted. Devon and Stephen found themselves forced onto Bourbon Street. Stephen couldn't speak. He heard a siren's bleat, saw a flicker of blue and red lights fall across the intersection. A police car pushed its way through the crowd.

"Bomb threat," Devon said gravely.

Stephen felt light on his feet. He rocked from the pull of the crowd surrounding him. The thin line he had used to separate the present from the past picked up at both ends, whirled like a jump rope. "I know him," he said.

Four police officers were jostling and elbowing through the crowd.

"Omigod," Devon gasped. "The snow guy? From that night on the Fly?"

Stephen nodded.

"They call themselves the Army of God," said a voice Stephen had not forgotten.

Jeff was standing next to them. Stephen recoiled.

"Are the police doing anything?" Devon asked.

"Not much they can do. Third threat this month. We're trying to get them to tap the phones. But the manager told me this one came by fax." Jeff looked at the rainbow flag flapping overhead and then at Stephen. Quietly Stephen inventoried his physical details. Gone was the football player's natural bulkiness and width. Jeff had honed and pumped the parts he now thought others would admire.

"How you been?" Jeff asked evenly.

"All right," Stephen said. "How's your stomach?"

Jeff smiled slightly. Devon snorted. Obviously Devon was less than impressed with Stephen's manners.

*"Please clear the area until a thorough inspection of the premises has been completed!"* a police officer bellowed.

The mass of men surged through an intersection now barricaded by police cars. Jeff clutched Stephen's arm and guided him through the tight gaps between bumpers. When they came out on the other side, amid a crowd of tourists who had wandered down Bourbon to see the excitement, Devon was gone.

"Come on," Jeff said, striding out of the thickening crowd, toward the door to Madam Curie's Voodoo Shop, where the obese proprietor had squeezed herself out the door to watch the spectacle. He disappeared inside. Stephen followed him.

Jeff was inspecting a rack of shrink-wrapped gris-gris. A sign promised that the mud-colored bags of potpourri would induce the immediate thrall of the one you love. Crudely carved voodoo dolls perched on wooden shelves. Enigma oozed eerily from the mounted stereo speakers.

"Heard you were at Tulane," Jeff said without turning around.

"Yeah, well, my dad used to teach there, so I got a full ride," Stephen answered grudgingly.

Stephen glanced out the store's front door where he saw a mass of men washed white by the glare of news cameras. Devon was being interviewed, speaking vociferously into the microphone, no doubt practicing for his days lobbying on Capitol Hill for the Human Rights Campaign. Devon was decrying the power of hate.

"LSU. Going on my fifth year," Jeff said, facing him now, illuminated by the store's harsh track lighting.

"You drive in every weekend to work at the bar?" Stephen asked.

"No big deal. Just an hour from Baton Rouge. A guy in my Econ class got me the job. He's a dancer."

Stephen smirked. The dancers at Sanctuary were booked via legitimate talent and modeling agencies and more than one was known to show overeager patrons a picture of his wife and kid that he kept in his thong.

"Only started a couple weeks ago. That's why I'm stuck in the Pool Bar," Jeff said, looking down at the floor between Stephen's feet.

"Right. Because the manager knows fags will flock to the cute new straight boy bartender."

Jeff's eyes met his suddenly, stung. A knot of regret tightened in Stephen's chest. Jeff turned back to the rack. Stephen moved for the doorway.

On Bourbon Street, the clamor of voices had blended into a sloppy rendition of a song that seemed vaguely familiar. Stephen halted in the doorway and saw a mini-kickline of drag queens, spot lit by the cameras, and belting Gloria Gaynor's "I Will Survive." The crowd had parted, cheering, giving them the street for a stage.

"Look. I know I should have called you or something."

Stephen jumped. Jeff was standing behind him in the doorway in a cruel parody of the position they had been in during their first kiss on the Fly.

"That was high school, Jeff." He descended the steps, stopped, and turned. Jeff's silhouette blocked the light coming through the store's front door.

"It's kind of ironic, though," Stephen continued, "because if you were really gay then you wouldn't be able to draw in nearly the amount of tips you do now. Once the fresh-meat factor wears off, you're screwed if you're gay. All those fags really want in there is a straight boy they can chip away at once they get him in their grip. And that's what you are. For now."

Stephen fumbled for a Camel Light. He knew that all Sanctuary bartenders were required to carry lights to assist the patrons. Jeff made no move to light Stephen's cigarette.

"Trust me," Stephen said, through an exhalation of smoke. "I've been going there for two years."

"I know. That's why I took the job," Jeff told him.

Stephen flicked on the overhead light in his bedroom. He didn't have the energy to pretend to give Jeff a tour. Jeff studied the wall of framed posters from Stephen's Cannon theatre career. Stephen lingered in the doorway. He hoped his mother was asleep.

Stephen looked at Jeff, hands bunched in the pocket of his jeans. He was still wearing his Sanctuary T-shirt, which featured a Saturn-like globe girded by rainbow-striped rings.

"I have to tell you something," Jeff said. "I saw them." He paused. Stephen felt his own confusion tighten his face. Jeff shook his head. "Greg Darby and Brandon Charbonnet. The night they . . . the night they did that to your new car. I was driving home and they were in front of me and I . . . You remember the note about Miss Traulain?"

Stephen shook his head. This wasn't just awkward anymore. It was starting to hurt.

"Well, I put that in your mailbox. So I knew how to get to your house and I had been at this party that night and they were there, too, and they were talking about your new car . . . And I saw them on the way to your house and I—"

"That was five years ago, Jeff," Stephen cut in.

"They were such assholes and everyone knew it, but Brandon usually had people so scared . . ."

"Jeff!" Stephen's voice rose with anger.

"I saw them turn at the intersection and I knew they were going to your house. They'd been bitching about your car all night."

"And what the hell would you have done?" Stephen's fists had clenched at his sides. He glared at Jeff. "Are you trying to tell me you've spent the last five years overcome with regret that you didn't play the noble hero, rushing to defend the poor fag? Give me a fucking break. It happened five years ago and it happened to *my* car. *I* don't even think about it anymore!"

"You're lying," Jeff said.

Stephen cocked his head. "You think you never did anything for me?" he asked, a crooked, bemused smile on his face. "You think taking me to the Fly and getting me drunk and letting me blow you in the backseat didn't mean anything? Come on, Jeff." Stephen laughed gently. "I can't think of a better gift."

Stephen slowly crawled across the mattress to where Jeff stood at the foot of the bed. He grinned. "What's the matter? Was I being crude?"

"I think about what happened that night. A lot," Jeff said evenly, his face fixed.

Stephen's smile faded.

"Do you?" Jeff asked.

Stephen rose to his knees and beckoned to Jeff. Jeff hesitated and then approached the edge of the bed. Stephen unzipped Jeff's jeans. Suddenly, Jeff's hands shot down and grabbed Stephen's wrists, holding them firmly in place. Stephen jerked his head up and glared at Jeff with bewildered anger. Jeff released Stephen's wrists before pushing him flat onto his back. Jeff dropped to his knees beneath Stephen's dangling feet and unbuttoned Stephen's jeans with his teeth.

She watched Jeff's shoulders disappear out of the frame of Stephen's bedroom window. She waited until the light blinked out. She sat there for a while in her mother's Acura, confident that Stephen had someone, if only for a moment. Then Meredith Ducote turned the key and pulled away from the corner, the car's taillights swallowed by the fog that had blown in off the river, dappling the streets with suggestions of ghosts.

# 5

"**I** think Stephen's found someone," Monica said.

Elise sipped her wine. This was the first time Monica had broached the subject of her son's homosexuality at lunch. Although it was by no means a secret, they had never discussed it in the four months since they had started lunching together.

Elise had tripped on the wording. "Found someone"—did Monica think her son was that desperate? Five years earlier, Elise had considered homosexuals as tragically misguided; two men having sex together was a horrifying thought. Two men together had no control. But since then she had grown more acquainted with desperation. "Do you know who it is?" she asked.

Monica was twirling her wineglass in small circles. "No. But I think I caught a glimpse of him the other night. Well, morning actually . . ."

"So he slept there?" Elise asked.

Monica nodded.

"Do you think it's a character flaw that I still pray for my son even though I stopped believing in God years ago?" Monica asked.

"Maybe it's a character flaw that I've stopped praying for one of mine . . ." Elise said. "At least you're a mother to Stephen. With Brandon, I'm just a bystander." She stabbed at romaine leaves with her fork.

"You would have turned into a bystander the minute he hit eighteen anyway, Elise," Monica said.

"Wrong." Elise's curtness surprised them both. "I would've been something else. A spectator. I would have watched him go off to school, grow up, get married. Now . . . All the crap that's made him so . . . ill . . . Well, none of it was my fault. But here I am knowing my son is a sick person. Stuck waiting for the next horrible thing he might do. That makes me a bystander."

Monica said nothing. In the pain game they often played, Elise held the winning hand that afternoon.


Jordan found Roger leafing through a stack of mail on the kitchen counter.

"Where's your mother?" Roger asked.

"Mom went to lunch with Monica Conlin," Jordan said flatly. He watched Roger carefully, trying to gauge his reaction.

Elise had admitted her new friendship with her former Garden District nemesis only after Jordan had pressed her. He wanted to see if this bit of news was as shocking to Roger as it was to him. Roger shook his head and tore open an envelope notifying him of the imminent end of his subscription to *The Wall Street Journal*.

Jordan waited until he heard the sound of his father's Cadillac pulling out of the driveway, followed by the metallic clang as the gate shut behind him.


Brandon's room was a time capsule from 1995. It had been cleared of personal belongings. Dust on the comforter indicated that the bed had not been unmade since Brandon had been packed off to Camp Davis. A framed photo of the 1995 Cannon varsity football team hung over the bed. In the photo, Greg Darby gazed stoically out from the team's ranks. He had longer hair than most of his teammates. He wasn't soft or feminine, but he was prettier. He was the only player whose eyes caught the sunlight falling on all of them. By contrast, Brandon's face was so set with fierce determination that he looked as if he might rear up and tackle the camera. His grimace was adolescent, comical.

Jordan felt like an intruder. He had not gone into Brandon's room since his arrival several weeks earlier. Finally, the shut door across the hall from his was too much of a lure. But when he realized his palms were sweating, he turned from the picture, his hip knocking into a nightstand that wobbled, its drawer sliding open a few inches. Jordan reached down and righted the nightstand, relieved that both of his parents were out of the house.

His younger brother stared back at him from inside the drawer. He eased the drawer open to reveal a picture. Three children. He recognized Greg Darby standing next to his brother. Jordan was surprised by how accurately his nightmare a month earlier at Princeton had recreated Brandon at age thirteen. He recognized the girl but could only remember her first name, Meredith. She was holding onto Greg, both arms around his chest. The picture had obviously been taken by Elise. The trio was standing in front of the Charbonnet residence, their bikes lay defeated at their feet.

Four bikes.

Jordan then noticed the thin outline of a fourth figure who was holding onto Meredith, a fourth friend whose form had been meticulously filled in with a black marker. Jordan tried to imagine Brandon steadying his hand to stay within the body's lines. Brandon had been an impatient kid brother, prone to tantrums. Steady hands had never been his forte. Jordan glanced up from the picture to where Brandon leered out from the ranks of the 1995 varsity team. Now his grimace no longer seemed comical.

The Bishop Polk bell tower was visible through Brandon's bedroom window, Jordan noted, as he slid the photograph into his shorts pocket. He knew his mother had heard the gunshot that killed Greg Darby, but he had no idea where Brandon had been on that night. The possibility that perhaps Brandon had seen some muzzle flare or human form inside the portico's windows made Jordan nauseated. He stepped out of Brandon's room, shutting the door behind him.

The only thing that made the ache in his stomach wane was his sudden determination to find out who was the fourth black silhouette clinging to the periphery of his brother and his two best friends.


"Your father wants to take you to dinner."

A month earlier, Trish Ducote would have made this pronouncement with a cigarette hanging from her lip. Now she forced herself to smoke outside the house.

Trish had forced Ronald to put Meredith's 4-Runner up for sale. They found a buyer a week after Meredith returned home. Apparently her car was not the only thing she would have to sacrifice as penance for her drunken stupidity.

"Shit," Meredith whispered, and slammed the refrigerator door.

"He sounds very concerned. And apparently this girl he's with is kind of serious," Trish continued, unfazed.

Meredith took a slug from her water bottle. "Serious?" she asked. "Does that mean she pays for dinner?"

Trish bowed her head to repress a smile. "She's a therapist."

"I'll go. But only if I can have two martinis."

"Meredith!"

"Joke, Mom."

"Not funny, Mer," Trish said. She handed the phone to Meredith and sped to the back door. Meredith knew a pack of Benson & Hedges waited on the lounger by the pool.

"Commander's Palace?" Ronald Ducote suggested when she said hello.

"No, reminds me of dinner before senior prom," Meredith said, gripping the phone tightly and trying to be difficult.

"Work with me here, Meredith," Ronald urged her.

Fuck you, Dad, Meredith thought: Try working with Mom again first.

"Debbie likes Emeril's," Ronald said with an exaggerated sigh. Only he said *em-uh-rools*, his yat accent in evidence. An accent he no longer had to conceal since he had left his Garden District wife.

"Emeril's is really good. How about tomorrow?"

"Cool. What time?" This conversation is now over, Meredith's tone said—save your crap for dinner.

"Seven?" Ronald asked tersely.

"Cool. Bye."

Andrew Darby reached for the phone, clearing his throat as he brought the receiver to his ear.

"Hello?"

"Hi. Mr. Darby," said the voice on the other end. Andrew knew who it was, but he was still surprised. It had been years since he had received one of these phone calls. The kid sounded drunk, his voice a parody of a little boy's.

"Can I speak to Greg, please?"

"Greg's not here anymore, Brandon."

Andrew waited until Brandon Charbonnet hung up on him before sinking back into bed.

# 6

The first thing Jordan noticed about Rich was that he was fat. His former Cannon teammate had been thrown out of the University of Alabama, his football scholarship revoked after he missed three games due to hangovers. Now Rich had landed one of the few jobs he couldn't drink himself out of—bartender at one of the nicest restaurants in New Orleans. Rich said getting Jordan a job as host would be a cinch because the manager "was a fag" and Rich routinely flirted with him.

The restaurant was packed with well-dressed conventioneers, the light through its plate glass windows illuminating the otherwise desolate Warehouse District of art galleries and studio apartment buildings. Rich occasionally threw Jordan leering grins from behind the bar as he flirted with the wives who had snuck away from their tables to have a cigarette. Rich's last job had been as a bartender at Fat Harry's, a bar they had all frequented in high school with their fake IDs.

When he arrived at work that night, Jordan asked Rich a question before he said hello. "Did you ever see my brother at Fat Harry's?"

"Once," Rich said.

For someone who usually padded his sentences with a joke or a crude one-liner, Rich's sudden case of clamp-mouth contributed to Jordan's sense of unease. "How long ago?" he asked.

"About a year ago, I think. I had just started there."

Jordan froze—a year ago? It didn't make sense. Not if Brandon was still in Camp Davis. Jordan tried to conceal his shock, knowing it would only contribute to skittishness.

"How was he?" Jordan asked evenly.

"What do you mean?" Rich asked, fingering the buttons of his white oxford shirt.

"I don't know. Was he . . ."

"I had to throw him out," Rich blurted out.

"Why?"

"He got into a fight in the back. He was with some guys I didn't recognize. They got into a fight with this gang of frat boys over by the pool table. I didn't want to do it, man. I told him I knew you . . ."

"And what did he say?" Jordan asked, aware of the sweat in his armpits and hoping it wouldn't stain through his blazer.

"I don't think he heard me, dude. He was too busy swearing at everybody. One of his friends had . . . Well, he'd, like, broken a pool cue across his knee. He was holding one of the pieces to this other guy's throat. It was bad. We almost called the cops."

"Jesus."

"Did Brandon mention it to you or something?"

Jordan shook his head no.


He had just returned from his coffee break in the employee lounge when he saw the host stand was empty. His cohost Leslie was seating a table at the far end of the main dining room. Rich's arm swung out from behind the bar and hooked him firmly on the shoulder.

"Dude!"

"What?"

"Over there . . ."

Rich pointed to the table that Leslie was seating. A man and a considerably younger woman were taking their seats slowly. Another young woman, maybe twenty, was already seated, her back to them, a plume of black hair spilling down her strapless dress.

"Do you know who that is?" Rich asked.

"Who?"

"The girl. That's Meredith Fuckin' Ducote, man."

"Meredith . . ." Jordan mumbled.

"Cannon homecoming queen nineteen ninety-seven. You didn't hear about that?"

"I didn't come home on holidays, Rich. You honestly think I kept up with homecomings?" Jordan responded. Meredith's arm appeared as she lit a cigarette. The man and woman shared a glance as the first curl of smoke rose from Meredith's head.

"She used to date that guy. What was his name? The one that popped himself in the bell tower—"

"Greg Darby," Jordan answered, his mouth dry.

"Right. So whatever. He died. She's like the shit at Cannon. Miss Everything. Booster Club. Cheerleading. Whatever. Then her senior year she gets elected homecoming queen. Big popularity contest, so it's not a surprise. Then the night of the homecoming game with the whole Mothers' Club and the Court out there on the field during half-time, holding a fucking bouquet of roses and a crown for her, the bitch *doesn't even show up!* Everyone said after that she didn't talk to anybody. Stopped going out. She was like a ghost until graduation," Rich finished.

A stocky conventioneer leaned over the bar, clearing his throat at Rich before plucking a cigar from his suit pocket. Rich took the man's order. Meredith was still a shock of black hair in a swath of cigarette smoke. Jordan had to find a way to get her to talk to him.


"I work mainly with sexual compulsives."

Her name was Debbie. She was employed at Bayou Terrace Hospital, the city's largest facility for the mentally ill.

"Sexual compulsives? Like people who can't stop fu—"

"Meredith, please!" Ronald Ducote looked like he was in a cold sweat. Meredith sucked another drag off her cigarette.

Debbie gave a resilient, determined smile. "Actually the majority of them can't stop masturbating, if you're curious. Obviously I can't go into any specifics."

"Obviously," Meredith responded too quickly.

Ronald was massaging the bridge of his nose with a thumb and forefinger. "I also deal in passive-aggressive suicide attempts," Debbie continued.

Meredith could feel her father tense up at the word suicide. "And what are those?" she asked.

Debbie seemed to realize her mistake. "Unsuccessful ones," she responded softly.

"Oh, so it's not, like, I'm going to kill myself if you don't do the dishes."

Debbie managed a laugh.

"Debbie's very good at what she does. In fact, Masters and Johnson is considering her for a position as . . ."

"Mom quit smoking in the house, Dad," Meredith interjected.

Ronald lifted his eyes from his open menu and gave her a hard stare.

Debbie clasped her hands on the table in front of her. "I am aware of some of the things you've been through . . ."

Meredith's smirk vanished.

"Your boyfriend and his . . . suicide . . ."

"Did you know he hit me?"

"Meredith!"

"He did. See this, Dad?" She tapped her chipped front tooth, leering at her father like a clown. "He did this to me sophomore year. I think you were with Sara at the time."

"Meredith . . ." Debbie said, one hand raised to Ronald as if to hold him in place. "What I'm trying to say is that if you ever need anyone to talk to . . . Well, I would do so freely."

A silence fell over the table. Meredith couldn't tell whether Ronald was more furious with his daughter or his girlfriend. "Don't you know better than to offer your potential stepdaughter counseling the first time you meet her?" Meredith said, surprised by her own candor.

"It's not counseling that I'm offering. It's an ear. And maybe some advice," Debbie responded firmly.

"Can I ask you a question?" Meredith said, lifting her head from where she had been studying the table.

"Sure," Debbie said, eager to placate.

"Did you ever treat Angela Darby when she was in Bayou Terrace?"

Debbie looked as if someone had thrown a drink in her face. She glanced at Ronald, as if seeking help. He offered none.

"Meredith, Angela Darby is still in Bayou Terrace."

When Meredith half-rose from the table and pushed back in her chair, Jordan saw her nearly knock it over backward. He jerked up from the host stand as if to rush forward. She was definitely the same girl as in the photograph.

As she walked across the restaurant, heads turned to take in her breasts swelling through her Betsy Johnson dress, and her delicate face wreathed in black hair. Meredith strode past the host stand and rounded the bar, passing Rich, who was gaping at her as he polished a martini glass. She disappeared down the corridor to the women's room. Jordan abandoned the host stand and followed her.

On the other side of the door, Jordan could hear the unmistakable sound of vomiting. He planned to give her a minute, then knock and ask her if everything was all right. Then he heard her gag and dry heave.

Jordan knocked twice, firmly. "Is everything all right?"

"Fine," Meredith croaked. He heard the toilet flush and backed away from the door a few inches. Meredith opened the door and smoothed her dress. "I'm fine," she said.

"Sounded pretty bad. I'm sorry to bother you, I just . . . Well, I'll be honest, if your little problem in there had something to do with the food then I represent those parties responsible," Jordan said, groping to hide his motives.

"I haven't even ordered yet," Meredith said, bracing the door frame. Even sick, she was striking, poised and defensively belligerent. She didn't seem impressed or awestruck by him. Jordan decided she was actually gauging his sincerity.

"Absolut, tonic, splash of seven, twist of lime. I'll wait right here," Meredith said.

"All right," Jordan almost stammered.

Leslie shot him a furious glance as he hurried to the bar. As Rich mixed the drink he asked, "Dude, you putting the make on her or what?"

"She said splash of seven. Not half vodka, half 7-UP," Jordan told him.

As Jordan handed the drink to Meredith, he slid through the half-open bathroom door and shut it gently behind him. Meredith took no notice. She was too busy guzzling the entire glass. When she finished, she wiped her mouth with the back of a hand.

"I knew your brother," she said.

"I thought I recognized you," Jordan said carefully.

She leaned against the far wall. Jordan stood next to the toilet, smiling sheepishly, as if his brother were nothing more than a source of minor embarrassment. Meredith burped and looked into the mirror. She didn't excuse herself. "How's he doing?" she asked, flipping her hair over her shoulders, raking her fingernails through.

"I wouldn't know," he answered.

Her eyes suddenly caught his through the mirror. She turned on the faucet.

"Greg's suicide affected him badly," he said.

"Tragedy brings out the worst in everybody," Meredith said evenly. She dried her hands with a paper towel before smoothing the front of her dress again, then surveying her reflection. "Although technically what happened wasn't a tragedy, because a tragedy requires a hero."

Jordan tensed, his shoulders rigid. "I never said it was a tragedy."

"Others have," Meredith answered curtly.

"I never said Greg was a hero either," he said, his voice harder.

Meredith turned to face him. "And your brother?"

Jordan didn't say anything.

"You want to ask me about him, don't you?"

"My brother's very ill."

She laughed. "Well, I haven't seen your brother since he went to that camp," she muttered, turning back to the mirror. He inched to the side enough to see that she was dabbing the underside of her chin. She caught him looking. "But you can ask me anyway," Meredith said.

Jordan was too furious to move or speak.

"Well then . . . let me tell you one thing," she said, a half-smile playing across her lips. "It could have been either of them in the bell tower that night."

Meredith stared at him, her face a mask of triumph. She went for the door. "Thanks for the drink," she said, opening the door as Jordan grabbed its edge and pushed it shut again.

"What the hell is that supposed to mean?" he blurted out.

"Take your hand off the door," Meredith said through clenched teeth.

"You can't just say that . . . to someone. He's my brother we're talking about."

"I'm not talking about anything with you anymore. Take your god damn hand off the door!"

Jordan's arm fell. Meredith's hand gripped the handle.

"I found a picture in Brandon's room. Four kids. You, my brother, Greg, and then another one. Only the fourth one is completely blacked out with a permanent marker. You can't even tell who he is . . ."

Meredith halted, half-in and half-out the bathroom door.

"*Who is it?*" Jordan asked her.

"What does it matter?" she asked.

He detected a new tone in her voice. He straightened against the tile wall, leveling his gaze on Meredith's back. He had scared her. "It matters because I have to know why my brother would do something like that . . ."

"Your brother's done worse things," she said, before squeezing through the door and shutting it behind her, leaving Jordan in the women's room by himself.


Meredith did not say a word for the rest of the meal. Debbie and Ronald chatted as if she were not even at the table. At the end of the meal Debbie handed Meredith her card. Meredith tucked it into her wallet.

Three hours after they dropped her off, Meredith called Debbie at her apartment.

"There is something you can do for me," Meredith said.

"What?" Debbie asked tentatively.

"I want to see her," Meredith answered.

"See who?"

"Angela Darby."

# 7

"Who's the fourth one?" Jordan asked Elise for the second time.

Elise studied the picture. "Where did you find this?" she asked.

"In his room," Jordan answered flatly.

"Exactly what were you doing in his room?"

He whipped the picture out of his mother's hands. "Well, let's see. I've been home a month and haven't seen Brandon once—"

"I told you . . ." Elise began.

"I know. Camp Davis. Odd though, considering that Rich had to throw him out of Fat Harry's just this past Christmas. Do the cadets take field trips to bars?"

Elise rose from her chair as if the seat were suddenly hot. She went for her purse on the kitchen counter.

"Considering everything, Mom, it's a pretty simple question. Who's the fourth kid in this picture?"

"I promised to meet Monica at two," Elise said, her purse over one shoulder.

Jordan held up the picture. "This is our house in the background, isn't it? You did take it?"

"You're just like Roger," Elise said as she moved toward the foyer. Jordan followed at her heel. "This question is going to lead to another and then to another. And the real question is why your brother's crazy, isn't it?"

"So now he's crazy! I thought he was just 'sick'!" he yelled.

Elise pivoted. "It's the same thing!"

Jordan backed up a few steps, turned, and slapped the picture on the kitchen counter. He took a deep breath. "Why am I the most arrogant person in the world for wanting to reach out to him—"

"Reach out, Jordan?" Elise shrieked. "For five years we get nothing from you, and now this? You're late. There's nothing to reach out to. Your brother is a shell. When Alex Darby was killed by a . . . by a garbage truck, and when Greg Darby did the stupidest, cruelest thing in the world, it took something from us, Jordan. It didn't make us any wiser. And delving into all of it isn't going to make you any wiser, either!" Elise inhaled deeply. "We all went to the same dark place. Only your brother never made it back. And no one can bring him back. So just shut up about it, already."

Elise let her arms fall to her sides. She waited for Jordan to give some response, but he just picked the picture up off the counter and looked from it to his mother. Elise turned and made for the front door.

"It's Stephen Conlin," Elise shouted back at him. "Monica's son!"

She slammed the door behind her.


Jordan was perusing the 1995 Cannon annual when the phone rang, making him jump. With color photographs on glossy pages, its inside and back covers scrawled with the generic signatures of high school classmates extolling his brother, the yearbook was the second item Jordan had taken from his brother's room. As he reached for the phone, he noticed a good picture of Stephen Conlin.

"Hello."

"Please speak English to me."

"Melanie," Jordan said as neutrally as he could manage.

"What time is it there? It's late here," she said, sounding slightly offended that he hadn't laughed at her opening line.

Fifteen-year-old Stephen Conlin stared up at Jordan as he pressed the receiver to his ear. "It's about three in the afternoon."

"I sent you a postcard yesterday. That was before someone bothered to tell me this hostel has a phone in it." A pause fell between them. "It's bad there, isn't it?" Melanie finally asked gently.

"Yeah," Jordan managed.

"Your brother?"

"Mom, too," Jordan said.

"Look. Take down the number here. Just to talk. Don't worry. I'm not keeping tabs on you or anything. I know we had a good run. Besides, I'm growing accustomed to rude, off-putting artist types."

Jordan let out a slight laugh, to satisfy her. As he took down the number, something occurred to him that brought his mind into alignment with their conversation. "Melanie, what was it you said that time. It was on our first date. About freaks . . ."

"Freaks?"

"Something about how I was a freak because . . ."

"Wait . . . Yeah, I remember . . . Freaks have a better vantage point from which to view the world. Something like that. My dad said it to me once. Only he was talking about writers. People who live outside society are the ones who can see how it works."

"Right," Jordan said, looking down at Stephen's picture. He told Melanie good-bye and promised to call her soon.

Jordan stared at Stephen's picture for several minutes. The boy's blond bangs falling across his forehead, his delicate features and his blue eyes, would have made him the enemy of other high school boys. Jordan felt he knew why.

Jordan had messed around with two guys in high school. Neither of them had looked like Stephen; both of them had been teammates, stocky and well-muscled. The shared blow jobs were drunken and almost utilitarian, defining Jordan's opinion of sex between men as a natural but emotionless act. Boys like Stephen stood in contradiction to Jordan's experience. Prettiness in males could lure a person into thinking sex between men was something other than simply letting off steam.

Jordan shut the yearbook.


"Is he good to you?" Monica asked.

Jeff and Stephen had overslept that morning. She had run into Jeff as he crept out of her son's bedroom, eyes still hooded from sleep. Monica had managed a polite hello. Jeff had nodded and descended the staircase. Monica had found Stephen in bed, still asleep. His naked back and a glimpse of bare hip were exposed from beneath the comforter. She had shut the door quickly.

"Yes," Stephen replied.

They were sitting in the rocking chairs on the front porch. Monica had returned from lunch with Elise an hour earlier. Elise had been sullen, uncharacteristically quiet. Monica needed talk from her son.

"How long have you known him?" she asked.

"He went to Cannon," Stephen replied, a glass of iced tea between his legs.

She nodded with numb surprise. "Are you being careful?" she asked quickly.

"You don't get AIDS from being gay, Mother," Stephen mumbled.

"Careful with your heart, I meant," Monica said and then giggled.

"Motherly advice courtesy of Hallmark." Stephen gave her a wry smile. "His name's Jeff."

Monica did not say what she wanted to—that Jeff certainly wasn't the boy in the picture she found in the back of his closet several weeks earlier.

She had been removing a pair of Stephen's loafers to be resoled when she came face-to-face with a shockingly handsome young man amid a pile of old tennis shoes. She had shut the closet door quickly, thinking she had stumbled across a photo of a secret boyfriend. Now she knew she was wrong. Who was the boy buried in the back of Stephen's closet?

# 8

Stephen drove down over Bonnet Carre Spillway at eighty-five miles an hour. Interstate 10 emerged from New Orleans and into the real Louisiana, its black water lit by the distant fires of oil refineries. Beneath the interstate, dams and locks contained the swamp water, occasionally unleashing it into the lake during heavy rains. His foot nudged the gas pedal, kicking up the Jeep's engine to nearly ninety. Stephen had an erection that he thought could split the seams of his blue jeans.

Jeff wasn't working that weekend and didn't feel like driving in from Baton Rouge, so he asked Stephen to visit him. He had offered a single instruction: "Don't dress gay." At first Stephen had been offended. He could feel a monologue building in his chest as Jeff dictated what Stephen was to wear. "Jeans, polo shirt, and a baseball cap. Wear the cap backwards," Jeff said, his voice excited.

Desire. Balance. Hunger. Their relationship had blossomed in the weeks following their unexpected reunion. In each other's presence they felt filled, each man answering some question that had been nagging the other all his life. They attacked each other's bodies with a mutual ferocity.

And now Jeff was taking Stephen to a frat party.


Sigma Phi Kappa had been booted off the LSU campus after a pledge drank himself to death during a hazing session. Jeff had been a pledge that year and amid the accusations and disciplinary hearings, his decision to decline the fraternity's bid went unnoticed. He was still welcome at the parties. "Sig Kap," as it was called, was now head-quartered in a Victorian house on the shores of a shallow pond, flatteringly named East Baton Rouge Lake. The pond was so shallow that the drunken students who drove their cars into it found that the water didn't rise up halfway past the doors.

When Stephen and Jeff arrived, the Sigma Phi Kappa house was a pounding blaze of light reflecting off black water. The house's paint was peeling. Cars were parked at odd angles across the front lawn. Stephen could hear shouts and bellows that conjured up memories of the Cannon locker room.

"Are you sure about this?" Stephen asked.

"Nobody knows who you are, Stephen." He curved one arm around Stephen's shoulders before tracing his hand down his boyfriend's back. "Besides," Jeff whispered, "you're with me."


Stephen straightened his back. His voice dropped a decibel. He held his arms firmly at his sides, not permitting his hand to wander and clasp. In the course of one minute, Stephen became a frat boy. Thick-necked football players shook Stephen's hand with a "Wassup dude?" or a "Good to meetcha" and in response Stephen delivered an Oscar-caliber performance.

They stationed themselves on the stairs, looking down on the living room-turned-dance-floor. Jeff recognized who Stephen was gawking at. "Señor Ass," he explained, had earned his nickname by always wearing the same pair of blue jeans with a large patch missing in the seat, revealing his bare skin. An LSU linebacker, "Señor Ass" was gyrating with a girl so drunk she looked like she was about to writhe out of her Gap tank top.

Jeff watched Stephen watching.

At Tulane, Stephen had steered clear of the objects of his desire, but Jeff had led him into the lion's den and now he was swollen with almost frantic longing. When Stephen's attention finally returned to Jeff, he was beaming. "Let's get out of here," he whispered.


Back at his apartment, Jeff pointed to the bed as he headed for the bathroom. He shut the bathroom door behind him and stripped down. Behind the shower curtain was his Cannon football uniform, shoulder pads, and jockstrap. He quickly dressed, starting with the awkward shoulder pads, which he thought would be necessary for girth. He fastened the Velcro straps, slid on the jockstrap—minus the cup—and wiggled into the blue Cannon jersey that read Haugh 33. He avoided glancing into the mirror, knowing if he glimpsed himself in costume he'd lose all his nerve.

Jeff cracked the door, stuck his hand out, and flicked off the switch for the bedroom light. He kept the bathroom light on and as he slowly opened the door a rectangle grew across the bed. Stephen squinted at him, fascinated by the effect. Jeff knew he was backlit by the overhead bulb and the outline of the shoulder pads had to be unmistakable.

Stephen rolled onto his elbows, looking as if he'd been caught in the wrong apartment. Jeff stepped toward the bed, his crotch level with Stephen's eyes. Jeff saw Stephen's chest rising and falling with rapid breaths. "Just do what you're good at, cocksucker," Jeff growled. The pitch of his voice was porn-star perfect.

Jeff grabbed the back of his neck so hard that Stephen lurched forward off his elbows, coughing as Jeff tightened his grip on the back of his neck. Jeff was trying to force Stephen's head into his crotch but Stephen's neck had grown taut, bone-rigid. Stephen's breath hissed through clenched teeth. His face wrenched forward, grazing the fabric pouch of the jockstrap. "That's it," Jeff grumbled. "That's the way."

Stephen's mouth opened, his breath flushing Jeff's growing erection. He grunted again, louder, pressing the back of Stephen's head into his crotch. Suddenly, Stephen's upper teeth dug in just above the shaft of Jeff's penis, his lower jaw pinning Jeff's scrotum.

"*Fuck!*" Jeff screamed. He stumbled backward, bright swaths of light dancing across his vision, and fell against his dresser so hard it knocked against the wall. His arms went out to his sides and he found himself sliding butt-first to the floor. As soon as he hit the carpet, Stephen's bare foot jabbed into Jeff's jaw, pushing his head back against a drawer handle. Jeff thought he was going to vomit. *What have I done?* he thought.

"*Fuck you!*" Stephen screamed. His voice ripped through the room as he fell back onto the bed. Jeff lay sprawled, back propped against the dresser, legs splayed out in front of him.

"I'm sorry . . ." he said between gulps of air, ready to cry.

"What?! You were proving yourself?" Stephen barked. "You had to prove you were still *one of them!*"

Jeff shook his head no, no. He opened his eyes and through tears he could see Stephen rising from the bed, blocking the bathroom's light. "I didn't mean to—"

"Didn't mean to *what?*" Stephen's voice was harsh, more anger than tears.

"I thought it was what you wanted," he said back, his voice desperate. "A football player." He could make out Stephen sitting on the edge of the bed, his head in his fists.

"That night on the Fly, I thought you were . . ." Jeff grasped for adequate words, "I thought you were an angel. I thought you made the snow fall. But whatever that was, it's gone. Brandon and Greg . . ."

"Don't say their names! Why do you *always* have to say their names?"

" . . . they *took* it from you. I thought maybe if I looked like them I could bring it back."

Stephen peered up from his palms. The light from the bathroom glanced across a sheen of tears on his face. Jeff rose, gripping the top of the dresser with one hand, tugging at the jersey with the other. The shoulder pads hit the floor with a thud.

Stephen's breath whistled. Jeff leaned over and took Stephen's hands in his before bringing them to his chest and holding them there.

"Tell me what they did to you."

Stephen did not finish his story until the sky outside had turned pale, pre-dawn gray. By the time the sun rose, he had nodded off to sleep against Jeff's shoulder as they lay on top of the bedspread, Jeff still in his jockstrap and Stephen fully clothed. Jeff held one arm around Stephen, unable to sleep for fear of any dream summoned by what Stephen had told him about a winter where snow drifted down, young boys died, and lives fractured.

"She was diagnosed as a schizophrenic after she was admitted."

Debbie's dour voice startled Meredith as they marched down the staff corridor of Bayou Terrace Hospital. There were no lunatics pounding on padded walls. The hall was lined with half-open doors to doctor's offices, through which Meredith could hear low, even voices. They passed a lounge, where the boisterous laughter of nurses struck Meredith as somehow sacrilegious. Debbie was leading Meredith through the "safe part" of Bayou Terrace, where those who worked daily among the mentally ill established their own niche of stability with laughter and pots of coffee.

Bayou Terrace Hospital had no bayou or terrace to speak of. Located several miles outside of New Orleans, the U-shaped building was concealed from the street by a hedge of oak trees. The hospital consisted of two starkly modern wings bridged by the Greek Revival original building. A haggard courtyard lay at its center. It was visiting day at Bayou Terrace, and Meredith could see a small congregation of pale-faced families waiting to visit their children in the Adolescent Ward.

Debbie walked, carrying a manila folder that Meredith assumed was Angela Darby's file. "Schizophrenic? Can someone just become schizophrenic overnight?" she asked quietly enough.

Debbie didn't answer.

Something wasn't right. First of all, Debbie had lost her authoritative calm. For a woman who had spoken with such expertise at dinner, Debbie seemed awkwardly silent on the subject of Angela Darby. They rounded a corner before halting in front of an oak door bolted with several locks. A plaque over the doorway read THE BORDEAUX WING.

"The Bordeaux Wing is the original hospital building. Built in 1856, I think. It's currently under renovation." Debbie fished her key ring from a pocket.

"They keep patients in here?"

"I'm sure you're aware of the circumstances under which she was admitted," Debbie said as she fit a key into a lock.

"Yes," Meredith replied.

Once all three locks were undone, Debbie pulled the door open and motioned for Meredith to pass through. The Bordeaux Wing was a long hallway with plaster moldings and paint peeling in thick curls from the walls. A scaffold littered with empty paint cans blocked the exit at the other end.

Meredith was acutely aware of the circumstances under which Angela had been admitted. She had been sitting in the pew behind Angela Darby when she yowled and clawed at her husband's arm. By the fourth time Angela had cried out, "They did it!" the priest paused in his eulogy and waited until Angela was escorted from the church. That night Andrew Darby was said to have discovered a draft of a letter Angela was composing to the mayor of Thibodaux, apologizing for her performance in the pep rally skit and asking the town's citizens to admit that they had orchestrated a plot to kill her younger son. Rumor went that Andrew had tried to tear up the letter. Angela had thrown a bottle at him and landed in confinement at Bayou Terrace the night of her son's funeral, several hours before her oldest son's death.

Angela's cell was actually a room, which looked to Meredith like an old administrative office. A faded rectangle in the oak door indicated it once bore a plaque with a doctor's name. Meredith stood on tiptoe to look through a small rectangular window in the door.

Next to a single bed, sitting on a wooden stool, Angela Darby stared out the room's single window at the low chain-link fence and parking lot.

"She's sedated?" Meredith asked quietly, looking at the red hair cascading down the back of the woman's hospital gown. She had not moved. "Where was she before?" Meredith asked.

"Violent admissions," Debbie answered.

"How long?"

"First week or so. According to her file . . ." Debbie hesitated.

"Let's get this straight," Meredith began. "Somehow she goes schizophrenic overnight. She's considered violent when she's admitted and now she's stashed here with no other patients behind a locked door."

Debbie said nothing.

"Does she get fed?"

"Of course she gets fed!" Debbie snapped.

Meredith again looked through the window. Angela's hair looked lustrous and a more violent shade of red than Meredith remembered. "What drugs is she on?" Meredith asked.

"She's not my patient, Meredith," Debbie retorted.

"That's in her file, isn't it?"

Debbie reluctantly extracted the file from beneath one arm. Something was very wrong here. Debbie had her own motive. She obviously wanted Meredith to see Angela, to note her condition, yet she wouldn't discuss the case. "Haldol," Debbie answered.

"Anything else?" Meredith asked.

Debbie shut the file. "Thorazine. Other tranquilizers. Milder. To help her sleep." She waved a hand in protest. "Meredith, the circumstances under which I obtained this file in the first place were false. I can't exactly go to her consulting therapist with questions about the drug regimen she's been put on without arousing some suspicion . . ."

"So in your opinion her medication is extreme?" Meredith cut in.

"My opinion is not that important, considering I'm not intimate with her file and her history. I wasn't even on staff here when she was admitted."

"She's catatonic, right?" Meredith said, struggling to keep her voice down.

Debbie looked as if she'd been punched in the stomach. She nodded.

Meredith gave one last look at Angela's back. "This way he doesn't have to tell her," she said, in a whisper of breath that fogged the window. "He doesn't have to tell her Greg is dead." She realized she had hit on Debbie's motive. Angela Darby was being held prisoner.

"Were you close with her?" Debbie asked.

Meredith didn't answer.

Meredith heard Debbie's voice calling after her as she sprinted down the corridor, bursting out the entrance door. Once inside her car, she gunned the Acura out of the parking lot. As she veered down the private drive running alongside the hospital, she saw the sun reflecting off Angela's window and she was a dark shadow on the other side of the glass. But Meredith could see what the window looked out on—an empty parking lot without a security guard.

Several days later, Debbie Harkness was summoned into the office of Dr. Ernest Horne, the head of Bayou Terrace's inpatient therapy, and questioned about the young woman she had brought into the hospital, the one who had been spotted running down the staff corridor. "Now I would like you to tell me in your own words if you feel you did something less than orthodox, Debbie?" he asked pointedly.

The doctor had been Angela Darby's therapist since she had been admitted. In Debbie's opinion, he was also a dinosaur and an asshole.

"My own words . . ." Debbie finally said.

"Yes, please," Dr. Horne urged.

"I would like to leave this facility before someone finds out what you're doing to Angela Darby," Debbie said. After that sank in, she continued. "I will keep this knowledge to myself on the condition that my leaving this facility does not jeopardize your recommendation of me to the Masters and Johnson program. As I said, my only interest is in not being on staff at this hospital when someone finds out about this case. I do not intend to cause any trouble."

Debbie knew a great deal about Angela Darby, none of which she had shared with Meredith. She had found out that Dr. Ernest Horne's wife was Andrew Darby's older sister. She had found out that the "violent episodes" mentioned in Angela's file could not be verified by the nurses. Angela Darby was no doubt ill, but also a victim of grief. Until Angela Darby had been placed in the previously empty Bordeaux Wing, there was no such thing as a grief ward at Bayou Terrace Hospital.

"Your recommendation will be mailed tomorrow," Dr. Horne said. "By that time, please have your office cleared out." Debbie left Dr. Horne's office without telling him one other person also knew about Angela Darby's condition.

# 10

**H**e's the boy in the picture, Monica thought.

Jordan Charbonnet looked up at her from the kitchen table where he was reading a copy of *The Times-Picayune*. "Sixth Bomb Threat Has Gay Community On Edge," the paper proclaimed. Monica's shock was evident. Jordan rose from the table.

"Nice to meet you, Mrs. Conlin," he said.

"Jordan?" Monica asked as she clasped his hand.

"Mom's upstairs getting ready," Jordan said. "Can I get you something to drink?"

Monica and Elise were going to hear the Louisiana Philharmonic. Elise had suggested the concert. The Philharmonic was performing Mahler's "The Resurrection."

Monica had swung by to pick Elise up. "No, thank you . . ." She swallowed. "The door was unlocked so I just . . ."

"Mom always forgets to lock it," Jordan said, and winked as if he and Monica shared an amused tolerance for Elise's carelessness. "You look wonderful."

"Thank you," Monica said with a nervous smile as she set her purse down. Having him compliment her looks made her feel desirable and guilty. The boy was beautiful, which saddened her. There was something distant and isolated about him. He moved with an exaggerated authority, as if he needed all the oxygen in the room.

"How's Stephen?" Jordan asked, opening the refrigerator door.

"He's fine. He's at Tulane. On break, right now."

"Summer," Jordan said, smiling as he poured himself a glass of orange juice. "You sure you don't want anything to drink?"

"Monica!" Elise's voice called down from upstairs.

"I'm here," she shouted.

"How'd you get in?" Elise called again.

"The door was unlocked."

"Jordan!" Elise cried.

"He's right here . . ." Monica answered. She noticed Jordan tense up before he capped the orange juice and returned the carton to the refrigerator shelf.

"Do you know Stephen?" Monica asked, a hint of suspicion creeping into her voice.

"Not really. He and Brandon used to be friends, right?"

"A very long time ago," she said flatly.

Elise sauntered into the kitchen, fastening one diamond earring. She was wearing a sequined, low-cut cocktail dress. Monica was startled. She didn't even know Elise owned such a dress. "I thought you had to go to work," Elise said to Jordan, sounding put out that he was in her house.

"I got cut," Jordan said.

"Cut? Is that bad?" Elise asked.

"No. It just means they had too many hosts scheduled so they let me go for the night," he said, taking a seat at the table, unfolding the news section of the paper again in a theatrical gesture that Monica thought indicated a sudden boredom now that his mother had entered the room.

"Ready?" Elise asked, as if she had decided to hustle her friend away from her son as fast as possible.

"As ready as I'll ever be," Monica said, her eyes moving from Jordan to Elise.

"Nice meeting you, Jordan," Monica said as she followed Elise into the foyer.

"Tell Stephen I said hi," Jordan said without looking up.

Jordan Charbonnet had a strange, dizzying effect on Monica. At first, she assumed it was simple shock when she realized he was the boy in Stephen's picture. Halfway through the first movement of Mahler's Second, Monica abruptly realized that Jordan reminded her of her dead husband, from his dark features to his apparent insensitivity to those around him. And she could see how anxiously Elise had reacted to Jordan, an uncontrollable presence. It was much the same way Monica had been with Jeremy during the early years of their marriage. In the end, Monica blamed it on the symphony. "The Resurrection" had been Jeremy's favorite, so naturally its chords would stir her memories of him.

• • •

Jordan found Meredith at Fat Harry's. Rich had invited Jordan to meet him and this girl he was dating for a few beers. The bouncer at the door, Jordan's old favorite wide receiver, Scott Sauber, patted him on the back as he ushered him into the smoky, raucous college bar. When Rich spotted Meredith at the video poker machines, he punched Jordan on the shoulder. "You two datin' or something?" Rich yelled over the jukebox.

Jordan walked over to Meredith. "Small world," he said to her. He had gotten off from work, lying to his mother about how he happened to be at home to check out Monica Conlin, and in hope of later finding Meredith here.

He sat down on a stool next to her and inserted a five-dollar bill into a machine. She kept her eyes focused on the display screen.

"Stephen Conlin," he said.

Meredith didn't answer. She bet four more credits and examined her new hand.

"The fourth one in the picture is Stephen Conlin." Jordan held three cards and dropped the rest with quick taps of his finger on the screen, losing seven credits.

"My brother was an asshole, wasn't he?" he asked, looking straight ahead and studying his new hand.

"Did you ever hear what they did to Stephen's car?" Meredith said to the screen. "They smashed in all the windows. Flattened every tire, just about. And spray painted the word cocksucker on the windshield. He'd only had the car for a day." Her machine let out an electronic belch, signaling that she was out of credits. Meredith stood up and retrieved her beer. Jordan saw how drunk she was, how wrecked— eyes bloodshot, face pale and gaunt, bangs combed haphazardly off her face.

"Greg told me all about it after. They were so proud." She lifted the bottle to her mouth and swigged. The movement of her arm shifted her weight awkwardly, and she fell back into the stool. It scraped across the floor. Jordan caught her with one arm around her waist. He saw heads snap toward them throughout the bar, including a few he recognized as Cannon alumni. The old missing homecoming queen and the all-American hero, separated by a few years, now supporting one another.

"I almost drank myself to death a month ago. That's why I'm a little tipsy . . ." Meredith said, shrugging Jordan's arm from her waist. He persisted, bracing her shoulders. Meredith pried his arm away and slapped it back to his side. "Answer me something," she said.

"What?" he asked.

"Why did you come back here?"

"This is where I'm from," he said, after a pause.

"That's the curse, isn't it?" Her bloodshot eyes locked on his. "We can never get away, can we? We always want to come home. Where it's easier to drink." She waved her beer bottle proudly. "And drinking makes it easier to watch everything rot." She leaned forward, jabbing a finger into his chest. "But really, what's the real reason? You think there's something in the water here, or you think maybe it's just easier to be someplace where everything's so fucked up?"

"I don't understand," Jordan said. He wanted to tease more out of her, even though each word of it stung.

"Bullshit, you don't understand," she said.

Jordan didn't protest. He did understand. No matter how far he strayed, New Orleans had never left him. Memories of slanting sunlight through oak trees had haunted him. He should have known that after a month the intoxicating charm of his hometown would lure him back into a world where homecoming queens staggered drunkenly around bars and brothers vanished into the cracks and gutters of the present. Meredith must have seen it on his face. She lifted her finger from his chest and caressed the side of his cheek. He saw pity in her eyes.

"You're all right, Jordan. You are. Believe me, you're a much better man than your brother."

Something started to give way inside of Jordan, provoked by the grief of Meredith Ducote, too drunk to stand up. Her boyfriend dead by his own hand. Her youth poisoned. It occurred to him that he might never find out what had happened to his brother, that maybe his mission was an excuse to cover for the fact that he had come home because returning to New Orleans was easier than beginning life. At night, he waited tables and by day he pondered where his brother could be; all the while his Princeton diploma hung above his childhood bed.

Meredith sobered slightly, backing away from him.

"Was it that horrible?" Jordan asked, barely audible over the jukebox. "So horrible that there's no possible way I can even know Brandon again? I'm an idiot for wanting to help him, isn't that right?"

"No, you're an idiot for thinking I can help you," Meredith said with surprising gentleness. "I don't know anything."

Anger flickered in Jordan's chest. His features hardened. "You're lying," he whispered.

She couldn't hear him but she could read his lips. She had passed into a state of sudden calm, as if she were studying him like a painting. "All I know is this . . . If your brother goes anywhere near Stephen, I'll hurt him. Badly."

She turned and moved out of the video poker booth. Jordan watched her weave through the thicket of patrons. Now he knew he had to talk to Stephen Conlin.


After the symphony, Elise Charbonnet had a few drinks with Monica at the Blue Room of the Fairmont Hotel across the street from the Orpheum Theatre. They sat at the bar as a pianist played Broadway favorites; Elise was determined to keep the conversation light. She mentioned Jordan only to bemoan the fact that he insisted on washing the car clad in only a pair of skimpy gym shorts. When she recounted how she had told Jordan he might want to strike some muscle-man poses on top of the car's hood, Monica laughed too loud.

On the ride home, Elise chattered about the two of them buying season subscriptions to the Philharmonic, and Monica blandly agreed. When they pulled up in front of the Charbonnet residence, Elise remarked shakily that Jordan's car—an old Cadillac Seville that Roger had bequeathed him—was not in the driveway. "I'm sure he went out," Monica reassured her.

"Call me," Elise said, distracted, halfway out the door.

Roger was dozing in front of the television. She pondered waking him before she realized she had no desire to talk to him. When he had just awakened, Roger was usually completely incoherent, jerking his head around like a newborn bird. When he was thirty it had been cute, but now that he was approaching sixty Elise thought it was a harbinger of senility.

She mounted the stairs, paused at the top. A year earlier the wall had been filled with a painted rendering of Roger Charbonnet Senior's dream of a country house, plantation style, nestled in swamp pine on the north shore of Lake Pontchartrain, an hour out of the city.

The house had never been completed. Roger had inherited the architect's drawing as well as the parcel of land in Nanine's will.

The thought of the parcel of land—isolated, scarred with the foundations of unfinished houses and the frame of a guest cottage—chilled Elise now. She had removed the print from the wall. She believed that someone was living there.


Monica rummaged in Stephen's closet for Jordan Charbonnet's picture. Stephen had called earlier that day. He was still staying with Jeff in Baton Rouge. He had been there for almost a week now. Monica believed her motive was simple: She wanted to see if Stephen would notice that the picture was missing, and if he did, she wanted to see what he would do about it.

# 11

Several weeks after he had his sons cremated, Andrew Darby quit drinking and began smoking. He had quit cigarettes in his late twenties. For years, he had required glasses of Glenlivet to blot out the racket of his sons' voices and his wife's knack for entering any room he was in and moving things around. Now he relished each cigarette and the fact there was no one around to be bothered by the smoke. Andrew Darby liked living alone.

Following Greg's suicide, Andrew cashed out his son's college fund. He was hesitant to touch Alex's, even though it had accumulated significantly less interest. He retired from his position as head of sales at Schaffer Construction. No one threw him a going-away party. Along with his pension, he drew in annuities from the money he and Angela had saved for a place in Miami Beach.

He was not a man who had nightmares. After he came back from Bayou Terrace Hospital to find two police officers at his front door to inform him that his other son had put a gun to his head, Andrew Darby lost faith in the usefulness of grief. While he was identifying Greg's body, he came to believe that his sons had not died; they had simply slipped out of his reach, leaving him a solitude in which he could spend the day reading Tom Clancy novels and smoking.

The death of his family had given him a new life. The memory of Alex's body arcing back to earth had faded quicker than he had anticipated, with no one around to remind him of it in words. When he visited Angela, he was the only one capable of speech. Every Thursday he would visit her and read her *The Times-Picayune*. It was the only time he left the house aside from a few runs to the grocery store.

One Thursday morning, near the end of June, with heat shimmering outside of the room's single window and Andrew's voice fighting with the drone of insects in the trees outside, Angela Darby spoke to him for the first time in five years.

"Baby," she said.

Andrew glanced up from the paper, angry that a nurse had disobeyed Ernest Horne's direct orders by bothering them.

"Baby," Angela said again.

In disbelief, Andrew realized it was his wife who had spoken. *The Times-Picayune* fluttered to his lap. "Baby," she whispered again.

"What?" Andrew said sharply.

"You . . . called . . . me . . . baby . . ." Angela said, without looking at him. Her voice was flat and throaty after five years of silence.

With his fist he gathered a ball of her hair. He yanked her head back, straining her neck tendons. Angela looked up at him wide-eyed. "What?" Andrew bellowed.

Her eyelids shut, and after a moment it seemed as if she had said nothing at all. He released her hair and her head rolled forward. Several red strands had twined between his knuckles. He examined one of them; it was fine and soft.

When Andrew placed the strand of red hair on Dr. Ernest Horne's desk, Ernest looked at his brother-in-law with annoyed puzzlement.

"Someone's been brushing her hair," Andrew explained, as if to a child. "Do the nurses do that? Do they brush her hair?"

"They bathe her daily. Sponge bath," Ernest replied smoothly, his eyes moving back to a memo.

"I think someone's been with her."

"You're with her every Thursday," Ernest replied, disinterested. "The nurses make the rounds. When they deliver her medication, they're with her. Those are the only people that have been with your wife, Andrew."

Fury flared inside of him. The day of Alex's funeral Angela had plummeted into hysteria and Andrew had dragged her out of the service and back to their house. She had screamed, "They did it!" But when Angela said *they* she meant the Cannon varsity football team. If Greg had never been made second-string quarterback, Alex would not have rushed across the highway.

Angela's fervor increased that evening as Andrew dragged her into the house. Now she was turning on her husband. "If you hadn't been late . . ." was all that made it out of her mouth before Andrew slugged her and sent her slamming into the wall.

He had left the room in a rage. When he returned fifteen minutes later, Angela was lying on the living room floor. He could not move her. She would not speak.

Andrew had called his sister Colleen's cell phone and summoned Ernest from the service. He examined Angela, and tested her reflexes. The deal had been Colleen's idea. Ernest was fascinated by catatonics. If Andrew was willing, Ernest could study her closely and with relative freedom. Andrew had taken no time to answer: Mourners would be visiting the house as soon as the service let out. Andrew wasn't about to let them see Angela curled into a ball, a massive bruise on her jaw and cheek.

When the mourners arrived to pay their respects, Ernest and Colleen had already taken Angela away and Andrew's story was prepared. Friends and family held Andrew's hand as he told them how he had found a letter drafted to the mayor of Thibodaux. "Angela thinks it all has something to do with that pep rally skit," he told them, letting them imagine the rest. The story was picked up by the channels of Garden District gossip and turned to myth overnight.

The deal had ended up benefiting Ernest more than Andrew. In lengthy sessions Ernest had tried to rouse Angela, jotting meticulous notes cataloging her reactions to pinpricks, pokes of a pen. Angela jerked, writhing entirely with her body, her face registering a faint smile at all times. He had told Andrew that Angela might have always had a "shadow syndrome" of autism but the theory never flew because she developed no ritualistic behaviors. Angela Darby had simply shut down.

After a year of fiddling with medications, Ernest set Angela's regimen of Thorazine and Haldol at nearly the maximum levels. Andrew wanted it that way. He had assured Ernest that Angela had no living relatives except him, and only a few friends, most of whom Andrew hadn't liked and had pretty much managed to drive off.

"If I find out that someone's been with her, I swear . . ."

"Swear to whoever you want, but in case you've forgotten I'm the head of this hospital. I can continue the terms of our agreement or I can make things difficult for all of us!"

"This is about Angela!" Andrew countered.

Andrew saw a wry smile curl Ernest's mouth before he turned his attention back to the file on his desk. "If you would like, I'll submit a letter to the board asking that they install security bars over the windows. They might consider it a little odd, given that there's a million-dollar renovation coming up and this is an area of the hospital that's supposed to be used for storage."

"Write it!" Andrew snapped before storming out of Ernest's office.

# 12

On the last Saturday in June, Jordan went out to dinner with his parents for the first time since he had been home. He ordered a gin and tonic as soon as they sat down; he knew he'd need at least one drink in him to do what he planned. Elise rolled her eyes. Roger spoke up in his defense. "If our federal government lets him have a drink at dinner, we should, too," he said.

"Most of us wait until after dinner to order our drinks," Elise mumbled and splayed her napkin across her lap.

Jordan said nothing until the waitress brought his drink. He took a sip, swallowed, and inhaled deeply, which washed the gin's sharp sting through his chest. He looked from his father to his mother, both of whom were studying menus. "I called Camp Davis today," he announced.

Over the top of her menu Elise's eyes met his with the force of a shotgun blast. Roger looked as if he had been punched.

"I spoke to a receptionist in the office," Jordan continued, locking looks with his mother. "It seems they're not really a military camp per se. They're a training program. Which—let's see, how did she put it— which attempts to instill discipline in young men with a blatant disregard for authority. I think it was a little bit more eloquent than that . . ."

Roger bowed his head. "Jordan, please . . ."

"I was more interested in the specifics of the program," Jordan reported. "The normal stuff you'd expect. Regiment exercises. Training drill. Work projects. A program that is supposed to last three months."

Jordan took a sip of his drink. He set it on the table. "Where is he?"

"Jordan, you have to understand . . ." Roger began miserably.

"Understand *what?*" Other diners snapped their heads at the shrillness in his voice. "Neither of you have had any idea where Brandon has been for the last four years! How am I supposed to understand that?"

Elise rose from the table, holding her napkin, dropped it on the chair, and moved off into the restaurant. Roger watched her go.

The waitress arrived. Would they like to wait until their third diner returned?

"I think she just went to the bathroom," Roger mumbled. The waitress smiled and moved off. "Jordan, we have tried so hard to get some kind of balance back here—" Roger started to say.

"Balance? Forgetting that Brandon was ever alive because he *threw a chair*? That's balance?"

"He did much more than that and you know it," Roger retorted.

Jordan stared with dumbfounded revulsion at Roger. Roger sank back into his seat, anger giving way to misery. He drew one hand to his forehead and held it there. He shook his head slightly. When he brought his hand away, Jordan saw the glimmer of tears in his eyes.

"I don't know what to do," Roger said, voice quavering. "Is that good enough for you? I don't know what a father's supposed to do when his son turns into a monster."

"You're afraid of him?" Jordan asked.

Roger nodded emphatically.

Jordan sank back into his chair.

"And maybe you should be, too," Roger said.


When Jordan and Roger returned home, their footfalls in the foyer echoed through an obviously empty house. After half an hour Elise had not returned to the table. They had finally ordered and eaten their meals in silence.

Jordan volunteered to see if she had gone to visit Monica.

The Conlin residence's verdant front yard curtained the light emanating from the windows. He rang the bell three times before he saw a shadow through the door's frosted panes. Monica seemed to hesitate for a long moment before her head appeared through a crack in the front door and the gate in front of him let out a harsh buzz.

Monica remained in the cracked door as he crossed the front yard and mounted the porch steps.

"Jordan?" she asked, sounding both excited and wary.

"Hi, Miss Monica. Is my mother with you by any chance?"

Monica shook her head no and stood taut as a cat in the doorway.

"Do you mind if I come in?" Jordan asked.

She stepped back from the door and he opened it further before passing into the foyer. "Is something wrong?" Monica asked.

"Nothing's wrong as long as you don't tell my mom that I came here tonight," he said.

"Can I get you something?"

"Do you have gin?" Jordan asked.

"Several bottles." Monica turned and headed toward the wet bar in the front parlor. Jordan scanned the surroundings. The house was more opulent than his own, all porcelain vases and dark velvety hues.

"Is Elise all right?" Monica called from the front parlor.

"No," Jordan said.

He lingered in the front parlor doorway, observing Monica's response. She turned from the wet bar to face him, clutching a bottle of Bombay that she had not yet uncapped.

"What happened?"

"It's my brother," Jordan answered squarely.

Monica nodded and poured Jordan's drink.

"Is Stephen home?" Jordan asked.

"No. He's not." She carried Jordan's drink to him and put it in his hand without offering him a place to sit. "He went to a movie with a friend. Just left a few minutes ago, so he shouldn't be back for about two hours." Jordan took a sip of his gin and trailed one hand over Amelia Conlin's grand piano. Monica studied him as he prowled the room. "Why do you think my mother never told me about what Brandon did to your son's car?" he asked.

"I'm sure she wasn't proud of it."

"And she wouldn't want to ruin your new friendship."

"We've known each other for a long time, Jordan," Monica said.

"But you weren't always friends," Jordan said, sprawling into a high-backed antique chair against the far wall.

"No . . ." she answered weakly.

"I want to talk to you about my brother," Jordan said firmly.

"I don't know anything about your brother other than what your mom's told me—"

"And what he did to Stephen," Jordan finished.

Monica glowered at him. She turned to the wet bar and began pouring her own drink. "You know you're a very handsome young man, don't you?" It wasn't really a question. She turned, took a sip of her drink. "People usually defer to you, don't they?" The bite in her voice was evident now. "Have you had a lot of experience at intimidating women twice your age? Do you practice on your mother?"

She was watching the impact of her words, so Jordan did not move or flinch. "You were a freak, weren't you?" Jordan asked quietly. "That's why you were never friends with my mother. Because you were from the wrong side of Magazine Street, and to make it all worse you were ten times prettier than she was."

"I'm going to have to ask you to leave . . ."

"I remember thinking, even when I was a kid, that she didn't like you because you were different. When you came along and moved into this house, you upset her equation. Threw things out of . . . balance. Well, that's what I'm doing. Because I have questions and I want them answered, but we both know the only way people in this neighborhood deal with anything difficult is to smile and offer it a drink."

Jordan could not read the expression on Monica's face. Maybe she was mildly impressed.

"What has my mother told you about Brandon? Did she tell you he was—"

"Camp Davis. Yes," Monica said, swallowing some of her drink.

"Did she tell you it was a three-month program?"

Monica furrowed her brow, looking genuinely puzzled, then drank.

"He was admitted four years ago," Jordan added quietly.

"What do you want, Jordan?" she asked.

"I want to know what's wrong with him."

"Then you're asking the wrong questions," Monica whispered.

He sat forward in his chair. "What should I be asking?"

She crossed the room to the window. Beyond her profile, through the gaps in oak branches, Jordan could make out the spire of the Bishop Polk bell tower.

"You should be asking about the night Greg Darby killed himself," she said to him.


"It was the worst thing I had ever seen. And my mother was a drunk who used to shit the bed so I've seen some things, let me tell you." Monica laughed bitterly and brought her third shot of Chambord to her lips. "It was horrible, not just because we all had children and we all knew we could end up like Angela Darby in one second, with just one wrong turn, or one cross of the street. But because it made the adults and the children the same. At the funeral, the parents . . . They didn't know what to do. I watched them. Stephen and I sat in the balcony and I saw all those parents trying to comfort their children and doing such a bad job of it . . ."

She paused, sipped her drink.

"She won't talk about it now," Jordan interjected. "But when she first called me after it happened, she told me she thought she heard the gunshot . . . when he did it."

Monica locked eyes with his. "We all heard it," she corrected. She went to the wet bar, pouring herself another tumbler of Chambord. With her back to him she continued. "I heard two things that night, actually. The first I only remembered later, but it sounded like one of the bells . . . You know, the bells haven't been used in years. They use some recording or something—that's what Stephen told me."

"They don't sound like real bells," Jordan agreed.

Monica swayed back, her chair tipping slightly as she settled into it.

"Well, earlier that night, I guess it was about—oh, God, I don't know . . . It sounded as if one of the bells had tried to go but couldn't. It was like this strange hum. I remember because that's when the dogs started barking." She looked out the front windows again. "I don't know. For a while I thought I might have imagined it. It could've been something else. A plane, or I don't know, a truck on Jackson."

She went quiet, either drunk or pensive.

"And the gunshot?" Jordan asked gently, urging her to go on.

"I'd say around ten or eleven." Monica fingered the hem of her dress. "It was loud. Too loud. I mean, you should know a lot of the times we can hear guns from over in the St. Thomas Projects. They're a few blocks away, but this was . . . I knew it was too close the minute I heard it." Monica looked at Jordan and for a moment her eyes couldn't focus. "Stephen wasn't home."

"What are you saying?" he asked.

"My husband. Jeremy. He used to have this office on the third floor. It's still pretty much the way it was. He was a writer and there's so much . . . Anyway, when the gunshot went off, that's where I was. I was flipping through books."

Jordan figured she was diverting him. "He wrote this poem many years ago, one of my favorites. It's called 'To a Child Not Yet Born.' But for some reason I've never been able to find the first draft." She waved her hand and let it flop. "This is all very boring, but Jeremy was quite detailed with his notes. He'd take notes, hammer out a first draft, and then polish a final for submission. He kept them all in notebooks. Anyway, the only copy I have of his poem is the final, and I keep it in his study."

Her eyes closed. ". . . I was reading it when I heard it. You see, Stephen was having a rough time in high school . . . Your brother." Monica glanced at Jordan, who smiled wryly and bowed his head.

"'What fires burn the heart,'" she whispered. It took Jordan a second to realize she was quoting the poem. "'From which God did these agonies start. . .'"

Monica halted and said, "I thought about reading it to Stephen." She shook her head slightly. Slower. Drunker.

"I heard someone in the house. After I heard it, I waited on the porch for a while. I heard the sirens. I went inside and . . . Stephen wasn't in his bed. I went back to the study. I was trembling. I thought that . . . Well, I was waiting for the phone to ring. I was waiting for the police to call and tell me . . . Then I heard footsteps. But I wouldn't leave the study. I wasn't even thinking. I remember, I got Jeremy's old pistol out of his desk drawer. It was the same one he used." Monica stared out the window as she whispered, "I found Stephen in bed."

Jordan felt a twinge of disappointment tug at his shoulders. "But you said he wasn't home?" he asked gently.

"I don't think he was . . ."

"But you heard footsteps?" Jordan asked again, a note of insistence in his voice. Careful, he told himself, don't blow this.

Monica stood and wobbled, clutched the chair's arm to steady herself, and wafted deliberately from the room. Jordan sat confused as he heard her climb the stairs. A few moments later, she returned, carrying a bundle of fabric. He had a faint memory of his grandfather's funeral. His grandfather had fought in World War II and at the service Jordan had accepted the flag that had draped his grandfather's casket, folded into a tight triangle, just like the flag Monica set on the coffee table in front of him. This one was not American.

"Stephen was lying wrapped in that," she said quietly.

"Wrapped?" he asked incredulously.

Monica nodded. Her hand quivered, sloshing the liquor in her glass. "I was able to get it off him because he wasn't just asleep. He was unconscious," she said, her voice thick.

Jordan traced a hand over the flag.

"That's the Episcopal flag. Bishop Polk is an Episcopal cathedral, of course," Monica said. She downed another slug of Chambord. "Do you think I'm a bad mother?" she asked, her voice tinged with grief and rage. "No, I never asked him about it. I stayed up all night checking his pulse. Making sure he was breathing. But I never asked him about it, do you want to know why?"

Jordan couldn't answer.

"Because he was alive. Because he's still alive. And I spent half of his life thinking that he would either be killed by your brother and Greg, or he would end up killing himself just like his father. But he didn't. Whatever happened, he lived through that night. And Greg Darby didn't. And he can never do anything to harm my son again."

Monica drained her glass and banged it down on the table. She walked toward the door.

"My brother's still alive, Monica," Jordan said.

She paused in the doorway, shock creasing her face.

"And no one knows where he is," Jordan added quietly.

"That's why you're here then?" she asked, as if speaking from a realm where no fresh pain could occur.

"Meredith Ducote told me that if my brother ever went near Stephen she would hurt him. Hurt him badly, she said." Maybe this would console Monica.

"Meredith Ducote has not seen my son in years. I'm not willing to bequeath to her what I consider to be my responsibility," Monica said tightly. She shuffled up the stairs. "Take the flag if you want," she called down the staircase. Jordan left it on the coffee table.


"I guess in the end it wasn't that hard. I mean, I figured out early on what I had to say for him to hit me, so as long as I didn't mention Stephen's name it was all right." Meredith guided the brush through Angela Darby's hair in a clean sweep. "He only hit me twice. I guess I'm kind of surprised." Angela sat motionless on the edge of the bed. It had taken Meredith less than a week to figure out the guard's schedule. He made rounds in his white pickup truck every twenty minutes. There was a shift change at midnight, during which time the parking lot outside the

Bordeaux Wing was empty for a full twenty minutes, which gave her ample time to dash across the parking lot and scale the chain-link fence. Once over the fence, darkness camouflaged her as she approached the windowsill. A nurse always turned out the light at eight-thirty each night.

By the end of June, Meredith had visited Angela four times. Angela had not said a word or acknowledged her. Meredith got drunk on the way to Bayou Terrace, and by the time she was safely ensconced in Angela's darkened room her words flowed easily, more effortlessly than they had in years, even since she was a child, in fact. Meredith felt strangely comforted, as if visiting Angela had become a more powerful addiction than her drinking.

"The strange thing about it, though," Meredith said, drawing the brush out of Angela's frayed ends, "was that he never seemed angry when he did it . . . I mean there was no, like . . . I don't know. He always hit me in a panic. I know it was meant to make me shut up, but there was always this look of pain on his face. It was so sad."

She broke off, a hot rush of tears stinging her eyes. She breathed deeply, collected herself, and continued. "Brandon's brother is back in town." She worked the brush just above Angela's forehead, tossing her red bangs back over her scalp. "I don't know if you ever met him. He was always just a picture before now."

"Baby—"

Meredith let go of the brush, where it dangled for a second, twined in the hair just above Angela's left ear, before it fell to the floor. Angela didn't move. Meredith recoiled, flattening her body against the wall. She sank to the floor, pulled her knees to her chest, and held them.

"Baby."

Meredith tapped her feet on the floor, mystified. "Greg used to call me baby," she whispered. She rocked forward on her heels and crawled across the floor to where the brush lay next to the stool. She stood and with a steady hand she threaded the brush through Angela's hair again. After a half hour of silence, she set the brush down on the bed, checking the window for the guard before jimmying it open. One leg craned over the ledge when Angela spoke again.

". . . 'e called me baby wen de truck it," she said.

Meredith had no time to turn back. She landed, both feet in the mud, rose, and slid the window shut. Halfway to the car, she deciphered Angela's slurred speech. "He called me baby when the truck hit."

Angela Darby was teaching herself how to talk again.

# 13

Jeff had to report to work by ten. At nine-thirty, he knew he and Stephen were never going to make it in time. Jeff's Honda was in the shop so Stephen had offered to shuttle him in from Baton Rouge. Jeff had to work the entire Fourth of July weekend at Sanctuary, since a lot of out-of-towners came in for Independence Fest, a gay block party that sent most of the straight tourists into self-imposed exile from the Quarter. Jeff was trying to earn extra money so they could get an apartment together after he graduated that winter. Stephen was speeding.

The French Quarter was a traffic nightmare. The Independence Fest merrymakers mixed with two conventions—one for optometrists and the other for Internet design consultants—plunged the labyrinthine network of narrow French Quarter streets into near gridlock. It took Stephen twenty minutes to travel four blocks from Rampart to Bourbon Street. Jeff offered to get out and run.

"I can make it," Stephen insisted. "Besides, it gives us more time together."

They finally reached Bourbon, blocked by a throng of gyrating and shirtless gay men. Devon leaped out of the crowd and bounced on the car's hood. "Asshole!" Stephen cried out. Shirtless and drunk, Devon rapped his fist against the window. "I gotta go, babe," Jeff said, leaned over, pecked Stephen on the cheek, and climbed out of the car. "Don't wait up!" he called after he disappeared into the crowd.

Devon leered through the window. "So tell me all about it!"

"I'm sending an account to *Jock* magazine. You can read it then!"

"Are you keeping the part about the snow falling on his humpy football shoulders, or is that too literary?"

"Good-bye!" Stephen announced.

"You're parking?" Devon asked, prying himself free from a coked-up drag queen trying to engage him in the lambada.

"No, I'm going home," Stephen shouted, already powering the window up. "I want no part of this fag nightmare, thank you!"

"Have I ever told you you're wracked with self-loathing?" Devon yelled after him.

"Watch my boyfriend. Make sure he doesn't get molested."

"What if I'm doing the molesting?" Devon laughed.

"Then you're both dead. Good night!"

Stephen powered the window all the way up. For a moment he felt as if he were surrounded by a riot. He accelerated the Jeep slightly and pushed forward through the crowd, which parted with shrieks and howls.

At ten-forty-five, two Jefferson Parish patrol officers arrived at the house of one Edna Bodier in the suburb of Kenner. Both officers knew Edna. She had the irritating habit of phoning the police and pleading with them to investigate strange sounds that were usually caused by the filtering station emptying the canal that ran behind her house into Lake Pontchartrain. She lived alone except for her Welsh corgi. Both Edna and the dog met the officers on the front porch.

"This way!" she ordered them.

The officers rolled their eyes and followed Edna and the corgi down the side of the tract house to the drainage canal that ran behind her house. Edna gestured a frail arm toward a torrent of garbage—empty beer cans, water-swollen cardboard beer cases. The officers were about to lose their patience when Edna asked, "Do you see the hand?"

By eleven o'clock the medical response unit had arrived and two medics dragged the body of thirty-one-year-old Eddie Carmagier from the drainage canal behind Edna Bodier's house. An audience of shocked neighbors had clustered on both sides of the canal. Eddie was wearing only his underwear. A clean bullet wound was discovered in the back of his head. Twenty minutes after his corpse was loaded into an ambulance, Jefferson Parish police learned from Eddie's wife that he was a driver for Plantier Liquor Service. He was supposed to have gotten off work around five, but he hadn't come home. His wife had assumed he'd gone out to his favorite bar, Parkway Tavern, with friends from work.

At eleven-forty-five, the fax machine rang in Sanctuary's employee lounge on the third floor of the bar. The evening manager was downstairs chewing out Jeff Haugh for tardiness when a curl of paper unfurled from the fax machine, revealing a single bold-faced word.

REVELATION.

By the time Jeff Haugh took up his post checking hand stamps at the re-entry door, Stephen was running a shower, and the Jefferson Parish police had finally tracked down Reynolds Plantier, Eddie Carmagier's former employer.

"I told Eddie he could just take the van home this weekend after he made his last run," Reynolds told the police. They had evidently awakened him; a woman, not his wife, waited in the other room wearing his wife's robe. When they asked him about Eddie's last scheduled stop, Reynolds answered, "That queer bar on Bourbon."

A call came to Jefferson Parish police headquarters just before midnight. Eddie Carmagier's empty truck had been found in a parking lot near the airport.

Sara Miller had begged her husband to take her to New Orleans for the optometrists' convention. A Midwesterner, Sara had never been farther south than St. Louis. In college, her friends trekked down for Mardi Gras but she had declined because of the long drive. She and Ted could use a little fun, carousing in the Quarter. She imagined they might find their love again.

They were having a romantic dinner at The Chart House, on Jackson Square, several blocks away from Sanctuary. The waiter had just brought their entrees when a bottle of Merlot flew across the table and landed in Sara's lap. For a second, Sara actually believed her husband had thrown the bottle at her, but as her chair toppled backward in a shower of cutlery she saw only her own legs. Plates shattered on either side of her head.

When Sara was asked later to describe the sound of the explosion, her sentence made every major newspaper in America. "It sounded like God cracking a stick across his knee," she said.

Sparkles Aplenty would wake up in Charity Hospital with doctors rudely calling him Jim Warshauski and declining to tell him what they'd done with his wig. "I remember thinking that one of the strobe lights had popped or something because suddenly you could see right through the doors. This press of bodies and all those hot dancers on top of the bars. It got so bright you could even see the sweat on the dancers' chests, and I almost turned to my friend and said, 'Cut me off a piece of that!' But before I could . . ."

That was all Sparkles could remember. Sparkles's friend Jose, who had been standing next to him and was hurled through the same glass window, died a day later of third-degree burns. Three hours before his death he clutched a nurse's arm and slurred through charred lips, "Tell them the devil exists." No paper quoted him.

There were only three parties left at Emeril's that night and one of the waitresses had quit, so Jordan was serving an older couple their yellow fin tuna when all the plate glass windows rattled in their frames. The older woman whispered, "Earthquake." Jordan said reflexively, "We don't have earthquakes here!" He straightened and scanned the dining room. Everyone seemed as startled as he was.

"It felt like an earthquake!" the older woman insisted.

In her bedroom, half a city away, Meredith heard a dull thud and thought it was an usually loud firework. She turned her attention back to the first entry she was composing in her secret notebook since high school.

Singing to himself in the shower, Stephen heard nothing over the patter of the water other than a dull thud coming from above. Upstairs, Monica had dropped one of Jeremy's notebooks when she heard a crack followed by a resounding boom.

Jeff Haugh was flung from Sanctuary's front door, fire carried him over Bourbon Street. For a brief instant, he knew he was flying. Objects slammed into him: other human bodies. Devon Walker was crushed by a slab of Sanctuary's front wall. Jeff's flight ended when he collided with a lamppost, his spine cracked on impact. He sprawled on the pavement, face toward the sky. In the second before his heart stopped, Jeff mistook the fire raining down over Bourbon Street for snow and thought of Stephen.

# 14

"**M**rs. Conlin?"

Monica didn't recognize the voice. She held the cordless phone to her ear and let her eyes survey Jeremy's darkened office. One of his notebooks lay open on the desk in front of her. The wails of sirens and the screams of reporters wafted up from the television in her bedroom, one floor below.

"Who is this?" Monica whispered.

"It's Meredith, Mrs. Conlin," Meredith answered. Her voice trembled.

"He's here, Meredith," Monica said. She could still hear the shower running.

"He's home," Monica added.

"*. . . as you can see behind me, Canal Street is gridlocked with ambulances and other emergency vehicles trying to rush to the scene. We have unconfirmed reports that several fires are still burning out of control as a result of the initial explosion . . .*"

Monica could hear that Meredith was watching the same news broadcast, which came to her now in an eerie stereo.

"*Melissa, can you give us any further information on the precise location of the blast?*"

"*Stan, we're working entirely on speculations right now, but obviously there's talk here of the several bomb threats received by the Sanctuary dance club over the past month . . .*"

The shower stopped. "Thank you . . ." Meredith stammered before hanging up.

Monica brought the phone away from her ear, setting it on the desk next to Jeremy's old notebook. Monica would now give Jeremy a chance she had never allowed him. She would see if maybe he had been right, that maybe there was something in his poems that she had missed. She scooped the notebook off the desk and teetered out the door.

As she entered her bedroom, she noticed that Stephen was blocking the television. He stood motionless, his back to her, arms limply at his sides. He clutched a towel around his waist. His hair was still wet.

*"Okay, this is definite confirmation now from the New Orleans Fire Department, coming to us here at the scene. The origin of the blast was the Sanctuary dance club on Bourbon Street . . ."*

Stephen's knees buckled cleanly. He collapsed to an awkward seated position on the rug next to her bed. Slowly, he rocked back and forth, his bleats turning to low moans.

"Stephen?" Monica ventured. His name caught in her throat.

She lowered herself to her knees and crawled across the floor, the notebook still in one hand, and gently touched his naked back. He ignited under her caress, leaping to his feet, the towel tumbling to the floor. He stood naked before her, wide-eyed, incredulous, outraged.

"Jeff's there!"

"Stephen . . ."

"Jeff's there!" he yelled, stepping away from her. His tone implied the obvious thought: *Don't you see, this can't happen, this didn't happen because Jeff is there right now.*

Monica embraced her son hard. She knew he would try to recoil. He writhed for a second and then she felt his chest heave and he pitched into her, disturbing her balance. They fell together, the notebook pressed beneath Stephen's back.

*"What do they want?"* Stephen moaned into her ear.

They. As Stephen rocked against her, an image reared up in her mind—how at the funeral for her seven-year-old son, Angela Darby had shot up from her pew, crying, "They did it!" This was the *they* of death, the *they* of murder. The unseen hand that plucked people from the streets. Death was so much easier to understand when it was the work of others.

Jordan and the two waiters who had closed Emeril's were lingering on the corner of Julia Street watching a battalion of MedVac helicopters sweep by overhead and disappear behind the thicket of downtown buildings. The night was filled with sirens. Just beyond the Sheraton Hotel, several blocks ahead, the night sky glowed orange.

"Plane crash . . ." one of the waiters decided. A reason for them to just go home.

"Downtown? A plane crash, downtown? We would've heard it," a waitress hissed.

"It's a fire," Jordan said.

They fell silent and watched the orange halo grow.


The French Quarter was on fire.

When the news broke in on *David Letterman*, Elise sat up and hunched there, studying the television screen. It had happened so fast even the newscaster couldn't seem to make sense of it. A terrified reporter stood in the middle of Canal Street, flailing his arms amid a blaze of fire engines and ambulances. Now the television screen in the Charbonnets' bedroom filled with an aerial view of what looked like a giant footprint impressed on several blocks of the French Quarter, a footprint etched in flame.

"Jordan's at work," Roger had said instinctively, anticipating a mother's initial fear.

When the reporter identified the explosion's origin as the Sanctuary bar, Elise threw up her arms in frustration. The name meant nothing to her.

"It's a gay bar," Roger muttered.

Then came the talk of bomb threats. The mayor arrived at Canal Street, looking dazed, dressed in a T-shirt and jeans and a light jacket, addressing the reporters amid the whirl of ambulances and fire trucks screaming past him into the French Quarter. He spoke so softly the microphones could barely pick up his voice. No, he didn't know anything new. Yes, he was aware of the bomb threats Sanctuary had received over the past month.

At around 1:30 A.M., Elise was still watching the news when the story of Eddie Carmagier and his stolen liquor truck was broadcast. The plot was unfolding live on television. In the living room, where he'd gone to make himself a drink, Roger flipped through the channels to see the French Quarter burning on every major network, including CNN.

As Elise watched, she remembered a decimated Jeep parked in front of her house one morning like a gift, a word sprayed across its windshield in red paint.

At two-thirty, a weary-looking anchor announced to Monica's bedroom that no survivors had been found in the still-smoldering ruins of the Sanctuary bar. She muted the television off just as they cut to footage of body bags lined up on Bourbon Street.

Stephen's sobs had abated and he lay, still naked, curled into a fetal position on her bed with his back to the television. She slid into bed next to him, the notebook still in one hand.

"Stephen, I want to read you something."

He didn't stir.

"Your father wrote this. For you, I think." She flipped through the notebook pages to the final draft of "To a Child Not Yet Born," written in Jeremy's severe cursive.

As she read aloud, Sara Miller's face filled the television screen. She was bleeding from a thin scratch across her forehead and her husband braced her from behind. She delivered what would become her world-famous quote.

"What fires burn the heart,
From which God did these agonies start?
Our cobwebs strung from death to death
Are too thin. Our lies the greatest sin.

I will hold you, child not yet born,
And tell you not to forget,
But not to know.
You will soon be dense with memory
And your memory dense with souls.
What fires burn the heart?
From which God did these agonies start?

I hold you, child not yet born.
Yet I am not your god.
Ask me not to stop the pain.
The lies I'll offer

You need not gain.
I cannot tell you how or why.
I can only teach you
That this world calls for you to cry."


Twenty miles across the black bowl of Lake Pontchartrain, where the sirens could not be heard and the night sky was free of helicopters, a shout erupted from the dense, swampy forest. It was joined by another, equally as strong. Birds startled from their branches and veered into flight over the lake's expanse, where the night sky and the black water met and the Causeway was a deserted strip of pavement leading to the distant shore. Five voices blended into one guttural triumphant roar that echoed between pine trunks and over black water, on the small parcel of land that Nanine Charbonnet had passed on to her only son, Roger, and his wife, Elise.

*Part Three*

# The Army
# of God

*"Give your soul to God and pick up your gun,*
*It's time to deal in lead.*
*We are the legions of the damned,*
*The Army of the already dead."*

—Robert Jay Matthews

# 1

At the end of the first week of July, Jordan clipped an article from *The New York Times* and slid it under his mother's bedroom door.

## WHO IS THE ARMY OF GOD?

### New Orleans Mourns Seventy Dead in Gay Bar Bombing
### Investigators Left with Rubble and Bodies

Its name was layered with meaning, a place where gay men were free to dance, drink, and express desires deemed unacceptable in your local bar. Now Sanctuary stares out at investigators from the debris sprawling over three blocks of the New Orleans French Quarter. Its brightly painted sign with a neon-pink planet encircled by rainbow rings that signify diversity is one of the few intact pieces remaining after a homemade bomb exploded in its rear liquor closet last Saturday, the eve of Independence Day. FBI Investigators now believe semtex, dynamite, and a crudely made timer reduced an entire block to ruins.

But even before the last bodies were pulled from the wreckage and the rumors of a gas leak were disproved, many Americans reacted to the previously unknown terrorist organization believed responsible, the Army of God. On the Sunday after the bombing, seventeen people were injured in Los Angeles when a riot broke out between angry motorists and protestors barricading Santa Monica Boulevard, in the city of West Hollywood, home to a large gay and lesbian population. Several demonstrators were injured during a similar altercation in the Chelsea neighborhood of New York City, when counter-protestors arrived at a candlelight vigil for the seventy dead, carrying signs depicting the shell of the Sanctuary bar beneath the proclamation, "The Work of God."

Even before the ATF released a report citing a bomb as the source of the blast, news spread of threats to Sanctuary over the previous month by fax and phone. Phone calls and a fax traced to a Kinko's copy store in suburban Metairie made vague promises to Sanctuary's manager. "Sodomites Beware" read one; "Revelation Approaches" an anonymous male caller promised. After a month of threats that both police and managers believed to be hollow, New Orleans is now coping with the fact that they were, in fact, warnings.

It appears that the threats from the Army of God had become so commonplace throughout the month of June that neither the bar's managers nor the New Orleans Police Department were taking them very seriously. A trace of the only threat received by fax yielded only twenty-four hours of security tape from a Kinko's on which the FBI had found "nothing and no one to point them in any direction," according to a spokeswoman.

"Everything that can be done will be done," New Orleans Mayor Anthony Morrison promised residents in a local televised address broadcast early Friday morning. "This tragedy is not a local one. The entire country mourns those we have lost. Now is the time for contemplation and patience."

Mayor Morrison's words might be more than an attempt to comfort a grieving city. They might be sad reality. According to the National Anti-Defamation League, "The self-proclaimed Army of God is a previously inactive hate group, implicated in no other acts of hate or terror," which makes investigators' jobs harder. Despite the discovery of semtex traces amid Sanctuary's wreckage, the FBI has been honest about the lack of progress in their investigation. Any possible links to a threat received the night of the blast were incinerated in the explosion.

This Saturday, a candlelight vigil will be held in Jackson Square, several blocks from the blast site. Beneath the spire of St. Louis Cathedral, New Orleans will mourn the seventy slain with a half hour of silence. Police Chief Ronald Fontenot told reporters that crowd control will rival that used during the Mardi Gras season.

But for now, there is much wreckage to be cleared before traffic through the French Quarter returns to normal. July has arrived in New Orleans with its typical, oppressive humidity, somehow more stifling than ever this year given the ghostly silence that holds the city in thrall. For some, the silence still resonates with the sound of an explosion that tourist Sara Miller described as "God cracking a stick across His knee." It is a sound that will force many to question whose God, or whose army.

Jeff Haugh's parents showed up at the Conlin residence the day of the candlelight vigil, a week after identifying their son's broken body. The Haughs had phoned several days earlier and asked Monica if they could see Stephen. Monica did not tell them Stephen had refused to come out of his room. Instead, she suggested that they drop by any time they liked.

Monica opened the door to the couple. Susan Haugh was a short, stocky woman, her husband, Bruce, leaner and taller. Their faces were pinched by grief as Monica led them into the front parlor and offered them a drink, which they both declined. Stephen came down the stairs a minute later.

From the kitchen, Monica listened. Their conversation was quiet and clipped.

"We were clearing out his apartment in Baton Rouge. We found a pair of underwear labeled with your last name," Susan explained evenly. "I still had a copy of the Cannon directory. There was only one Conlin."

Monica could tell from Stephen's silence that he realized Jeff's parents needed more to witness him than to hear his words.

Bruce Haugh's deep baritone voice took over to explain it was probably a good thing that Jeff's ulcers had ended his football career because at LSU he had shown a natural talent for the sciences. Susan commented wryly on Jeff's potential to become a physician with an ease that implied their son was still alive. The conversation drifted on, in fits and starts.

As they said obligatory good-byes, Susan Haugh embraced Stephen and then broke down into sobs. Bruce led her out the front door, offering Stephen a simple "Thank you."

In her room at Bayou Terrace, Angela Darby learned nothing about the bombing because Andrew skipped all articles in *The Times-Picayune* referring to it. Angela had not spoken again. Andrew avoided stories about the bombing because he thought they might upset Angela.

Ronald Ducote called his wife to ask if Meredith was all right. Trish didn't question his motive; in the week following the bombing, New Orleans residents often phoned to check on each other. Trish and Ronald had a gentle and relaxed conversation. When Ronald mentioned that Debbie had been transferred to another hospital, Magnolia Trace, Trish expressed a wish for her happiness that surprised both of them.

By the afternoon of the Candlelight vigil, the number of dead was finally established at seventy-one. Fifteen were labeled as "bystanders" or "nearby residents," not "patrons" or "workers at the club." Jordan Charbonnet showed up for work to find Emeril's darkened and locked, with a typed message taped to the front door: "EMERIL'S IS CLOSED TONIGHT. WE ENCOURAGE ALL EMPLOYEES TO ATTEND THE VIGIL IN HONOR OF . . ." Three names followed. Jordan spent the entire drive back to his house trying to connect faces to his three dead co-workers who had been at or around the bar that night. He couldn't remember one.

He retrieved a beer from the refrigerator and watched the vigil on television. He could hear Roger upstairs pacing in his office. The Bishop Polk bell tower was a looming shadow through the living room's window.

Jordan and Elise had not said a word to each other since the bombing. Jordan didn't know that his mother was now the proud owner of a .35 caliber revolver.

# 2

Jackson Square was bathed in silence. The spire of St. Louis Cathedral rose toward a darkening sky flecked with clouds. As dusk fell, the cathedral was thrown into a flickering silhouette by the candles burning beneath it. The only sound was the low moan of a ship's horn as it passed down the Mississippi. The gates of the square had been opened and the statue of Andrew Jackson astride his bronze horse rose up out of a sea of shoulders. From the roofs of the Pontabla apartment buildings flanking the square the news cameras recorded a sea of celestial, winking eyes. The Pontabla residents had gathered on wrought-iron balconies overlooking the square. The silence began at seven o'clock and lasted until seven-thirty.

Several rows back from the cathedral's façade, amid the low and staggered sobs, Stephen clutched a candle that burned to a waxy stub in his hands. The pain was welcome.

At first, the idea of Jeff's death had been too immense to comprehend. But with each day of the past week, singular memories had brought the tears back: Jeff's voice unfurled in a whisper from the drapes around the window, his dimpled smile, his drowsy brown eyes. Jeff Haugh was now a picture, and while Stephen could recall scraps of conversation he could not remember his touch.

Stephen felt a hand brush his shoulder.

"Fear cannot touch me . . ." a voice whispered, speaking to Stephen across eight years. He felt hot breath racking his ribs as he ducked through alleyways of mausoleums, eluding the pursuit of Greg Darby. "It can only taunt me . . ." Meredith Ducote continued.

"It cannot take me," he answered as he faced her.

"Just tell me where to go," Meredith finished.

They held each other for the rest of the vigil. The news cameras craned over them and the surrounding mourners saw them as a girl and a boy grieving for the murdered men. Meredith and Stephen also cried for four kids on bicycles, illuminated in their memory by a slanting sun, and now gone forever.

Elise ordered another screwdriver.

The restaurant was emptying out and the waiter had already brought their check. Both televisions above the bar had been tuned to the vigil. The somber images killed all of the business at the bar, but the bartender's brother had been among the dead and he watched the televisions defiantly as he polished beer mugs and wineglasses.

Monica cradled her chin in both hands, elbows propped on the table.

"You want another?" Elise asked. Monica shook her head. She was drunk already. She had been drinking for an hour before Elise picked her up for dinner.

The waiter brought Elise her drink. She sipped the screwdriver and finally broke their silence.

"I want to apologize for what my mother-in-law did to you that day," she said. "Nanine was the kind of woman I'm glad I didn't become."

Monica paused, asked, "She's dead?"

Both of them erupted into bitter, deep-throated laughter, struggling to contain their guffaws. The waiter shot them an annoyed look.

"Yes, Monica, she's dead," Elise choked out.

"Who isn't these days?"

Elise snorted, thought, This is the New Orleans way of dealing with death: alcohol.

"Ladies," the waiter said, forcing a smile as he dropped the revised check on the table.

"Calm down, young man," Monica told him. "There's a hefty tip in it for you if you keep the screwdrivers coming . . ."

"I'll have another," Elise said, lifting the glass she had already drained.

"Whatever," the waiter muttered as he took the empty glass.

"Oh . . ." Monica gasped, as both hands kneaded her forehead. Elise could tell that the only way she could anchor herself was to speak, as soberly as she could manage.

"I never wanted motherhood to be just one thing. One fear, over and over again," Monica said. "I'm not one of those people that thinks life is going to be taken away by some . . . enemy. I've always thought life was the real killer. That it just grinds down a person." She locked eyes with Elise. "Suicide."

Elise was thinking of the envelope buried at the bottom of her purse, the one she had planned to give Monica earlier that summer, before Jordan had come and scared her into stasis. She was convinced the other woman knew why Elise had first called her, why Elise needed to go to lunch again and again. "Your husband loved you, Monica," she said in a hushed, loving tone of voice.

Monica's face grew entirely unfocused. Elise knew she had to get her home and put her to bed.


Stephen and Meredith poured the remaining scotch into plastic Mardi Gras cups and sat cross-legged beneath the Conlin mausoleum. Meredith had dropped the bottle when she scaled the cemetery wall. Although the top of the bottle had shattered, the base was still intact, and only half of the Glenlivet had spilled.

Stephen was half-illuminated by moonlight. Meredith listened carefully as Stephen told the story of Jeff Haugh from start to tearless finish. She tried to look him full in the face, but she could not see his blue eyes amid the shadows.

He bowed his head slightly, his eyes fixed on the scotch in his plastic cup.

"I almost died at school," Meredith said.

"How?"

"Drinking."

They both laughed. "Have you seen anyone?" Stephen asked.

"One guy . . ." Meredith said, shaking her head indifferently. "Teddy. He was . . . well, he lasted just a week. Freshman year. The sex was good, though."

Stephen nodded. The mention of sex disturbed the moment, silencing both of them for a few awkward beats. Long after they had depleted the scotch, their conversation meandered easily, intimately. Meredith told Stephen about her secret notebook, her vodka-induced writing sessions. Yes, Stephen could read it if he really wanted to.

"So you're a writer," Stephen said, and Meredith knew it wasn't a question.

She was startled. "I'm too used to being the drunk," she said, studying the cup.

"Most writers are drunks. Like my father."

"Let's not even get into fathers," she said. They both laughed again. But her laughter was strained because she knew she had told Stephen a half-truth. She did not feel she could be a writer because she lacked the courage to let anyone read her words.

When she glanced up from her empty cup Stephen was leaning against his father's grave, the moonlight outlining his profile. He told her about what he called the light in the darkness. Life, according to Stephen, was not a journey out of darkness into light. In fact, darkness and light were two arbitrary categories applied to the human spirit in a vain hope that it, too, with all its fleshy influences, would be as orderly as the rise and fall of the sun. The light in the darkness, as Stephen explained it, did not chase away the shadows of fear and regret: It merely illuminated the fears worth fighting. It lit the paths dictated by fate and choice, rather than casting a celestial glow on the way to a better and more perfect world.

Although he did not say it outright, Meredith knew Stephen was talking about the events of that winter five years before, the deaths of Alex and Greg Darby. There between the tombs, Stephen was explaining how everything that had happened—that horrifying chain of events culminating in Greg's suicide—had acquainted them with the truth of the world: how dark and light overlapped, pulled at the soul in intermittent, unsatisfying tugs.

Death, tragedy—whatever you wanted to call it—gave human beings the opportunity to absorb the world's true nature. Many people ignored this chance. Most people opted for denial and despair. Stephen had chosen neither, and in a subtle way he was asking Meredith to do the same. Meredith vowed to herself that she would.

They talked for hours, the only voices among the city of the dead.


Elise had managed to strip Monica down to her bra and panties and ball her into the bed, draping the comforter over her. She stood over Monica for several minutes, checked her pulse twice. It wasn't good for middle-aged women to drink this much, Elise thought.

Finally, Monica let out a sob. "Drunk crying," Roger called that sound—tears that came at a point of utter inebriation and exhaustion, when anything could provoke a rush of sorrows. Elise placed a hand firmly on Monica's forehead.

"He was a bad man . . ." Monica stuttered, not bothering to open her eyes all the way. "Why can't I just admit he was a bad man?"

Elise's hand against Monica's forehead went rigid in the minute before she brought it away.

"I'm cold . . ." Monica whispered.

"Do you have another blanket?"

"Closet . . ." Monica said, shivering, gathering the comforter around her neck. Elise opened the closet door.

Her oldest son stared back at her. Elise almost screamed.

Monica began to snore. Elise looked away from Jordan's picture and tossed the blanket over Monica's body. Grabbing her purse from the nightstand, she left the room. She climbed the staircase to the third floor and entered Jeremy's study. With nausea rising in her throat, she dropped the envelope containing the first draft of "To a Child Not Yet Born" on Jeremy's desk and left the study before her own memory of it could return.

Elise ran at full gait across Third Street, eyes stinging with tears of both guilt and grief. She would probably lose the woman who had convinced her she had a soul.


Jordan could smell the vodka before his mother opened the door all the way. He sat up in bed as the sliver of hallway light fell across his bare chest. Elise was a dark shadow framed in the door. He had been half-asleep. A silly thought seized him as the comforter fell down to just above his navel: She doesn't know I sleep naked.

"Stay away from Stephen Conlin," she said.

Jordan caught another whiff of the vodka as she spoke. He couldn't remember the last time he'd seen his mother this drunk. "Go to bed, Mom," he said and burrowed himself back into the comforter.

She finally closed the door.

# 3

"**H**ave you ever had to nurse your mother through a bad hangover?"

Meredith could hear Stephen chewing between his sentences. "No," she told him. She shifted the phone to her other ear.

"It's not fun. She didn't get out of bed all day. And she's watching soap operas, which is always a bad sign."

Meredith laughed. "You want to go for coffee later?" she asked.

"Sure. But later, because I have something I have to do today," Stephen said, more distant now.

"Just call me. When, do you think?" she asked.

"I don't know . . ." Stephen paused. Meredith detected the click of a cigarette lighter and then a sharp exhalation of breath. "I go to the Fly every day for, like, an hour."

Meredith almost dropped the phone.

"It's where Jeff and I first . . . Going to a tombstone isn't like real to me. So I go there."

"I used to go to the Fly," she said.

"Really?"

"In high school . . ." She stopped. They were wandering into dangerous territory.

"Listen, I still want to read your notebook, if that's cool," Stephen said, obviously changing the subject.

"Sure," Meredith said. She would have to ponder that more.

"Cool. I'll call you when I get back, all right?"

"Sounds good."

"Okay . . . Bye."

"Later." Meredith hung up. She knew they still had a long way to go.

• • •

Jordan Charbonnet watched from his father's Cadillac as Stephen slipped out of the front gate of the Conlin residence, a lit cigarette in his mouth. In one fist, he held the stem of a dead white rose as if it were the handle of a shovel.

Stephen backed the Jeep out of the driveway and pulled off down Chestnut Street, unaware that Jordan Charbonnet was tailing him.

Jordan's strategy was haphazard, rushed. When the Jeep made a drastic right turn through Audubon Park, he knew where Stephen was headed. He, too, had visited the Fly in high school, mostly to drink stolen beers after practice. Jordan parked the Cadillac in the Audubon Zoo's lot. It wouldn't be wise to tail Stephen right onto the riverbank. Jordan was wearing Umbro shorts because the afternoon heat was pushing ninety degrees. But he was also wearing a polo shirt, which wasn't appropriate if he wanted to look like he had casually gone running. Jordan stepped from the car and shed his shirt. A mother shepherding her two toddlers from the zoo glanced at him lasciviously as she passed, and he jogged toward the Fly, acting on instinct and affirmed by the power of his exposed torso.


Stephen made his way down the rocky steps toward the river's edge and tossed the rose into the muddy water. A while after Stephen had told Jeff about Greg Darby's suicide, Jeff had surprised him with a bouquet of white roses. By the time of Jeff's death half of them had already withered. Stephen had resolved to throw the dead roses into the river one by one.

Stephen sat on the last bank of rocks before the water. He thought about how hard it was to think about Jeff. Not because it was painful, but because since the catharsis of the vigil, it was now more difficult to single out one memory and allow it to make him cry. When he heard the footsteps come to a stop behind him, he didn't turn around. Then he heard panting breaths.

When Stephen turned he saw Jordan Charbonnet bent at the waist and grabbing his ankles to stretch. His breath clenched in his sternum.

Jordan Charbonnet straightened and met his gaze. Shirtless, glistening with sweat, and trying to catch his breath, Stephen's god of the Cannon corridor stood before him in three dimensions.

"Hey," Jordan said nonchalantly.

Stephen said nothing.

"Oh . . . hey!" Jordan said again. "Stephen?"

Stephen nodded.

"I'm Jordan. Elise's son."

And Brandon's brother, both of them thought at once.

"Hey," Stephen managed.

"What are you doing?" Jordan asked in a friendly, even tone of voice.

"My friend was at that bar. We used to come here."

Jordan remained a few feet away. If he approached Stephen he'd be crossing an invisible line; Stephen made that clear by his stance. Jordan was wearing penny loafers. No one went running in penny loafers.

"Our mothers are friends now," Stephen said, to see what reaction he might get.

Jordan nodded and attempted a smile. "You said your friend was . . ." Jordan began and then stopped as Stephen's chin jerked back to the river. This was too much—a Charbonnet asking about Jeff Haugh.

As if sensing he had upset Stephen, Jordan stepped down over the curb, maneuvering down the slope before slowly sinking to his haunches several feet from Stephen. Stephen directed his gaze back out at the river, and Jordan joined him, as if they had the water in common.

"I'm sorry," Jordan whispered.

Stephen turned his head to him. "He worked there. At the bar," he said, as he tugged a pack of Camel Lights from his jeans pocket. "You want one?"

Jordan took one and Stephen produced a lighter from his pocket. Stephen kept his eyes from Jordan's while he lit the cigarette. Jordan inhaled. The runner was not only wearing penny loafers, but smoking; Stephen had to smile a little bit at the curious transparency.

"He was just your friend?" Jordan asked.

Stephen's eyes narrowed. He felt gooseflesh spread across his arms and back. He looked hard at the boy who had first struck him in Cannon's Administrative Hallway. If he answered Jordan's question then he would be confessing his true self—who he had been on the day he'd stolen the picture. Who he was now.

"No," Stephen said, "not just a friend."

Jordan put a hand on Stephen's knee. "I didn't mean to upset you," he said, his voice low and conciliatory.

The hand felt familiar, awful, warm. No man had touched him since Jeff had an hour before he was murdered. Stephen knew he had to keep talking.

"He got me through a lot. I went through some shit in high school and he helped me more than he knew." Stephen took a breath. "Jeff. His name was Jeff."

Jordan turned to face the river as Stephen wiped tears from his cheeks. Focusing on a distant point across the Mississippi, Jordan squinted, and Stephen realized that this encounter was beyond him somehow. He had not come here just to convey his sympathy.

"You went through some shit in high school?" Jordan asked, not looking at him.

Stephen didn't answer.

"Since I kind of ruined your day, can I take you out for a beer or something?" Jordan's gaze returned to Stephen. "We could talk about it."

"Talk about what?" Stephen asked, an edge in his voice.

"What you went through."

"He's still not back yet," Monica told Meredith for the third time that evening, her voice icy with irritation. Meredith wasn't sure if her tone signified anger at the fact that this was Meredith's third call or was a product of her nasty hangover.

"He told me he was going to call. We're supposed to do something."

Monica sounded more put out. "Well, I'll ask him to call you when he gets in, Meredith, but I don't know when he will. He didn't even say good-bye before he left."

"He doesn't have a cell phone?" Meredith asked.

"No, he doesn't," Monica answered, tersely.

Meredith found no way to articulate the fierce protectiveness that had welled up in her since last night. She had spent the afternoon rearranging the furniture in her room and smoking her mother's cigarettes. "I'm sorry. I'm just worried," she told Stephen's mother.

"Stephen's a big boy now, Meredith," Monica declared, and then hung up.

"Bitch," Meredith whispered into the phone.

# 4

The Sunday night crowd at Fat Harry's was thin. Jordan held the door for Stephen, who ducked clumsily through it. The jukebox was playing Matchbox 20 and the sounds of Tulane frat boys shooting pool in the back was a muted clamor.

"I've never been here," Stephen said as they perched on stools at the bar. He ordered a Corona, Jordan a Crown and Seven.

"How's your brother?" Stephen asked, after an awkward pause.

He glanced up from his beer. Shouts erupted from the back of the bar as someone sank the eight ball prematurely.

"How well do you know Brandon?" Jordan asked.

Stephen leaned away, snake-bit. He clasped his hands around the bottle. "My opinion of your brother isn't very high," Stephen said before swallowing a third of the Corona.

"Nobody's is," Jordan said quickly.

Stephen looked at him again, trying to gauge him. Jordan sat with one elbow on the bar, fist pressed against his chin, his brown eyes leveled on Stephen with a reporter's intensity.

"I know what he did to your car," Jordan said.

"He didn't do it by himself," Stephen replied.

"Greg?" Jordan asked. "Do you think that's why my brother lost it? Because of Greg Darby's suicide?"

"I can't answer that."

"You knew my brother."

"I didn't *know* your brother!" Stephen snapped. "I was *hated* by your brother. There's a difference, all right?"

A few feet away, the bartender watched them as he polished glasses.

"What do you despise?" Jordan asked, in a low, conspiratorial tone.

"By this you are truly known," Stephen said. "Frank Herbert." He raised his beer bottle in a mock toast.

Jordan knew the quote because the Cannon senior whose picture had been right above his in the yearbook had used it as an epigraph. He guessed that Stephen had learned it from the same place.

Stephen straightened himself on the stool. "Football players and fags," he said in a forced singsong voice. "It's a common phenomenon. You went to Cannon. Hell, you played football. You should be able to figure it out. We need each other." He lit another cigarette.

"*Need* each other?"

"Symbiosis," Stephen said.

"Stop fucking around with me, Stephen."

Stephen smiled wryly as if savoring Jordan's frustration. "Give and take. In high school, football players are this iron wall of perfection. They're everything a male is supposed to be. So naturally, fags like me, who have no way to prove their masculinity, who might not even have any, begin to worship them . . ."

"This has nothing to do with—"

"Let me finish," Stephen said. "But the part no one talks about— what makes the whole thing a symbiotic relationship—is that football players need fags, too." He paused and swigged his beer.

"Football players are gods," Stephen went on, "and gods need to be worshiped. And there is no better worship than another male swallowing your dick. Why? Because it's total, absolute prostration. A little fag with no pride and no self-esteem sucking on your dick is richer worship than you can get from any cheerleader. Because men aren't supposed to suck each other's dicks, so when a man sucks yours, it means he's giving you everything he has! And that is *worship*!" Stephen jabbed a finger into the center of Jordan's chest.

"What does this have to do with Brandon?" Jordan asked, trying to keep his voice steady. He felt enveloped, sickened.

"Figure it out," Stephen said without emotion.

"You and Brandon used to . . ." Jordan's elbow slid off the bar as he sat upright, confronting Stephen head-on.

"Greg Darby?"

Stephen's eyes met Jordan's, but he wouldn't speak, wouldn't urge Jordan on. For Stephen to confess anything, Jordan would have to say it first. "So what does the fag get in the end?" Jordan asked, low enough not to be overheard. "The football player gets worship. But what about the fag?" Jordan asked, as dispassionate as he could manage, as if he were discussing physics.

Stephen didn't smirk or look away. He seemed satisfied that Jordan had chosen to debate him point for point. "Validation," Stephen offered. "Brief affirmation."

"No love?" Jordan asked.

Stephen's jaw tightened, his authority leaving him. Jordan leaned forward to whisper into Stephen's ear, "Are you telling me there's no possibility you could have gone with Greg Darby into that bell tower because you were in love with him?"

Jordan sat back on his stool. He felt that Stephen had known the entire time what he wanted.

When Stephen's beer bottle shattered, both of them flinched.

The bartender spun around and slapped a rag down on the counter over the shards and foam. He swept the remains of the bottle into an ice container beneath the bar.

Stephen swabbed his hands across his thighs, leaving beer stains. Jordan was struck by the strange beauty of the moment, by the abrupt vigor of Stephen's rage. Stephen looked up at him, dazed, groping for words. "When I was a freshman, I stole a picture of you from school," he managed, his voice trembling. "I stole it and I took it home and I jerked off to it for the rest of high school. You want to know why? Because you were everything that was right with Cannon and everything that was wrong with me. And that got me off."

He leaned toward Jordan. "And that is not love."

Stephen released his grip on the bar's edge, swung his legs to the floor, strode across the bar, and left Fat Harry's.


Jordan parked the car in his driveway, cut the engine. Cold sweat had broken across his shoulders and was trickling down his back. After Stephen had left him in the bar, he had quietly drunk three more Crown and Sevens.

The Charbonnet residence was dark. Jordan entered the kitchen and gently shut the back door. He was even more careful with the door to Brandon's bedroom, taking a full thirty seconds to click the door behind him. He sat on the edge of his brother's bed.

Stephen Conlin would tell him the truth, Jordan was sure of that. But, why do I have to know? Jordan asked.

Maybe there was no finding or saving Brandon. But Jordan didn't know if he cared anymore. He shifted his weight on the bed, studied the thick black shadow the bell tower threw across the wall. He wanted Stephen out of his head, his wide blue eyes and the mess of questions he stirred. Greg Darby had probably wanted the same thing. But how far did Greg go?

Jordan turned onto his side, toward the window. A light was glowing inside the bell tower's portico.

# 5

The grounds of Bishop Polk Cathedral were bordered by a cast-iron fence crowned with six-inch spikes. Jordan walked along the fence, out of the halo of street light. Beyond the fence he saw a black opening like a small mouth on the bottom side of the cathedral's western wall, leading into a basement labyrinth of offices.

As he hoisted one foot on the fence's crossbar, he swung his other leg between two metal spikes. It struck him that he was following the trail of Greg and Stephen. The spikes pressed his thigh like a vise. Jordan swung his other leg up, shifting his weight over the top of the fence. He fell six feet into the shrubbery on the other side, toppling onto his side with arms and legs splayed out. He spat leaves and groped branches to pull himself to his feet. He found the open window to the church basement.

Jordan was blinded by pitch-blackness before his foot touched the top of a desk right beneath the windowsill. He stepped forward, expecting to hear the sound of pencils rolling to the floor. The desk's surface was clear, though. He brought his other leg through the window and crouched on the desk, adjusting to the darkness.

For several minutes, he wandered the offices beneath the cathedral. The sudden change in temperature indicated that he was entering a vaster space where the heat rose toward a high ceiling. He was in the foyer of the cathedral.

He shuffled into the middle of a patchwork of dim light cast down from nearly thirty feet overhead. Jordan gazed up into the interior of the bell tower's shaft. The faint light came from a single bulb, its glow fractured by the portico's uneven floorboards. He could see a human figure pacing back and forth thirty feet above, footfalls creaking the floorboards.

"Stephen?"

He was frightened by how his hoarse voice resonated.

The figure overhead stopped pacing. Jordan backed up several steps and something hard grazed his left shoulder. He groped a splintered piece of wood. He realized he was holding the bottom rung of a wooden ladder.

He began to climb. Thirty feet up, the floorboards stopped and solid darkness outlined the bowls and clappers of three suspended church bells.

Jordan made it to the top of the ladder, where the top rung was secured with metal bolts in the shaft's concrete walls. He hauled himself through the opening, before collapsing into a ball on the floorboards, gasping for breath. When he looked up, he saw Stephen.

Stephen opened a bottle of Bombay gin and swigged it as Jordan tried to get to his feet. Dizzy and breathless from the climb, Jordan sank to the floor, several feet from where Stephen sat in the frame of one of the portico's arched windows, knees to his chest. The single bulb dangled overhead from a chain. Beyond Stephen, Jordan saw stars and the canopy of oak trees through the window's wooden slats.

Stephen lifted the bottle, offered Jordan a sip. Jordan waved it away. Stephen shrugged drunkenly, capped the bottle. His eyes moved to the slats.

"It started as a contest," he said. "Before sixth grade, I think. Or maybe the summer after. Meredith was out of town on a trip with her mom, so me, Greg, and Brandon were all at Greg's house one day and Brandon and Greg were laughing about how if you went up and put your dick in one of the vents in Meredith's pool it felt just like a blow job.

"I didn't say anything because I had never done it. They noticed I wasn't talking so Greg wrestled me to the floor, teasing me. Brandon started yelling, 'Stevie doesn't know how to jerk off!' so naturally I threw a fit and told them I did it all the time, which was a lie. I was afraid to touch myself down there."

"Why?" Jordan asked.

"Because of what I thought about when I did."

He took a slug from the bottle of Bombay. Jordan sat down crosslegged. The floorboards creaked beneath his weight. He tried to ignore the thirty-foot drop visible in uneven patches all around them.

"So Greg finally has me pinned to the floor and I'm screaming over and over again that I know how to jerk off, so finally . . . Greg . . . no, it was Brandon, I think . . . says 'prove it' and then just like that Greg hops off me and falls onto the bed next to Brandon. I stand up and I realize they're both staring at me. Waiting for me to prove it.

"I'm not going to lie. I already knew some things. I knew Brandon and Greg both had this weird effect on me and that whenever they walked into a room I would change. I know it made Meredith angry but she never said anything about it.

"So anyway, I'm standing there and finally Greg says, 'You have to take it out, stupid!'

"Brandon laughs really loud so I unzip my shorts and take it out. They both go quiet but they still have these smug smiles. I was scared as hell but proving this was important, especially to them."

"So I take it in my hand and Brandon says, 'Back and forth,' but real calm, almost like a school teacher. So I start to do it and finally I get a rhythm going and they're both just watching."

Stephen paused and gulped a mouthful of liquor. Beyond him, the Garden District extended for blocks, dark interlocking oak branches beneath a dome of stars.

"I know it might not make sense, but we used the words *fag* and *gay* all the time. They don't really have any kind of practical application when you're in grammar school. Stupid things are gay, and people who say stupid things are fags. So, whatever, my point is that there didn't seem to be anything 'gay' about what we were doing . . .

"So I'm doing it and I start to get goose bumps and then all of a sudden it was like . . . I thought, Oh shit, I'm going to pee. I shut my eyes and felt this burning. I didn't want to open them because I thought I had pissed all over Greg's floor. But then I heard Greg hit the floor on all fours and I open my eyes and see that he's staring down at this white glob that landed three feet away from me. And then Brandon screams at the top of his lungs, 'Jesus Christ, something came out?'

"I mean, I guess we knew what it was but we'd never seen it. They hadn't. So that's how the contest started."

The contest. Jordan felt hollow at the word.

"The game was simple. Who could come first. But who could make something come out was the real goal, though. Brandon and Greg both wanted to make something come out. Every evening, once Meredith had to go home, we'd gather on Greg's bed. Brandon would lie against the headboard, Greg against the wall, and me against the footboard. Greg suggested that we take our shirts off. We all assumed that would be a good idea. Put us more in the mood or something. The door was always locked because we were old enough to know that adults were really afraid of penises.

"Finally, one night, Brandon won the ultimate prize. It was quite a victory for a thirteen-year-old. He cursed and spat and jerked harder at himself before, I'd say, about three drops of come landed on his stomach. I always finished first, so I was just watching, but Greg was having a hard time with it. After Brandon shouted 'fuck' and came on himself, Greg rolled his eyes. 'For the love of God!' he grunted. He had to be pretty upset if he used an expression we heard his mother use time and again. Greg sounded so pathetic Brandon and I just stared at him. Greg was jerking harder, trying to coax the magic white stuff out of himself, but it wasn't working.

"Brandon's eyes had this sort of hazy, drugged look to them when he stared at me.

"'Help him, Stevie,' he finally said. I had no idea what he was talking about, but when Greg gave me this puppy-dog look I felt so bad for him I asked, 'How?'

"'Just help him out,' Brandon said, as if it was the most obvious thing in the world. Then, I understood what they were suggesting. Everything inside of me turned cold. I was only thirteen, but I did realize at that moment that we were doing something bigger, important. I remember how it tasted, and I remember Greg let out this sort of startled gasp when I finally had my mouth around him, and the sound of it made me sick. It was too human, too real, having a penis in my mouth, I guess.

"And then the sick feeling went away. Just like that. I shut my eyes and imitated the women we'd watched in the porn movies we stole from under Brandon's . . . well, under your father's bed. Those movies where the women moaned and loved it when they got fucked and we thought that was a miracle because we thought all females were like Meredith, always guarding their sacred secrets.

"So the sick feeling died. Forever. It would never come back. If it had, things might be very different from the way they are now."

Stephen stopped and looked at Jordan. A car gently rushed by below them down Jackson Avenue.

"So then what?" Jordan asked.

"He won. Something came out," Stephen answered. "Suddenly, he stopped me. He put a hand on my shoulder and I stopped and Greg wrapped his fist around his dick and started pulling. It got on my face. A minute passed and nobody said anything and then suddenly Brandon screamed, 'We have a winner!'"

Jordan burst out laughing, the sound echoing through the portico, down the shaft. He doubled over, his hands on the floorboards in front of him. "I'm sorry . . ." he stammered through his guffaws. But Stephen was laughing, too, low, and under his breath. "We have a winner!" Jordan cried out, pumping one arm in the air triumphantly.

Gasping between laughs, Stephen accidentally knocked the bottle of Bombay from the ledge and it rolled across the boards. Jordan grabbed it, uncapped it, and drank.

He rose and moved to the ledge. Stephen slid his leg off the ledge to allow Jordan to sit across from him. Jordan handed the bottle of gin back to him.

Stephen took another drink. The gin washed his laughter away. He wiped his mouth with his arm.

"At the end of eighth grade, Greg called me. I rode to his house and he met me outside, pushing his bike out of the driveway, and his first words were, 'Don't tell Brandon, okay?' I just nodded. I knew this was a big no-no. Meredith was a girl and the boys could do stuff without her, but two of the boys without the third? That was unheard of. Just like going to the cemetery without all four of us was unheard of, too.

"But I followed him to the cemetery. We made it there, but the gates were already locked so Greg said we could hop the wall on the other side, the side on Coliseum. We left our bikes under a bush and helped each other over the wall, onto the top of a mausoleum.

"I knew Greg wanted to show me something, but I wasn't sure what. Finally he brought me to this really old tomb and showed me where the wall had been cracked near the platform.

"'What's in there?' I asked. I was imagining skeletons and rats. I was totally freaked out when Greg crawled through the opening. For a moment I thought he had hit his head or something because I couldn't hear anything. 'Greg?' I asked. And then his voice rang back from inside: 'There's nothing in here. It's all gone. Just some dirt.'

"I crawled in after him and found myself in total darkness. I panicked before I felt Greg's hand on my shoulder.

"'I want to do it again,' he said.

"My hand groped for something to hold onto, and it hit his chest . . . or shoulder . . . I can't remember, but he wasn't wearing a shirt. We did like he wanted to only this time he held the back of my neck and slapped my back during it. He was into it. He loved it. But he didn't do it to me and I didn't ask.

"Afterward, we hardly said a thing. We used the same mausoleum to climb over the wall. Greg went over first and his foot landed on something big and metal. He tripped and fell flat on his ass. I was on top of the wall still and I could see what he had fallen on before he could."

Stephen paused. From the look in his eyes, Jordan could tell he was seeing it again.

"It was the wheel of his bike. Brandon had found our bikes and torn them to pieces—pulled out the spokes, shredded the seats, pried the gears apart. Sliced the tires into flaps. The frames, or what was left of them, were bent. I remember thinking, How could he do that without tools or something? How could he just rip them apart like that?"

"Like your car," Jordan said.

Stephen's head jerked slightly. Jordan bowed his head. "Can you turn that off?" Stephen asked, pointing to the lightbulb overhead. "It was on when . . ." Stephen halted, guided the bottle to his mouth.

Jordan got up and yanked the bulb's chain. The portico was plunged into blackness, until the dim light through the slatted window carved shapes across the floorboards and threw Stephen into silhouette.

"Better?" Jordan asked quietly, taking his seat on the ledge again.

"He called me," Stephen whispered. "The day of Alex's funeral."

Stephen turned his gaze from the window to Jordan. "I was happy that day," he whispered. "I was happy. Not because Alex was dead but because . . . Because I thought that somehow all of Cannon had been made to feel for at least one day what I had felt ever since I started school there. I remember how at the funeral Mom and I sat in the balcony because there was no room below. I watched Greg the entire time. Even when Angela lost her shit, Greg didn't even move. He couldn't. He just sat there with his head forward. It looked like someone had clubbed him in the back of the neck and it was too painful for him to lift his head up."

Tears dribbled from Stephen's eyes. "So when he finally called me that night in this weird way, I thought I'd won." He swigged from the bottle again.

"'For passion, like crime, does not sit well with the sure order and even course of everyday life,'" Jordan recited softly. When Stephen's tear-filled eyes met his with a flicker of recognition, Jordan finished. "'It welcomes every loosening of the social fabric, every confusion and affliction visited upon the world, for passion sees in such disorder a vague hope of finding advantage for itself.'"

Stephen managed a swallow. "Where did you hear that?"

"It's from—"

"I know what it's from. Where did you hear it?"

"My mother gave me a copy of *Death in Venice* as a gift when I graduated from high school. She said it was her favorite book. She had underlined that quote." He pulled his eyes from Stephen's.

"My father had that quote on his study wall," the other boy said.

Silence fell again. Stephen hunched slightly over the gin bottle, his head now inches from where Jordan leaned against the window frame. "I was so stupid," he whispered.

"What did Greg Darby do to you, Stephen?" Jordan asked, trying to keep his voice as neutral as a doctor's.

Stephen leapt off the window ledge onto the floor, clutching the bottle of Bombay in one hand. He lingered before the bells, brought the bottle to his mouth, and turned to face Jordan. "When the phone rang that night, I knew it was going to be him. I just knew. I answered and he said, 'Stephen?' I could tell he'd been drinking since the funeral. 'My mom's in the hospital, Stevie,' he said. 'Did you know that?'

"'No,' I said. I didn't know.

"And then he didn't say anything and I could hear him rapping a beer can against the kitchen counter. He started asking me all these questions. Did I remember Alex? Did I know what he looked like? Was I at the game? I kept answering no. But I was trying to be, I don't know, sympathetic. And then finally he asked me if I had ever been inside the bell tower. He said he'd been up there once when he failed Physical Science and had to work in the chaplain's office during summer. He said the view was awesome . . ."

Stephen took another drink, paced between the window and the bells. His free hand went out and traced the metal flank of the nearest bell.

"We met just outside the fence. He showed me how to get in. He even helped me over. They don't lock the basement windows because they figure the fence is high enough. He led me . . . downstairs, you know, through the offices . . ."

"I know," Jordan said, nearly breathless.

"We made it up the ladder. He had me go first. It was pitch-dark up here and I remember not being able to see . . ." Stephen stopped, took a deep, labored breath.

"I remember thinking something was weird when he didn't switch on the light right away. But when he did, his hand was already on the back of my neck. I remember seeing . . ."

Stephen's fingers trailed down the bell's curved skirt. "This is where he slammed my head into the bell. I couldn't see anything after that."

Jordan felt himself stand up from the window ledge and move to Stephen. Steadying himself with one hand on Stephen's shoulder, he reached out with his other, his fingers probing the bell.

"I remember. He told me, 'You wanted me this way! You wanted me to lose!' He kept saying it over and over again. I could hear him even as I . . . I couldn't see. I'd hit the bell so hard I could see just black and bright swaths of colors. I didn't know which way was up or down. I just knew he was on top of me. Pinning me to the floor. 'You wanted me this way!' he kept saying."

Stephen withdrew his hand and backed away from the bell. "He was right. I did want him that way. I wanted his trophies broken at his feet. I wanted him to lose a parent. I wanted him to lose a lot."

Stephen raised the bottle to his mouth, spat in sudden protest, then hurled the bottle at the far wall.

"But the next morning, it felt like he was still inside me. That's how I knew what he'd done. I woke up and my mom was there, and she told me he was dead, but I could still feel him inside me."

"You didn't do it?" Jordan asked firmly. "Because I would understand if you had."

"I couldn't have," Stephen said, his voice soft. "I could never have done . . . that."

He slowly knelt on the floorboards. When his arm shot out to steady himself, his hand glanced off the floorboard from under him. As Stephen erupted into sobs, Jordan's arms encircled him, lifting him to a seated position. Jordan felt Stephen's tears like a heartbeat within his own body.

Jordan held Stephen without rocking him. "I'm sorry," he murmured, again and again, a refrain meant to lull Stephen into the present.

• • •

Moonlight glazed the oak branches overhead and a low fog ushered the sounds of the river through the Garden District. Their footsteps echoed as they walked down Chestnut Street. Neither man had said a word by the time they came to the corner of Chestnut and Third, outside the Conlin residence.

"You going to be okay?" Jordan asked hesitantly.

The expression on Stephen's face was inscrutable. His eyes had gone cold, but they were still bloodshot.

"Why did you have to know?" he asked, his voice low and urgent.

Jordan shook his head. Stephen bristled. "Good-bye, Jordan," he said, and crossed the street.

"Stephen . . ." Jordan called after him.

"I'm going to bed," Stephen said, unseen on the front porch of the house. Jordan lifted one arm as if he were about to begin a final entreaty, but he stopped as he heard the sound of the front door shutting behind Stephen. "Shit," he whispered.


Stephen strode up the stairs too quickly to see Monica sitting in the darkened front parlor. She turned her gaze back out the window, where Jordan's shadow dwindled down Chestnut Street. She clutched the contents of the envelope Elise had left on Jeremy's desk.

The first draft of "To a Child Not Yet Born," dated August 1976, was legible in the dim moonlight through the front windows.

# 6

"Where've you been?" Angela Darby asked Meredith.

Meredith eased herself through the window and knelt down on the floor, surprised. Angela sat primly on the edge of the bed, hands folded across her lap. It was the first question Angela had ever asked Meredith.

"I was trying to find Stephen," Meredith answered. She had left the house and driven blindly across the city, checking Fat Harry's, where she suspected Stephen might be, but finding no one. Her journey had finally led her down to the French Quarter around dusk. The Sanctuary bar was a pit in the earth bordered by several charred, skeletal timbers. The pit was littered with rotting flowers. The few standing timbers were plastered with notes to loved ones, some pasted with smiling photographs of the dead. An old woman stood at the edge of the crater, studying the pool of muddy water. Meredith remembered why the dead were entombed aboveground in New Orleans. The water table is so high that coffins would float to the surface.

She walked down Bourbon Street, desolate beneath the halos of street lamps. A few bars were open. Most had been boarded up with plywood, their side walls gouged by the blast. The filigree ironwork of their balconies had curled and melted where it had not been blown free in huge chunks.

"Stephen," Angela was saying. Her cadence was drunkenly slow, her eyes sluggishly scanned the room. She effortlessly tugged out a large clump of hair.

Meredith jumped to her feet. Angela did not flinch as Meredith took her hand and gently pried it open. The strands fluttered from her palm to the bedsheet. Could this be the medicine? Meredith thought. Is it making her hair fall out?

"He pulled it," Angela said.

"Who pulled it?" Meredith asked.

"He . . . He doesn't hit here. He only pulls . . ."

Andrew Darby had somehow pulled out an entire clump of his wife's hair. Meredith made for the window before halting, feeling as if she had nowhere to go. She began to cry.

"Crying's what we do before we're broken," Angela answered. "Have you ever been to El Paso?"

Meredith shook her head numbly.

". . . lights . . ." Angela said. ". . . so many lights . . . just over the border. Andrew said we couldn't go there, 'cause it was Mexico. We were going to California . . ."

Her memories are coming back first, Meredith thought. Maybe if I come back again and again she'll realize where she's ended up.

"Andrew used to get lost all the time . . ." Angela said.

Her words were still labored, but her reactions were quicker, more natural. The medication, Meredith thought again. "No one noticed that he pulled out your hair," she said, rocking forward onto her thighs. Angela didn't look at her, but shook her head.

"I'll be back," Meredith said as she rose.

"Tonight?" Angela asked.

"Yes. Tonight. I'm going to try to come back tonight . . ."

"Please come back," Angela said as Meredith swung one leg over the sill. Meredith squinted at the disappearing taillights of the security truck as it left the parking lot and swerved right, down the hospital's private side street. Meredith's Acura was parked in the rear lot of a strip mall, separated from the Bayou Terrace parking lot by a line of shrubs.

"Please . . ." Angela said.

Meredith turned with one leg jutting over the window ledge and nodded. Angela nodded in return, but Meredith could tell she was just mimicking her. She clambered out the window and sprang to the earth, then bolted across the parking lot, already calculating how long it would take her to get home, steal her mother's diet pills, and return to Bayou Terrace.


"She's dancing," Thelma said.

Dr. Horne gazed at her, baffled.

"Angela Darby," Thelma repeated. "She's dancing."

The nurse led him into The Bordeaux Wing, where he peered through the window in Angela's door. She was now standing with one foot propped on the edge of the bed, having lifted up her robe to reveal the hair on her legs. She was rubbing her hand up and down, and then slapping her palm to her face.

Oh shit, Dr. Horne thought.

"She was dancing earlier," Thelma insisted. Dr. Horne thought of Andrew Darby in his office, his face red at the sound of his wife's first words in years. "How?" he asked the nurse.

"She was . . . twirling," Thelma said. The doctor smiled wanly through the window at Angela. Thelma squeezed beside him, as if to make sure Angela was not smiling back. She was twirling again.

"Let her dance," Dr. Horne said. I hope Andrew sees it and pisses his pants, he thought to himself.


Holding the phone between chin and shoulder, Jordan sat forward in Roger's desk chair as the rental information he had requested an hour earlier streamed out of his father's fax machine. Jordan watched the real estate agency's emblem appear inch by inch.

"Hey," he said.

On the other end, Stephen cleared his throat. "Hello."

Jordan could tell he was still in bed and possibly hung over. "Listen, I'm going out of town for a while. My parents used to rent this house in Florida, just outside of Destin," he said, and then plunged on, "I thought I might go there for a few days. Clear my head."

"Okay. Have a good time." Sarcasm.

Jordan yanked the rental agreement from the fax machine. The bottom half caught in the tray and tore off.

"Shit . . ." Jordan cursed. "I want you to come with me."

Stephen didn't say anything, which unnerved Jordan enough to say more. "I don't want to talk about it . . ." Jordan started. He snorted, annoyed with himself. "I didn't sleep last night, Stephen."

The top half of the rental agreement now curled on Roger's desk. "Gulf Sun Rentals" promised Jordan 231 Dune Alley Lane for two days, starting tonight. Jordan scrutinized the fax's slightly blurred text, trying to get a bearing on his motive.

"When?" Stephen asked, his voice lower as if the trip had suddenly become a secret.

"Tonight."

"All right."

"Okay. Good then." Jordan's tone was abruptly businesslike, proper. "How does eight sound? It's a four hour drive and . . ."

"Eight's good. How long?"

"Four hours."

"Jordan, how long are we going to *stay*?"

"A few days," he mumbled.

"Eight o'clock, then," Stephen said.

Jordan hung up the phone, propped his elbows on the desk, and clasped his forehead, kneading the knots of tension that had just formed in his skull.

Stephen slipped on a pair of boxers and found his mother on the third floor, squatting on the floor of the study. A pile of flattened cardboard boxes sprawled like a deck of cards on the floor next to her. She was leafing through a leather notebook.

"I'm going out of town for a few days," Stephen said.

She nodded. Jeremy's desk, which Stephen knew she had not touched in nineteen years, was now bare. His father's Selectric typewriter sat in a cardboard box. With the exception of the quotations still plastered on the walls, the study looked nude.

"What are you doing?" Stephen asked.

"When I'm done, you can have it," Monica said. She closed the notebook and dropped Jeremy's collected works from June to December 1980 into the box.

"Have what?"

"This," Monica said, waving at the room. Stephen noticed a glass of liquor on the windowsill. Absolut and Chambord Royale, his mother's favorite. It was early, even for her. He wanted a sip. Monica bent down and stacked the books tumbled inside another box.

"We'll go to Hurwitz Mintz and get new furniture. Once school starts, I think it'll make a good study. Better than studying in your room." She squinted at him, sluggishly thoughtful. "Or maybe Scandinavia if you want more modern stuff."

"I study at the library," Stephen pointed out.

Monica stood up, unapologetic. She was clearing away all evidence of his father for a reason she did not volunteer. He turned from the doorway, headed downstairs. "You're not supposed to drink before noon, Mom!" he yelled back over his shoulder.

"Who are you going with?" she asked.

"Jordan Charbonnet," he shouted up the stairs. "Elise's son!" Stephen slammed his bedroom door and retrieved a duffel bag from under the bed. He assembled some T-shirts and shorts as his mother stomped and thudded overhead, packing the remnants of his father's life into boxes.


"Sorry about coffee," Stephen apologized.

"That's cool. What about tonight?" Meredith asked.

"Can't."

"Okay," she said, slightly wounded.

She had called from her car. The tinny blare of the radio filled the silence. Trish had finally awakened her and ordered her to drop off some transfer forms at Tulane; she had either not noticed or decided to ignore the fact that Meredith had commandeered a hefty portion of her new prescription "diet pills"—speed intended to skyrocket the metabolism. And of course Meredith didn't tell her mother that she would also be buying any books she could on psychotropic medication at the Tulane bookstore.

"I'm going out of town," Stephen said matter-of-factly.

"Where?" Meredith asked.

"Florida."

"Cool. With your mom?" Meredith asked.

When Stephen didn't answer immediately, Meredith felt a pang of nausea in her stomach. Her hand tightened on the cell phone and her foot slipped off the gas pedal, the odometer falling as she coasted down St. Charles Avenue.

"No, it's kind of weird . . ."

"What's weird?"

"Do you know Jordan Charbonnet? Brandon's brother?"

Meredith sailed through a red light.

"Not really," she mumbled, her head feeling airy, weightless.

"Is something wrong?" Stephen asked.

Meredith clamped the phone between her ear and shoulder and aligned the Acura with both hands on the steering wheel. No cops were in pursuit, thank God.

"Isn't he kind of a prick?" she asked.

"I guess I'll find out," Stephen said.

"I heard he was."

"Well, he is Brandon's brother," Stephen admitted.

"You two messing around or something?"

Stephen didn't answer. Meredith veered randomly onto a side street that she hoped would take her into Tulane's campus. "Sorry. That was kind of crude . . ." she muttered.

"Uh-huh," Stephen agreed, his voice gravelly. "I'll call you when I get back."

"I'll give you my notebook if you still want to read it."

She could hear the panic in her voice. She pulled the Acura into a parking space labeled FACULTY ONLY.

"All right, Meredith," he said gently.

"Bye," she said and hung up. She punched the steering wheel with one fist. The horn honked and she jumped. She inhaled deeply to quiet the storm of panic. Contrary to what she had thought, Jordan Charbonnet actually had the balls to go after Stephen.

Angela, she thought, focus on Angela. It's all you can do.


At six-thirty, Monica decided to walk to the Charbonnet residence. She rang the doorbell. No one answered. She looked over her shoulder and saw Roger's Cadillac parked at the curb. A suitcase sat in the backseat.

The door opened and Jordan Charbonnet stood before her. She glanced at the car and then back at Jordan. "Is your mother home?"

"No," Jordan answered.

"Where did she go?" Monica asked, as if she were asking the whereabouts of a murder suspect.

"We have no idea."

Monica nodded. She looked up at him with humming rage. "You hurt Stephen, I'll hurt you. Is that perfectly clear?"

Jordan said nothing, and Monica pivoted and strolled down the front steps with exaggerated dexterity.


"Meet me here," Jordan said when Stephen answered.

"Why?"

"Your mom just paid a visit." He heard the sound of a door slamming. Stephen's silence suggested to him that Monica had just entered the room. "Okay," he said, and hung up.


At seven P.M., Elise Charbonnet drove her Ford Explorer through the tollbooth at the south end of the Lake Pontchartrain Causeway. On the passenger seat lay folded a map on which she had highlighted her route across twenty miles of lake to the north shore. Highway 190 would take her into Mandeville.

The .35 caliber revolver rattled in the glove compartment. She was ten miles down the causeway and only halfway across the lake when fat drops of rain tapped the windshield.

# 7

Two-Thirty-One Dune Alley was tucked behind a bank of storm battered sand dunes. Standing on the back deck, Stephen could make out the distant glow of condominium high-rises marking the shore's distant bend. The house was on one of the few empty stretches of beach. The night was windless and the Gulf was placid and black, swells lapping feebly against the sugary sand. Stephen understood why people loved the ocean: It was the farthest you could get.

He shut his eyes briefly, smelling salt air for the first time in years. He was startled by the sound of Jordan setting two beer bottles onto the table behind him. He took a Corona from him with a nod of thanks. "How long since you've been here?"

"Last time we came down I was seventeen." Jordan took his seat on one of the weathered benches behind Stephen.

"Is it like you remembered?"

"No," Jordan said before downing half his Corona. "That's a good thing, though. All I remember is noise. My parents fighting about how far we should drive for dinner. Brandon bitching and being put in time-out." He put the bottle down and leaned back, out of Stephen's line of vision. "I've always wanted to come back alone."

"Alone?" Stephen asked.

"You know what I mean," Jordan said easily. "Sit down. You're making me nervous."

"Move first," Stephen said.

"What?"

"Move. The way you're sitting, with your back to the house. I can't see you. You're just a shadow."

"Afraid of shadows?" Jordan teased.

Stephen snorted, still not turning. In truth, he was afraid of people in shadow: the black silhouette of Greg Darby reaching for the light cord before hurtling him headlong into the bell; the featureless form of Jeff Haugh looming in the doorway of Madam Curie's Voodoo Shop, saying that he had taken a job at Sanctuary just so he might run into Stephen again.

"I'll stand then," Jordan said, clearly. He crossed the deck and stood next to him. Stephen was acutely aware of the space between his left shoulder and Jordan's right.

"Want to go swimming?" Jordan asked.

Stephen faced him, frowning and quiet.

"What?" Jordan asked.

"Exactly what are you doing, Jordan?"

"You don't like it here?" Jordan asked.

"Don't play stupid," Stephen said, his voice accusatory. Jordan sighed and slumped against the deck rail. Stephen settled onto one of the benches, propping his beer between his bare feet.

"You didn't have to come," Jordan said.

"You really thought I'd say no?"

"I'm not a mind reader."

"You're not answering my question," Stephen said, glaring. "I'm all out of stories, Jordan."

"You didn't have to tell me!" Jordan snapped, turning. He held his bottle in front of him like a weapon. "But when you left the bar, you knew I would follow you. And you knew I'd see the light go on inside the bell tower. You wanted me to follow you."

"I don't know where your brother is," Stephen said.

"I don't care!" Jordan barked.

Stephen's eyes narrowed. Some fresh power in him was aroused by Jordan's anger. "Do you want your picture back?" Stephen asked, his tone low and gruff. He rose from the bench. Jordan snorted a half-laugh in response, which he tried to down with a slug of beer.

Stephen bounded down the steps to the beach. Then he halted, yelled, "Follow me," to dare Jordan, then danced across the white sand toward the purr of the surf.

He could hear Jordan following him, grunting as his sneakers sank into the sand, then panting as he jogged to get closer.

"Just stop, all right?" Jordan cried out.

They had moved past the last house in the beachfront row and both of them stood several yards apart in darkness. Stephen faced him, waiting for an answer that Jordan would have to glean from a part of himself he rarely touched.

"You're a witch," Jordan finally told him.

"A *what*?"

"I bet it's so easy for you to think you're just the victim. I bet all of it's easier to remember if you tell yourself it was just hatred. But it's not. It's more." Jordan shook his head.

Stephen wanted to throttle him, slap him quiet in quickening rage. "What was it then?" he spat.

Jordan sputtered, thought out loud. "Why didn't he just find a quiet place and put the gun to his head? Why did he even have to bother with you, Stephen? Have you ever thought about what that meant—"

"I *know* what it meant!" Stephen shouted. "He wanted to destroy me. Break me. And then he realized what he'd done and that's when he killed himself. Greg Darby didn't want to die that night." He bristled with anger. "He probably brought the gun because he was going to use it on me!"

"No," Jordan said. His voice was calm and authoritative.

Stephen's mouth opened, but nothing came out. Jordan lifted his eyes to Stephen's.

"You had power over him. You suggested something else . . . This other world outside the boundaries of what he knew . . ."

"This is fucking bullshit!" Stephen growled. He strode off across the sand. Jordan didn't follow, but he raised his voice.

"You had power over him! That's why he called you! That's why he asked you to go with him. That's why he wanted you to be there when he took his own life, because he wanted you to know what you had done to him!"

"He raped me!"

"I know, but *why*? Why not just kill you?"

Stephen stopped, his eyes useless against the black water. Anger hummed inside of him like an engine filling with fuel.

"You're a witch, Stephen. You have a power over people you don't even realize. It's a curse." Stephen was moving toward him now, but Jordan continued. "You killed Greg Darby without even lifting a hand."

Stephen slammed into Jordan with so much force that Stephen could feel Jordan's body slam into the sand and bounce. Before he had time to struggle, Stephen was rolling him over onto his stomach, pinning his wrists. His mouth opened in protest and Stephen saw sand spill into his throat. He brought one knee between the back of Jordan's legs, pushing it into the underside of his crotch. One hand pressed Jordan's face deeper into the sand. Jordan tried to twist his neck beneath Stephen's grip. Stephen's other hand yanked the back of his shorts, pulling the waistband down.

As Stephen glimpsed the off-white skin of Jordan's ass, Jordan screamed into the sand, a muffled, retching bellow, filled with enough panic and horror to unsaddle Stephen from his back.

"*Was that power?*" Stephen cried.

Jordan lifted his head from the sand, coughing. He braced both hands in the sand and hauled his chest from the ground to a crude half-pushup. When he opened his eyes, Stephen saw he was crying.

"*Was that power?*"

Jordan sat up, his chest braced against his bent knees, trying to breathe. Stephen backed away from him, his anger flushed with shame. "How would you know?" Stephen spat out, with his last shred of fury. "How would you know?" He tried to summon his anger again to combat the threat of sobs.

Jordan rose to his knees as Stephen fell onto his back against the dune. He watched as the god of everything he wasn't righted himself and approached. Jordan sank down into the sand next to Stephen. Stephen reflexively turned onto his side, as if anticipating the first swift punch of Jordan's vengeance. He gripped Stephen's shoulder and easily pulled Stephen onto his back.

"Because you've done the same thing to me you did to Greg Darby. That's how I know," Jordan whispered. He touched Stephen's chin, craning Stephen's face toward him. Stephen waited to be hit.

Then Jordan brought his other hand to Stephen's cheek, framing Stephen's face as if surveying it.

Stephen raised a hand, his fingers tracing a path from Jordan's brow to his upper lip, and then over his mouth, catching his lips briefly before outlining his jaw. Stephen smiled. "You could destroy me without even realizing it," he whispered.

Then he remembered: something he thought had died in him in that explosion of hatred weeks before. The expression where the face goes lax as the body suddenly takes control. The eyes drowsy, the mouth slightly parted. Before Jordan's mouth met his, Stephen almost said it out loud—the whisper face.

# 8

Greg Darby stood wreathed in shadow next to the pond, his form outlined by the torrential rain.

Greg usually arrived when the rain did, as he had on that first afternoon at Camp Davis, when Brandon glimpsed him through the window of the mess hall. On that first day, all of the cadets had been forced to sit before their empty food bowls because fifteen of them had passed out during the regiment's run. Greg had said nothing to him. Brandon had looked from the window to the squad captain, who stared back at Brandon with a gaze so penetrating he immediately believed the man was possessed of the ultimate knowledge. Brandon rocked back on his bench and collapsed to the floor. They had not been fed for twenty-four hours.

Inside Nanine Charbonnet's half-finished guest cottage, Troy was screaming at his cousin. "Where are the fucking grenades? You promised fucking grenades!" The cousin had made good only on the promise of combat rifles and semtex. Ben and Rossi had been caught in the rain near the firing range. Brandon wondered if the storm would interfere with their chances of a kill. He wasn't sure whether or not snakes slithered from the rain.

"Pestilence . . ." Greg whispered to him this time. Brandon nodded.

The others were becoming a problem. Troy's cousin turned out to be less than reliable, and now there was his bullshit about wanting to join up. Before that, they'd had no trouble scaring off the Klan. The Mississippi boys in their pickup truck abandoned all talk of "unity and incorporation" when they saw the four soldiers of the Army of God emerge from the fringe of the clearing with their twelve-gauge combat rifles cocked against their shoulders.

"Pestilence," Brandon answered to the rain. I know, Greg, give me a break. This was the best way to start out, wasn't it?

Greg was gone in a gust of raindrops.

Troy slammed the door, jarring the dead water moccasins where they hung from nails along the plywood wall. Their thick black bodies swung from arrow-shaped heads, driven through with nails. "Dammit, if he ain't my cousin!" Troy said, sinking onto the step.

Years earlier, Troy's father had taken a liking to sodomizing his only son during fishing trips. The practice lasted until Troy sent his father off the stern, headfirst into the propeller. Troy's behavior didn't go over well in his hometown of Boutte, given that his father had been recently elected sheriff. His mother couldn't prove her son had killed her husband. She asked her two brothers to meet Troy in the driveway when he came home from school one afternoon. He was going to spend some time away, they told him as they loaded him into the back of the van. Troy rode to Camp Davis sandwiched between two of his uncles, one of them a cop, the other a shrimper.

Troy had told Brandon and the others that there was a gay bar outside of Boutte called Earl's, a nondescript roadside shack given away by a rainbow-colored BUD LIGHT neon sign in the front window. As soon as Troy's cousin got his ass in line, Earl's would be the Army of God's second strike.

Troy was their leader, Brandon their frontal lobe. Ben and Rossi were the foot soldiers. Troy always joked that the other two were "in it for the snakes." But lately Troy was starting to joke too much for Brandon's taste. Ever since the first strike Troy had relaxed and lost focus. Brandon was surly and impatient; he needed a strike to get his blood pumping. And worse, Greg was also appearing less and less frequently.

Rossi had shot the liquor truck driver and made the delivery himself, which made him "something." Troy had finally calmed him down, but Brandon didn't have the patience for that kind of shit and they all knew it.

"Says he's got a new contact down in Venice. Works for Shell. Says he can get his hands on all kinda stuff they use for dredgin'," Troy said, more to the rain than to Brandon.

"Not worth anything if he can't get some fucking triggers next time. That shit held us back more than a month," Brandon said, his voice low.

"Timers are better 'n triggers," Troy added, dropping his voice, not wanting to start a fight. Brandon wanted triggers. Watching it on a TV with shitty reception defeated the whole purpose. He wanted to be there, see it.

They heard the report of a combat rifle off in the distance before Rossi let out a cry audible over the patter of rain.

"What you thinkin', Brandon?" Troy asked.

Brandon looked at Troy from where he sat on the edge of the porch. "Snakes around the columns of the temples of salvation," he told him.

Troy forced a smile that revealed his chipped front tooth. Troy had picked up the phrase from a pastor back in Boutte, and they'd adopted it as their mission statement. On the night of the strike, the four of them had grouped around the television, watching *Letterman* with the sound off, softly chanting the words until the BREAKING NEWS banner blazed across the screen. They'd fallen respectfully silent at the sight of the French Quarter in flames.

Brandon looked back to the shadows by the pond where Greg had stood. He didn't know the right way to tell Troy he was thinking about a bell tower and the boy who had started the pestilence.

Troy rose to his feet as Ben and Rossi stomped through the mud toward the guest house. He turned and went inside. Brandon hesitated, then followed.

Two cottonmouths were draped over Ben's neck. The long body of a black moccasin trailed over Rossi's shoulder as he held the head in his other hand.

"Nails'll fix that," Ben said.

The rain spattered through the holes in the ceiling. Brandon sat cross-legged at the foot of the half-built staircase just inside the front door. The rain made Troy nervous, and he paced across the cement-floored room, an unfiltered Camel dangling from his lips.

"Any word?" Rossi asked as he dropped the moccasin to the floor.

"When there's word, I'll tell you," Troy snapped.

Ben held up one of the cottonmouths for Brandon to study.

"Smaller."

"Ain't a moccasin," Ben said, sounding wounded.

"Big ones look better on the wall," Brandon said.

"Shit, Brandon, what you gotta be so particular for?"

Rossi had found the hammer and was trying to mend the moccasin. The tool slipped and crashed to the cement floor. "Goddamn it!" Brandon screamed.

They were all skittish. "You do inventory yet?" Troy asked Rossi.

Rossi's eyes were on Brandon, who turned and walked back to the window. Troy batted Rossi's chin to get his attention.

"What the hell I gotta do inventory for every day?" Rossi asked quietly.

"Goddamn thing's belowground. Gotta check for leaks, cracks. All that kinda shit," Troy said. A spray of rain doused his Camel. He spat it out and ground it with his heel.

Rossi set the mutilated moccasin down on the cement floor as he ducked out the door, disappeared through the rain toward the tool shed they referred to as the "storehouse." It had once housed the construction equipment used to lay the foundation of the guest cottage. Now its racks contained low-grade explosive devices, purloined by Troy's cousin for a small fee.

Ben had stretched out his two cottonmouths on the floor. He was sharpening his Bowie knife, and the sounds the blade made as it grated the stone were sure to irritate Brandon. "Ben. Quit!" Troy said, his gaze drifting to Brandon, who paced slowly in the door frame.

"Ever seen how a snakeskin looks when you, like . . ." Ben began, still dragging the knife across the stone.

"Just quit!" Troy interrupted.

Ben paled and set the stone down on the floor. "How long till next strike?" he asked quietly.

Troy shook his head.

"Thibodaux," Brandon said loudly.

Both boys were quietly surprised. They had all agreed months ago that Earl's in Boutte would follow Sanctuary in New Orleans. "Brandon . . ." Troy said tiredly.

"Thibodaux!" Brandon shouted, before turning his back on both of them. "That's where it started," he whispered under his breath.

On that December night, secluded in his bedroom, Brandon had seen the shadow of Greg Darby in the portico of the bell tower. He had been sitting at his desk, inking the image of Stephen Conlin out of an old photograph.

Stephen Conlin. Not listed among the dead found in Sanctuary's ruins.

*"What the hell!"*

Brandon turned, startled by the sudden high pitch of Troy's voice. Strange light slid across the far wall, just above where Ben sat, the cottonmouths' carcasses at his feet.

"Son of a bitch!" Troy yelled. A second later the light congealed into the twin beams of a car's headlights.

"*Posts!*" Brandon roared.

Rossi hurled through the side door, panted, "There's someone . . ."

"*Posts!*" Troy echoed, punching both fists against Rossi's shoulder, pushing him toward the twelve gauges leaning against the wall.

The headlights grew as Ben and Rossi dashed out the side door. Troy rushed up the stairs bound for the upstairs window. Brandon balanced the butt of his rifle against his thigh and flattened his body against the edge of the window, just inside the front door. He peered out to see Ben and Rossi lugging their rifles into the darkness on either side of the clearing.

They had practiced this, but not in the rain. Their vision was limited. Troy had babbled about floodlights but there hadn't been time. Their intruder would drive into the clearing in complete darkness. Ben and Rossi would fire a warning shot, signaling that the approaching car was alien to them. After that, they would ignite a dynamite charge in the center of the clearing.

Brandon kept still as the headlights beamed through the window and landed on the opposite wall. The car had rounded the bend fifty yards from the entrance to the clearing. The only sounds now were the drum of rain and the wet rasp of his own breathing.

"Brandon!"

The voice was soft and thin, muffled by rain. The car had reached the edge of the clearing, where its front tires had dipped at a point where the gravel road gave way to open mud. The vehicle was large, probably a Jeep.

"Brandon!"

Elise Charbonnet got out of the Explorer, splayed one hand in front of her face, shielding her face from the rain. The skeleton of the guest cottage looked desolate through the haze of rain. It was overgrown with weeds and vines. There were no signs of life. Elise pulled the gun from her raincoat, unnerved by the swamp darkness.

"*Brandon Charbonnet!*" Elise screamed as a rifle shot thundered behind her. She pivoted, aimed the .35 into the darkness of pine trees, and squeezed. The kick set fire to her arm and knocked her backward into the mud.

She saw a flash of gunfire from the upstairs window. The slug from the twelve gauge slammed into the Explorer's nose, popping the hood and shattering both headlights.

Elise fell and rolled toward the car, which in spite of the gunfire seemed to be the only refuge. Another explosion, this one from the other side, fractured the passenger-side window, and shards of glass spiraled outward. Male voices shouted from the guest house. Elise could barely make out "... *fucking mother's asshole! My fucking mother* ..." before she heard the blast of her son's rifle tear through the rotting insulation of the house. In a flash of yellow light that lit up the interior of the cottage for a brief instant, Elise saw the boy's death. It wasn't her son, she knew, as the slug hit the boy in the crotch, folding him in half. He flew up before thudding to the floor.

She hugged the mud under the Explorer's nose as the second blast from a twelve gauge ripped the front driver's-side tire. Pellets of rubber seared her face and she screamed, pulling the trigger on the .35. The muzzle flare lit the muffler and engine in a brief flicker. She held the trigger, foolishly thinking it would fire endlessly from under the car. It let out another slug, rocking the gun upward where it rammed something metal she couldn't see. From the trees beside the road she heard a noise that sounded like a cat in heat. She knew it wasn't her son—she knew his cry—as the victim howled in agony.

It took Elise a second to realize she was no longer holding the .35.

In darkness, she groped for the gun. Then she heard it, barely audible over the drum of the rain. It was a movie sound, a cartoon sound—a sputtering hiss that was more insistent than the rain. Blue sparks briefly illuminated a ragged young man, bracing himself against a pine trunk as he dropped the flickering end of a fuse to the mud at his feet.

She scrambled out from under the Explorer and flung herself to her feet, slapping her hands against the driver's-side door before finding the handle. Behind her she could hear a boy retching and cursing. She slid behind the steering wheel.

A burning fuse marched across the clearing, its light reflected on the hood's frayed metal edges.

Elise threw the Explorer into reverse. The car coasted backward. She gripped the steering wheel with both hands.

"Jesus . . ." She formed her panic into one word. "Jesus, Jesus, Jesus . . ."

As the dynamite exploded, the Explorer was rolling backward down the gravel road, picking up speed. The hood was ripped from the Explorer. Elise saw a folded flap of metal fly up and crack the windshield into spiderweb formation, then tumble over the roof like a flag twirled by a gust of wind.

Elise turned to see all smoke where the charge had detonated. And then there was silence.

She yanked the steering wheel, spinning the vehicle into a sharp 180 as the Explorer veered to face total darkness. No headlights, Elise thought. Gasping, she pulled on the steering wheel. The car's rear slammed into a tree. Elise whipped forward, her forehead banging the steering wheel, and then she bounced flat against her seat. "Jesus," Elise said again.

There was someone in front of the car.

As she leaned forward, her vision blurring, she saw a crumpled body where it had fallen, struck down by her first blind shot into the woods. She thrust her foot on the accelerator.

The pine tree held to the Explorer's tail for a moment before releasing its grip, taking the rear fender with it, but slingshotting the Explorer forward and the body crunched under the tires like rocks. For half a minute, Elise drove blindly down the road, expecting to careen into the trees. Gradually, adrenaline cleared her mind, helping her to remember where the bends were. When she saw the blaze of the Texaco station's mustard lights through the thinning pines, a sob escaped her chest.


Greg led Brandon into the woods, running away from the fire. Brandon heard the sound of the pep band and his rain-drenched clothes became his sweat-soaked football pads.

"Go deep!" Greg commanded.

"Don't fuckin' taunt me, Darby!" Brandon yelled to the rain.

"Come on, Bran, my man, you got more in you than that!" Greg called back.

Brandon didn't hear it when the kerosene he had poured and lit finally embraced the storehouse. A flash occurred at the edge of his left eye, but otherwise, there was only the dark, the rain, and the voice of Greg Darby urging him deeper into the swamp.

The Texaco station cashier dropped the phone at the sight of the middle-aged woman caked with mud.

"Phone!" Elise gasped.

He stared at her dumbly, ignoring the tinny anger of a woman's voice from the dangling receiver.

"I found them!" Elise gasped. She stumbled into the candy rack.

"Who?"

Elise groped at the counter, grabbed it, and collapsed to the floor, an inventory of candy bars, cheap sunglasses, and magazines tumbling onto her face.

"The Army of God," she whispered.

The candy rack crashed down onto her and at the same moment the window behind the cashier shattered as a mixture of semtex and dynamite tore a hole in the earth three miles up the road, hurling fire and pine trees toward the sky.

# 9

Two-Thirty-One Dune Alley had a single phone, in the kitchen. Just after midnight, it rang.

Stephen was watching him silently as Jordan awoke to Stephen's warm breath against the nape of his neck. He opened his eyes: His own naked body was entwined in Stephen's limbs. Stephen's hand came to life on Jordan's chest, his fingers spreading slightly. At the phone's third ring, Stephen cocked his head like a dog's.

"Jordan . . ." he murmured.

Jordan separated himself and twisted off the edge of the bed. Stephen drew his knees to his chest and watched as Jordan plodded beautifully over the carpet and across the linoleum in the kitchen. The phone's ring ended abruptly. After a moment of silence, Stephen heard the noise of a drawer shutting. Jordan didn't return.

Stephen moved to the bathroom, closing the door behind him. He switched on the light and was shocked by his ruddy reflection. He was surprised to see no bruises or blood on his naked body. It had begun with necessary violence, a violence that Stephen knew was not rape, but rather physical evidence that this encounter required Jordan hand over something and not Stephen.

He turned, examining himself with almost clinical detachment. The fire at the bottom of his spine where Jordan had pressed himself into him lingered but was waning. It had burned at first. Stephen's back had arched like a cat's and he had buried his face into the pillow to muffle the reflex of protest. Jordan had steadied his hands on Stephen's shoulders, and Stephen's body relaxed beneath his, vertebra by vertebra. They seemed to fit together easily. It should have been more difficult.

Stephen emerged from the bathroom to find Jordan had grabbed a beer from the fridge and was sprawled across one of the living room sofas. He stared out at the Gulf, the dome of sky flecked with stars. He set his beer on the coffee table, leaned forward, and brought his hands to his temples, and Stephen could tell he was fixing the dance of this night into his mind.

"Jordan?"

He glanced up to see Stephen, who had wrapped a bedsheet around himself. Jordan looked down at his own nudity, embarrassed, and Stephen felt pleased that for once it was the other man who was more naked and vulnerable. Neither of them spoke. But the space between them was heavy with questions. Stephen moved to the deck door, feeling vaguely disappointed. "Who called?" he asked softly.

Jordan rose from the couch and padded to the kitchen cabinets. He took the phone from one of them and placed it on the counter between them as if it were a prize catch. He had unplugged the cord from the wall, severing their only line to the outside world.

When Stephen lifted his eyes to meet Jordan's, he felt his face soften. He's not going to punish me, Stephen thought.

Stephen came to him, releasing the sheet from his shoulders. Jordan bowed his head as Stephen curved both arms around his back. Jordan gave his weight over to Stephen's frame. "I'm tired," he whispered.

Stephen took Jordan's hands to lead him back to the bedroom.

He turned down the comforter and both of them eased into bed. For several minutes they didn't touch. Jordan lay on his stomach, face grazing the pillow, and Stephen lay flat on his back, drawing the comforter to his chin. Then Jordan traced the rim of Stephen's navel. Stephen gripped his hand before turning onto his side. Jordan nestled against Stephen's back, keeping his hand curled against Stephen's stomach.

As they fell asleep, Nanine Charbonnet's parcel of land was still scattered with dying flame.

The Cadillac barreled down Interstate 10 through tracts of swamp pines. Jordan had already threatened to eject Stephen if he changed the dial one more time. Stephen had put the radio on scan, filling the car with maddeningly brief snippets of songs. They half-listened to a news report about the imminent hurricane season. One of the season's first storms had just developed off the coast of western Africa, but was not yet strong enough to earn a name. Jordan finally reached into the armrest's container and retrieved a mixed tape Melanie had made for him that long-ago last spring, and inserted it into the cassette player. It was night by the time they sped past downtown New Orleans, Business 90 taking them alongside the Superdome's mushroom swell before they saw the exit sign for St. Charles Avenue. Neither of them said anything when the Bishop Polk bell tower came into view.

They pulled up in front of the Charbonnet residence. Two NOPD cruisers were parked against the curb. An armed police officer stepped out of the first car and approached the Cadillac. Jordan got out. Stephen remained in the passenger seat, watching as the officer greeted Jordan. He noticed the officer's hand rested on his belt, inches from his pistol. As they exchanged words Stephen saw the officer snap the gun holster shut with a slow, innocuous motion of his right hand.

He summoned his nerve, kicked open the door, and stepped out of the car. He opened the rear passenger door and pulled his duffel bag from the backseat. He tried to ignore what Jordan was saying.

"Destin, Florida. A few miles past Fort Walton Beach," Jordan explained.

"Uh-huh," the officer replied in a bored tone of voice. "For the time being we're going to have someone on watch. It'll be an unmarked car after tomorrow."

Stephen shut the car door and swung his duffel bag in front of him. Jordan's expression was unreadable, but he held Stephen's gaze intently. Stephen shook his head slightly, waiting for Jordan to give him a sign.

"Stephen, do you need me to bring you home or can—"

"I'll walk," Stephen said softly. Jordan would know where to find him if he needed him. He turned and crossed Philip Street. He paused on the corner and shot a glance back at the Charbonnet residence. Jordan and the officer had not moved.

"How long has it been since you talked to your brother?" the officer was asking. Stephen turned and rounded the corner, trying to assuage fear with each step toward his house.

The officer led Jordan into the kitchen where Roger sat at the table nursing a glass of straight scotch. The policeman nodded and then left. Roger did not look up as Jordan slouched against the table, studying *The Times-Picayune*'s headline:

## SUICIDE BLAST DESTROYS ARMY OF GOD'S NORTH SHORE HEADQUARTERS

"Did you turn the phone off?" Roger asked, his voice thin. He took a sip of scotch. Jordan didn't answer. He sat down opposite Roger and scanned the paper. The subheadline read: THREE BODIES FOUND, FOURTH MEMBER BELIEVED MISSING. Brandon's face, a Cannon varsity football team photo, filled a square beneath a photo of Nanine Charbonnet's blackened lot.

"Why did you turn off the goddamn phone?" Roger barked. "I called you seven times, Jordan. Do you know they sent the highway patrol to look for you this morning? You must have missed them by minutes."

Jordan tossed the paper to the table. "Where's Mom?"

Roger shook his head and again gulped the liquor.

"Where's Mom?" Jordan asked again, his voice edged with anger.

"Upstairs," Roger said to his scotch.

When Jordan nudged open the bedroom door, the light that fell across the bed did not stir or rouse her. Elise had wrapped herself in a cocoon of blankets. Her hair, usually styled, had clearly not been washed in three days since an ATF helicopter had ferried her across Lake Pontchartrain. A red scrape stretched across her forehead. Jordan held the edge of the door.

"Seventy-one people are dead because you couldn't handle it when your son threw a chair," he said.

"Get out," Elise said, eyes on the ceiling.

Jordan's knuckles whitened on the knob. His mother lay still, as distant as she had been when he had returned home from college. "I did what I was supposed to do," she said, her voice low and disarmingly even. She didn't look at him. "I went there and I did what I was—"

"He could have killed Stephen!" Jordan shouted.

He slammed the bedroom door behind him, went downstairs, brushed past Roger, and out the front door.

Elise sat up in bed. "Stephen," she whispered as she heard Jordan clatter down the front steps. "Oh Jesus . . ." She shut her eyes again and sank back onto the pillow. She remembered a summer day, her bare back warm upon a wooden floor, a framed quotation looming on the wall above her head as the strains of Mahler's Second Symphony drowned the sounds of her desire. "For passion, like diseases, does not sit well with the sure and even course of everyday life . . ."

Meredith was sitting beside Stephen's bed when the doorbell rang. Stephen did not flinch. Monica was downstairs but apparently didn't want to answer it.

Meredith had gone to the Conlin residence every day since the story hit the news, half-expecting she would find the house in flames, with the devilish figure of Brandon Charbonnet dancing on the sidewalk. Stephen had not been there, which had only made the nightmare vision more acute. Earlier that afternoon, Monica had invited her to come in and "wait" with her. They'd said very little to each other. Monica had offered Meredith a drink, which she had declined. When Stephen opened the front door, hoisting his duffel bag, he had halted at the sight of them in the parlor. Meredith had studied Stephen's face.

He had not cried as Monica explained what had happened. His knees had not buckled. They had not been forced to carry him up the stairs. When Monica finished, Stephen just looked at her, jaw slack.

"Brandon killed Jeff," he said, as if it were a fact he had forgotten.

He had turned and with one arm knocked the foyer console table to the floor, shattering a porcelain vase. He'd mounted the stairs and shut the bedroom door. "Sit with him," Monica had urged her.

Now she stood in his half-open doorway, listening to a muted argument downstairs. She recognized the male voice and Monica's furious "Please!" Meredith heard Jordan protest, followed by the slam of the front door. Jordan was climbing the stairs toward her.

"What are you doing here?" she asked.

Jordan pushed her gently out of the way and walked into the bedroom. Jordan rounded the bed and sprawled on it, reaching out for Stephen's clasped hands.

Monica appeared in the doorway behind Meredith. They watched Jordan pry Stephen's hands apart and guide one to his own mouth, kissing it gently. Stephen made no sound to interrupt the shocked silence.

"I have a gun," Monica said. "If your brother decides to pay us a visit, I'll use it." She withdrew toward her bedroom.

Jordan finally lifted his eyes to Meredith, poised in the doorway.

"Did you two have a nice time?" she asked in a sharp whisper.

"You can go now," Jordan answered.

"You disgust me," she said.

"Was he trying to kill me?" Stephen asked, calm.

"I don't know," Jordan managed. "But . . . Let me stay here for a while." Now Meredith felt confused. She shook her head numbly.

"You think he's going to come after me?"

Jordan just kept looking at him.

"Stay," Stephen finally said.

Meredith turned and descended the stairs.

# 10

On the first Sunday in August, *The Times-Picayune* printed a front-page story detailing the findings of the Bureau of Alcohol, Tobacco and Firearms in the aftermath of the explosion that had leveled the Army of God's alleged headquarters. ATF investigators informed the city of New Orleans that the explosion had been caused by human action, confirming the theory that it had been an attempt to destroy all evidence the two acres of land might have yielded. More important, the explosion provided a cover for the escape of a group member whose body was not discovered among the ruins—Brandon Charbonnet.

All three dead men were pictured with yearbook photos that ran down the left margin of the front page. Their criminal records were printed beneath the photos. Signs of "gunshot wounds prior to incineration" on all three bodies suggested an internal fight among the soldiers.

Trish Ducote passed Meredith the article after she had read it herself, noticing that the article said very little about Brandon Charbonnet beyond a brief quote from the local FBI: reassuring readers that all law enforcement agencies were on the lookout for the suspect.

Later that day, Trish went to Meredith's room to hand her the registration forms and orientation packet that had arrived in the mail from Tulane. Classes started at the end of the month. Meredith took the pages in one hand without glancing up from what Trish now referred to as her "damn notebook."

"What are you writing?" Trish asked.

"I don't know yet."

Trish swallowed her irritation, began again. "Do you think that maybe you should talk to the police considering that you . . ."

"Don't be an idiot, Mom," Meredith said, scribbling.

"I'd appreciate it if you didn't call me names like that," Trish said as she left.

Meredith had left the newspaper on the kitchen counter. Trish scanned it again, then read a smaller article at the bottom of the page. The small storm that had developed earlier off the coast of western Africa was now a tropical depression, unnamed, but on a determined course for the Caribbean. She thought about the four or five hurricanes that aimed for New Orleans during the past decade and the pointless panic they had caused. Every single one of them swung eastward.

The second Monday in August, Jordan finally returned home to get some clothes. Roger met him at the door.

"I need some stuff," Jordan said.

"Where have you been?"

"Stephen's."

"You might want to tell Monica to drop by for a visit. Maybe she can talk to Elise," Roger suggested, coolly. Upstairs, Jordan gathered essentials into a duffel bag. He passed by his mother's bedroom door without a word or a knock.

"My dad asked if you'd go see my mom," Jordan said when he returned to the Conlin residence and found Monica in the front parlor restocking the bar. She nodded, lining the bottles of Bombay and Glenlivet on the cabinet's top shelf. Jordan knew she would not go.

"How's the thing going upstairs?" he asked her, with forced politeness.

"What thing?"

"The room on the third floor. I saw the boxes and stuff . . ."

"Fine," Monica said shortly.

"I guess I don't have to stay here if you don't want me to," Jordan blurted out. Monica stopped, turned from the liquor cabinet. She studied him long and hard, alert and seemingly sober.

"Just remember what I said," she replied evenly.

Jordan nodded and climbed the stairs to find Stephen.

• • •

Tropical Storm Brandy was one hundred miles from Cuba on the day a Bayou Terrace nurse saw Andrew Darby punch his wife. Although she had been on staff at Bayou Terrace for a mere three weeks, the nurse was already suspicious of the circumstances surrounding the strange internment in The Bordeaux Wing. She needed no further incentive to call Security than the sight of Andrew's fist colliding with Angela's jaw. A guard pulled him from the room as Angela Darby stammered the question that had provoked her husband. "Where's Greg?"

Two guards dragged Andrew Darby down the corridor. As they passed Dr. Horne's office, Andrew yelled his brother-in-law's name. On the other side of the door, Ernest pretended to peruse a file. Angela Darby had been dancing since the end of July, and he had not informed her husband.

Andrew Darby was furious by the time the guards got him to the front door. In his anger, he made the mistake of calling the black guard a nigger. The guard lunged to tackle him, a nightstick in one hand, but Andrew dove into his car and peeled out of the parking lot.

At home, Andrew made himself his first drink in five years.


Meredith had not talked to Stephen since the night he returned from the Gulf Coast. When she called, Jordan picked up. "You're answering his phone now?" Meredith asked.

"Do you want to talk to him?" Jordan countered.

"Yes."

"Hold on."

Stephen came on the line. "Meredith?"

"How are you?"

"All right." He sounded icy and remote.

"What's up with you and Jordan?" she asked.

"He's staying here. He doesn't want to go home since . . . He had a fight with his parents."

There was a heavy silence. "Are you two . . . ?" she asked.

Stephen didn't answer and she felt herself flush with embarrassment.

"I don't want to get too personal. I just think it's kind of weird," Meredith said quickly, annoyed by her own defensiveness.

"You're right, it's weird," Stephen said dryly.

"I want to see you soon, okay?"

"Can you come over?"

"I've got to register for classes today," Meredith answered. Suddenly she didn't feel up to the task of telling Stephen about her encounters with Jordan—nor did she have the will even to avoid the subject. She doubted Jordan had been open about it either.

"School. Fuck," Stephen said.

"Yeah. We'll be at the same school again," she said, half-surprised by this realization.

"You're right. We'll . . . we'll be at the same school again."

Meredith heard the strain in his voice. A simple statement had knocked both of them askew.

"I'll let you go," she said, her voice thick.

"Bye-bye," Stephen said. Bye-bye, like a boy. Not good-bye, like a boy trying to be a man.

"I love you," she said before hanging up.

That evening Tropical Storm Brandy was upgraded to a hurricane as it pummeled the southeast corner of Cuba, its winds gusting to a hundred miles an hour.

## Part Four

# Heaven's Answer

*"And I saw as it were a sea of glass mingled with fire;*
*and them that had gotten victory over the beast,*
*and over his image, over his mark,*
*and over the number of his name, stand on a sea of glass,*
*having the harps of God."*

—Revelation 15:2

# 1

The mud was moving.

Warner Doutrie watched from the porch of his shack. He had built the house with his friend Earl, who'd been in his squadron in Vietnam and seen the same boys blown in half, thrashing legless through rice fields, calling to gods they didn't believe in. Warner and Earl had shared a desire to live far down pitted roads, away from civilization. They were both Louisiana boys, from Lafourche Parish, south of New Orleans, assigned to the same platoon by coincidence. After the war, they had built the shack together. Earl had died two years earlier and until the day the strange half-naked body stumbled out of the swamp, Warner had lived alone.

"Boy, come looka this!" Warner exclaimed, as the mud quivered.

Warner called Brandon "the Boy" because Brandon had said nothing to him in the month they had lived together. Warner talked, his rusty vocal cords creaking into use again, and Brandon listened. Warner had cleaned, fed, and praised him as if he were a swamp changeling come to keep him company.

The mud was shifting in folds emanating out from the inlet's banks. As Brandon walked onto the porch, a throng of red pinchers surfaced, masses of crawfish rising in sluggish tides of mollusk shells.

"Ain't datta sight!" Warner hooted.

Brandon slumped against a post and watched. Greg had not appeared to him since the night he ran from the fire. But this sight was most assuredly a sign. The crawfish migrating out of the water, branching around either side of the shack. Go forth from this place.

"Hoo yah, 'sgotta be sumtin wit da weatha, I tell yah," Warner whistled through his teeth.

Yes, Brandon thought, the weather. He's speaking to me through the heavens now. This has been a necessary exile but the heavens will send an answer soon enough.

For several days after the fire, Brandon had wandered the stretch of swamp across the north shore. By the time he came across Warner Doutrie's shack, he had eaten only a nutria and had had only two nights of fitful sleep. To chase away the demons he recited aloud the verse he lived by.

He'd been prepared to kill the old man fishing off the dock, but Warner Doutrie had greeted him with the frank expression of outcasts. Brandon had passed out, and when he woke Warner had washed him in the swamp water and laid him out on the floor.

Warner's incessant talk revived Brandon's strength. Warner had spoken about wars, but Brandon did not share his own soldiering with Warner. He spent his days hiking the swamp, looking for Greg. When he inhaled the pungent scent of Warner frying catfish, he would head back to the shack, where the older man would already have a plate ready for him.

*Go forth from this place.*

"Pestilence was born in Thibodaux," Brandon whispered, his lips scratchy as sandpaper.

"Wat dat yoo say?" Warner asked.

"Pestilence was born in Thibodaux," Brandon repeated, rapidly, like a child's tongue twister. He moved across the porch. Warner looked frightened of him for the first time since he'd come out of the swamp. Brandon sank down onto the porch next to him. He was shirtless and Warner saw a welter of scratches on his shoulders, signatures of brush. Brandon balled a hand into a fist and held it out, as if he were about to release a butterfly. Warner stared at him before balling his own fist and touching it to Brandon's, as if they were conversing in sign language.

"The world," Brandon said. His dark eyes gleamed with reverence. "God and the devil! God . . . one thing. The devil . . . many, legion . . ."

Warner nodded dumbly. What did this have to do with the crawfish?

"The devil is sprinkled. Peppered. Like God, see, he just took his great big hands and cast the devil down onto the earth, where it spread itself around. It's in cracks and corners. It's in people!"

Warner nodded emphatically. He'd met many men he thought were the devil.

"It's waiting, too. It can take lots of different people, but you see . . . it's never just one thing. You gotta root it out . . ."

He pinched the knuckles of his fist with the fingers of his other hand, grinding his teeth together to feign exertion as he rooted out the devil. Suddenly he went lax, sucked breath, exhausted by his revelation of pure truth.

Brandon gazed at the tide of mollusks passing beneath the boards of the porch. "How many men have been lost to their own desires because of pestilence?" he asked in a low, flat voice.

Warner gazed at Brandon in awe. "Pestilence," he agreed.

Brandon could still see the rivulet of blood that had trickled from Greg's nose five years ago. After he had slugged him, after Greg had leaned in and Brandon had reared his legs, wheeling kicks at Greg until he writhed out of the door of Brandon's Cadillac. Forced Greg into the pestilence that awaited him.

"Stevie," Brandon whispered.

Stephen, guardian of the bell tower. Who had filled its portico with his pestilence, lured Greg Darby in a moment of weakness, within.

"Who?" Warner asked.

Brandon looked at him. "I need to go soon," he said tersely.

Warner nodded, looking disappointed to see the Boy leave so soon. Brandon stood and went inside the shack. Warner could hear him mutter, mesmerized by his thoughts.

The old man regarded the crawfish. That morning, crawfish migrated across southern Louisiana, dogs bit and snapped at their chains, birds took to the air in strange formations. The pressure was falling. The sky was thickening.

# 2

**R**oger had helped Elise to the living room sofa and tucked a blanket across her shoulders. She slouched in front of the television set and watched *The Young and the Restless* as her husband packed their clothes into three suitcases.

She was staring blankly at the television screen when Jordan entered. A message scrolled across the bottom of the screen: "HURRICANE BRANDY IS ON A DIRECT COURSE FOR SOUTHEASTERN LOUISIANA. MAYOR MORRISON ASKS ALL NEW ORLEANS RESIDENTS TO EVACUATE OR SEEK SHELTER."

Upstairs, Jordan found Roger squatting on the floor next to a pile of suitcases. "Can you get the shutters for me?" Roger asked his son as he stuffed the clothes into the suitcase.

"I'm staying," Jordan announced.

Roger shook his head, exasperated but not surprised. "Do you have any idea what's going to happen if it hits the mouth of the river?"

"I want to be here." He smiled.

Roger snorted. "Can you close the shutters then? Make sure they're locked. I put tape on all the windows. Move the living room furniture into the kitchen, just in case."

Jordan nodded.

"And say good-bye to your mother."

Jordan went downstairs and lingered behind the couch, waiting for Elise to sense his presence. On television, *The Young and the Restless* had given way to the mayor, who addressed a huddle of reporters. "We are using every possible structurally sound building as a storm shelter. The media has been given a list of these places, which includes the

Superdome. We're asking everyone who can to get out of New Orleans now, but those who can't should proceed immediately to these shelters . . ."

"Mom?"

Elise turned with pained slowness.

"I'm going to stay," Jordan said.

"This is what you've been waiting for, isn't it?" she asked him.

In the living room, Jordan dragged furniture away from the windows. Through the panes he saw how Philip Street was eerily quiet, the oak branches still an ordinary blue. Not one car was parked on the street.

The news stations had been advising all day that this was merely the calm before the storm. Last night Stephen and Jordan had noticed that the television reporters were energized by the imminence of Brandy's strike, acting as if it were the night before the Super Bowl. By morning, with Interstate 10 clogged all the way to Baton Rouge, the reporters and news anchors had grown more somber, their eyes heavy with the possibility of a storm that might tear down their own homes.

His mother was half-right. Jordan wasn't going to miss this for the world.

Three days before the official warning, Meredith had bought a generator and had waited in line for three hours at the Schweggman's grocery store to buy enough bottled water and canned food to last a week. Trish Ducote had busied herself by telling everyone, including Meredith, that Brandy was not going to hit. A year earlier, Hurricane Georges had given New Orleans a similar scare, resulting in a lot of useless panic, she said.

Meredith had paid no attention. She had stored all of her supplies in the guest house behind the Ducotes' swimming pool that was jokingly nicknamed the Manger. At parties Meredith had overheard her mother often say, "When there's no room in the inn, you stay in the Manger!"

On the second floor of the guest house, Meredith stretched Xs of duct tape over the bedroom windows. She hoped the tape would hold the glass in place should the storm batter the windows. Now sobered by the prospect of the storm, Trish saw the Xs as she crossed the yard. "You damn well better get in the car with me!" she called up the stairs.

"No," Meredith said flatly. She was changing the sheets on the queen-sized bed.

"This is a hurricane, Meredith!" Trish shouted. "It's not any safer to stay out here than in the house."

"If it gets bad I'll go to Aunt Judy's in La Place," Meredith answered, throwing a comforter onto the bed and adjusting the corners.

"Judy's already gone. They went to Mississippi this morning."

"Just go, Mother," Meredith said.

Trish started to cry loudly. Meredith rolled her eyes and went down the stairs to her, looping one arm over her mother's shoulders.

"Mom, you need someone to stay here. I know how much you hate floods, so . . ."

"Oh, please!"

"If you put a lock on the liquor cabinet, will you feel better?"

Trish shrugged off Meredith's arm. "You're old enough to know when you're being an idiot, and I'm too old now to stop you," she declared, striding toward the door to the yard. Meredith, relieved, didn't follow her.


"Maybe we should just fill the bathtubs with gin?" Stephen suggested.

Jordan laughed from the front porch where he was securing the window shutters. Monica emerged from the kitchen.

"Want a drink, Mom?" Stephen asked as the shutters rattled closed over the window behind him.

"Yes, please," Monica said. "Did you fill the bathtub in your bathroom?"

"Yeah. What do you want to drink?"

"Something alcoholic," Monica said, implying that Stephen should know already. She glanced out the living room window where Jordan was unlatching the shutters from their locks on either side and rapped on the pane with her knuckles.

"Not the front door!" she called.

Jordan seemed startled but nodded before closing the shutters between them.

"He's not a butler, Mom," Stephen muttered as he added a tiny splash of gin to Monica's tumbler of tonic. Jordan's footsteps echoed over the front porch as he moved down the side of the house. He would nail plywood strips to the kitchen windows.

"We should talk," Stephen said.

"No, we shouldn't," Monica said firmly, taking her drink from Stephen. "If you need me, I'll be on the third floor . . ."

"Mom, what is *up* with the third floor? Don't you think Dad's office can wait?"

"No. I'm going to dump everything in it tonight," Monica said. "When the water gets high enough outside."

"That's kind of weird," Stephen remarked.

"Yes, it's all very weird." She shot a glance at Jordan through the front windows and mounted the stairs, burdened with the knowledge that Jordan made Stephen happy. This truth made the task of clearing out Jeremy's office utterly crucial.


Warner Doutrie's battered 1978 Ford pickup slipped past the highway patrol before the roadblocks were set up at the north end of the Lake Pontchartrain Causeway. Spanning twenty-one miles of shallow, tempestuous lake water, the Causeway had been closed as an evacuation route. They had reached the dead middle where no land was visible on either horizon of the darkening sky. Ahead, the Causeway was a desolate strip of concrete that seemed to lead nowhere. The Boy had asked for one of Warner's shotguns and Warner had consented. He could spare one for a soldier of truth. He'd also given the boy a white T-shirt ripped around the armpit, exposing a pectoral behind a flap of white cotton.

Brandon was rooting around in the mess of tools behind the seat, making Warner nervous. Brandon extracted a spool of metal fishing line.

"I need this," Brandon announced as he set the spool on his lap.

Warner eyed the spool and then Brandon.

"Das good stuff. Yoo could hold a twenny poun' catfish on dat."

"I need it," Brandon repeated.

Warner didn't say anything. He'd given the Boy a shotgun. Why did the Boy need his strongest fishing line? "You gonna be doin' any fishen?" Warner asked, with a smirk on his lips.

"I need it," Brandon said again, his voice lower.

"C'mon, boy, you can take my bes—"

The first blow sent Warner's head into the steering wheel, beeping the horn. He could taste blood on his tongue. The second blow connected with Warner's shoulder blades, jerking his head. He spit a stream of blood on the dashboard.

"I fucking need this!" Brandon wailed.

On the third blow, Warner slumped back. The steering wheel spun free from his hands, and the left side of the truck plowed into the cement guardrail, shattering the left headlight. Brandon saw the rail whizzing past the passenger window.

Blood dribbled down Warner's chin.

"Goddamn it!" Brandon cursed. The truck slowed as it rode, kissing the guardrail, then dragged to a halt against the cement. Its tail swung outward forty-five degrees as its nose crumpled into the guardrail.

"Boy . . . Boy," Warner moaned.

"Shit! Fuck!" With one sweep of his arm Brandon smashed the wheel of metal fishing line into Warner's face, snapping the bridge of his nose. Warner's last two breaths were haggard whistles as he saw Brandon kick open the passenger door. The door struck the guardrail with a thud. He watched Brandon squeeze out of the truck and leap to the cement. As Warner died, Brandon was marching down the desolate Causeway toward the blackening horizon, the spool of fishing line in one fist.

# 3

Andrew Darby watched the news as he drained the Glen-livet, speculating that his house might be washed away that night. The revelation caressed him through the alcohol haze. He turned off the television and poured the scotch into a plastic cup. Convinced he was leaving his house for the final time, he drove to Bayou Terrace.

As he pulled into the hospital's parking lot, he saw three Orleans Parish prison buses idling at the curb outside the entrance as nurses dressed in rain slickers directed the buses as if they were jet planes taxiing on a tarmac.

He walked through the lobby to the front desk. The nurse there scrutinized him as if he were a confused, wandering patient. "I'd like my wife, please," he asked quietly, setting his cup of scotch on the desk between them.

"Mr. Darby?" the nurse asked. Andrew nodded. "I'm going to have to ask you to leave. If you'd like to arrange a discharge, you can do so after the patients are transported to Magnolia Trace, but you'll have to talk to—"

Andrew knocked the cup across the desk, spraying her face with scotch. As the nurse screamed, Andrew dashed through the hallway door.

"*Angela!*"

The doorway to Angela's room was open. A security guard rushed down on him from behind, grabbing his arms in a vise. Andrew glimpsed an open window, a gap torn in the chain-link fence.

Twenty minutes later, he was loaded onto the last bus bound for Magnolia Trace Hospital, sixty miles north of the city. His hands cuffed behind his back, Andrew muttered "baby" under his breath before he fell back against the seat, grinding the metal cuffs into the small of his back. When he started to sob, several other passengers followed suit.

• • •

"Bugs!"

Angela had been silent. As soon as the Acura merged onto Jefferson Highway, she grabbed Meredith's wrist.

"Bugs!" Angela screamed again.

"Angela, there are no bugs!" Meredith said calmly.

Angela Darby had not ingested Haldol and Thorazine in twelve hours and her fog was lifting, inducing fits fired by hallucinations. Jefferson Highway was desolate, its storefronts boarded up. Gas stations emerged from the prestorm gloom. Meredith slowed the Acura to thirty as she passed a battalion of state trooper cruisers and National Guard trucks ferrying sandbags to the subdivisions scattered along the Mississippi.

"Hand me my purse off the floor," Meredith instructed her.

"But they're all over it!" Angela whined.

"I'm not afraid of the bugs, okay. Just hand me my purse," Meredith said. Angela picked up the strap, her hand trembling, and dropped the bag in Meredith's lap. She tucked her legs to her chest, thrashing in her seat to crush the bugs crawling under her robe.

With one hand, Meredith fished out her mother's diet pills. She tapped four from the bottle into her open palm and extended them to Angela.

"Take these!"

"Meredith, I see them!"

"Angela, if you swallow these, the bugs will go away. Trust me. I'm taking you somewhere safe, remember?"

Meredith held out her free hand. Angela took the pills and swallowed them with a grunt. They drove in silence as Jefferson Highway wound uptown. Overhead, black fingers of clouds crawled across the sky, heralding Brandy. "There's a storm coming, isn't there?" Angela asked, her jaw resting on her knees.

"Yes," Meredith answered. When they finally pulled onto St. Charles Avenue, she pondered what she was going to say to Andrew Darby when she called him. She knew. She was carrying out a lunatic mission: If Andrew Darby wanted his wife back, he would have to rectify everything he had done to her. He would have to set her free. If not, Meredith would expose him and the administration of Bayou Terrace at the risk of facing criminal charges herself.

There were entering the Garden District. Meredith felt she had nothing to lose.

Angela slumped onto Trish's guest bed, hands curled against her chest as she whispered into the pillow. Meredith listened to the phone ring on the other end. When the machine picked up, an old recording of Angela's voice, strangely even in tone, asked if the callers would be so kind as to leave their names and numbers. Andrew had not changed the message on his answering machine since the death of his two sons.

He left, Meredith realized. He left her.

An hour passed. Angela, finally quieted, whispered, "They're all gone. Greg's gone, too . . ."

Meredith nodded.

"That's good," Angela said, sounding strangely normal, like her voice on the machine. "That's good, because I know he would have come to visit me. I know he . . ."

"No," Meredith said abruptly. "He wouldn't have come." She began to explain as the first rain pattered against the second-floor windows of the guest cottage.

In the Cadillac's rearview mirror, Roger Charbonnet watched black clouds churn across the sky. Elise regarded the graying landscape out of the passenger window. Green Lawn Cemetery stretched along the side of Interstate 10. Ahead of them the Interstate dipped beneath a train trestle so severely they couldn't make out the taillights of the cars ten feet in front of them.

They'd been stuck in gridlock for nearly five hours.

As the rain tapped the windshield, Elise reached to turn on the radio, but Roger grabbed her. She pulled her hand free. "I told you not to get on the fucking Interstate," she growled.

She scanned the stations. Nothing but snatches of music and the titter of static. And then suddenly a bellowing male voice filled the Cadillac. "The wind is really picking up . . . It's black as night out here . . ."

"Where is he reporting from?" Elise asked.

"Pretty soon we're going to have to get a . . . Jesus, okay . . . The National Guard has just informed us that we need to leave the area . . .

These are the first storm bands of Hurricane Brandy coming to shore now in Grand Isle . . ."

Roger and Elise both paled. Grand Isle lay at the mouth of the river, less than an hour from New Orleans.

Lying in the crook of Jordan's arm, Stephen could hear Monica lugging cardboard boxes around upstairs. The wind was stronger now, rattling the plywood boards and storm shutters. On television, a reporter practically screamed into her microphone, the winds angling the hood of her rain slicker over her face. "Anyone who has not evacuated should do so now," she was saying, sounding as if she wished she were in Memphis. Stephen felt Jordan's laughter vibrate through his chest. "Yeah," he said, "as if you could ever get away."

When the news cut to a shot of lightning spiderwebbing over the downtown skyline, Stephen sat up in surprise. Ensconced inside the shuttered house, he hadn't known night had fallen so quickly.

"Jesus . . ." he whispered.

"How old is this house?" Jordan asked.

"Old. It was in my dad's family for like a century or something."

"That's good. It's survived a storm before, then."

"This isn't just a storm."

Jordan's face was bright with excitement. "You love this, don't you?" he asked Stephen.

"It's kind of thrilling."

On television, the next report showed crowds of people huddled along the Superdome's stairwells. Children skipped and played before the cameras. An angry woman complained that all they were serving was hot dogs.

"Stephen?"

"What?"

"Why didn't you tell your mom about it?" Jordan asked.

"About what?"

"Greg?"

Stephen propped his elbows on Jordan's chest, puzzlement in his eyes. "She knows . . . She brought me home that night."

Before Jordan could ask more, they heard what sounded like giant fingernails scraping across the façade of the house and then the study window upstairs shattered. Monica screamed. Stephen leapt off the bed and bolted up the stairs.

He found her cowering against the far wall. Splinters of glass had fanned out on the floor. The wind was whipping through the study. A piece of paper blew past him and he grabbed it. At the top of the page of writing entitled "To a Child Not Yet Born," Stephen glimpsed Jeremy Conlin's severe cursive: *"Elise—Give this to him."* A shard of glass pierced Monica's bare foot as she crawled toward him. She tried to snatch the paper, but the wind danced it out of Stephen's fingers and through the splintered window.

"Help me get the boxes downstairs!" she screamed as her right foot trailed blood on the floorboards.

The front door was the only unbarricaded entrance. Blindly obeying, Stephen helped Monica carry the boxes down the stairs before setting them in the open doorway, where, to Stephen's astonishment, Monica wrestled them out onto the porch. The rain was falling in torrents that shook the branches. Monica moved to the edge of the porch, wind whipping her dress up from her waist before she caught it with her fists.

Four feet of water swelled across the front yard, flowing through the wrought-iron fence. Through curtains of rain Stephen could see that Third Street was flooding.

"Not high enough yet!" Monica pronounced.

"Mom, this is insane!" Stephen barked from the doorway.

The wind tore across the flood, whipping the surface into erratic rippling footprints. Across the intersection of Third and Chestnut, the water had swallowed five feet of the transformer pole. With silent awe, Stephen saw that the water seemed to be swallowing everything at various depths—the pole, the fence across the street, the oak trunks: The flood revealed the unevenness of the earth it covered.

"Mother." Stephen moved to her and gently took her shoulders.

"Go be with Jordan," she said. "Let me do what I have to do."

"Don't do this because of me!" Stephen cried out. "I don't need you to erase him for me!"

"You deserve the room!" Monica shouted back evenly.

"I don't want it! The only reason—"

An enormous oak branch splashed into the intersection. A whirlpool sucked it down.

"It's different for me, Mom. You knew him. He betrayed you, but you knew him at least. Not me. The parts of me that come from him—he was never here to tell me which ones they are."

"They aren't in these boxes!" Monica answered. "You won't find anything in these boxes!" She raised a hand to pull her windblown hair from her eyes.

Stephen released his grip, backing away from the veil of rain. He retreated into the house where the roar outside was softer. The chandelier in the foyer rocked slightly, its crystalline light scattering over the floor and staircase.

Stephen was halfway up the stairs when he saw Jordan waiting at the top.

"Is she all right?" Jordan asked.

"We won't have power much longer. It's flooding."

"What's she doing?" Jordan asked.

"Just what she said she was going to do. Let's go to bed," Stephen said, taking Jordan by one arm. Jordan flinched and made as if to descend the stairs. His eyes were locked on the open doorway and the stormy chaos beyond.

"We need to leave her alone right now," Stephen said, his voice insistent, irritating. Jordan brushed past Stephen into the bedroom. Stephen followed. He had stopped locking the bedroom door behind him weeks ago. Within an hour, Stephen and Jordan had drifted into a sleep shaped by the hammer of branches against the side of the house.

# 4

The lightning kept Roger and Elise in the Cadillac even as other motorists abandoned their vehicles, their arms full of clothing, precious framed pictures, and stuffed animals, some of them bearing guns and all of them darting into the shadows on either side of the Interstate. One bolt struck, erupting from the center of Green Lawn Cemetery in a perfect blossom of blue sparks.

"Roger!"

Elise saw it first. In front of them, the dip beneath the train trestle was swelling with water. A station wagon rose up suddenly in front of them before pitching forward. The flooded dip in the road swallowed it up to its doors as the water surged up the slope in the Interstate toward the Cadillac's front tires.

"We can't . . ." Roger barked.

"Roger, please!" Elise wailed. "We can't stay here!"

Roger shook his head vigorously. They were staying put. Elise released her grip on his arm and kicked open the passenger door. The wind shrieked through the car. Needles of rain stung Roger's face as the wind hurled the passenger door shut behind her.

When Roger flung open the driver's-side door, he was wrenched from the car and thrown against the hood. The water rose to his ankles. He spun around, confused for a moment. Then he made out cars surrounding him and the train trestle looming down the highway. He could hear car doors being slammed repeatedly by the wind. Detritus lapped at his feet: smashed milk cartons, water-soaked clothes, swollen loaves of bread.

Roger climbed onto the Cadillac's hood. He saw Elise crawling up the grassy rise on the side of the freeway through the mud toward the railroad tracks. She was heading for Green Lawn Cemetery. When he called out her name, his voice was muffled by a roar of thunder. The lightning was so bright he shielded his face with his hands, almost losing his balance. When he parted his fingers, a jet of sparks was spiraling downward. The bolt had struck a crossbar of the railroad tracks.

Elise was nowhere in sight.

Roger splashed to the side of the freeway, hesitated a moment, and then leapt across the tracks. A gust of wind tripped him and he somersaulted through the mud before colliding with a chain-link fence. He reached out and pulled himself to his feet.

The field of mausoleums stretching before him was roiling with black water. Roger saw coffins riding the flood. He sank to his knees and squeezed through the torn opening at the fence's hem, the tattered chain-link raking his back like claws. When he emerged on the other side, he could make out the distant silhouette of Elise, wading between mausoleums, hunched over, reaching out to the side of tombs for support. It looked as if she were knocking on them for admittance.

Roger tried to follow, lurched, and fell headfirst into the water. He began to swim, stroked into the mahogany flash of a coffin, gasped for breath, and was inside a mausoleum before he realized Elise was sitting next to him. He groped her trembling jaw. His other hand felt the floor of the mausoleum and noted that only several inches of water seeped through the broken door.

Elise was shivering. Roger backed into the opposite wall. "Elise?" he called out to her. "Grab my hand!" he shouted.

She found his wrist and yanked him close. His cheek brushed the soft swell of her breasts. "I didn't . . . I didn't think pe-people were pun-punished like this . . ." Elise stammered into his ear. "I th-thought people just had to live with what they had d-done!"

Both of them relaxed in their embrace. As Elise's hands slid down Roger's back, he found her face in the flickering stormlight.

"What did you do, Elise?"

Elise began to speak. Roger could not hear her over the roar outside. He craned his ear to her lips, catching her in mid-sentence.

" . . . she-she asked me if-if I wa-wanted to go in and lo-look around and I said ye-yes . . . Na-Nanine did-didn't wa-want me to . . ."

"I kept the knife in my pocket during the whole funeral," Meredith said.

Angela and Meredith heard the groan of the furniture downstairs as the water crept in under the guest house doors. "I knew that he was going to . . . I knew he was going to snap," Meredith said, eyes focusing on a flurry of tree branches outside the window. "It was my weapon. It belonged to my dad, actually. He left it behind when he moved. I never gave it back to him. He said it was his grandfather's and that he had used it in World War Two . . ."

She paused and inhaled the electric air as if it were the drink she was craving.

"At the reception . . . At your house, Mr. Andrew told us that you had gone to the hospital. Greg didn't say anything. He just took me up to his room. I was supposed to be at his side again, you know, the comforting girlfriend or whatever. Once we were in his room, he tried to . . ."

Her eyes locked on Angela's. "He was mad. About you being sent to the hospital. At the funeral he'd been crying, but he hadn't been mad . . ."

"Did he hurt you?" Angela asked.

Startled, Meredith shook her head. No. They heard a tinkle of glass as one of the French doors downstairs collapsed from the pressure of water. Neither of them moved. "I had the knife," Meredith said. "He wanted to have sex. Right there. He was like . . . an animal and when I told him no he pushed me onto the bed. He didn't know I already had my hand on the knife. When I got it . . . When I got it to his throat he looked so shocked. I almost, I don't know, lost my nerve. I wasn't going to hurt him . . ." She curled herself into the chair, to feel her own body warmth.

"He hurt you," Angela answered.

"I think he was going to." Her words made a knot in her chest.

"Afterward, are you going to take me back there?" Angela asked. "After the storm's over?"

"Do you want to go back, Angela?"

There was a long pause before Angela Darby made her first real decision in five years. She shook her head. No, she didn't want to go back. "I like talking to you . . ." Angela said, her eyes darting to the window. With this wind the X of duct tape would not hold the glass in place for long. "I'm starting to remember you," Angela said.

Meredith lowered her legs to the floor. "What do you remember?"

"You always seemed so sad."

Meredith ground her teeth together to stop her jaw from trembling.

"Keep talking to me," Angela said gently. The wind blew open a shutter.

"I put the knife to his throat and I told him he couldn't hit me anymore. Ever again. I told him I was sorry about Alex but that didn't give him the right to . . . hurt me. And I told him . . ." She had to stop.

On the night of Alex's funeral, Meredith Ducote had told Greg Darby that children die all the time, that there was nothing special about Alex Darby. Meredith held the knife to his throat. He had cursed and spit, but his words had been clipped by the blade against his Adam's apple.

When she withdrew the knife, Greg reared up and leapt across the room. She rose from the bed, still gripping the knife, her black skirt hiked over her thighs. Greg flexed his arm to hit her. She had not relied on the knife to shield herself. Instead, she had said, "I know what you and Stephen used to do."

Greg's hand had frozen. Meredith watched with sick fascination as his face blanched.

"If you ever hit me, if you ever hurt me, I'll tell people. I'll tell everyone."

Before he could react, Meredith sprinted out of his bedroom and down the staircase. She had not stopped running until she reached her house. She secluded herself in her room. Several hours later, when the phone rang, she answered the call. Meredith listened as Brandon vented his rage through the phone. *"He's fucking lost it!"* Meredith had listened quietly. She had envisioned Greg's world crumbling; one more question would destroy him.

"Do you know what he and Stephen used to do together?" she asked Brandon.

Brandon hung up, a response Meredith had not expected. The triumph had soured inside her chest as she returned the receiver to the cradle. Bad, she thought, I just did something . . . bad.

Meredith surfaced from her memory when she heard a faintly familiar noise. She shut her eyes, believing she was caught between the present and her memory. But she had not imagined the metallic bang that resonated over the howl of rain and wind. Meredith stood abruptly.

"I have to go," she said.

"Meredith?"

She dashed downstairs, answering the chimed call of the Bishop Polk bell tower.

Jordan awoke to the hiss of the transformer ramming into the spokes of the front fence. His eyes opened into pitch-blackness. He noticed the absence of the bedside clock's green glow. The power had gone out.

He sat up in bed suddenly.

There was no tug of weight next to him. He patted Stephen's pillow. When he called out Stephen's name, he couldn't hear his own voice over the wind against the shuttered window. A glare he took for lightning briefly illuminated the bedroom.

He felt his way to the top of the stairs where he saw the front door yawning open. A thin sweep of water blew in through the front door, soaking the Oriental rug on the foyer floor. He descended the stairs blindly, missing the last few steps, then fell against the doorframe before another shock of yellow light illuminated the front yard. The water was lapping at the porch. Ink-smeared papers rode a current past his feet and into the house. Third Street was a river with tiny rapids around the topmost spokes of the front fence. In the middle of it all, Jordan saw a patch of floating cloth.

It took him three seconds to make sense of it.

It was the back of Monica's dress.

He dove off the porch. His head surfaced and he saw Monica floating facedown, almost close enough to touch, entwined in a crepe myrtle branch that shed its soaked purple blossoms around her.

Something materialized behind her. The downed transformer was lodged on the spokes of the gate, the power line strung behind it, dancing a mad gavotte over the intersection, up to the pole across the street. The only thing keeping the transformer from dislodging itself from the gate was the erratic tension of the wind, tautly pulling on the power line.

He called out Monica's name as he dog-paddled toward her. Water the taste of raw tobacco filled his mouth, burning as he swallowed. He gripped her shoulder and gave it a good yank, wrenching her from the branch. She rolled onto her back. He was kicking to stay afloat, the soles of his bare feet churning the soft cushion of submerged fern leaves.

Jordan finally encircled his arms around her and hoisted her onto his chest, which forced him under the surface, beneath her. Something brushed his leg as he struggled up. He shut his eyes and locked his arm under her back, kicking as the sensation repeated itself down his thighs, across his calves. Jordan shut his eyes and kicked madly, disrupting the swarm of rats migrating beneath the surface.

Monica glided against the porch's top step. Jordan jabbed his right foot down, finding one of the bottom steps. He hauled her onto the porch and climbed after her, scooping Monica in both arms like a bride about to cross the threshold. By the time the transformer toppled into the intersection of Chestnut and Third, he had thrown Monica onto the bottom steps of the staircase. He turned to see a maelstrom of electricity ignite the front yard; beneath the surface at least fifty rats were silhouetted like bacteria suddenly illuminated under a microscope slide. The howling wind covered the sound of the transformer's explosion. The flash ended quickly. The bodies of the electrocuted rats floated and bobbed, then they were swept through the spokes of the gate by the current toward the Mississippi blocks away.

Jordan lifted Monica's lolling head from the third step. Water oozed from her mouth. She was out cold. He shook her. More water bubbled from her lips.

Jordan didn't know CPR, but he did know he must lay her flat. But this seemed wrong. Fighting panic and working fast, he bent her forward, driving a knee into her stomach. He felt a warm wash on his foot. He rammed his knee deeper into her stomach and Monica's whole body rebelled against him, muscles tightening against the torque of his leg.

A flash of lightning caught her face, contorted into the squint-eyed mask of a newborn. He put his lips to hers and exhaled. Half of the breath escaped down her cheek, but suddenly her lips twitched inside his mouth. One of her hands pawed his right shoulder. He brought his mouth away.

She was trying to speak.

"Monica!" Jordan shook her again, rattling her head against the step. Her eyes wouldn't open. Jordan placed one hand on her forehead and carefully forced her eyelids up, revealing glazed whites before her pupils slid into place.

"Stephen!"

Breath returned to her as her mouth opened around that first ragged word.

"He took Stephen!" she gasped.

# 5

"**S**tevie?"

The wind had changed. It was no longer the incessant roar that had lulled him to sleep against Jordan's chest. The sound was deeper, hollowed-out.

"Time to see God, Stevie!"

He jerked at the voice, feeling where the metal fishing line carved into his wrists. He was holding something. He knew he was no longer in his bedroom. He groped for memory—remembering the sudden blow to his temple, thinking the bedroom window had blown in before darkness had enveloped him, bringing him to this familiar voice.

A single slatted window blew inward in a hail of splintered wood. A shadow next to Stephen pitched forward in response. What was under him?

Stephen squirmed. As his chest grazed cold metal, he realized in horror where he was.

He was thirty feet above the ground, bound to one of the bells in the Bishop Polk bell tower. Around him was the racket of the tiled roof, shaken by the howling wind, and the motionless bell.

Stevie. No one had called him Stevie in years.

Brandon backed away from the bell's flank, to which he had bound Stephen with the spool of wire. He looped it around Stephen's legs, which circled around the entire width of the bell, using the last of it to secure Stephen's wrists to the bell's lug nut.

Brandon watched in fascination as wind sucked out the first floor-boards through the window. He stepped back before the boards shifted, revealing a glimpse of the thirty-foot drop into the dark shaft. "Listen to the wind you've brought," he cried.

Stephen opened his mouth to scream, but found himself tasting the bell's flank. He could see Brandon's shirtless shadow in the flickering storm light as he approached the bell. "Brandon . . ." he managed, feeling blood sticky on his lips. He could hear the sound of two more floorboards sucked out the window, the scrape of ceramic tiles peeling from the portico.

"Snake," Brandon said into the wind.

Stephen fumbled for some response and found rage instead. Not the frustrated anger of the unrequited lover, the survivor shredded by grief. This feeling was untapped; it had gone unused during each overheard whisper, each slur against him; it had failed him when a brand was slapped on his back for the rest of his life. It had been wrenched out of him when Greg Darby lured him to the same spot five years earlier and raped him unconscious. This rage washed the heavy sludge of self-pity from his soul.

"If I don't die here, Brandon, I'm going to kill you."

Brandon slammed the empty coil against the bell. It sang. "This is where you're going to see God!" Brandon screamed, with a child's fury. "This is where you killed Greg . . ."

The wind gnawed at the frayed edges of the window before the timbers above it suddenly split. It sounded like the pop of a giant knuckle. The wind's whistle increased in pitch.

"I didn't kill him," Stephen said through clenched teeth, clearly, so the storm would carry it.

"Liar!"

"He killed himself."

"You were waiting the whole time. You had a snake in you, Stephen! You had a fucking snake in you and you wanted it to bite us both, didn't you? You were fucking waiting for him and you know it!" Stephen felt Brandon's hand on his neck, suddenly pulling him off the bell, etching the metal wire deeper into his flesh. Stephen wailed.

Brandon brought his mouth close to Stephen's ear. "Wanna know what God does, Stevie? God owns the devil. And when he made the world, he took a big fucking handful of evil and threw it on the earth. It's everywhere, only it tries to bury itself. In people. It's in you, Stevie. I've known that all my life, and you know it, too. You're a monster and you need food. Greg was a fucking meal to you!"

Brandon clutched Stephen's head six inches from the bell. Stephen's face grimaced. The twine dug into the back of Stephen's neck, blood dribbling across Brandon's fingers.

"The-the real m-monsters . . ." Stephen coughed and spat a thin bolus of blood across Brandon's cheek. ". . . the real monsters are the ones who think they see God . . ."

"Snakes around the columns . . ." Brandon retorted.

Four more floorboards danced out the window. The hole revealed the bottom end of the metal scaffolding that held the three bells in place.

". . . of the temples of salvation . . ."

"You be-better leave now, Brandon . . ."

Outside the wind had stripped the last of the ceramic tiles from the portico's roof, exposing the pliable timbers. The six-foot cross was ripped free from the portico's crown overhead.

"I remove you from the earth. I cleanse the earth . . ."

Rain lashed down on them, funneled from a patch of open sky where the cross had been ripped free. A weak gray light illuminated their faces, inches apart. Their eyes met. Stephen's mouth contorted into a leering smile.

"Fear cannot touch me," Stephen shouted.

He saw the shadow before Brandon did.

Brandon heard the first line of the rhyme and punched Stephen's head into the bell. Stephen felt a shudder of pain in his forehead, but it didn't matter. "It can only taunt me . . ." he cried through clenched teeth.

Then Brandon saw the shadow. He sank to his knees beside the bell. He stared into the darkness at the top of the ladder.

Stephen knew what Brandon beheld: Greg was taking shape.

Several floorboards clattered through the air. The rain swirled down from the opening overhead. The wind buffeted the window's frame. But none of it touched Greg as he climbed into the portico.

"It cannot take me," a voice answered.

The voice was not Greg's.

Meredith Ducote rammed a floorboard into Brandon's left shoulder. Its nail pierced Brandon's skin, nicking the bone beneath before she retracted it. Stephen saw her form, then watched Brandon crawling across the splintering floorboards.

"Just tell me where to go!" she cried.

Meredith brought the board down into the small of Brandon's back. The nail lodged as his body reared up, his arms flailing in the air before he collapsed. She yanked the board from his back. A section of the portico's shell tore free and a jet of wind roared through the interior.

Meredith rocked back onto her heels. As the wind knocked her several steps backward, Brandon righted himself and turned on her. Stephen cried out in warning.

When Brandon saw Meredith, he froze.

"I can either follow . . ." Meredith hissed. "Or stay in my bed . . ." She raised the board and brought it down like a hammer. Brandon's arms went out to block the blow. The nail tore into his open palm. Brandon growled like a rabid dog as he saw his hand was impaled on the floorboard, which was stuck to the timber shell of the portico wall above his head, trapping him there. Meredith grabbed his free hand.

"Say it with me . . ."

"Snake!" Brandon screamed.

"Finish it with me!" Meredith yelled. "I can hold on to the things that I know."

"Snakesaroundthecolumnsofthetemplesofsalvation . . . Snakesaroundthe . . ." Brandon's words were all mania.

"The dead stay dead. They cannot walk. The shadows are darkness . . ."

Stephen saw one of Brandon's legs flex. "Meredith, watch out!" he screamed. Instantly, she swung one hand into Brandon's crotch and closed her fist around his balls. His eyes widened, his body writhing against the trembling wall of the portico, blood dribbling from his impaled hand down his arm.

"And darkness can't talk . . ."

Stephen's screams were suddenly louder. Brandon's eyes fell on hers with weary defeat. "He murdered him . . . Stephen murdered Greg . . ." he tried, his voice careening with panic.

"You're wrong," Meredith said. The floor beneath them quaked, the wall behind Brandon was trembling like a sheet on a laundry line. She backed away from him, steadying herself against the pummeling rain. His gaze followed her, eyes wide with shock. She turned, balancing on the remaining floorboard.

The crack above the window had opened all the way to the portico's crown, scattering patches of gray light around her. Stephen knew there was no way for her to get him down in time. She looked at the vibrating floor underfoot and saw a thin metal bar running beneath the floorboards. Above her, the wind chipped away pieces of battered wood, revealing the bell's metal holdings set firmly within the concrete base of the shaft.

As Brandon howled in incoherent fury, Stephen felt Meredith's hands inching up his arms to the twin strands of wire that bound his wrists to the lug nut. She looped her own wrists under the strands. The twine bit into her wrists.

Brandon was prying at the board that pinned his palm to the wall when the portico cracked. He vanished.

The wind struck Stephen and Meredith with a force that twisted their bodies together. The bell began to sway as they found themselves beneath a sky studded with lightning and roaring with the angry promise of heaven.

Clinging to a lamppost, Jordan believed he was hallucinating as the portico's shell split into two pieces and hovered fifty feet above the ground, before one half collapsed into the seemingly magnetic center they had held for several seconds. The two halves obliterated one another, dissolving into what looked like a mad flock of birds taking flight over the intersection.

Jordan tucked his head to his chest and prayed the debris wouldn't hit him. The lamppost heaved under him and pitched forward, angled from its cement foundation. When his forearms touched the water's surface, he realized the post had tilted almost forty-five degrees.

He looked up. A face stared back at him.

The post's bulb had caved into the chest of a male body, stripped of its clothes by the wind. It took Jordan a moment to realize he was staring at his brother. "Brandon." Jordan's voice was inaudible even to himself.

Brandon couldn't answer. The post keeled farther and Brandon's dangling feet met the rushing surface. As he sank, Brandon stared back at Jordan, his face drowsy and placid.

The post stopped. Jordan watched as Brandon's body slipped off the shattered lamp, the weight of wood pulling him down, his head loose on his shoulders. Jordan clutched to the post, pressing his forehead to the metal, as Brandon's body drifted down Jackson Avenue in an eddy of flotsam.

Jordan lifted his head. The wind had died down. The water spiraled elegantly as it flowed past him. Bumpers of cars were revealed by the abrupt absence of swirling rain. One of Bishop Polk's front doors had been torn from its hinges and sprawled there, looking worn out. And now, the bells were ringing.

Jordan studied the remaining scab of the portico atop the thirty-foot shaft. It looked like a gnawed fingernail. The metal skeleton of the bell's holdings jutted out from the concrete walls. The three bells rocked, out of synch with one another. Impossibly, two forms clung to the left bell: Meredith and Stephen.

Above, flocks of seagulls shrieked and circled, caught in Hurricane Brandy's eye.

Jordan sloshed through the waist-deep water that had flooded the church foyer. The cry of seagulls guided him to an open patch of gray sky, obscured by the skirts of the bells. The ladder was partially intact. Jordan scaled it.

The only recognizable part of Stephen was his face pressed to the metal flank, an oval of pale skin, one cheek and shut eye visible to Jordan as he gripped the last rung of the ladder, several feet below. Twine had trapped him and scored his flesh.

He reached for the metal crossbar, the only remaining piece of the portico floor. He balanced himself with one foot on the ladder's top rung and one hand on the bar, leaning over the thirty-foot drop. *"Meredith!"* he screamed. From below he saw her gripping the top of the bell, her teeth gnawing the twine that looped around the bell's lug nut. Jordan realized she could not hear him. The bell's gongs had deafened her.

Meredith extracted the last coil of twine from the lug nut. She slid down the side of the bell, the end of the twine in her teeth. He watched, giddy, as the twine whipped around the lug nut in a metallic swirl, hitting Stephen's body. Her crotch banged into Stephen's head. His limp body peeled off the bell's flank. Jordan screwed his eyes shut, one arm shot out. He felt the sudden tug of loose twine.

When he opened them he saw Stephen, his body dangling like a rag doll, still bound by the twine, the end of which Jordan held in one tense fist. Above him, Meredith had struck the metal crossbar, her bloodied hands pressed between the bar and her breasts as if she were about to do a series of mad pushups. The weight of her legs pulled her backward across the bar. She swung with both arms holding to the single crossbar, thirty feet in the air.

Stephen's body swayed in the twine net. Jordan gripped the loose strands of twine even as Stephen's weight threatened to pull him off the ladder. Jordan's other hand clung to the ladder's top rung. He knew he could not help Meredith if she fell. He looked up at her gouged wrists.

Meredith let go of the bar.

She fell cleanly down the thirty-foot drop, splashing into the dark water below. Jordan could see the white froth foam up in her wake.

With Stephen dangling from his right arm, Jordan began to descend, holding each descending rung with his left. Halfway down the ladder, he saw Meredith standing in the waist-high water below, arms raised toward him. He continued. Stephen's body rocked in the twine encasement dangling from Jordan's fist.

Jordan lowered Stephen's body into Meredith's arms. When Meredith secured one hand under Stephen's neck and the other under his feet, Jordan jumped into the water beside her.

"Like this!" he cried to her. They held Stephen above their heads, Meredith with both hands on Stephen's shoulders, Jordan with one hand holding Stephen's ankles and the other pressed against the small of his back. Held aloft, the rank and polluted water could not touch Stephen's lacerated flesh.

He swayed on the platform of their arms. The water rose up to their chins. A plastic garbage can slid past Meredith's chest. Somehow they buoyed Stephen out of the building and toward the drowned intersection of Chestnut and Third Street.

Monica Conlin fell to her knees at the sight of Jordan and Meredith carrying home Stephen's lacerated body. They passed through the front gate. Monica waded toward them. The cry of seagulls had died and the wind was picking up again. The eye was leaving New Orleans behind. But Stephen was home.

# 6

Jordan and Meredith sat on the front porch watching the sun rise. As the water ebbed, the front gate emerged inch by inch. Meredith rocked gently, holding her bandaged wrists to her knees. Jordan did not disturb her, but sat several feet away at the porch's far corner. The first light of dawn revealed the devastated neighborhood. Upstairs, Stephen slept with Monica's head to his chest, ear monitoring the rhythm of his strained heartbeat.

"I have to go," Meredith said. She stood unevenly as Jordan nodded. "I have to get Stephen something," she said, then waded through the waist-high water toward the gate, and down Third Street.


Meredith found Angela floating on her back. The turquoise blue of the swimming pool had faded into a muddy green. Angela suddenly reared up when she saw Meredith make her way around the corner of the driveway. She swam to the pool's edge and rose to her feet on the submerged flagstones, her breasts visible through the hospital gown.

Angela gestured and Meredith followed the quick movement of her hand. An oak tree had crashed through the second floor of the guest cottage, its lacerated trunk disappearing through the side wall. Angela shrugged, as if the sight alone would explain why she was floating lazily in the backyard. She had disobeyed Meredith and she was sorry. Her eyes narrowed on Meredith's crudely fashioned bandages. She splashed toward her and took Meredith's hands in hers, studying them intently. Slowly, she lifted her hands to Meredith's head and ran her fingers through Meredith's disheveled hair. She combed it back into place, finding the natural part.

Meredith's sobs finally came to her. Angela embraced her and Meredith cried bitterly into her shoulder.

Angela held her. "I can't remember their faces . . ." she whispered.

Meredith craned her head and gazed at the older woman. Angela's eyes were bright and animated. "I can't remember," she said again, and a faint smile played at her lips.

Meredith nodded, wanting to believe her. "Can you remember anything?"

Angela thought a moment before answering. "El Paso."

Monica found Jordan on the front porch and put a hand on his shoulder. It was the first time she had ever chosen to touched him.

"He's awake," she said. "The wounds aren't that deep. They just bled a lot. If we keep cleaning them he should be fine. If not, then we'll try to get him to the hospital. He's awake, though." Monica summoned the strength to say it. "He's asking for you."

Upstairs, Jordan slid into the bed next to Stephen and tossed the blanket away, studying the cuts and abrasions. Stephen stirred and eased back against Jordan, concealing the wounds he had been examining. Jordan held him tentatively, with one arm draped across Stephen's side.

"Did you see him?" Stephen whispered.

"Yes," Jordan answered, and realized that was all they were ever going to say about Brandon.

A fetid odor of mildew settled in the house. Three days after the storm, they still lacked water and power. Despite the stifling heat, the doors and windows were kept shut. Monica had spotted snakes swimming down Third Street the day after the hurricane. Stephen drifted in and out of sleep. Every couple of hours Monica would walk him to the back porch, lean him against the rail, and allow him to relieve himself into the four feet of water that filled their driveway.

Jordan and Monica cleaned out the house. Monica collected glass shards and wadded paper while Jordan attempted to reassemble the furniture. Most of the rugs could not be salvaged. He threw them out.

On the third day after Hurricane Brandy, Stephen awoke and sat up in bed, alone. He heard the sound of footsteps before he noticed a tattered blue spiral notebook on his desk. It was labeled *Meredith Ducote—Freshman Biology*. Stephen slung one leg to the floor, fervently hoping that the lacerations would not burn again. He eased into the desk chair, flipped open the notebook, and began to read about the first time Greg Darby hit Meredith Ducote.

Jordan cracked the bedroom door. Stephen look up at him briefly and held the notebook so he could see the name on the cover.

Meredith sat on the front porch watching the street take solid form, waiting for Jordan.

# 7

"**A**fter your brother called me, I knew Greg was going to do something to Stephen," Meredith said. Her legs dangled over the edge of the porch, the soles of her bare feet almost touching the muddy water. Jordan leaned against the Doric column next to her. Dread filled him as Meredith continued.

"When we were little, I was the only girl. I was always afraid the boys were going to run off and leave me. So I figured out where everybody's hidden keys were, just in case. Angela always kept one in the geranium pot outside the back door. Monica keeps hers in the flower bed inside the driveway." Meredith paused, took a resolute breath. "The night of Alex's funeral, after your brother hung up on me, I went to Greg's house. No one was home. Andrew was taking Angela's things to the hospital. I took the key, got inside, and went to Greg's room . . ."

Jordan watched as Meredith's eyes went distant. An oak branch splayed across the spokes of the wrought-iron fence directly in front of her, but Jordan knew she was back in Greg's bedroom. "It was a . . . mess," she said. "He'd torn open drawers. Thrown shit everywhere. Obviously he'd been in some kind of a rage. And then I saw the picture. It was on the bed. I had a copy, too. We all did. Your mother took it and gave us all copies. Greg had blacked Stephen out with a marker. That's when I went to look for the gun.

"Greg had always bragged about his dad's gun when we were kids. I remember I used to tell him not to, because of Stephen's dad. But he did anyway, and he used to always say he knew where it was. He'd never tell us, but I think that's because we all knew that if Brandon found out where it was he would go shoot birds or something."

Meredith bowed her head. The mention of Brandon's name had

thickened the air between them. Jordan glanced away, tried not to remember his brother's body wedged on the lamppost, sinking beneath the water.

"I went to his parents' bedroom next. The closet door was open and for a second I thought maybe Greg had torn apart the whole house. But everything was in order except all of Angela's clothes were gone. Andrew had taken them to the hospital with her. I found the gun in the nightstand; it wasn't even hidden."

Jordan straightened against the column. This was getting real.

"I sighed. I remember. I sighed out loud when I saw the gun sitting there. Greg didn't have it. But it only lasted for a second. Because I knew I should probably take the gun myself and find him."

Meredith's jaw went rigid. Jordan heard the gurgle of water past the front porch.

"I was going to the cemetery. And then I heard it."

"The bell. The bells hadn't rung in years. When we were at Bishop Polk everybody used to talk about how fake the bells sounded. It's because they were a recording. Only this sound was real. Metal. I could hear it from outside Greg's house."

"Everyone heard it," Jordan whispered.

"Yeah," Meredith said sharply, "but nobody bothered to figure out what it was. It was Greg slamming Stephen's head into the bell."

Jordan felt his throat constrict. He lifted one hand and massaged his neck. Meredith did not move, her bandaged hands folded across her lap.

"I couldn't see anything. I was holding the gun in front of me. Letting it bump into walls. I ripped the shit out of my pants when I jumped the fence and my leg was bleeding. I didn't know how bad, but I could feel it. And then I heard Greg's voice somewhere over my head and he kept saying, over and over again, 'You wanted me this way!'"

Tears trickled down Meredith's cheeks, but her voice remained even. Jordan watched her, gripping the column.

"Greg was naked. He didn't even hear me. I held the gun in front of me with both hands and I remember not being able to decide whether I was going to look at the muzzle or at him. Stephen was underneath him. I thought Stephen was dead. I had never imagined what Greg was doing to Stephen. I thought if boys were going to fit together that way, then one of them would have to die in the process.

"For a long time I tried to convince myself that's why I did it. That I pulled the trigger as a reflex when I thought he killed Stephen. But that's a lie."

Hot tears blurred her vision.

"Why did you do it, Meredith?" Jordan asked.

"Because we'd been lied to," Meredith said. "Because a part of us would die each day after we started Cannon and Brandon and me and . . . Greg. We lost whatever we had." Meredith paused and wiped her forearm across her nose.

"But not Stephen. Stephen got to keep it. He paid the price. But no matter how hard Brandon and Greg tried to, and no matter how many times I stood back and let them, they couldn't kill that part of Stephen. The part that told me not to be afraid of the rain.

"And Greg was going to take that from him. And I couldn't let that happen."

Meredith's mouth trembled, like a little girl's. "I fired," she said. She brought one hand to her mouth and held it there, breaths whistling through her knuckles.

Jordan stood still. There was no comfort he could offer her. Her crime was hers alone, as it had been for the last five years of her life.

The details of the killing itself she told him dispassionately, like the plot of a novel she had read years before. Greg hadn't seen her, even after she brought the muzzle of the gun to his temple, just above his left ear. This random position had saved her. Without realizing it, she had mimicked the position of a suicide bullet by firing at close range on the left side of the body. The muzzle flare blinded her and the sound rang in her ears. She dropped the gun and it thudded to the portico's floorboards. She moved to Greg and pulled on his shoulders, trying to pry him off of Stephen. After some effort, Greg's body rolled onto the floorboards on its back. Then she noticed the rise and fall of Stephen's back. Meredith took Greg's T-shirt and wrapped it around the handle of the gun before placing the trigger in Greg's hand. With the shirt she wiped the slick puddle of Greg's semen from his belly.

"There was only one way to get Stephen out of there," Meredith went on.

Jordan had moved closer to her. Meredith had not turned to look at him.

"I slid myself underneath him and managed to grab his arms. I pulled them around my neck, and I remember saying over and over again, 'Please, Stephen, please, Stephen.' He didn't make a noise, but I could feel him breathing against my back. To be safe, I took his shirt and tied it around both his wrists, sliding them over my head, so his hands held onto the back of my neck. I had to keep him between me and the ladder. I got his head on my shoulder . . ."

She pointed to where Stephen's head had rested on the nape of her neck.

"He was naked, so I laid him down in the lobby and stole one of the flags off the wall. I wrapped him in it. I went out the front doors. There was no way to get him over the fence. I wasn't even thinking. I carried him home."

Jordan sat down on the porch next to Meredith. Neither of them spoke as they surveyed the ruined neighborhood around them. In the near distance, the remains of the Bishop Polk bell tower jutted up among the splintered oak branches.

"It's all in the notebook," Meredith finally said. She rose from the edge of the porch.

"Where are you going?" Jordan asked.

She lingered on the top of the steps. Faced him for the first time that morning. Her eyes were now dry. "I did what I wanted to do that night," she said.

Jordan nodded in weak agreement.

"You tell Stephen that I love him," she added.

"*You* love him," she ordered quietly before walking down the steps and into the black water.


By dusk, Stephen had read the last pages of Meredith's notebook. When he finished he let out a sound Monica could not interpret when she heard it all the way from her bedroom. She went to his door and found him sitting at his desk, the notebook open in front of him. As he cried, she strode to the desk and picked up the notebook. She read the last words.

> *You told me about what you called the light in the darkness. About how life was neither good nor bad, but a combination of both and occasionally good things pop up in the middle of tragedy, but they still don't make tragedy go away.*

*They can't protect you. They're just light.*

*But what you didn't say is that sometimes, certain people can be a light in the darkness.*

*There are some people in this world who are worth saving when other people decide they shine the wrong kind of light on the wrong kind of things.*

*You have been and will always be my light in the darkness.*

*I love you,*
*Meredith.*

# 8

Jordan awoke to the drone of the National Guard Hummers winding their way through the streets. A week and a half after Hurricane Brandy, the water had receded enough to allow people to return to their homes. At the window, Jordan watched as a Hummer loaded with returning evacuees crunched through the debris over Chestnut Street. New Orleans was coming to life again, in a clamor of engines and propellers.

Trish Ducote knelt on her front porch and tried not to cry as the Hummer pulled off down the street. Her house was intact. Only one of the shutters had been torn free and miraculously the window had not broken. Trish had been almost thirty miles outside New Orleans when she abandoned her car. The stranded evacuees were picked up by National Guard envoys that had rushed them to nearby shelters. She'd spent the past week eating cold red beans and rice in the cafeteria of Destrehan High School, sharing conversations with strangers and clustering around a few television sets, where they all silently watched the aerial footage of a drowned New Orleans, the city built below sea level.

Roger and Elise Charbonnet had left the mausoleum once Brandy passed for good. Without touching, they waded through Green Lawn Cemetery. Roger led Elise all the way to the gates, not waiting for her to catch up or extending an arm to help her. A harbor patrol cruiser ferried them to the Superdome downtown.

When they were bused back to Jackson Avenue, Elise disembarked first, leaving Roger behind in the crush of passengers desperate to see if their homes had survived. She walked back to her house quickly. Roger found her standing in front of the gate of their house, one hand gripping a post. The Charbonnet residence no longer had a roof.

Through the skeletal timbers Elise and Roger could discern the remnants of their bedroom. The mattress and box spring, stripped of their sheets, leaned against the doorframe. Roger realized that there was no possible way he could leave his wife.

The cleaning of Stephen's wounds had evolved from dreaded task to a solemn ritual. Monica handed over the job to Jordan several days after the storm. Stephen lay on the bed. They heard the clatter outside, the hiss of truck brakes. Stephen chuckled as Jordan dabbed the rag down the back of his naked thigh.

"What?"

"You always do that," Stephen murmured.

And then Jordan understood. When he cleaned the wounds, Jordan instinctively followed the path of the twine, from the top right cleft of Stephen's butt to the back of his left thigh.

"The water's gone?" Stephen asked.

"Yeah . . ."

Jordan thought of his parents and paused in his ministrations.

"Where's Mom?"

"She's downstairs. She's turning everything off because if the power comes back on it'll blow the wiring," Jordan said, swabbing the back of Stephen's right knee down his left calf, and then his ankles.

"I can go outside then," Stephen said, sighing. He had not been permitted to leave the house.

Jordan finished, dropped the rag on the bedside table, bent down and nibbled Stephen's earlobe. Stephen laughed.

Jordan found Roger on the front porch with his head propped in his hands. Roger regarded him as if he were a stranger.

"Mom?" Jordan asked quietly from the front walk.

"Inside. Taking it all in, I guess," Roger said, patting into place a few moist strands of hair on his head. "Obviously we won't stay here."

Jordan nodded.

"I assume you won't come with us?" Roger asked.

"I need to be with Stephen now."

Roger glared at Jordan, a look Jordan assumed was hatred. Roger rose, turned, and disappeared through the front door, shaking his head. Jordan waited, hearing the sound of his father's choked crying coming from the welter of demolished walls and broken glass. He gripped the gate, unable to pass through it. The fact that it was destroyed only made the house seem less like his home.


Trish Ducote was planted on the porch, struggling to get the shutters open when she saw the tall blond man walking down Chestnut Street toward her house. She stared at him. "Stephen?" Trish finally managed. "Stephen Conlin?"

Stephen smiled slightly and nodded. Trish shook her head. She had not laid eyes on Stephen Conlin since he was in high school.

"Is Meredith here?"

Trish's face darkened. She remembered the note on the counter. *"House is fine. I'll be fine, too, if you don't try to find me. Love, Meredith."*

Trish shook her head.

Stephen didn't say anything. Trish looked away from him and back to the jammed shutters.

"Thanks, Mrs. Ducote," Stephen said, and turned from the gate.

Stephen was halfway down the block when Trish's voice called after him. "Stephen!"

He halted.

"You've really grown up," Trish said loudly.

She felt immediately ashamed that she had said it.


Angela was asleep when Meredith saw the lights. Blossoming on the side of the interstate, stretching out for miles in a glittering blanket. Meredith reached over and touched Angela's shoulder. Angela stirred and awoke, the lights of Mexico playing across her face.

"El Paso," Angela whispered. She locked eyes with Meredith, desperate to see if Meredith was serious. Years earlier, Andrew Darby had told his wife there was no way in hell they would cross the border, not for a minute. It wasn't on their way.

"Mexico," Meredith responded.

Meredith looked back to the quilt of lights, impossibly close, piled on the roofs of shacks, the fires of oil refineries stretching out through Ciudad Juárez. A glittering star marked the dark presence of mountains. Meredith was no longer sure whether she would tell Angela that she had killed her son.

# Epilogue

October brought the first chill, blotting the summer's lingering heat. In the month since Hurricane Brandy's landfall, seventy thousand dollars had been raised to reconstruct the Bishop Polk bell tower. The shell of the Charbonnet residence had been demolished at the beginning of September and the lot on Philip Street was sold.

Stephen had finished repainting his father's study when the postcard from Meredith arrived. It featured an anonymous beach and a seashell. On the back she had printed, Writing . . . Love, Meredith. He tacked it to the study's bulletin board.

Monica checked for Stephen in the study. He was gone. She noticed that the space reserved for his new desk was directly opposite where Jeremy's had been. She wondered if Stephen had done this consciously. She noticed the postcard. At five forty-five, she left the house, bound for the cemetery.

Halfway through her drive into New Orleans, Elise realized she had forgotten her sweater. She could not go back to get it, as she had promised Monica they would meet at Lafayette Cemetery at six. In her later years, Nanine Charbonnet had returned to her native town, Convent, thirty miles north of New Orleans. Her last home, a two-bedroom cottage, had remained in the family for years, and now Roger and Elise had moved in.

The tombs slanted the sunlight as Elise walked toward the Conlin mausoleum. Monica did not turn as Elise sat down on a cold slab of stone across from Jeremy's tomb. The inscription, once a plate of white marble, was still covered with silt. Elise tugged a pack of Parliament Lights from her pocket. Monica flinched at the sound of her butane lighter.

"Give me one," Monica said.

"I didn't think you smoked," Elise replied. She extracted a cigarette and handed it over. Monica turned and took it, then extended her hand for the lighter. She lit the cigarette without returning the light, avoiding Elise's eyes.

"He said he might tell you," Elise said, her voice low and reverential. Monica faced Elise now. She was not startled. She didn't even seem offended. She seemed impressed that Elise had immediately broached the reason for their meeting.

"Was he drunk?" Monica asked.

Elise locked eyes with her for a beat, then she looked to Jeremy's epitaph. *Beloved Husband, Beloved Father.* She inhaled a whiff of smoke, trying to summon petulance. An apology for what she had concealed for twenty-three years would not come easily now. Too much else had happened to grieve over. Brandon's body had been identified among scores of corpses pulled from drainage canals and pumping stations. Roger had refused to give him a marked grave.

"Why do you think he didn't tell me?" Monica asked, her tone flip.

"I don't know," Elise mumbled before taking a drag off her cigarette. She exhaled, leaned against the tomb. "He said he might tell you to prove a point. That there was no need to be afraid of women like us because we could be fucked just as quickly and just as easily."

Monica's laughter sliced through Elise's chest, cleaving the icy resolve Elise had hoped would get her through this. Monica shook her head slightly, as if aware she was laughing at a crude joke. Elise felt tears salt her eyes. The cigarette in her hand quivered.

But even as her rage surrendered to dread, Elise knew that she deserved Monica's laughter. It dispelled the mystery from that moment in Jeremy Conlin's study when the Mahler had drowned out her moans as Jeremy guided her across the top of his desk, running her skirt over her thighs, growling into her ear. She had foolishly believed he was discovering parts of her she didn't know existed. Any presumption that they had actually made love on that summer afternoon died with Monica's laughter.

"What do you want me to say, Monica?" Elise said, her voice thick with tears.

"Nothing!"

Elise's mouth opened onto silence. She could feel tears trickling down her cheeks. Monica saw them. She did not soften, but she backed away, glanced at Jeremy's epitaph again.

"We never tell them," Monica whispered.

Elise nodded. She forced her lips to move. "We've lost too many children."

Monica looked at her again. Elise saw something in Monica's eyes, a flicker of recognition behind the veil of rage. Elise knew she was surveying her for the last time, weighing whether or not their newfound, fragile friendship would survive this revelation. When Monica turned and moved off down the alleyway, Elise realized that the other woman was already attempting to forget her.

"I'm sorry."

Monica paused. "What for? It's only a memory now."

Elise waited until Monica had rounded a bank of tombs before she let the sobs wrench free from her. She cried for an hour in front of Jeremy's tomb. It was the first time she had visited him.

Monica had easily repaired the picture frame Elise had broken that afternoon more than two decades before. She had glued the wooden sides back together and kept the picture on her nightstand. In the photo, she and Jeremy smiled in front of the Reno wedding chapel where they were married before a lattice altar strung with plastic flowers. She angled the picture so she could see it from bed.

Down the hallway, Stephen emerged from the shower, the towel around his waist failing to conceal the red scars that striped his skin like the map of a road . . . only without a beginning or end. Jordan flipped over Meredith's postcard and examined the postmark as Stephen slid into bed next to him.

"Mexico?" Jordan asked, replacing the card on the nightstand.

"They're not fading," Stephen said.

"They probably won't. They don't hurt anymore, do they?"

"Sometimes. At weird times, though. Like in the middle of the night I'll wake up and they won't hurt but I can feel them."

Jordan switched off the light. "That'll probably never stop," he whispered. "You'll probably always feel them."

Underneath the comforter, Jordan traced the route of the scars across Stephen's chest. Stephen let out an easy breath as Jordan's hands glided down to his stomach. Stephen turned onto his side, as he had learned to do, and Jordan nestled against his back, mouth to the nape of Stephen's neck. They slept like two halves cut from the same stone, one floor beneath the room where Jeremy Conlin and Elise Charbonnet had conceived Jordan on a summer afternoon in 1976.

Monica prayed for sleep. The wedding picture would remain on her nightstand as penance for every day she did not inform Stephen and Jordan that they shared a father.

Stephen now dreamed in music, a clamor of remembered voices, a density of souls in which no individual spoke the truth, but in which the accumulated layers of lies and loss gave way to a truth rare and great and capable of stripping wounds from a part of the world.

In Stephen's dreams, Meredith sat beneath a star-studded sky free of clouds, her legs tucked to her chest, gazing out at open ocean but hearing the resonant fall of remembered rain.

# Acknowledgments

Stories belong solely to the author. First novels do not. To the following I give part-ownership of A *Density of Souls*:

Sid Montz and DeLauné Michael can consider themselves the proud parents of this novel by providing with me a format in which to present the short story that was its inspiration. The Spoken Interludes reading series continues to be a literary spark on a Los Angeles landscape that glitters with stories that often go untold. DeLauné Michael welcomes these stories, as she did me, with a grace and dignity I can only attribute to our shared Louisiana heritage.

Sid Montz's continued friendship has guided me toward the subjects that compel me and convinced me that the friends we hope for, but never expect to find, will find us in the most unlikely of places and take us on a journey toward the locus of what makes our dreams worth turning into stories.

I was blessed with friends who read this novel in the earliest stages and gave me the courage to continue. They are the brothers and sisters of A *Density of Souls*. Julia DiGiovanni, you have lead me through the darkest times reflected fictionally in these pages and you gave me courage to believe that such times could be the stuff of stories—stories that you desperately requested the final pages of, even as I was still writing them. Todd Henry, your fondness for certain lines compelled me to preserve them even through the most stringent of copy edits. Leigh Butler, your voice of criticism was a necessary light that pierced the delusional haze that can envelop a beginning writer who is not yet aware that he is writing for himself only if what he writes is of relevance to others.

Lynn Nesbit gave me her faith. She knew me as a child and her belief that I could become an adult capable of turning this story into a novel will make me forever, yet happily, indebted to her.

My editor, Jonathan Burnham, clearly saw the landscape of this novel through the first glimpse I offered him. With a dedicated and persistent guidance, he led me to explore its territory further, find its truth, and then offered me the chance to lay it out before the reader.

David Groff coaxed out this novel's necessary language and cadence with the gentlest of touches. Kristin Powers created imagery that represented the interplay of light and darkness which set the novel's characters on their course through the landscape I was allowed to let them inhabit.

John Craft Crane (1978–1995), may you have been brought to the peace I have found in completing this novel.

The following is an excerpt from Christopher Rice's new novel, *The Snow Garden*, to be published in February 2002. *The Snow Garden* is a story of sexual menace and murder on a snowbound university campus. As in *A Density of Souls*, Rice explores the dynamic within a tightly knit group of young people driven by obscure desires, and haunted by sexual uncertainty and fears.

# PART ONE

# Atherton

*Not slowly wrought, nor treasured for their form*
*In heaven, but by the blind self of the storm*
*Spun off, each driven individual*
*Perfected in the moment of its fall.*

—HOWARD NEMEROV, "Snowflakes"

# One

I

The neon yellow sign atop the Yankee Savings & Trust Building flickered to life at just past three in the afternoon, its light-sensitive timer tripped by the advancing tide of gray clouds that rolled in off the Atlantic, casting downtown into a gloomy winter shade. Since the building's completion in 1984, the old joke for the "townies" who lived at the base of the hill was that the tallest and newest building in Atherton's meager skyline liked to send everyone home early during winter by announcing nightfall several hours prematurely. By five thirty, the last of the insurance adjusters and bank tellers made the short walk to the train station where they would board commuter rails that would carry them as far as Boston and Connecticut, leaving behind a downtown that would become an empty stage set of art deco entrances and sidewalks blown clean of litter by increasingly ferocious winds off the bay.

As the city below drained of life, the crown of Atherton Hill glowed with a corona of light. A verdant green swell in summer months, winter stripped the hill to a scabbard of skeletal branches spider-webbing between Gothic spires and Victorian rooftops. Streets snaked up the hillside toward the university campus, begging for a blanket of white they might not be granted. The waters of the bay usually warmed potential flakes into dreary sheets of rain.

By seven o'clock, on the evening of November fourteenth, fat flakes filled the halos of the streetlamps lining the paved banks of the Atherton River, a black vein curving its way around downtown. The snow fell with rare and determined force, clinging to the pavement with a refusal to melt. Shouts erupted across the crown of the hill. Dorm room windows were raised, and students burst from the library headed for the nearest cafeteria and its piles of trays that could be used as sleds. Almost an hour later, the Hill had quieted, the continuing snow blanketing the campus with an eerie hush. At the base of the hill, squealing brakes and an abrupt shatter of glass broke the silence.

II

"Phil?"

Headlights danced across his three rearview mirrors in succession. The brake pedal groaned and stuttered under his foot and the Tercel almost went into a skid. He threw out his arm, hooking one of his wife's shoulders and driving her back against the passenger seat. There was an abrupt silence and he felt as if the world had suddenly been put on pause.

Then he saw it: the Volvo that had come out of nowhere, arcing silently through the air fifteen feet from the angled nose of their car, a torn section of guardrail hooked to one of the Volvo's shattered head-lights. It vanished as quickly as it had appeared.

"Oh, shit . . . Phil! Shit!"

Silence again except for their own gasping breath.

Where the hell did it go? he thought. It just disappeared.

But he knew better.

When he kicked open the passenger door, his wife bucked against her seat belt, one arm reaching for his. But he slammed the driver's side door shut behind him, extinguishing the dome light. His wife became a dark shadow behind the windshield, still pulling frantically at her seat belt. He jogged breathlessly to the torn opening in the guardrail, went to brace himself against it and then withdrew his hands suddenly like a man about to get his fingerprints on a murder weapon.

Black water embraced the Volvo's upended taillights. Escaping air out the shattered rear window bobbed a flotilla of rent metal and ice. And after the shrill shriek of the brakes and the shattering glass, now the only sound was the disgusting, rhythmic thump of the air pushing itself out of the Volvo and to the river's surface in cartoonishly large eruptions. Without thinking, he turned.

Colonial Avenue was a dark swath cutting down the hill to where his Tercel sat angled in the intersection. To his right, downtown was a warren of shadows. No headlights in either direction. He was startled by the sound of the door alarm and turned to see his wife running toward him across the thirty-foot-long bridge, one arm raised over her bent head, trying to shield herself from the driving snow.

He met her halfway, grabbing both of her shoulders, practically lifting her off her feet for an instant as her shocked eyes met his.

"Get in the car!"

Could she smell it? He certainly could. And Jesus Christ, hadn't she been the one who made the crack at dinner? *One more glass and we'll be toasted.*

"We have to call someone!"

"Just get in the car—"

"Phil, this is insane!"

But he had already taken hold of her shoulders, was driving her back toward the Tercel. She tried one last time, whipping her body around against his bracing arm, grabbing at his forearm with both hands, as if trying to get a peek over his shoulder at the Volvo which was now. . . . He didn't dare turn around.

He threw her against the door and her chest hit the roof of the car with a sickly thud, her breath coming out of her with a groan. And this time when she turned, her eyes landed on him, not what might be going on beyond the rail, and he saw equal parts disgust and fear. Was he really going to make them do this?

"We'll pull over. We'll use a pay phone."

The apology in his voice sounded pathetic and he pondered exhaling right into her face so she could smell the one and a half bottles of Cabernet Sauvignon. But she was already climbing back into the car, and by the time he joined her, she had rolled her head to one side, gazing out the passenger window and the hole punched through the guardrail, crying silently.

"I'll pull over."

He turned the key in the ignition and the entire car screamed before he realized he hadn't bothered to kill the engine.

### III

Kathryn Parker couldn't move her feet. She looked down and saw they were wedged under the wooden crossbar of the railroad tracks. She heard the low, mournful moan of a locomotive's horn somewhere in the distance, and then the tracks stretching out on either side of her erupted in a concert of metal against wood. She was blinded by the headlight of an approaching train, roaring toward her out of darkness that had been immaterial only seconds before. Her arms went up to stop the inevitable.

She awoke to the theme from *Shaft.*

Strange shapes drifted across the far wall of her dorm room and she sat up, groping for the knob on the halogen lamp next to her bed. The torchère sent a halo of light across the ceiling, its panels still scarred by the design of beer bottle caps that had been embedded in them on the day she moved in. Flakes fell past the window, casting their shadows on the cinderblock wall on April's side of the room. Now that the roar of her nightmare had retreated, she could make out the persistent and grating music of Stockton Hall, a pulsing four-story beehive of disconnected adolescents announcing their new identities with stereos turned too loud, shouted punch lines followed by forced laughter. Next door, the sounds of *Shaft* gave way to televised conversation and she remembered that the engineering freaks were holding their weekly *Babylon 5* party. April had been the first one to point out that white Jewish boys from outer Boston seemed to have a propensity for all things Superfly. She didn't know how she could sleep through it all.

It was Randall's story that had caused her nightmare, and she reached for it where it lay on her desk.

*The town of Drywater, Texas exists because a woman named Elena Sanchez was killed by a train.*

Randall Stone was her best friend at Atherton—maybe her *only* friend—and now he had managed to infiltrate her dreams thanks to a short story she could only describe as bizarre.

*Elena's only son Ricky didn't find this out until he was thirteen.*

She dropped the story to her desk and swung her legs to the floor, padding barefoot across the threadbare rug April had bought only a week earlier, and across the chilly linoleum to the poor excuse for a vanity set into the wall between the room's two closets.

Since arriving at Atherton University, her dreams had become increasingly bizarre and she had developed the odd habit of checking herself in the mirror after every one to see if nightmares left any visible traces on her face. She raked one hand back through her sandy blonde hair, revealing her wide eyes, still brown and no, not *that* bloodshot. Her fingers instinctively traced a path down to where her hair hit just above her shoulder, searching for split ends. She caught herself, forcing her hand down to her side, staring dead on at a pretty enough girl who had stopped being called mousy once she entered high school, whose breasts had exploded at fifteen before refusing to expand another cup size. After several seconds of the masochistic exercise, she found herself unable to turn away from her own image. The hand she had forced down earlier traveled back to her throat. Even as she told herself to stop, her fingers were prodding the soft flesh at the top of her neck, trying to find the lump of her lymph nodes. Bigger than yesterday? Bigger than the day before that?

She clasped her hands in front of her face, breathing into them.

Was it the nightmare that had left her this shaken, or was it the reality that this compulsion had not left her as quickly as she thought it would? How many more test results would have to come back before a mild sore throat could be just that, a fucking sore throat?

The door flew open and she backed away from the vanity as if she had been caught fondling herself. She expected Randall—he had stopped knocking long ago—but it was April who shoved her way through the door. She was bundled in her favorite leather jacket with the faux fur collar, black braids flecked with white flakes. "It's snowing!" she announced flatly, before letting her book bag slide off one shoulder to the floor with a thud.

"How was the meeting?" Kathryn asked, standing awkwardly as April got down on all fours and dove headfirst into her closet, two feet deep with a tattered curtain instead of a door.

"I need a beer."

She tossed a pair of Gucci boots out behind her, which landed at Kathryn's feet.

"April?"

April rose, shoving the curtain aside on its rod. "Did you know there was a Black national anthem?" She tore several hangers from the rack before depositing the pile of shirts onto her extra-long twin. "No, I didn't," Kathryn answered, realizing that April's worst fears about attending a meeting of the Afro-American Student Alliance had been confirmed.

"It was like the first day of high school. I walk into the center and the only person that would even talk to me is Marcel. And you want to know what he told me after the meeting? It doesn't matter that his mother's Irish and his father's black. But with me, see, that's a problem, because all the women there think I'm going to steal all the good men. Good black men who really want white women. How's that for unity?"

April froze, her back to Kathryn. "Did you tell them you were a dyke?" she asked with as much humor as she could muster.

April's laugh was strained. But at least she had responded. It was a reliable joke. In the first week of living together, Kathryn had gone from calling April a lipstick lesbian to a Neiman Marcus lesbian. "Screw them, April. Give the GLA a try. Trust me. I went with Randall once. They're hurting for patent leather and side-zip jeans."

"Great," April responded. "And in a month I'll be out on the green trying to turn dykes into Girl Scouts. Or Girl Scouts into dykes. No thanks. Politics isn't my calling anyway."

April dug into her jacket pocket and removed a crumpled pink flyer which she handed to Kathryn. Kathryn unfolded it as she crossed to her side of the room. Andy Warhol's face stared up at her, superimposed on top of a spiral design that looked like it had been designed by a third-grader.

"Burton House?" Kathryn asked incredulously. "The literary frat?"

"They don't card. And we're going. So get dressed."

"These are the losers that march a pledge naked on the green and make him do tequila shots while they dance around in llama costumes, right?"

"Kathryn, who are you to talk? You've been napping since we got here."

Kathryn tossed the flyer aside and fell back onto her mattress with a groan. "I've got work."

"Waiting for Randall is not work!" April shot back. "Besides, I think he's going."

"No, he isn't," Kathryn responded, sitting up suddenly.

April shot her a look. "Why? Because he didn't clear it with you first?"

Kathryn rolled her eyes. April's suspicions of Kathryn's deep affection for Randall had become old hat. But truth be told, Kathryn didn't know where Randall was going that evening. She had dropped by his room earlier, daring to knock even though it might result in a face-to-face with Randall's roommate, Jesse, and maybe whatever completely naïve freshman he was bagging that evening. But both Randall and his walking penis of a roommate had been out and she was greeted only by the sight of those inane construction paper signs announcing the room's occupants in bright letters cut of neon colored construction paper. The RA had taped them to the doors of every room on the first day of orientation, but most students had removed or disfigured theirs. Randall's and Jesse's signs remained intact, as if highlighting the odd pairing that lived together on the other side of the door.

With a jolt she realized April had been talking to her for the last minute.

". . . guy looked like Paul Bunyan on crack but we both took a flyer and Randall said he might be going." April turned suddenly. Kathryn hoped she didn't look caught, but April saw something in her eyes because she crossed to Kathryn's bed and sank down on it. "If you don't snap out of this I'm going to buy those special light bulbs I read about. The ones that simulate sunlight for little West Coast girls like you who turn suicidal during winter."

"I'm from San Francisco. But nice try."

April smiled, pleased that Kathryn was sparring with her again. "April, don't you remember my rule about frat parties?"

"Oh please. It's a *literary* frat, Kathryn!"

April rose, shaking her head before her gaze landed on Kathryn's desk. She rose and crossed to it, picking up Randall's story. "What's this?" she asked. Feeling a strange stab of panic, Kathryn rose from the bed, too. "I didn't know Randall wrote stories," April said distantly. No sooner had she flipped the first page than Kathryn had tugged the story out of her hands gently. April looked to her with a surprised, slightly offended smirk.

"Sorry. I just don't know how many people he wants reading it."

"Can you tell me what it's about?" April sounded slightly offended, and when Kathryn looked up from the story on her lap, she realized that despite her wisecracks that implied Kathryn felt something deeper than friendship for her best friend, April was also intimidated by the strength of their bond.

Kathryn managed a slight laugh. The story was so bizarre it defied instant description. "It's about this kid who grows up in this small town in Texas—"

"Randall's from New York."

"That's why it's a story. Do you want to know what it's about or not?"

April rolled her eyes and returned to her bed.

"When he's a little kid, his mom gets killed in this car accident. Her car stalls out at this railroad crossing and she gets hit and like dies instantly. Then the county finally decides that it should put up gates and warning lights because she's like the ninth person to get killed in that spot. So then . . ." April was holding up a collared shirt that looked like it was made out of aluminum to her chest and examining herself in the full-length mirror. "April, are you listening?"

"Uh-huh."

Kathryn knew she was pre-med and had little patience for fiction beyond Michael Crichton.

"All right, so when the boy turns fifteen he finds out that this entire town he grew up in only exists because the county put up the gates and people finally thought it was safe to live near the tracks. Basically, his mother had to get killed before anyone would build his home-town. So the kid just . . . snaps. And one night, he derails the train."

Startled, April turned.

"How?" she asked, her sense of logic obviously offended.

"He saws through some of the crossbars."

April's eyebrows arched.

"I don't think he really means to do it. I think you're supposed to believe it's an accident."

But even she wasn't sure. The descriptions of propane tanks lying in the smoldering cavities of Airstream trailers had been too emphatic, demonstrating a love of fire even as it consumed humans, and more than that, a kind of rage she had never seen Randall Stone exhibit in day-to-day life. Now, the five-page story had a dizzying effect and she slid open her desk drawer and deposited it inside. When she turned, April was studying her, seeming to have sensed the strange spell the story had cast on her.

"What's a Warhol party, anyway?"

"I don't know." April brightened at Kathryn's first sign of surrender. "Drugs?"

"One condition."

"Here we go!"

"If Jesse Lowry shows up, then I'm out of there."

April lifted both hands in a gesture of defeat. "Fine."

## IV

Eric Eberman wasn't sure what had awakened him: the mournful wail of the siren carried by the wind that was buffeting the walls of the house, or the feel of the boy's finger tracing a slow path down the center of his chest before circling one nipple. The bedroom window was rattling in its frame and outside tree branches jerked in the wan halo of light from the street, their shadows dancing over Randall's face, hiding and then revealing his pale blue eyes and his slight smile.

"I have to go," Randall whispered.

He bent down as if to give Eric a formal kiss on the cheek, and in response Eric curved an arm around his shoulders and brought the young man's body on top of his. Randall let out a gentle, almost placatory laugh before his head came to rest on Eric's chest. Most of the sounds that came out of Randall Stone seemed strangely adult given his soft, boyish features: full lips and baby fat padded cheeks that could transform from a pout to a smile in a second, a jawline that added years to his face when tensed in anger.

Eric allowed his hands to wander down Randall's naked back. Wondering how long he could let his fingers traverse the smooth flesh before the first stab of guilt would come, that sudden weight that yanked him down from the delirious high that came from freely touching what had previously been taboo.

Randall let out a labored breath and brought one fist to rest against his head as if he were about to return to sleep. But when Eric's fingers touched the first scabbed scar on the back of his thigh, Eric could feel the young man tense a bit, and then think twice, before forcing himself to go lax.

"Do they hurt?"

"Never," Randall answered.

"I'm sure they did at the time."

Randall grunted slightly as if to say he couldn't remember.

"How did you . . ."

"My mom was preparing for this big dinner party. I was three and she put me up on the counter so I could watch. I barely remember . . ." Randall paused as if trying to summon the recollection. "I just remember this entire pan going up in flames. It was like this big curtain of fire."

The first time Eric had asked about the burns covering Randall's legs his description had been more vivid. The pan had tipped. His mother had screamed when she knocked it over. Three-year-old Randall had blacked out the moment he saw his legs burning.

"I thought you blacked out."

Randall lifted himself off Eric's chest.

"I must have." He kissed Eric's forehead gently. "Because I don't remember any pain."

Outside, the first siren was joined by a second in discordant chorus.

Randall slid out from Eric's arms and swung his legs to the floor. He reached for his pack of Dunhill Lights on the nightstand and extended one to Eric. Eric didn't need to shake his head "no." Randall knew he wouldn't smoke. But of course, their silent and shared joke was that the man who had just cheated on his wife with one of his male students wouldn't be caught dead with a cigarette in his mouth. Randall lit it and crossed to the bedroom window. Eric saw the snow for the first time, framing Randall as he stood naked in front of the glass, one arm braced against the panes over his head where a slow curl of smoke crept from his fingers through the street light's frail glow.

"Where are you going?" Eric asked.

"A party."

"So I was just a pit stop."

Surprised, and no doubt amused, Randall turned from the window.

"Are you asking me to stay?"

"She's not coming back."

"I know." Randall returned his attention to the fat flakes falling with determined force past the window.

"Sometimes I think she might stay," Eric added, unnerved by Randall's silence.

"That would be easy, wouldn't it?"

"What do you mean?"

"I mean it would be easier than leaving her."

Silence fell as Eric realized they had wandered dangerously close to forbidden territory, and he felt the urge to appropriate one of the few sayings of his generation Randall frequently used: Don't go there.

"You made the rule yourself, Eric. Can't spend the night, remember?"

"We have rules?"

Randall's only response was an amused exhalation of breath that couldn't qualify as a laugh.

"It seems more real with rules. Otherwise all we are is a bunch of stolen moments lined up in a row. Both of us are too afraid to actually give this a name, and when it ends, both of us will spend the rest of our lives trying to figure out the best ways to call it a mistake. It's not fair to me when you think about it."

"Why is that?"

"Because I'll live longer than you."

"What makes you think that?"

Randall turned from the window, no longer a softly lit profile. A dark shadow staring back at him. The sound of Randall's breathy laughter startled him. Randall's shadow moved to the chair draped with his clothes. By the time he heard the tinny rattle of Randall's belt buckle sliding to his waist, Eric spoke again.

"Randall."

He could see Randall's head turn.

"I'm asking you to stay."

Randall was still for a second before he moved to the foot of the bed, crawling across it on all fours until his mouth was inches from Eric. Eric didn't move. Randall was still shirtless, his jeans unbuttoned. His gelled and spiked hair was slightly mussed and matted from being twisted against the pillow. He stared at Eric, eyes bright, teeth sinking slowly into his lower lip, and Eric felt his stomach tighten with anticipation. And then Randall slowly shook his head "no."

"No. I like you better when you don't get everything you want."

Randall's kiss was brief but firm and Eric fought the urge to lean in and draw the boy's tongue out of his mouth. Randall's weight left the mattress and Eric slouched back into the pillows, rolling over onto one side as Randall left him alone with the mournful song of several sirens which no longer seemed to be approaching or departing but had joined together in a consistent, off-key wail that was impossible to locate because of the distorting wind.

V

"Want to cut through the Elms?"

"Shut up, April."

"They're a good shortcut if you're not loaded. Or you don't have an overactive imagination."

The snow was driving and they were forced to walk with their shoulders hunched. Kathryn could hear sirens coming from the city below the hill. April had brought her jacket up over her neck. Kathryn shot a glance at the dark expanse of suggestive shadows to their left. To bypass it they had to walk through residential streets.

"I don't get it," Kathryn said.

"What?"

"How much money did they spend to build the Tech Center?"

"Loads, probably."

"And they still haven't managed to build on the Elms?"

The trees were thinning out and up ahead the four houses fringing Fraternity Green were fishbowls of light. Strobe lights inside Burton House cut stained glass shapes across the snow-blanketed lawn. "You think they should put a dorm there just because it gives you the creeps."

"No, it's just weird that Michael Price can't get his hands on a piece of prime real estate."

"Please. Be grateful. If someone doesn't stop that jerk, he's going to coat the entire campus in chrome!"

Michael Price was one of Atherton's most prominent alumni. The world-renowned architect had made a point of bringing cold and sterile modern architecture to his alma mater, which students and faculty alike found glaringly inappropriate for a predominantly Gothic campus.

"You know the Pamela Milford story, right?" April asked. Kathryn shook her head "no." They were steps away from Burton House and the bass pounding of disco was already audible. "I think it was the '80s. She wandered out of some party here, drunk off her ass, stumbled into the Elms and drowned."

"How did she drown?"

"There's some kind of creek, I think."

"All the more reason to raze it."

On the front porch of the house, Kathryn looked back to the Green.

"He might be inside. Can we just go in?"

April tugged on her shoulder.

Inside, they were swallowed by the shoulder-to-shoulder throng clogging the front hallway. The living room had been transformed into a poor man's Studio 54. Every other dancer wore a neon-colored wig and a Warhol film was being projected onto the ceiling. A rail-thin boy done up in drag shoved a tray of Jell-O shots in their face. April took one, shot it and then handed one to Kathryn.

"I told you they didn't card!"

"What's in this?" Kathryn asked the drag queen.

"X," he shouted back, before vanishing into the adjacent dance floor.

April brought one hand to her mouth. "He was probably kidding," Kathryn said, as she dropped her shot onto the stair above her head.

"Whatever. If I'm still awake in four hours, cuddling up against you in bed and stroking your hair, then these freaks are going in front of the Disciplinary Council!"

Kathryn hooked her by the shoulder. "Let's find Randall."

The kitchen was as crowded as the rest of the house, but Kathryn spotted an open back door. A hand slapped her ass. When she turned she saw April several steps behind her, and whirled to face the offender. Tim Mathis grinned back at her, raising dimples. His cherubic cheeks had the blush of too many drinks and to an ignorant observer it might have looked like the short, stocky peroxide blond with the bicycle chain around his neck was making an ill-advised pass. That illusion was broken when Tim threw both arms skyward with a squeal before enfolding Kathryn in a sloppy embrace. "It's my favorite couple!"

"Have you seen Randall?" Kathryn asked as she pried herself free.

"Nope. No sign of the Ice Queen. But his *roommate* is certainly here, though!" Tim said, exaggerating the word roommate with a sexual suggestiveness that turned Kathryn's stomach. "He's out on the dance floor bumping and grinding with some twelve-year-old."

"Who?" Kathryn asked, before she could stop herself.

"Someone who doesn't know any better," April cut in, grabbing one of Kathryn's shoulders.

"What's the guy's deal anyway? Randall wouldn't give me any of the dirt. Is he a member of the spur posse or something?" More drunken guests were shuffling into the kitchen and Kathryn was being pressed up against Tim's chest. April's hand didn't leave her shoulder, ready to pull Kathryn away from a conversation she knew Kathryn didn't want to have. "I mean, don't get me wrong. Jesse Lowry is a Bruce Weber photo waiting to be *snapped*, but forgive me for thinking that a man who sleeps with that many women doesn't have something to prove!"

"Have you quit smoking yet?" April asked her.

"No."

"Let's go have one. I can't breathe in here."

"No, I wasn't talking. Really," Tim cut in. "And aren't you a med student?"

"Nice try. Biomedical ethics. And aren't you a music major?"

"No!"

"Then why don't you try talking without *singing!*"

"You're just pissed because you're a dyke."

"I'm also black. Which fills me with rage. Kathryn, cigarette!"

"No, no. Not so fast!" Tim grabbed Kathryn's other shoulder. "Seriously, Kathryn, now I know how you and Randall are. You two probably did the whole finger-pricking, sharing blood thing. And I hate to be the first one to tell you but I think there might be more going down behind that door when you're on the other side . . ."

"No offense to you or your kind, Tim, but Jesse Lowry is as heterosexual as they come," April cut in.

"Bullshit. He's sexual. When are you girls ever going to learn the difference?"

Kathryn guessed that Tim had had no idea how much his flip comments had disturbed her, but the hand on her shoulder had begun to grip and pull. "Maybe you can interview Jesse for your column, Tim," she managed.

"Screw that. I'm about to quit. They think if they make me a news editor then I'll stop trying to rile shit up. I mean, do you guys even read the *Atherton Herald*? It's like three pages long and the major headline is always something real scintillating like, 'Sophomore Plants Tree.'"

Kathryn laughed.

"Have I told you I'm claustrophobic?"

"Jesus, April. All right. Tim, if you see Randall tell him I'm looking for him."

"Yeah, right. Like I ever see Randall anymore," Tim managed, raising his plastic cup in a sarcastic toast as April dragged Kathryn toward the open back door.

On the patio, smokers shivered in huddles. Trash cans lined the back wall spilling flattened beer cases.

"That was rude," Kathryn finally said.

"The guy bugs me. He talks about the *Herald* like it was the *Washington Post* and he's just trying to milk you for info on Randall with all that Jesse bullshit. He needs to move on."

Kathryn was silent, knowing that April had dragged her away from Tim solely because he had mentioned Jesse's name. And it wasn't just because Kathryn happened not to like her best friend's fanatically arrogant, albeit incredibly attractive roommate. The one time Kathryn had voiced her opinions on guys who sleep with a different girl every other night and refuse to call any of them back, April had accused Kathryn of being a puritan.

"Are you rolling yet?" Kathryn asked.

"Shit. It's Svet."

"Who?"

"Svetlana."

Kathryn followed April's frightened stare to where one of April's previous girlfriends of the moment stood smoking next to a trash can, shooting slant-eyed glances around the patio as if any number of the other guests might jump up and try to oppress her.

"Is that Abba?"

"I told you not to call her that. You and Randall need to start learning people's names. You're sociopaths."

The girl had claimed to be Swedish royalty, so rather than risk embarrassment in attempting to pronounce her name, Kathryn and Randall had agreed to nickname her after the famous Swedish singing group.

"How royal is she?"

"I have to talk to her."

"Why? You dumped her last month."

"That's why I have to talk to her. It's like noblesse oblige. Wait here."

"For what?"

But April was already crossing the patio. Kathryn turned, instinctively scanning the other guests to make sure no one was staring at the girl who had just been left standing awkwardly by herself.

Where the hell was Randall?

She shoved her way back inside. There was no sign of Tim in the kitchen, so she moved into the front hallway. She stopped in the doorway to the living room, scanning the dance floor and narrowing her eyes against the flashing strobe lights. There were plenty of blond heads, some with the same military-short buzz cut that Randall sported. But none of them belonged to Randall.

When her eyes met Jesse Lowry's, her breath came out in a startled hiss.

He was halfway across the living room and his dance partner was a rail-thin brunette who clung to Jesse's broad frame as if she were in a drunken swoon. They were engaged in a slow, swaying embrace completely out of synch with the uptempo disco. Jesse wore his UCLA baseball cap, with the bill shading his eyes from the flashing strobe lights, but Kathryn could make out his slight, suggestive smile; a smile that implied Kathryn had been watching Jesse for hours. The cap was a permanent fixture and she guessed his hair was dark under it. He wore a tight, cable-knit sweater which accented the broad swells of his chest. Most girls went weak in the knees—not unlike his current dancing partner, and chosen one-night stand—when Jesse bothered to look their way. Kathryn had trained herself to react with a mixture of disgust and suspicion.

After several seconds of this icy eye contact, Kathryn saw that it wasn't alcohol that had turned the girl in Jesse's embrace into a limp noodle. One of Jesse's hands disappeared behind the unbuttoned, slightly extended waistline of the girl's jeans, and she rocked up onto her toes, trying to bring her mouth to Jesse's before her intended kiss turned into a defeated gasp against his cheek.

Jesse withdrew his hand from the girl's pants. Kathryn left the doorway right before Jesse brought his finger to his mouth.


VI


When he returned home from the department meeting that evening, it had still been light out. Eric descended the stairs to the pitch-dark first floor, where the view out the living-room windows glowed brighter than anything inside the house. Parked cars along Victoria Street sat beneath layers of white and the snowfall had thinned to frail flakes that danced on their descent; the evening's blow had turned into a dusting.

He wasn't sure what prevented him from turning on any of the lights. Randall was long gone and his paranoia was probably just that. But he crossed to the gas fireplace in the living room without flicking a switch. With a flick of the wrist, he turned on the gas and lit it with the fireplace lighter, the flames catching with a sudden whoosh as they punched through the plastic, charred coals. The firelight was too weak to illuminate the framed prints on the walls and they looked like hanging patches of deeper black.

Halfway to the kitchen, something hard banged his knee and he stepped back, realizing he had walked into the liquor cabinet door, which Lisa had left standing open. Angrily, he pushed it shut before realizing that he was hardly in any position to curse his wife's forgetfulness. Never mind that Lisa had spent the last three years of life fomenting scotch and Darvon as staples of her diet, he could still taste Randall in his mouth.

In the kitchen, he flicked on the overhead light, glancing at the phone. Lisa had left one of her usual notes, they were also cursory and by now unnecessary.

"Went to Paula's . . . Paula had a bad week. Back Mon. Prob Late."

He had popped open the fridge when the phone rang, startling him.

He turned and crossed to the phone. His hand was almost to the receiver when his eyes landed on the note, written on the banana-shaped stationery usually reserved for grocery lists. Instead of picking up the phone, he picked up the note, raising it closer to his face even though he had no trouble reading it at all.

I SAW. I KNOW.

His breath didn't catch, it simply stopped. Then a painful stab in his chest reminded him to breathe, and when he sucked in his first breath he realized the phone must have been on its tenth ring.

"Hello?"

"Is this Eric Eberman?"

An unfamiliar female voice, its tone clipped and professional.

"Sir, is this . . ."

"Yes. Who is this?"

"My name is Martha Kellerman, sir. I'm afraid I have some bad news."

"Lisa . . ." There was no shock or urgency in his voice. He had answered on instinct.

"Your wife has been in an accident."

He looked down at the note he held in one hand. The urge to tear it in two struck him with such sudden force that he almost dropped the phone. Instead, he opened the nearest drawer with one hand and slid it inside, shutting it slowly so as not to be heard on the other end. By the time the woman was explaining that a patrol car was on its way to pick him up, Eric remembered the wail of sirens which had only come to a stop twenty minutes earlier.

## VII

Burton House shook with the bass thud of disco. Tim rested his head in both open palms as Kathryn fished a cigarette for him out of her jacket pocket. He took it with a weak smile and popped it into his mouth, before she lit it for him.

"This kills, you know?" he managed after exhaling his first drag.

"Shit. Why didn't anyone tell me?"

Silence settled.

"Sorry about earlier," Tim muttered.

Kathryn feigned ignorance with silence.

"So what's his deal anyway?"

"Jesse?"

"No. Randall."

Kathryn had assumed that Randall's fling with the guy she had referred to as the "junior reporter guy" was over simply because the last time Kathryn had asked about it Randall had commented, "He's too earthy. He makes his own soap."

"He's from New York," Kathryn responded, unsure of how much she should be divulging.

"Only child, right?"

"Yeah. I guess that explains a lot."

"The New York thing explains a lot more." Tim sucked a drag. "Sorry. I just realized we've been on a few dates and I barely know a thing about him."

"I didn't think you guys actually went on dates."

Tim smiled wryly. "He tells you everything, doesn't he?"

"I don't ask for all the details."

Tim's eyes were downcast and Kathryn felt a stab of sympathy when she realized that Tim was still smarting from the sting of rejection, albeit a silent one.

The door to the house popped open and April emerged, tailed by Svetlana and three other lesbians Kathryn didn't recognize. "We're going to the Hole!"

"Gross. Be sure to shower," Tim commented.

"You coming?" April asked, eyes on Kathryn as she punched her fists into her gloves.

"Some of us don't have fake ID's."

"I can get you in," one of the lesbians offered. Kathryn attempted a grateful smile and just shook her head "no."

"No sign of the Ice Queen?" April asked.

"Looks like my nickname stuck," Tim said proudly.

April shot Kathryn one last disapproving look before turning to her entourage. "Let's head out, girls!" They shuffled down the steps past Kathryn. "We might meet you!" Kathryn called after them, and April only responded with a wave over one shoulder.

Kathryn stared after them before noticing a dark shadow striding down the path toward Burton House, moving a determined and familiar gait. On instinct, Kathryn rose and descended the front steps of the house. Randall's eyes lit up when he saw her, glancing briefly over to where Tim remained seated behind her. He hooked an arm around her waist and kissed her on the cheek. "You were waiting?" he asked, tone apologetic.

"No. It's cool."

She heard Tim rise to his feet behind her and turned to see him brushing off the seat of his pants. He gave Randall an acidic forced smile and Kathryn felt a current of tension pass between both men before Randall returned the smile with a stiff and formal one of his own. "Tim," was the only greeting he managed.

"*Randall*," Tim responded mockingly, descending the steps. "All right, Bopsey Twins. I'll see you guys later." He passed them and Kathryn heard him add, "Maybe," under his breath.

Once he was gone.

"I know. The soap," Kathryn said.

"What did I miss?"

"Nothing. But you might still be able to see Jesse reel in tonight's catch."

"I'm sure I'll run into her later."

Randall tugged his silver flask from his inside jacket pocket, uncapped it and handed it to Kathryn. She took a slug and winced. "Christ, Randall, can't you add soda or something?"

"Lightweight. Come on." He took one of her hands and began leading her off the sidewalk and onto the lawn.

"Mind if I ask where we're going?"

"Madeline's."

Kathryn yanked her hand free. "No, Randall. I hate that place."

"I'll let you change. They'll only card you if you're dressed like you are right now."

His playful smile indicated he was only half-serious, but when she didn't show any signs of giving in he formed his mouth into a slight pout and stuck out his lower lip. "Don't," Kathryn said. Randall furrowed his brow, jutting his lip out further. His expression had transformed from baby-faced pleading into a monkey scowl and by the time he had raised his hands to push his ears forward and complete the effect, Kathryn had grabbed one of his wrists. "Fine!" she barked, to choke off her laughter. "Stupid of me to think you could hang out with anyone who doesn't wear Prada."

"This is Gucci," Randall said in a small voice.

"Don't push it!" Kathryn made a sharp turn, leading them back toward the sidewalk.

"Where are you going?" She turned and saw Randall gesture with one arm toward the Elms. "Are you kidding?"

"Come on. I'll protect you." He curved an arm around her shoulders. Kathryn let out a defeated groan and allowed herself to be led into the dark woods. To her surprise, they were easily navigated. There was no underbrush and the only obstructions were shoulder-height tree branches that were hard to make out in the darkness. Randall pressed her head down and pushed branches out of their way with one gloved hand as they went.

"You don't even want to know what I saw your roommate doing tonight."

"Now I do."

Randall came to a sudden halt. Kathryn looked down and saw they were standing at the edge of a five-foot drop down into a creek swollen with runoff from melting snow. She looked to Randall, who stared down the drop as if it had foiled his plans. "I didn't know it was so wide down here," he mumbled, eyes scanning the creek bed.

"I thought you knew your way."

"Come on," Randall said, taking her hand and leading her up the bank. The trees began to thin out, revealing houses beyond. "So?" Randall asked.

"He and the girl he was dancing with needed to get a room," Kathryn said, instantly regretting that she had brought it up.

"Is there any reason you can't refer to him by his first name? He's always My Roommate, or That Asshole."

"He's both," Kathryn responded. They came to a sidewalk with a stone banister that crossed over the top of a large drainage pipe which emitted a crystalline mixture of black water and miniature ice floes extending from the bottom lip of the opening like white teeth. Kathryn's breaths were more steady now that they were on the solid ground of the sidewalk. The welcoming halos of Brookline Avenue's street lamps beckoned up ahead.

"I think it's interesting how some people make concessions for the beautiful, but you hold them to a higher standard," Randall said.

"He's not beautiful, Randall. He's hot. There's a big difference," Kathryn said, thinking of the magazine ads of shirtless, buff male models Randall used to bridge the gaps between posters on the cinderblock wall of his room; models who bore a striking resemblance to Jesse in their perfectly proportioned frames and inscrutable, distant facial expressions which suggested they were permanently aloof as well as physically indestructible.

"You might want to sleep with him. Just once."

"I'm going to pretend you didn't say that."

"Why? It might take away his mystique."

"He doesn't have any mystique."

"That must be why we're talking about him, then."

They had arrived at the stop light across the street from Madeline's. Brookline Avenue's only hip restaurant had made its ten o'clock transformation into a nightclub. Its front door emitted a long and impatient line of the university's best dressed, shivering in the cold as they waited to pretend they were in Manhattan for the rest of the night.

Randall had turned to face her, still holding one of her hands in his.

"What's next?" he asked gently. "Campus-wide outreaches for one-night stands gone wrong?"

"You've played the messages for me, Randall."

"For fun."

"Every time it's a different girl. It wouldn't bother me so much if I didn't think those messages were getting him off as much as the act itself."

"Fine. No more messages," Randall responded. "I don't think I should be indulging this fixation on Jesse's sexual habits."

"You know every time I talk about him, you and April make me out to be this Puritan."

"You talk about him a lot, Kathryn."

A note of concern had crept into Randall's voice and it took Kathryn a second to decide whether it might be condescension. Slightly wounded, and now feeling like a neurotic, she met Randall's gaze, unable to give voice to why she kept returning to Jesse as a conversation topic. Recognition flickered in Randall's eyes and leaned into her, reaching an arm around her waist and cupping the back of her neck slightly in one hand.

"Kathryn. I know better. All right?"

She didn't say anything else, she didn't need to. Once again, Randall had exhibited his knack for cutting straight to the truth, and doing it gently. Maybe this was one of the major reasons they had fallen into such a deep and all-inclusive friendship. Kathryn only had to do half of the work, because Randall could usually intuit the rest. Did this make her lazy?

She returned his embrace before giving him a surprise slap on the ass. He jerked.

They were both startled by a high-pitched whistle.

"Break it up, you two!"

Kathryn steeled herself at the sound of a familiar voice. Jesse's date clung to his shoulder, and let out a short, barking laugh as they approached down the sidewalk. Kathryn's eyes immediately shot to the girl's crotch to see if her jeans were buttoned.

VIII

Candles on wall sconces lit the interior of Madeline's. The bar was clogged with Armani- and Gucci-clad students downing shots between boisterous fits of laughter. Anemic, black-clad waitresses maneuvered between the cramped tables carrying trays of drinks on their rail-thin arms. A strange mix of acid jazz and ambient music pumped from unseen speakers, a stark contrast to the flickering images of the local eleven o'clock news Kathryn watched on the television above the bar.

Kathryn sipped her club soda and shot a glance over one shoulder. Through the plate-glass windows, cardigan-clad students made the walk back to their dorm, weighted by overloaded book bags and shooting withering glances at the designated hangout for Atherton's Euro Trash and designer-drug addicts. Kathryn prayed none of them noticed her.

"Where's Randall?"

Kathryn didn't bother to look at Jesse as he slid onto the bar stool next to hers.

"Bathroom."

"I thought you two were like attached at the hip."

Kathryn took a sip of her drink. "What's her name?"

"Don't know yet." Jesse sipped his drink and Kathryn finally made eye contact. He lifted his glass. "7-Up."

Kathryn nodded, as if impressed.

"You?"

"Club soda. I thought you were a Schlitz man, Jesse."

"Not when I have to perform."

Kathryn's smile hurt her cheeks.

She looked toward the bathroom, praying Randall would emerge. Instead she saw Jesse's brunette, filing out of the women's room with three other girls. The brunette's eyes shot in both directions before she clasped her hands as if in prayer, using both index fingers to wipe at her nostrils. Kathryn noticed one of the other girls applying a liberal amount of Chap Stick. She read the group's behavior in an instant. They hadn't gone to the bathroom together to put on make-up.

"Hey?"

Kathryn turned, startled, to see Jesse leaning toward her with one bent elbow braced on the bar. "Mind if I ask you a question?"

"Never," Kathryn answered.

Jesse laughed, eyes not leaving hers. "No, I'd just love to know what it is I do that pisses you off so much."

"I think it's really important you find one girl who won't sleep with you."

Jesse leaned back onto his stool and gave her a slight nod, not in agreement, but as if satisfied to get an explanation for the constant chill she greeted him with.

"You know, I think it's kind of cool what the two of you have."

"What do you mean?"

"I just remember the way you guys were during Orientation Week. Everyone else was hanging out in the lounge making bullshit conversation, spouting off those statistics about how ninety percent of married couples meet their other half in college, or going to those stupid ice cream social things. Not you and Randall. You were always out in front of the dorm smoking."

"I don't exactly recall you bonding with our dorm unit, either."

"I didn't," Jesse responded, without pause. "That's why I think it's cool."

Puzzled, she waited for him to continue. "Jesus, it's like everyone on our floor. They're all rushing to join some club, or they've got some whacked-out major like April with a hundred requirements and they've already gone to three classes by the time I wake up. It's like they're working their asses off to be anything other than what they are."

"What are they?" Kathryn asked.

"Kids. Away from home. But if you ask them they'll tell you they're a major. Not us, though," Jesse continued. "The three of us. You, me, Randall. It's like we didn't get taken up into the fold. Everyone else here, they're like Stepford Child freaks. It's like they're still high on all that bullshit they tried to feed us at Orientation."

"April says I use Randall to avoid making new friends," Kathryn said carefully, reminding herself who she was talking to. She left out April's other point, she used Randall to avoid meeting a boyfriend as well.

"I don't know," Jesse said nonchalantly. "We've only been here, what? Two months? It's like the two of you have taken vows or something."

She was reminded of Tim's comments about finger-pricking and sharing blood.

"So who's he dating anyway?" Jesse said.

"Randall? No one."

"That's weird. What happened to that reporter guy?"

"That's over," Kathryn responded.

Jesse's eyes narrowed.

"What?"

"He's just been staying out really late."

"No, he hasn't," Kathryn said, unable to restrain the hint of anger in her voice.

"He leaves after you two get back."

The brunette suddenly slid between them, perma-smile plastered on her face, pupils dilated. Kathryn was definitely sure the girl was high and she watched as she leaned in to Jesse and whispered into his ear. She withdrew, laughing slightly, but Jesse's face had gone blank. Kathryn was startled to see him cup the girl's chin in one hand and gently push her face back several inches, surveying her.

"What?" the girl asked.

Jesse reached up and swabbed at the girl's nostrils with one finger.

"What are you *doing*?" the girl cried indignantly.

Jesse turned his attention to his 7-Up as the girl's eyes moved from him to Kathryn, having watched the entire scene. "Oh, I get it!" She snorted and turned on one heel. "Asshole!" she barked over one shoulder before making a beeline for the front door. Jesse didn't look up from his glass.

"High as a kite," Kathryn finally said.

Jesse's eyes shot to hers.

"How could you tell?"

"Experience."

Jesse arched his eyebrows suggestively.

"Not me. I had friends in high school whose entire weekend was an eight ball."

"But you never touched the stuff?"

"Never," Kathryn answered, her gaze unwavering.

Randall sidled up to the bar in between them. He shot Kathryn a curious glance, obviously wondering how long she and Jesse had been bonding. "Can I get an apple martini?" he asked the bartender.

"Randall, someday you're going to introduce me to a homosexual who can drink something that doesn't have a visible shade in candle-light!"

"Wait!" Jesse piped up. He grabbed one of Randall's shoulders and turned him, cupping his chin and examining his eyes.

"Mind if I ask what you're doing?" Randall said.

"He's clean," Jesse said to Kathryn with an unnerving grin.

The bartender delivered Randall's drink and he paid in cash. He turned his back on Jesse and leaned in. "What the hell was that about?" he asked, voice low.

"Inside joke. You're on the outside. Sorry."

"You two have inside jokes now? I was only in the bathroom for ten minutes."

"I know and we wanted to know why."

"Are you saying that the two of you actually bonded?"

"Mmmm. No, not really." Kathryn grabbed his chin. "But let me see something…"

"I don't do drugs."

"Then why do we keep coming here?"

"Damn!" Jesse barked. "Check that out!"

He pointed to the television screen above the bar, where Kathryn saw the mauled remains of a Volvo station wagon being hauled from the black water of the Atherton River. Police lights flared on the bridge overhead.

"Turn it up!"

It took Kathryn a second to realize Randall had shouted at the bartender, who was occupied on the other side of the bar.

On television, the news report cut live to a reporter at the rail of the bridge at the exact moment when Kathryn thought they were going to be given a glimpse of the person behind the Volvo's wheel. The volume bar suddenly appeared on the bottom of the screen. Heads around the bar jerked at the sound of the reporter's voice, now fighting with the music. Kathryn turned to see Jesse, bent over the bar, holding the remote.

". . . trying to chase down the anonymous caller who placed the 911 call reporting the accident, but so far they are short on leads. And also, no comment on whether or not that caller might have been involved in tonight's fatal accident which claimed the life of forty-one-year-old Lisa Eberman."

The reporter cut to footage of paramedics rolling a gurney towards the flaring light of an awaiting ambulance, smeared halos through the driving snow.

"As we told you earlier, Eberman was the wife of noted Atherton art history professor and published author, Dr. Eric Eberman."

"Dude!" the bartender snapped, before yanking the remote out of Jesse's hand. "This isn't a sports bar!"

Kathryn turned to find Randall staring rapt at the television screen.

"Do you know her?" she asked.

Randall turned, eyes glazed over and distant.

"Her husband. I'm in his course," he said.

Kathryn nodded as Randall gripped the stem of his glass and took a slug.

Jesse rose from his stool. "Looks like I've got work to do," he said, gesturing with one arm to the rest of the bar.

"Good night, Jesse."

Jesse departed into the crowd milling around the tables.

"You ready?" Randall asked.

She was surprised to see he had downed his entire drink.